SHOOTING BUTTERFLIES

Also by T.M. Clark

My Brother-But-One

SHOOTING BUTTERFLIES

T.M. CLARK

First Published 2014
Second Australian Paperback Edition 2015
ISBN 978 174369332 2

SHOOTING BUTTERFLIES
© 2014 by T.M. Clark
Australian Copyright 2014
New Zealand Copyright 2014

Except for use in any review, the reproduction or utilisation of this work in whole or in part in any form by any electronic, mechanical or other means, now known or hereafter invented, including xerography, photocopying and recording, or in any information storage or retrieval system, is forbidden without the permission of the publisher.

This book is sold subject to the condition that it shall not, by way of trade or otherwise, be lent, resold, hired out or otherwise circulated without the prior consent of the publisher in any form of binding or cover other than that in which it is published and without a similar condition including this condition being imposed on the subsequent purchaser.

All rights reserved including the right of reproduction in whole or in part in any form.

This is a work of fiction. Names, characters, places, and incidents are either the product of the author's imagination or are used fictitiously, and any resemblance to actual persons, living or dead, business establishments, events, or locales is entirely coincidental.

Published by
Harlequin Mira
An imprint of Harlequin Enterprises (Australia) Pty Ltd.
Level 4, 132 Arthur Street
NORTH SYDNEY NSW 2060
AUSTRALIA

® and TM are trademarks of Harlequin Enterprises Limited or its corporate affiliates. Trademarks indicated with ® are registered in Australia, New Zealand and in other countries.

Printed and bound in Australia by Griffin Press

MIX
Paper from
responsible sources
FSC
www.fsc.org   FSC® C009448

AFRICA

TANZANIA
ZAMBIA
Lusaka
ANGOLA
MALAWI
Harare
ZIMBABWE
NAMIBIA
Francistown
Musina
(Messina)
Windhoek
BOTSWANA
Polokwane
(Pietersburg)
MOZAMBIQUE
Pretoria
Johannesburg
Upington
Kimberley
Hluhluwe
Bloemfontein
Durban
Port Shepstone
Margate
SOUTH AFRICA
Stellenbosh
Cape Town
Port Elizabeth

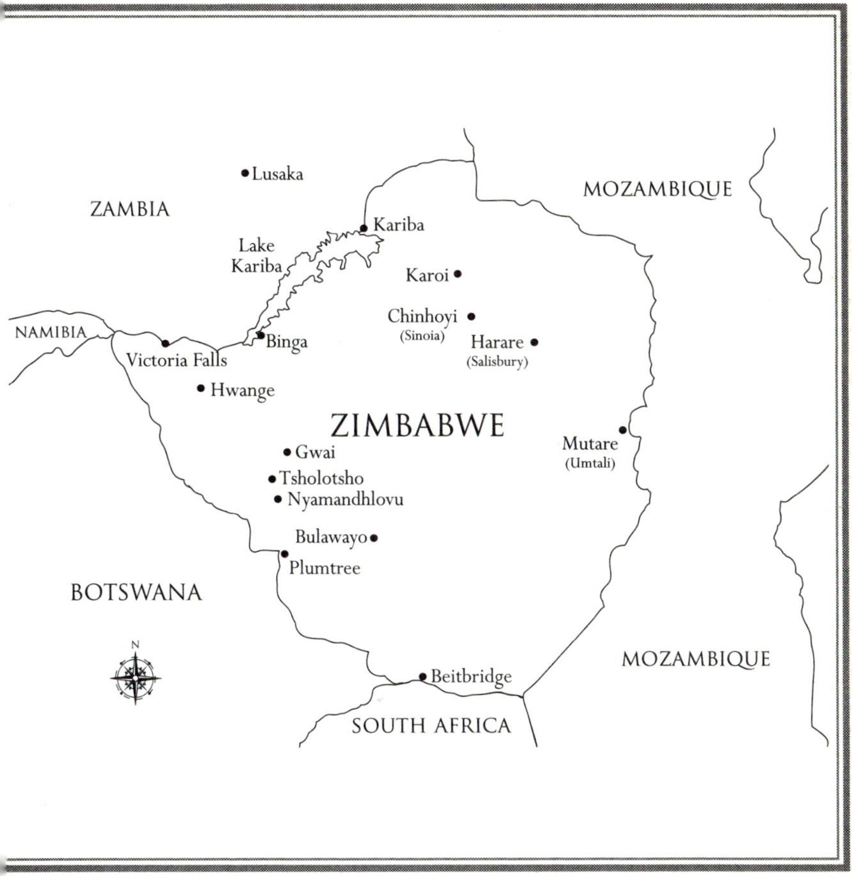
Lusaka
ZAMBIA
MOZAMBIQUE
Kariba
Lake
Kariba
Karoi
Chinhoyi
(Sinoia)
Harare
(Salisbury)
NAMIBIA
Binga
Victoria Falls
Hwange
ZIMBABWE
Mutare
(Umtali)
Gwai
Tsholotsho
Nyamandhlovu
Bulawayo
Plumtree
BOTSWANA
N
MOZAMBIQUE
Beitbridge
SOUTH AFRICA

To Shaun,
My sounding board, and first beta reader. The one who tries to change my 'nonsense' sentences into language that everyone will hopefully understand, and the person who is always brutally honest with what I have written.
Thank you for not being the stereotypical macho male, but for being what is perfect for me!
Love you more.

To my mother Carole Wilde,
Because you had a belief in your own family who I too grew to love.
Thanks for always trying to do the best you could for us, for your sacrifices along the way.
Love you Mum.

PART ONE

The Chrysalis

CHAPTER

1

The Karoi

**Mission Station Outside Sinoia, Southern Rhodesia
1946**

The hunting dogs went ballistic. Their excited howling rang through the African bush.

'See, told you there were animals here. They have something cornered,' Kirk said as he ran next to Impendla. 'Come on, run faster.'

Impendla stopped.

'No, *mukomana* Kirk, we go no further. Call your dogs, bring them back.'

'What? No, listen, they have something.'

The dogs continued their baying, the noise high pitched and foreign in the bush.

'We go no further. Bad muti here. Look,' Impendla said as he pointed to a few feathers strung together like a bunch of leaves and hung on a tree.

'How can you tell that's muti? That looks like just some stuff in a tree!'

'No, *mukomana*. There is evil in this place. We must not go closer.'

Kirk looked at the tree. Luckily there were no thorns. It was just a leopard tree, its bark changed colour in patches of green and silver. The trunk was slim but solid. The bark was rough beneath his hands, but it made digging the toes of his boots in easier as he climbed up and onto the first branch. He reached downwards, his fingers edging towards the bundle.

'*Aiwa*, don't touch that. The *Nehanda*, she puts those where you must not go. This ground it is sacred to her, like a church is to you. No one must touch that, the *tokoloshe* will get you. Spirits sent from the *Mwari*.'

Kirk laughed. 'My father says you natives are all talk and there is no such thing as bad magic. And he says your *Nehanda* and the *sangoma* are lost souls who need saving.'

'*Aiwa*!' Impendla shook his head. '*Mwari* is the one Shona god, the high god.'

'Impendla, you live in the mission. My father taught you in school that there is only one God, and he's not Shona.'

'There is muti here. The *Nyamhika Nehanda*, she's a spirit, the voice of *Mwari*, and she said her bones would rise up again. We must not be the ones who disturb her. She can be a *mhondoro*, a lion spirit, and if we disturb her, she can pass into us and then we will hold the spirit.'

Kirk shook his head. 'That's not true, Impendla. Who told you that?' he asked as he drew his hunting knife and cut the bark twine holding the crude bundle in the tree.

It tumbled to the ground.

Kirk shinnied down the tree and kicked it with his foot. The feathers tied around the bundle parted and it split apart. A strong stench of carrion swamped the boys, and something else, something worse than any rotten eggs Kirk had ever smelt.

For a moment they just looked at it, then Impendla dropped to his knees and hung his head and began to wail. 'Do you know what you have done, *mukomana*? You have angered the *Mwari*.'

'Pish-posh,' Kirk said, 'that's nothing except a bit of powder with a bad smell. The *sangoma* probably collected it somewhere near the hot springs or something. Come on, I'm going to see what the dogs have got us.'

He hitched the rifle higher on his shoulder and strode towards the howling dogs, but realising he was alone, he turned back to Impendla. 'You coming with me?'

'*Aiwa. Aiwa.*' Impendla shook his head.

Kirk shrugged and continued to follow the sound of the dogs, smacking the tall grass away from his face as he went.

'Superstitious native!' he cursed.

The howls of the dogs became more frantic and he began to a run. Hunting for meat rations for the kitchen in the mission station had recently become one of his responsibilities and he took it seriously. His father had told him if the boys didn't get fresh meat, the people would eat only vegetables and *sadza* for dinner.

He hated the vegetables Sister Mary always put on his tin plate, and couldn't understand why he should be grateful for mushy carrots, smelly turnips and a wild spinach mixture that tasted terrible. But since he always felt hungry he knew better than to complain about the food, because his father would make him feed his meal to someone in the sick bay. So he made sure they shot something each day, a rabbit or a fat guineafowl. Sometimes he'd shoot a small duiker and the tender meat would be used to make biltong to store in the pantry.

The thicket of trees and tangled bushes that pressed up next to the grassland narrowed, pushing Kirk forward. He broke through the long grass into a clearing and stopped dead. His father's dog pack yipped and yelped even more now he had joined them, and they knew they would be rewarded for doing their job.

In a tree was a black woman, screeching and throwing bean pods. Although the pods hit the dogs every now and again, they were well trained and kept their prey cornered. As one dog fell back, another rushed to take its place. Their heads swung to check that he'd seen what they'd acquired for him, and they wagged their tails excitedly and yelped a few more times.

'Heel!' he shouted, and the dogs backed away and came to stand at his side. Quiet but alert, their ears erect, not ready to give up on their prey just yet. The oldest bitch whined. 'Heel, Mylani!' he commanded.

She rushed closer to his side and sat close beside him, submissive to her little master, but she remained alert and watched the tree.

Kirk stared as the woman climbed down and approached him, her knobkerrie raised. She shouted at him in a native language he couldn't understand. He couldn't even catch a few words, it was gibberish to his ears.

Her chest was bare and painted in white, with dark red stripes and dots across her belly. At her waist she wore a leather thong decorated with strips of different animal skins that had curled as they dried. Many of the pieces of skin flashed different colours as the hair had not been removed from them, and the leather was untanned. But his eyes were drawn to the mummified remains attached to the bottom of each strip. Small cats, rodents and even tiny jackal heads all seemed to look at him at once, their beady black eyes taking him by surprise.

Kirk took a step backwards. He pulled his hat off his head and crossed his chest. 'God the Father, God the Son and God the Holy Ghost,' he said as he repeated the cross.

His other hand touched Mylani's back and she growled, her hackles standing up. He gripped the skin on her neck, more to steady himself than to stop her aggression towards the stranger. Mylani snarled.

But his eyes were no longer on the witch.

In the lower branches of the tree, just high enough not to be mauled by any passing hyena, were five children, not much older than him. Three boys and two girls. They were hanging by their feet like pigs in the smokehouse. The boys had fresh warrior marks carved in the skin on their faces. Across their young cheeks and over their chests the blood, red even on black skin, was akin to battle paint on a warrior. Bound to the side of each boy was an assegai and a small fighting shield.

The girls were also suspended by their feet, hanging like huge cocoons around the tree. Mummified animals were arranged on their skin skirts, which dangled around their necks like the lace collars the white ladies wore to church on a Sunday. The girls' chests were bare and he could see that each girl had just started to come into her bosom, the tiny nubs hardly visible beneath the patterns that had been painted on their bodies in the same white and red that decorated the *sangoma*. Their eyes were blank in death, the flies thick all over their lips and crawling inside their noses.

He closed his eyes to try to erase the scene and put his hands over his ears as the children called to him in his head.

'Help us, help us.'

But when he opened his eyes, he could still see them. The image was real, but their earth-bound calls for help had long since been squelched.

Mylani took a step forward and her growl changed pitch. Kirk quickly looked back to the *sangoma*. She seemed afraid to come closer to the dogs but stood shouting and waving her knobkerrie around, gesturing at him. She began to sing. It was unlike any singing he'd ever heard, and he'd listened to lots of black people singing, in church, while they tended the garden, even when they were clearing trees in the forest. The singing quietened the children's voices in his head, but it made the dogs more aggressive.

The *sangoma* ignored the warning from his dogs and stepped closer. Kirk didn't see the knobkerrie swing, but Mylani dropped to the dirt and was instantly silenced.

Suddenly Impendla was behind him, pulling him away. As Kirk turned to run, his father's rifle slipped from his shoulder to fall in the dust.

'*Mhanya!*' Impendla shouted as Kirk turned back to retrieve it. 'Leave it. She's going to kill you!'

Kirk ran.

The boys fled back through the grass, the dogs with them, as if they realised their roles had changed from the hunters to those being hunted. The *sangoma* pursued them, wielding her deadly knobkerrie.

Impendla tripped and Kirk stopped to help his friend up. 'Come on, come on,' he said. Now that he was running he didn't want to stop. He wanted to get as far away from the dead children in the tree as they could. Away from poor Mylani lying dead. Away from the *sangoma*.

The boys ran for the safety of the mission station. The dogs ran too, their pink tongues lolling out the side of their mouths, saliva drooling.

'*Mhanya,*' Impendla said as he hurried Kirk on when Kirk slowed. They could no longer hear the *sangoma* chasing them but they knew she was out there still.

At last the mission came into sight, the wood smoke from the donkey boiler curling into the green canopy of bushland around it. They could hear the sounds of men cultivating the vegetable field, the heavy thud of *budzas* as they dug furrows and removed unwanted weeds, an easy rhythm, as the steel scraped the ground and then returned to the air to strike the dirt again. Singing wafted up to them, the melodious sound of African voices joined in an age-old tune.

Kirk stopped and bent over to catch his breath. A stitch in his side pulled the muscles taut. He gulped air as he straightened and stretched his cramping stomach.

'My father's rifle!' he panted. 'I have to go back.'

'No *mukomana*, you can never go to that place again. We have angered the spirits of the ancestors. Only bad things will happen if we go back.'

'Maybe tomorrow she'll have gone away?' Kirk asked. He straightened and began to walk towards the mission at a slower pace, still holding his side.

'No, she's everywhere. She's a *sangoma*! A spirit medium for *Nehanda*. A *Karoi*—what you would call a "little witch". You know the Chirorodziva Pool at the caves? The deep one with the blue waters? The *sangoma* is the person who calms the spirits that catch your stone if you toss one into the waters. If you throw a stone, you stir up and insult the Shona heroes who were killed by the Nguni raiders, you cause unrest in the ancestors' bones at the bottom of the pool, where they are watching, still protecting their homelands. They come to get you while you sleep. They take you away and no one ever sees you again.'

'No one believes in that stuff.'

'*Aiwa*, do not say that, *mukomana*. It is true. The *sangomas*, they are the only ones that can take away the curse the ancestors put on the man who throws the stone. Only the *Karoi*.'

Kirk looked behind them then continued to walk towards the mission.

'What else do your people say about the caves and the blue water?' he asked.

'That there are many bones in the pools, not just those of the Shona people. But also some maybe from the great Mzilikazi's *amawarrior*, and some from the white people who came here long ago. They wait forever in the cave, trying to get out and go home to their own hunting grounds and *ikhaya*.'

'But that was years ago. The Matabele wars—'

'The ancestors, they never forget. The *Karoi* can choose to save you or she can choose to help the spirits if that's what she wants. If you want a person to die and they have not cast a stone, then you go see her and she can call those spirits.'

'My father says that's all native superstitions. None of it is real,' Kirk said confidently. 'We visited those caves on the way to Salisbury last month. My father stopped and we ate lunch there beside the blue water. The white people call it the Sinoia Caves. The only ghosts we heard were our echoes as we called out hello.'

'The Reverend can say anything because he only believes in his one god that he says is more powerful, and is gentle, but that is not our way, *mukomana*. That is not the way in Africa.'

'Kirk! Impendla!' Sister Mary called out loudly and waved to them from the mission.

Impendla turned to Kirk. 'Come on, better get back and tell them that the dogs found nothing.'

'But Sixpence will want to know where Mylani is. He'll go looking for her,' Kirk said.

'Don't tell him about Mylani. If he asks, tell him she never came back to us when we called while hunting and we'll go look for her tomorrow. Even though we know she's dead, we can never tell him. We cannot return to bring her body home. The *Karoi*, she will find out and call the spirits!'

'But what about my father's rifle?'

Impendla shook his head. 'It is lost to you.'

Kirk was dressed in his hunting clothes as he entered the mission church. He had his large knife in its sheath and carried an assegai that he'd made with Impendla. The thick thatch of the building's roof cooled the interior and the wooden framework of the tall structure created a cathedral-shaped ceiling. Its low exterior white-washed walls defined where the church was, and kept out the larger animals, but its open style ensured that the wind freely circulated through the building. His father stood tall talking with a group of black women, their coloured clothes bright against the red polished concrete floor as they sat, their legs stretched outwards. As always, some nursed babies on their laps or had them attached to their back with blankets, and small children sat quietly close to their mothers. Out of habit he looked up to check there were no bats hanging from the rough wooden rafters as he approached the circle. 'Father, have you seen Impendla? I've looked everywhere.'

'No. You spend too much time with him anyway. Remember that we're here to spread the word of God, not be converted to the native ways.'

Kirk pulled a face as his father ruffled his hair.

'Cook says that guineafowl is better without the lead fragments, Father,' he said, but he grimaced as he spoke. The dread of having to tell his father about the loss of his rifle sat heavy in his stomach. He knew that when he did tell him there would be trouble and he'd probably receive a belting. Perhaps he could sneak back later and get it, when Impendla had calmed down.

His father smiled at him. 'I agree with Cook. No, I don't know where he is, so off you go, keep looking,' he said. 'Make sure you don't go into the bush without him, though. Understand?'

Kirk half turned to go.

'Kirchman Bernard Potgieter, do you understand?' his father asked.

He knew his father meant business when he used his whole name, and there would be no going into the bush today without Impendla. He had to find him.

Kirk nodded, then ran over the polished cement floor, jumped nimbly over the low wall that was the outer structure of the church, and headed towards the compound, the only place he hadn't looked for Impendla. He'd already searched all the mission buildings, the orchard, the field of maize they had planted, where he had run his hands over the tops of the green plants that now grew almost to his waist, but he hadn't located him.

He entered the compound and inhaled the aromas. The smoke of the cooking fire, the fragrance of slow-cooked meat in a broth. The *kaalnek* chickens leapt out his way as he ran past, their feathers ruffled and their protests loud. But they soon returned to scratching and pecking in the dirt, searching for something tasty to eat.

He rounded a corner and looked at Impendla's *ikhaya*. The kitchen hut was the centre of Impendla's home, for many meals they had sat around the kitchen fire eating *sadza* and gravy from the enamel plates. There was always food to eat in Impendla's kitchen. Its neat thatched roof was trimmed in a pattern, and smoke clung to the thatch like a baby monkey to its mother. The top half of the building was whitewashed, and the bottom half was smeared with a black mixture of mud and dung. Next to the round kitchen was the sleeping *ikhaya*. Made of mud and cow dung, it wasn't as neatly decorated as the kitchen, but it was always in order and the floor well swept.

Impendla's mother worked in the hospital section of the mission. She tidied the beds and washed the floors, and it was her job to put the mosquito nets down over the patients. But today she wasn't in the sick bay. She was sitting in the doorway of the *ikhaya* holding a bunch of colourful feathers. Kirk looked closer. Among the feathers, he could see the mummified head of a rodent, and then he noticed that the skin it was attached to was the same colour red as the markings on the *sangoma*'s skin the day before.

A cold snake crept along Kirk's spine.

'*Mhoroi, amai,*' he greeted Impendla's mother. 'I'm looking for Impendla.'

She glanced up at him and he could see there were tears in her eyes, her face wet with those that had already run down her cheeks and onto her white uniform that was now brown from sitting in the dirt.

'He is taken.'

'Taken?'

'He is taken.' She nodded and sniffed, unconsciously turning the colourful package in her hands. Kirk stared. Constructed exactly like the muti bag he had cut from the tree, the crude leather pouch was decorated with bright feathers that had been sewed roughly onto the raw leather with *riempies*, and then wrapped in the pieces of skins with the heads attached, their eyes sunken in and dried. The package had a single drawstring, closing it at the top, but not sealing in the odour. He'd smelt the same vile stench just yesterday. Kirk's stomach heaved and he dry retched.

Terrible dreams of the mutilated children had woken him during the night and he'd screamed into the inky darkness. His father had rushed into his room with a candle to check on him. He hadn't told his father anything about the incident, about losing his gun, or about the dead children who had called to him to help them while he ran away and abandoned them to the witch.

He'd almost told his father.

Almost.

But as he opened his mouth he'd remembered Impendla, shivering, the sweat pouring off his forehead. Real fear. Impendla had been terrified.

Impendla had made him promise not to tell. A promise was your word, if you were black or white. It was your oath. So he'd kept his promise to his friend.

Impendla believed in the bad medicine.

Maybe it *was* real, and she would come for them. So he'd said nothing.

'We're cursed,' Impendla's mother said and she held the bag out for him.

He looked at her.

He looked at the bag from the *Karoi*. And he ran screaming.

'Father! Father! The *Karoi* has taken Impendla! Father!'

He barrelled into Sister Mary as he ran around the corner, still screaming, and saw his father rushing towards him.

'Whoa, Kirk. Slow down. Talk to me.'

'The *Karoi*. The witch. She had these bodies hanging in a tree and I didn't mean to disturb her when we were hunting. Then she killed Mylani with her knobkerrie and we ran. Then I lost your rifle, and now she's taken Impendla and his mother has the bag of bad muti from the tree. Father, the *tokoloshe i*s real!'

'Come, take me to this place,' his father said as he took Kirk's hand in his and ran towards the stables.

The horses were out in the field, and the groom was just putting new hay into the stalls, helped by his young son.

'Saddle the horses. We need a search party to find Impendla,' Kirk's father instructed the groom. He turned to the child. 'Tendai, quickly run to the church and ring the bell. Keep ringing it for a long time so that everyone comes in to the mission. There is bad trouble.'

Kirk watched as Tendai sprinted away to the church, the urgency in his father's voice clearly understood by the six-year-old. Moments later the dull clanging of the bell rang out, echoing across the valley and calling the people to the mission.

The reverend helped the groom to saddle up the mission's three horses and pull the two donkeys inside as well. Kirk stayed close as instructed and watched as the workers, worshippers, and people from the small kraals nearby gathered in the courtyard outside the church. He only ever saw so many people all together when his father handed out Christmas *bonsellas* in celebration of the birth of Jesus.

Tendai was still ringing the bell.

Clang-clang.

Clang-clang.

When the horses were ready, the groom passed the reverend the reins of his black stallion. Taking them, Kirk's father walked out of the stables and stopped in front of the crowd. A hush fell over the people. Someone had told Tendai to stop ringing the bell because it clanked once more before silence descended over the mission.

'One of ours has been taken from us during the night. He is in trouble. I know about the custom of giving up one of your children for a plot of land, or to the *sangoma* in exchange for the marriage of another child into a wealthier family. But Impendla was not given to anyone for muti, he is our friend. We need to find him. Arm yourselves with anything you can find, bring your picks and *budzas*, there is trouble! *Huya pano*, we need to save him. I pray that God be with us today in our search, and that the Almighty will protect Impendla wherever he is.'

He mounted his horse, and then reached down to help as the groom lifted Kirk up to sit in front of the saddle. The people of the mission station hurried to do his bidding. One of their own was in real danger. With hushed voices, as if scared of what they would find, the men and women gathered together, armed with tools from around the mission and their own kraals, including shields and assegais.

'Which way, Kirk?' his father asked.

Kirk pointed towards the bushes, to where he and Impendla had last seen the *sangoma*. They moved off slowly as a group, the reverend in front, his stallion's nostrils flaring as it tossed its head and played with the metal bit between its teeth, uneasy at the crowd that followed.

More people joined them, emerging from the bushes after they passed the fields, armed with their traditional shields, hunting *assegais* and knobkerries. Ready to fight.

Soon a soft church hymn began from within the mob. Men, women and children joined in, the song grew louder as people heard it and added their voices, so that the gathering was united in a song of prayer. The procession moved through the bush, not knowing what they were heading into, but ready to help the reverend out of a deep respect for him, and face whatever they needed to.

Seated against his father, Kirk found the courage deep inside himself to save Impendla now that their secret was told. The seven remaining hunting dogs ran in front, yelping in excitement, as if knowing that something else other than hunting was happening.

Soon they came to the place where the foul bag of feathers and leaves had fallen to the ground. Only it had been removed. Kirk looked upwards. It was back in its original place, tied to the tree, but now there was a black marking carved deep into the tree branch underneath it. And new feathers. Blue and purple feathers, like that of the lilac-breasted roller, showed bright against the brown and green bark. The same feathers that had been tied around the bundle left with Impendla's mother.

A warning.

A promise.

The mission people refused to go any further. The women sat down and started wailing, the hymn forgotten. The strong realisation that they were dealing with a *Karoi* and the *tokoloshe* sat heavily upon the sombre crowd.

'They are in there, Father. They hang on a tree.' Kirk pointed. Now that he had unburdened part of the story, it was easier to tell his father the rest.

'Hunt!' his father commanded the dogs.

Released, the dogs streaked off into the bush and moments later the people heard their hunting call.

Something was still there.

The reverend addressed the crowd once more. 'I know you believe in the *sangoma*, the *Karoi* and the *tokoloshe*, but God will help us at this crossroad. He is testing our strength, to see if we are ready to enter the kingdom of heaven. One of your own is in there. Those who follow me will be the ones who trust in the Lord Jesus, the Almighty God. I ask that those of you who will not come with us stay here and pray for us. Let us know that even if you can't be with us in body, that your hearts are with us as we go into the darkness and seek out Impendla.'

The reverend urged his horse further into the long grass. Kirk looked back over his shoulder to see who had followed them. The groom was closest on his horse, followed by a handful of men, their assegais ready. The two old men who rode the donkeys kicked at their ribs to hurry them along. A few women followed as well, including Impendla's mother, a pick held in her hands in a death grip as she walked hesitantly behind her husband.

Somewhere ahead the dogs were going mad, yipping, barking and baying, calling to their humans to hurry up and come and see what they had to show them.

The stallion cleared the grass and stepped into the clearing, and the reverend pulled him up in an abrupt halt. The stallion's nostrils flared and his skin shivered. His body twitched.

'Impendla!' Kirk cried out and started to jump off the horse, but his father restrained him.

Impendla hung by his feet in the tree, the reverend's hunting gun and a warrior's shield tied to his body. His blood dripped from the fresh warrior wounds carved into his skin and onto the dry dust of the African continent.

Now there were six children's bodies hanging in the tree, and no sign of the Karoi.

'Holy Father, help us. What have these savages done now?' The reverend began to pray.

CHAPTER

2

The School Yard

Mozambique
1978

Shilo Jamison Khumalo breathed deeply. Seated on the bench running along the inside of the Dakota plane, he could feel the vibration of the engines. The jump light was still not illuminated. Opposite him Kwazi winked. Shilo smiled at his friend.

'Stand up. Hook up!' the despatcher hollered.

The paratroopers stood up awkwardly, the drop bags at the front of their thighs making it hard to balance. Simultaneously they connected the static line snap hooks to the cables running the length of the cabin roof.

The two assistant despatchers moved quickly down the centre of the aircraft, checking all the hooks were properly connected and safely pinned. They gave the thumbs-up to the head despatcher standing near the door.

A terse acknowledgment to the pilots over the intercom, and they were ready.

Shilo rolled his head on his shoulders, easing the stress building there. Waiting for the drop was always the hardest part.

Finally the stand-by jump light illuminated the aircraft with its red glare.

'Stand by the door!' yelled the head despatcher.

Clutching their drop bags with one hand and pulling their hooks along the cable with the other, they shuffle-marched as one towards the door. 'One-two, one-two,' they shouted as they marched one foot forward then shuffled the other foot to catch up. It was a practised manoeuvre that helped the paratroopers to keep their balance. Just one of the moves Shilo had trained for and executed since the beginning of the war, when they had allowed black men to sign up and fight for the freedom of their Rhodesia, and he had become a paratrooper. Exiting the aircraft and leaping into the slipstream of the plane had become an addictive rush, an adrenaline high.

He stood opposite the dark chasm.

The drop light turned from red to green.

'Go!' screamed the despatcher and slapped Shilo's thigh.

He took one last deep breath and crossed his arms across the reserve pack on his chest, then stepped out as far as he could into the abyss. He felt the icy-cold rush of air and then the incredible noise of the engines and the air around him. He knew that, behind him, other men tumbled into the darkness as they emptied the plane quickly and fell like hail from the sky. He reached his four count. He heard his olive-green canopy snap open above him, its release controlled by the static line that was still attached to the plane. As it was designed to do, it had unwrapped his chute perfectly when he came to the end of the webbing. Relief surged through him that he wouldn't need to use the reserve on his chest.

His fall slowed. He could breathe again.

Shilo could hear the plane's drone somewhere in the distance, and in the near silence he drifted down towards the target drop zone over five hundred metres below. He quickly released the Capewell releases to deploy his drop bag which contained his webbing, rucksack and the rest of his deployment kit. He felt the drop bag jerk to a stop at the end of the two-metre lanyard, and mentally checked that off his list of how to execute a perfect drop.

The cold wind flapped at his jumpsuit and the familiar sensation of dread and anticipation sat low in his belly. The military parachutes had little sense of directional guidance. He was never under any illusion that he was in control of where he would land. He hoped that he would at least be within the vlei demarcated as the drop zone, and not drift into the trees along the edges. His adrenaline surged again with anticipation of his unpredictable landing.

Shilo watched the darkness beneath him change density and knew the ground was rushing up towards him. He felt his drop bag hit the ground and immediately braced for his para-roll. He hit the ground a second later.

Slightly winded, Shilo quickly opened the harness releases and rolled away from his gear. He glanced upwards to check no one was going to land on top of him, but the sky was too dark to see.

He unstrapped his weapon, cocked the action and made sure the safety catch was on. Despite not being his standard military issue, it was habit to collect his gear. Once he had packed it up he stood motionless and listened to the night sounds.

He could hear crickets and an owl hooted far in the distance. Other than that there was nothing. No sounds of animals stirring.

He removed his webbing and rucksack from the drop bag and strapped them on, then jumped up and down to make sure nothing rattled. Satisfied, he jogged towards the glow of a red flashlight where he knew Sergeant Riley had set up the rally point, and the other men from his platoon would all be gathering.

'Weapons check?' Sergeant Riley queried. The company men quickly confirmed they had checked their weapons. Standard Soviet Bloc weapons, AK-47s with the signature curved magazine. Each man had plenty of extra ammunition in spare magazines along with grenades in his chest webbing, a bayonet, and a .9mm pistol holstered on his belt.

Shilo looked around. They were all dressed in East German 'rice-flecked' pattern shirts and trousers, the standard issue of the

Mozambique People's Liberation Forces, so they looked exactly like any other Mozambique soldier would. Their disguise was perfect.

He knew his black skin shone at night, so he'd applied plenty of the camo cream the white men in his unit slathered over their faces to try to look as black as he did. But they failed. Their eyes always gave away that they were white men. Nothing would ever dim the blueness from Sergeant Riley's eyes. He noticed Sergeant Riley pull his bush hat lower over his eyes as if he was thinking the same thing.

The brief for their original mission had been a strike on a building that was being used as an ammunition depot. But on entering the plane, a new captain had joined them. He was from the Psychological Operations Unit – PSYOPS, as everyone referred to them, or, as they called themselves, POU.

Shilo knew they were in for a different mission now. It was common knowledge that the main emphasis of PSYOPS was to cause confusion in the black populations and undermine their morale so much that they would be unwilling to fight against the Rhodesians, and even further, be encouraged to defect from any communist groups they found themselves sympathetic towards.

He frowned as he listened to the changes to their original orders.

'… they must never try to re-form here again,' Captain Kirchman Potgieter was saying.

'Yes, sir,' the company said together, but Shilo had missed the beginning of his orders.

'Anyone addressing me as captain or sir from now on gets his nose broken. You'll only address me as Buffel.'

The men remained silent. The reputation of the mad PSYOPS Unit had preceded him. They would obey.

'Your final objective after the raid on the training camp is to round up the survivors. Then and only then do you assemble back at the vlei for helicopter retrieval. No one will stay at the school while I finish up. You will wait for me at the vlei before you take off and return to base. Understood?'

'Yes, Buffel,' the company said. But that didn't mean they liked it.

Just having the PSYOPS captain along on the mission made Shilo's stomach lurch. The man was up to something, and it wasn't above board.

'Remember ZANLA is using this school as a guerrilla training camp,' Buffel said.

Shilo had participated in previous cross-border raids into both Mozambique and Zambia. Many of those attacks had been on training camps such as this one. They were usually performed successfully. But judging by the coordinates of this school, the camp had been moved deep into Mozambique's interior in the hope the Rhodesian forces would not follow.

The gooks were wrong. The Rhodesian forces were there to take it down, which was nothing out of the ordinary, but the big difference was having a PSYOPS captain with them.

Shilo smelled a rat. They were being lied to.

He looked at Buffel. The man was huge, even as white man standards went. His shorts were cut shorter than regulation, the pockets sticking out below the hems, hanging against his hairy legs that he'd covered in blotchy patterns with camo cream. He wore *veldskoene* and no socks. His shirt was camo, like his pants, and bore no insignia. His green combat vest wasn't like any Shilo had seen before. It sat tight around him and had more pockets than army issue. He carried an oversized cargo bag, which wasn't usual for someone to jump with, and the bag was attached to him at all times, as if he couldn't bear to be without it. His beard, wiry and wild, covered most of his face and only beady brown eyes could be seen between the blackness smeared onto his skin and his jungle hat. But it was Buffel's hands that attracted Shilo's attention the most. The last two fingers were missing on his left hand and thick scar tissue covered the place where they should have been.

Shilo wondered what had happened to make this man into one who could live with himself and operate within the PSYOPS unit. The rumours of these men always involved mutilated bodies and unnecessary killings.

Sergeant Riley tapped Shilo on the shoulder to get his attention and made a thumbs-up sign. Shilo returned the gesture, and Sergeant Riley moved up to the next trooper, Kwazi, and repeated the same procedure. The men moved quietly through the thick bush, each trained by the top SAS officers that the army had, and each man, both black and white, fighting for a cause he believed in.

Silently, like leopards stalking at night, they carefully made their way through the darkness towards the target. Shilo held his AK-47 loosely to his right. The Russian-supplied weapons were not standard Rhodesian issue – they had been reconditioned in the armoury after they were captured from gooks. The standard-issue FN was more accurate and had better hitting power, and he wished he had one in his hands instead.

He stepped onto a large fallen tree branch and took a wide stride off the other side to avoid a bite by a puff adder should it be lying in wait. His eyes skimmed the bush around them. Although it was dark, he could make out the areas of trees and shadows.

The target, a whitewashed school building, quickly came into view. Behind a broken fence the camp looked deserted. Except that there were sentries posted on the corners of the wire fence, and the camp itself made noise that didn't belong in the night. A man coughed, and someone smoked a cigarette next to the building, the red tip glowing.

Schools were supposed to be deserted at night.

Shilo could see the equipment they had in the yard. A tall swing claimed prize place in the centre of the playground. Rope hung from the crossbeam at the top, knotted in strategic places so that children could climb, testing their strength or plummeting downwards if they didn't measure up, but not too far.

There was something about this camp that looked different from the other ones they had seen before, those run by Chinese and Cuban trainers. Always, in those camps, they had found the soldiers inside were barely men. Boys taken from their homes and forced into combat. The camps always reflected that they trained killers though. Human-shaped targets, and modified playground equipment. This school looked like any other school in a rural society. Its soccer field with goalposts. Tyres hung like curled-up black shongololos on ropes under the trees, which had obviously been planted to provide shade around the playground. These were children's toys, not military training equipment.

Questions flew around Shilo's brain.

Why was a school protected by a guard?

If this was in fact still a school, then why were they attacking it?

An uneasy feeling washed over him. He crossed his chest in the sign of the Holy Cross as he'd been taught by his mother, who had learnt it from the nuns at the mission station so many years before. Shilo Mission, after which his mother had named him.

Before those same missionaries, who had helped deliver him, had become victims of war.

Before the mission and church had been burnt to the ground by the terrorists.

Before he volunteered to become a soldier in the Rhodesian War of Independence, to fight the communists who were trying to take over his country.

He was a solider, it was not his place to question his superiors.

Carefully he made his way after Kwazi who walked just in front of him.

The signal to leopard crawl was passed from Sergeant Riley through the men. Shilo signalled to the next trooper and immediately dropped to his belly. He dug his elbows into the ground and kept his AK-47 ready while maintaining the same pace forwards. They broke through the bush and crawled across the patch of cut grass towards the outline of the fence.

Sergeant Riley held a section of fence open as Shilo slithered through and broke to the right. He wiped the sweat off his face with the sleeve of his camo smock and cleared the dust from under his nose as he continued to slither further along.

The sky was beginning to lighten and he could see better now. His eyes still straining in the half-light, he passed near the guard, who was smoking another cigarette.

The guard was dressed in overalls like a farm worker, except he carried an AK-47 assault rifle. Shilo strained to see if he had access to any of the other Soviet Bloc weapons they knew the ZANLA guerrillas were in possession of. They might not all be dressed in any type of standard uniform, but they were infamous for their access to Soviet and Chinese weapons. Like the RPG-2 and RPG-7 rocket-propelled grenade launchers and RPK light machine guns. Lately there had even been reports that the gooks had access to the larger weapons like 122mm multiple rocket launchers and 14.5mm heavy machine guns.

Shilo held his breath for a moment as he flattened himself into the ground. The lightening sky silhouetted Kwazi about one metre from him, and he dug down into attack position, low on his stomach, his weapon on the ground as he waited. A mosquito buzzed around and he silently lifted his hand to it, and crushed it between thick fingers, making no sound.

The guard coughed, blew his nose and continued to stare into space. He sat down on the small wall that ran along the few steps up into the building and turned his back on the unknown danger that lurked in the lengthening shadows of the schoolyard.

The sky lightened to a bright blue with purple overtones just as Shilo received the command to advance. The paratroopers struck at full assault. Within moments, a sharpshooter had taken out the guards on both corners of the building, and the troopers ran over the bare ground within the fence line, towards the building, their weapons ready.

Shilo breathed deeply as he rushed up the three steps, jumped over the downed guard and into the school, Sergeant Riley only milliseconds behind him. He ran through the open door and immediately dropped to one knee and searched for anyone inside. Kwazi was already on the right-hand side of the door, and signalled for him to move forward towards the next room.

Shilo shifted quickly and with purpose.

Soon he was ready at the next entry to the connecting room.

'Shilo, cover me,' Sergeant Riley said. Shilo adjusted his AK-47 at his hip and scanned the room. He kicked the door open. When no movement was detected Sergeant Riley stepped inside. Nothing attacked them. They could hear weeping. A boy cowered in the corner, almost hidden from view by an upturned kitchen table. He couldn't have been more than ten years old.

'Got a survivor,' Sergeant Riley said as he pulled the boy's arm.

The child was unarmed.

'Continue to clear the room,' Sergeant Riley said as he held the sobbing youngster.

Kwazi poked around the room and soon shook his head. 'Clear.'

Sergeant Riley passed the boy to another trooper. 'Buffel's instructions are to take survivors to the sports field, make sure this kid gets there.'

The trooper left back the way they had just come. Shilo watched as he exited, his AK-47 ready all the time.

'Shilo, cover me,' Sergeant Riley repeated as they came across a door at the back of the kitchen.

Shilo squared his shoulders, ready for impact as Sergeant Riley opened it.

The small room was obviously used as a janitor's room to store mops and brooms. Sergeant Riley shone his torch into the room and a young girl cowering in a corner raised her hands in the air, even as she ducked her head down between her knees.

'Come on, child, time to go,' Sergeant Riley said as he reached for her. She jumped up and brushed past him. Shilo caught her by the arm and quickly restrained her.

'Put her with the others,' Sergeant Riley said. 'Kwazi, you and I continue. Shilo, join us when you are done.'

'Yes, Captain!' Shilo said as he gently pushed the girl forwards while holding onto her arm.

Shilo frowned. Neither of the two survivors had been armed. The fight the troopers had just engaged in had been against light weapons, and scattered, not the heavy weapon fire they had expected. Something else was going on, and he suspected they had not been briefed on what their true mission was. This was not a training school at all. It seemed like a normal farm school where families were simply living together as a group to deter attacks from passing gooks.

He swallowed the panic that threatened him as he recalled the stories he'd heard about what the soldiers in the PSYOPS units did and exactly how they instilled fear into the people. If the PSYOPS trooper was here to create havoc, he'd just turned their unit from patriotic paratroopers into killers.

Shilo walked the young hostage onto the playing field. He should have bound the kid's hands at least or put a short rope between her legs to minimise her ability to run away, but it went against everything he believed in to treat a child that way.

'Put her with the others,' Buffel instructed. 'And tie her up.'

'I don't have rope,' Shilo lied.

Buffel yanked the child away from Shilo and tied her hands together with a thin cord. Once he was finished, he shoved her towards the other children.

The child quickly ran to her friends, sobbing. They huddled together, as if by touching they could share strength in their fear.

Shilo watched. Unable to move.

Sergeant Riley and Kwazi joined them with yet another hostage moments later.

There were ten survivors of the attack. Ten kids. Children. They had attacked a school filled with school children. Not terrorists. Shilo fought to keep the nausea back.

'Go now,' Buffel dismissed the paratroopers who had gathered around, looking at the children. 'There is work I need to complete here.'

He turned his back on them, expecting his instruction to be instantly obeyed. The paratroopers turned and ran together. Sergeant Riley signalled to his troopies to run for the fence, and the safety of the tree line after that.

Shilo's feet were leaden as he ran the five hundred metres across the bare sports field area, hating to leave the children with the unpredictable Buffel, but having to obey instructions given by a superior commanding officer. Forcing his feet to move he passed the fence line and the slashed area beyond. But just as they got into the tree line, Sergeant Riley tapped Shilo and Kwazi on the shoulder. He signalled to turn back.

Shilo smiled. Their sergeant didn't trust the PSYOPS captain either.

Sergeant Riley dropped to his belly and began to crawl through the bush, and Shilo and Kwazi followed as they crept back towards the school building. They lay as close as they could get in the bush cover, just beyond the cleared area where the bush had been cut short near the fence line, where they had a clear view. The sun had risen into a full dawn while they had executed their raid. No longer able to use the cover of darkness, they relied on their camouflaged clothes instead.

'Tell me your ages!' Buffel demanded in Portuguese. He had moved the children and they were now lined up against the wall of the school. Ranging from eight to about fourteen years old, the troopers saw the kids shake in fear. One had pissed in his pants and the strong smell of urine wafted towards where they hid, the scent sharp on the morning breeze.

Two answered in French and two in Portuguese, the others in Swahili.

He took one of the French boys and one of the Portuguese-speaking girls, then selected four of the younger Swahili children: four boys and two girls in all. He walked them over to the tree that held the tyre swings.

He took something out of his backpack and tossed it in front of the children standing at the wall. Shilo couldn't see what it was, but the children cowered away from it.

One child threw up.

Kwazi tapped his arm and brought his attention back to Buffel, who had drawn his handgun.

'No!' Shilo began to protest and he drew his legs up into a position to stand, to run to stop Buffel.

Sergeant Riley moved his arm over Shilo, his elbow digging deep between Shilo's shoulder blade to hold him down. 'He'll kill us too. We can't interfere. He's PSYOPS. They outrank us.'

Shilo watched in horror as Buffel executed the six children. Wasting no time, and as if this was a practised procedure, he looped six thick ropes over the lower branch of the tree.

He cut each boy's face with marks of a warrior from an older time, a time when Zulus ruled the bottom half of the African continent, when the Shona people lived in fear of the intruding Impis and when thousands died under the rule of a dictator. Buffel shredded their clothes with sickening confidence and slashed at their chests. They watched him strap an AK-47 to each boy's side with a single strand of rope. From the cargo bag he carried with him, he took traditional small shields made of cowhide, fashioned in the Ndebele style for fighting but the perfect size for the children. He fitted a shield to each child's left arm and bound more rope around the body, so that the shield was clearly visible once he was done. Then he hung the boys by their ankles, winching them up into the tree with the rope and fastening each one off securely. Just far enough off the ground to safeguard against predator animals, but low enough that a person could clearly see what had been done and look at the mutilated body at eye height.

He dressed the girls in skins he pulled from his cargo bag, and quickly hung them up by their feet in the tree too. Their skirts hung down and formed collars around their necks, decorated with small animal heads stitched on the skins. It looked as though the clothes had been custom made for the children. Buffel quickly cut the young girls with different markings, but unlike the boys who he made into warriors, he gave the girls baskets and stabbing spears. Both the girls he had chosen were already in their teen years, just blossoming into their womanhood.

Shilo looked on, his body shaking with unreleased rage.

The blood dripped from the children's wounds and soaked into the dirt of the playground.

Shilo gritted his teeth and closed his eyes to the atrocity in front of him.

Buffel had crossed a line.

This was murder.

The four children standing against the wall of the school building remained still. Their eyes were huge but they made no sound.

Shilo felt Riley pull at his arm and he followed him silently into the bush, his breathing shallow. Clear of the low bush, they fled. Minutes later they heard four shots. The bastard PSYOPS captain had killed the other surviving children anyway, after making them watch the horror that was his ritual.

They ran faster, making sure they were in front of the mad Buffel.

A hand clamped over his mouth and another held him down on his chest.

Shilo woke from his light rest while waiting for the pick-up helicopter, but didn't fight when he saw who it was that had silenced him.

'Sergeant Riley is dead,' Kwazi whispered. He removed his hand from Shilo's chest and signalled him to remain silent.

Shilo nodded. 'What?' He sat up, careful to keep his voice to a whisper. 'He ran out with us, he was not injured.'

'He confronted Buffel on those killings and he didn't survive the consequences.'

'Shit!' Shilo swore.

'You and me, we say nothing!' Kwazi said. 'We keep our noses clean and we keep quiet. I watch your back and you watch mine, just like when we were training. If this PSYOPS trooper can kill a white man and get away with it, he can bury us black guys six feet under and no one will notice.'

'I didn't volunteer to kill kids,' Shilo said.

'Me neither. But if we're going to survive our unit now being used as a PSYOPS one, we have to pretend we were never with Riley and we never saw that copycat ritual killing. No one must know that we know it wasn't a *sangoma* who did that. No one.'

Shilo nodded.

Riley had been their sergeant and he'd always been there to watch his unit's back. Even though he was white, he trained and lived with the black men. Like family.

Now he was dead.

Shilo and Kwazi had witnessed what Riley had. If the PSYOPS captain knew they had been with Riley, they would be next.

Guilt weighed heavy on Shilo's heart.

He'd never forgive himself for just standing by and seeing those children being murdered. He crossed his chest and prayed to all the gods to help him be a better person, to forgive him for not stopping the massacre. He prayed that if Buffel remained with their unit, he'd have the strength to stop him from murdering again.

CHAPTER
3

Imbodla's Race To Survive

**Whispering Winds Farm, Zimbabwe
September 1981**

'Please, Daddy,' Tara begged as she batted her blue eyes at her father. Six foot tall in his army boots, she nonetheless knew that she'd get her own way eventually. All it took was perseverance.

'*Please*, Daddy!' Tara said. 'Please let me ride with you. I really don't want to sit in the *bakkie* with Mum and Dela, they will be talking girl things all the time and singing silly songs. Please?'

'Okay,' Joshua said, his voice as soft as a sergeant major's could ever get. 'Fine. You can come with us. And, as a special present because it's school holidays, you can ride my Apache on the way home.'

'Thank you, thank you, Daddy!' Tara said as her father helped her mount his stallion and slip her feet into the top of the stirrup leathers above the irons, the stirrups hiked up as short as the holes would allow. The McClellan saddle was obviously too big for her, not that she'd ever care.

'Just remember, he might be big, but he's a gentle giant,' Joshua said to her. Then he pulled his horse's head towards his chest and said roughly into the stallion's ear, 'Take good care of her. I'll be watching you ...'

The stallion breathed deeply, his nose flaring as if he was listening to every word. He stomped his foot and tinkled with his bit, eager now that the day was nearly over and he was heading in the direction of home. Joshua smiled at Apache, once a proud warhorse. Together they had survived the Rhodesian Bush War during their time in the Grey's Scouts, and now he was being subjected to family pony rides. Apache snorted as if understanding Joshua's thoughts.

Joshua laughed.

'Just take care of her, you spoilt brat,' he said to his horse. 'This is the easy life now.'

'What about Gabe? Can he ride home too?' Tara asked.

'Not this time. His dad is waiting at the intersection for his drop off. The weekend is over, your cousin needs to go home, to his own house.'

'But Dad, why can't he just stay with us? It's holidays. It's not fair that he always has to be in his house on a Sunday night. That's a stupid rule his family has.'

'My cousin's house, his rules.'

'It's not fair, Dad. It's not like they ever do anything with him anyway. He might as well live with us all the time, it would be so much nicer for him and for me.'

'Don't say that, Tara. Their family might have their own problems, but they are family, and you can't speak about them as if they are bad. They are just different from us. Closed off. Private. You're lucky that his dad allows him to spend so much time with us, he could be nasty and not let him visit at all. Then who would you talk to all the time?'

'Dad,' Tara said. 'Uncle Stuart is your first cousin, hey?'

'Second,' Joshua corrected.

'So there is blood in there somewhere. So promise me that just because you have some of the same blood, you will never be like him, okay?'

'I promise I won't. His path and mine took different directions years ago. Now, we need to leave or we will be arriving home in the dark.'

'Thanks, Dad,' Tara said and she smiled.

Joshua's heart melted at the innocence in her smile. She remained totally oblivious of the harsh world that he and her mother protected her from. His heart broke to think that poor Gabe had to return home to his drunk, abusive father. But what happened behind closed doors within a person's home was their business. It was a rotten system.

Joshua turned to his twin, Jacob, who stood holding the reins of the other horses.

'Poor kid. Sometimes I wish I could smash Stuart's face in for what he continually puts Gabe through. I'm amazed the boy returns for holidays from university. I'd stay well away if I were him,' Jacob said.

Joshua nodded. 'Me too. To both Gabe staying away from home, and to wanting to beat up Stuart. But I think Gabe comes home for Mauve, to check on his mother, not for want of seeing his father. I don't know how we can actually be related by blood. Pity you can't choose your relatives.'

'Agreed. But I'd still choose you, brother, despite the fact that you are a total softy. You know you give in to Tara all the time, right?' Jacob said, but his face was soft too, the words said without malice.

'Thanks, but you would not have to choose me as your brother. Because you were born exactly three minutes after me, I would be the one choosing my younger sibling.' Joshua laughed and Jacob shook his head.

Joshua coughed, and his tone turned more serious. 'I know I give into her. She looks at me with that pixie face, bats those blue eyes and I'm toast. There's nothing in the world I wouldn't do for her. Not that I have ever heard you say no to her either.'

'That's my sworn duty as the doting uncle. Never to give her cause to doubt I'll say yes. Since your girls will be the only ones who will ever call me Uncle, it's my duty to spoil them,' Jacob said as he mounted his horse, Ziona. He took the lead reins of the five horses from his brother's hand, so that Joshua could mount up on the bay, Elliana. 'You, on the other hand, will face the wrath of your wife when we get home so late with your daughter. Give it another two hours and it will get dark while we stand around here talking. Even though the war is over, she still hates it when you are out in the dark. Especially if you have Tara with you.'

'She'll forgive us. She always does. Besides, she knows that Tara gets her horse-madness from me, and that she is happier on a horse than anywhere else. Maggie loves me, she always forgives me.'

'You're a lucky son of a bitch, you know that? First Maggie and now the girls. I tell you, I envy your life now that independence is here.'

'No you don't. You love being the footloose bachelor of the district. Think of the routine life I have settled into, the downside of being a lawyer from Monday to Friday. You would die trapped inside a courtroom.'

'That I would. Give me my trucking company any day ...'

'Come on,' Joshua said as he mounted. His brother passed him back two of the lead reins, and twisting in his saddle, Joshua touched Elliana's flank with his heels to begin their journey home. She needed no second urging and the horses on lead reins pranced behind her, free of their saddles that had been loaded in the back of Maggie's *bakkie*, they tossed their heads in high spirits, sensing they were on their homeward journey.

Joshua grinned at his daughter. It was hard to believe she was already twelve years old. With her pixie build, inherited from her mother, she looked about eight. Her ash-blonde hair, cut with a blunt fringe, was sticking up at all angles after their day spent at the district party at the Farmers' Club. Her dungarees were striped denim and she wore a cotton shirt. Maggie had told him that although Tara still had no bosom, she'd put all her T-shirts at the back of her wardrobe and would only wear thick, button-up cotton shirts so no one could see that she was a late bloomer behind the other girls at school. Her huge dark blue eyes noticed everything, and were like windows into her soul. Sparkling mischievously, they radiated her humour, her love for life and her passion for horses.

'Do I have to stay behind the lead horses on the way home, or can I ride next to you, Dad?' she asked as Apache automatically pushed his way forward to be nearer the lead, putting the mares and geldings behind him.

'Just keep Apache close to the front, honey,' he said. 'But don't let him get too far ahead of us.'

Tara patted Apache's thick neck as he tossed his head.

'Bye, guys, see you soon,' Gabe called as he aimed an old camera at them. Tara turned slightly in her saddle, waved and blew him a kiss. Gabe was the opposite of her in looks, and despite their age difference he was her best friend. His eyes were as green as bright emeralds, rimmed with thick lashes and heavy eyebrows. His thick sable-brown hair was cut short on the sides, and a little longer on the top, so that it seemed to fall like a horse's mane to the side of his face. She smiled, thinking of him cooped up with her sister Dela and her mum in the front of the *bakkie*, until the intersection of theirs and the Victoria Falls Road, where he had to get out and drive back into Bulawayo with his dad.

Her smile slipped from her face. She wasn't too fond of Gabe's dad. Once she had tickled Gabe when he was with them for a weekend, and he had winced away. She lifted his shirt, despite him telling her not to, and she had seen the biggest, blackest bruise on his side. When she asked what had happened, he told her he'd fallen down the stairs at home. But Gabe was swift and surefooted, and he would never have done that. So she kept asking, until eventually he told her that his dad had hurt him, and made her promise not to tell her parents, because if she did, then he wouldn't be allowed to come to their house anymore. She had never told a soul. She would rather see a bruised Gabe than never see him at all. And she made him promise to try to keep out his father's way. And he had – mostly. Soon after that he finished school and went away to university, but he still came home for holidays. Tara wished he came only to them and not to his parents' house.

Apache began to gain speed. Tara quickly brought her mind back to her horse and her hand back to her reins as the stallion followed her dad as he urged his horses into a trot, then a gentle canter as they left the farmers' club behind and headed homewards.

Dusk was just knitting its inky darkness over the African sky. The lengthening shadows had joined together and formed barriers of dark beneath the *lowvelt* bush. A quietness spread over the small riding party. Ahead of them, a big kudu bull leapt over the road, followed by another three. Their large twisted horns looked majestic as crowns as they nimbly negotiated their way into the thick bush on the other side of the road and disappeared from view, their grey coats and white stripes perfect camouflage, helping them to blend into the thorn trees. Dusty brown impala flicked their tails as they grazed along the shorter grass next to the road, ghosting silently back into the bush as the party of three humans and eight horses walked peacefully near them, the buck unthreatened by the riders on their horses. Beetles sang into the coming night, loud and high pitched. A go-away bird called, signalling their intrusion into the bush.

'Can we have a rest, Dad?' Tara asked as she yawned and arched her back to ease the ache that had begun to throb there. After riding for the past hour and a half, and having to keep Apache in check, her muscles needed a break.

'We are almost there, only one fence left. We're still on Potgieter's land, but soon we'll be home.' He turned to her and smiled, and she saw his teeth flash white in his tanned face.

She loved that face and knew every crease in it. There were times still when she would sit on his lap while he was in his armchair, and wrap her hands around his shoulders and listen as he read her the paper or talked to her mum. She'd watch his Adam's apple bob up and down in his throat and put her hand on it, feeling the vibration of his laugh. She grinned at the thought.

'Can you hang in there, *Imbodla*? Apache's looking after you, not hurting your hands?'

'Aw Dad, don't call me that. I get into trouble at school when the staff call me that. Matron Jones says if the staff have given me that name, it means I'm not being a proper lady, and I shouldn't be so friendly with them.'

'Ignore the old biddy, you should be proud that you have earned a Ndebele name. It's a sign of respect. Besides, a wildcat is a beautiful animal. You've seen them. Intelligent, sleek, supple, natural and affectionate, but always holding their own, and they walk a little on the wild side. That's my girl, an African wildcat, an *imbodla*.'

'I know. But you named me that, it wasn't given to me by any of the workers.'

'So you're saying I'm not a worker? I wonder who provides the food on the table, and pays the school fees and the gymnastic lessons for you then? You know, any Ndebele man or woman who belongs on this land would have called you that eventually. I remember the day I first called you *Imbodla*, your mother freaked. She said it sounded like a maid's name. Took quite some convincing that I was saying it with pride. You're my spirited daughter, my wildcat.'

A shot rang out loud, the sound foreign in the evening bush.

'Dad?' Tara said. She swung around in her saddle in time to see her uncle Jacob slump forward onto his horse's neck. Ziona pranced sideways but held her ground, her head up and nose flaring, uncertain. In slow motion, he slid down her side and hung from one stirrup, his head and arms on the road.

'Uncle Jacob!' she screamed.

A second shot cracked through the air. She heard a dull thud as it hit a target next to her and she turned back to look at her father. The breath caught in her throat as she saw him clutch at his chest, his big hands crossed over one another. Elliana shuddered but she too stood her ground, ears flicked back, the whites of her eyes showing.

Time stood still.

'Dad!' Tara screamed, starting to dismount, one foot out of the stirrup leathers.

'Run, Tara. Apache *ándale*!' she heard her father command. 'Home!'

Apache's ears pinned back flat against his head and he bolted into a full gallop up the road. He'd obeyed his master's command, the perfectly trained bush war horse. Tara clung to his neck as she looked over her shoulder. Her father was lying on the road and someone big dressed in camo clothes was leaning over him. Then her view was obscured by horses. The five lead-rein horses raced after her, joined by Elliana and Ziona. Their reins trailed as they snorted, flicked their heads and galloped in blind fear a few strides behind her.

'No! Dad!' she screamed and tugged on Apache's rein, trying to turn back and run down the person who had hurt her father. Apache snorted and ran on, his head held low, pulling the leather through her fingers. He listened to only one master.

'Dad! Uncle Jacob!' she screamed. She flattened her body against Apache's neck, clinging to his mane for extra stability, knowing that she had to be as small a target as possible. All the survival training from years before rushed through her head.

Small target.

Get away.

Only fight if in a corner.

Hide.

Be invisible.

Growing up on a farm during a bush war, staying for months at a time with only her mum, sister and the workers on the farm while her dad was away fighting in the Grey's Scouts, her dad had made sure she could always fight for herself. Defend herself. Defend her family. Survive if it became necessary. And today all that training was being tested. Someone had shot her uncle and her dad, and she needed to get help.

Her heart ached. She tried to pull on the reins to make the stallion slow a little as a bug hit her face and blinded her. She could feel him as he tossed his head, opened his mouth and pulled the slack from the leather reins out of her hands, still listening to the man who had trained him and spent years in the bush with him. He wasn't slowing.

Too scared to let go of the reins, she wiped her face on her arm and pressed her eyes into her sleeve. The bug cleared out and her vision returned.

She looked around her to find where they were.

She saw the cattle gate ahead at the end of the strip road. The wire concertina-style gate was higher than a normal gate, marking the boundary fence between the properties. She knew this place. They were almost on their farm.

She could hear the other horses as they thundered behind her, the sound clear over the beating of the blood rushing through her heart. Their hooves kicked up chunks of dirt as they followed their stallion.

She was in trouble.

'Stop, Apache! Stop, we can't jump that, it's too high,' she told him. He tossed his head again, but his ears twitched as he listened to her. She stroked his neck, thick with creamy lather. The skin shuddered and twitched under her hand. Alive and responsive.

'Come on, Apache, stop boy. You and I, we can't jump that. I need to open that gate so all the other horses can get through as well.'

She felt his neck twitch as he slowed and came to a stop at the gate with a jolt. The other horses stopped too, pressing in to him from behind. He held his ground, avoiding the barbed wire. 'Good boy,' she soothed as she looked at her uncle's horse, Ziona. One stirrup leather was missing from his saddle. Her uncle hadn't been dragged the whole way.

Another shot sounded. Loud and in the distance, but she could tell it was still close to her.

She shivered and Apache's ears flattened again. The other horses jostled in, grouped into a bunch, the whites of their eyes flashing. She could smell the fear from the horses as they pressed close around her. Looking for safety with their stallion.

A year ago she'd have been armed with her trusty .38mm she'd inherited from her granny on her father's side. But her dad had insisted that the Bush War of Rhodesia was over now that they had had an independence celebration and renamed the country.

But he'd been wrong.

The war wasn't over.

He'd been shot.

And she wasn't armed.

A weak target if the shooter pursued her. A lame duck caught up against a fence line. It was like the bad dreams she used to have at boarding school, but this one she knew she wasn't waking up from.

It was real.

Cold sweat ran from her body. She urged Apache to step closer to the gate. He pranced sideways, his ears pricked, listening for her commands.

She tried to open the gate while sitting on his back. It didn't move.

She wasn't strong enough to pull the closure wire off the concertina fence with her hands alone. Reluctantly she dismounted, jumping to the ground from her saddle. She wrapped Apache's reins around her arm and across her palm. 'Just don't leave me here, boy. Dad said to go home. We need to do that. We can get Mum and she can come and see what happened to Dad. We just need to get this gate open first and then you need to let me get up on your back again.'

She pushed her shoulder into the upright and pulled against the huge fence post with everything she had. But she couldn't budge the wire. So she stood on the wire at the bottom, jumping on it to get it to slide down the wood and loop off the bottom of the post, but it was so tight it didn't budge.

'No!' she muttered at the gate. 'Open! Come on, open!'

She knew she had to keep her voice low. Her voice would carry in the bush above the natural sound that the horses made. She couldn't attract attention to herself and as much as she wanted to scream at the gate in frustration, she would spook the horses and whoever her pursuer was might hear her and know she was in distress, know she couldn't get the gate open. Know she was defenceless and trapped.

She had to get away.

She kicked at the gate and shook it, and tried again to open it. Ramming her shoulder into the wood, she dug her feet into the sand and heaved, grunting as she strained against it. But the wire remained taut.

Apache's eyes rolled white and he pulled back on her arm.

'Shhhoooooo. No, boy, no. Come back. Sorry. It's okay, we can get through. Come on.' She quietened her voice even more, using a soothing tone as she'd been taught years before when she'd ridden for the first time – drop the tone in your voice and speak slower to calm the animal. Apache pushed his nose into her shoulder and breathed heavily. She patted his head. The pressure on her arm from the reins eased.

But the gate still remained shut.

She tried the top strand of wire again, pushing on it with her shoulder, trying to force it to shinny up and over. 'Oh, come on! Come on gate,' she hissed.

But the wire remained strained and tight.

Apache snorted and stamped his foot. The other horses snorted too.

Apache moved closer to her and whinnied. As if to protect her, his big body shuddered as he snorted and tossed his head.

Someone or something was close.

Tara stood dead still, holding her breath, straining to listen better above the natural noise of the restless horses.

'*Inkosazana* Tara ... *Imbodla.*'

Sweat broke out on her forehead and she could taste it on her top lip.

The voice was soft, but it was definitely that of a black man.

'*Ngubani igama lakho?*' she asked.

'My name is Shilo. You need to get on your horse, *Imbodla*. I will open the gate.'

She didn't know this voice, but whoever it belonged to knew her name.

'How do you know me?'

'I work for *Baas* Potgieter. I served you tea when you and your little mother came to his house a few weeks ago when his cattle broke your fence and were in your velvet beans. Do you remember me?' He moved to stand a little further in the open on the road, closer to the horses. She looked under Apache's belly and through the legs of the other horses. She could see the man's legs covered in blue overalls, his white *takkies* glaring against the yellow sand. But he stayed at a respectful distance, as if afraid of the horses.

He crouched down and she could see he carried no weapon in his hands, which he held in front of him in what seemed to be a 'trust me' gesture. Her eyes scoured the ground for a gun, but there wasn't one.

'You wore a green skirt,' he said, and then he held up one finger at her as if to remind her of something, 'but you had your shorts sticking out from underneath and your riding boots on. Your mother told *Baas* Potgieter that you weren't disrespectful for not wearing a dress to visit him this first time to his home. That you were just strong willed and spirited, like your dad's horses. Do you remember that?'

She did. And she remembered the house boy serving them on the veranda. He had a big grin when he'd served her from the tray, and put the delicate porcelain teacup in front of her, then filled it with fresh hot brewed tea. But that grin had turned into a frown when he was ordered to take the tray away again and had to lift her tea away before she'd had a chance to drink it. He'd slipped a Marie biscuit into her lap from beneath his tea tray when they visited their weird neighbour, just as Buffel Potgieter had suddenly deemed their visit was over. She'd hidden it in her hand until they were back in the *bakkie*. Afraid to eat it near Buffel in case he took that from her too.

She studied him.

The richness of his skin was the same as most of the other Ndebeles on the farm and had a shine to it, as if he was sweating excessively. His nose was broad, his eyes were chocolate brown, and he looked her directly in the eye. Not downcast as if he needed to show her respect. Eyes that pleaded with her to trust him. Big lips that attempted to smile at her, his straight white teeth flashed underneath. She recognised his face. He was the same man. Only he wasn't dressed in a white house boy's uniform, but in full blue overalls, as if he was working on the farm in the dairy or in the sheds. His hair was cut in the normal short shave most of the farm-boys wore.

'I know you,' she said. 'Why are you here, Shilo? At this gate?'

'That is a story for another time, *inkosazana*. Right now I need to help you back on your horse and you need to ride home. Fast as you can. It is dangerous out here alone.'

Tara knew that without him, she couldn't open the gate. If he wanted to kill or hurt her, he could have already done so easily.

'Come, you must get back onto your horse.' He looked down at the ground, a sign of respect, and she believed him.

'Okay,' Tara said. 'But he's too big. I need help. Come here and kneel down, I can stand on your back to climb up.'

'I can lift you up but you will need to bring the horses away from the gate so I can open it.'

'Are you scared of horses, Shilo?'

'No, but I don't trust so many together not to crush me. They don't know me. Hurry, Miss Tara.' She saw him look over his shoulder and move a little closer to the horses. There was urgency in his movement.

'Okay,' she said again, a waver in her voice as she swallowed the panic at the thought of the big man in camo coming after her. Leading Apache out the herd of horses, she stood next to Shilo. She lifted her arms up to allow him to slide his hands around her waist. Helping her on like this was not something that even Bomani had done. Only her dad, her uncle and Gabe lifted her onto a horse.

He gently lifted her upwards. His hands were warm, not something she'd expected. Tara grabbed the horn on the saddle and scrambled up, and put her feet back into the leathers. She released a breath and Shilo stepped away.

Apache snorted, unsure of the black stranger. His ears cocked backwards, listening and waiting for a signal from his rider.

'*Inkosazana*, tell no one I helped you. *Baas* Potgieter mustn't know I wasn't working. I will be killed if he finds out that I was out here.'

Tara looked at him standing next to her horse. His face wasn't ancient but he already had grey hairs on his head and with black people it was hard to tell how old they were. He was big and muscled, but not fat that would jiggle when he ran. And he was afraid of Mr Potgieter.

They had that in common.

The big German terrified her.

He was the only man she'd ever heard her dad say anything terrible about. This black man worked for Mr Potgieter, and she believed he told her the truth. If she ever said anything, he'd be what they used to call a *dead kaffir*, but now white people couldn't say things like that anymore. Not in the new Zimbabwe.

'Promise, *inkosazana*?'

'I promise,' she said, and she made a sign over her chest. 'Cross my heart.'

He turned to the gate and opened it, pulling the wire quickly to one side to avoid the horses becoming tangled in the barbed fencing. As Apache walked through she heard Shilo say, 'God speed, *Imbodla*. Be safe.'

He raised his hands in the air as if to attempt to hit Apache's rump or just hurry him along. Apache kicked out at him and then bolted, the other horses close behind. Tara turned her head to look back, but all she saw was that the gate was closed and Shilo had ghosted into the bush back from wherever he came.

The horses thundered up the road of Whispering Wind farm and didn't stop until they reached the stables, which were close to the house but outside the eight-foot security fence.

'Mum! Mum!' Tara screamed even before Apache stopped, the dirt skipping up from his front hooves. 'Dad's been shot!'

CHAPTER 4

Carnations

**Zimbabwe
1981**

He was dead.

He lay in a fancy coffin with silver handles and so many flowers it looked like a florist's shop.

'Yuck, that smell.' Dela put her finger under her nose.

'There is no smell,' Tara said, 'it's all in your stupid head.'

'Girls, not now,' Maggie said, as she moved to stand between her children.

Tara stared at her dad. She reached into the coffin and laid her hand against his cheek. Someone who had always been so vibrant and alive was now cold to touch. He looked like he was sleeping, as though if she shook him hard enough he'd wake up and tell her he was only pretending.

But it was real. He wasn't coming back. Even she knew that there was no return from death.

'Don't touch him,' Dela hissed at her.

'Dela!' Maggie said. 'Your sister can say goodbye however she wants.'

'But Mum, she's touching a dead person.'

'That person is your father. And it's perfectly fine to touch him and say goodbye.'

'I'm not touching him.'

'Suit yourself, Dela, but Tara and I are saying our farewell in our own way, and you will not spoil that for us. If you have finished your goodbyes, go outside and sit with your aunty Marie-Ann, she is waiting for you.'

'Fine,' Dela said and stormed out of the viewing room, her new skirt swishing as she moved.

'Come on, Tara. You know you can say goodbye to your dad, you're allowed to cry, honey.'

'But there are no tears, Mum,' Tara said.

'You're so much your father's daughter. He didn't cry easily either. They'll come one day, when you're ready. And when they do, you won't be able to stop them.'

'Sure, Mum,' Tara said as she picked a red carnation off the floral spray that sat against the side of the coffin. She kissed it and placed it in the coffin next to her father's head.

'I love you, Dad,' she said. She looked again at his face. Beneath the make-up, she could see the fine stitching where the big man had cut his throat, ear to ear, to finish him off. Ensuring he was dead. According to the policeman who had spoken to the family, the killer had also taken his pinkie finger. She shuddered to think that he was being buried with part of him missing.

The thought replayed in her mind of what might have happened if she'd stayed, of how she might have been able to run the killer down with Apache. He was trained for that. She might have saved her dad.

If her dad hadn't sent her away.

So many regrets swirled around her head, the fact that while he died, she'd been running away, and that she could tell no one a black man had helped her because he had sworn her to secrecy.

She wanted the big man in camo clothes caught.

She wanted him to pay with his life for her father's and uncle's deaths.

She wanted justice.

But deep inside, she was being torn apart by a promise she was finding it harder and harder to keep. She'd told the police about everything else that day – the ride, the shootings, the running away – but she'd said that she had been the one to open the gate. Not that she'd had help from Shilo.

She'd lied.

She knew that if the police had a good tracker, he might have seen Shilo's footprints in the sand.

If she told the police about Shilo, he might be able to help identify the killer. But then he would be dead, and his blood would be on her hands. She knew she'd be responsible for taking his life, and he'd saved hers. Having blood on one's hands was a reminder about the balance of life.

Tara remembered the moment the year before when she had shot a duiker, and it hadn't been a clean kill. The animal had cried like a human baby, a sound forever etched in her head. And as she'd slit its throat and it gurgled its last breath, the duiker's large amber eyes had looked into hers, pleading with her to stop the pain. Not knowing that she was the cause of that pain in the first place. Some people would say she was putting an animal out of its misery, but she couldn't come to terms with the fact that she'd been the cause of that misery in the first place.

She didn't want the blood of a human being on her conscience too.

Because even if she never pulled the knife across Shilo's throat herself, someone else would. He'd told her that, and she believed him. He'd made her promise. She wondered if, when he saved her life and extracted the promise, he knew she would then own his life? If she talked, he'd die, and as long as she was silent, he'd live. Being responsible for a human life was exceptionally harder than hunting and killing an animal.

She accepted that if she said nothing about Shilo helping her there was a chance her father's killer might not be caught.

He would go unpunished.

Until she was old enough to find Shilo alone, without the police tagging along, and speak to him. To follow up on what he'd said. One day soon, she'd go to Buffel's farm and find Shilo. It wasn't that justice would not be done, it just had to wait. She was sure her dad would understand.

Tormented, she put her hand on her dad's throat and traced the uneven skin. 'I'm so, so sorry, Daddy.'

She turned away and walked out of the room, tugging at the skirt she'd worn after losing the argument with her mother that morning. Her father didn't care what she wore when he was alive, why would he care now when he was dead? She was told that the skirt and new shoes with a small heel on them were not for him, but for her mother. Tara had worn them for Maggie, because in the end arguing with her mother wasn't something she wanted to do, the day was for her father, and Uncle Jacob, for goodbyes.

Tara walked through the connecting door from the viewing room and into the main hall, and stopped. There was no solitude in the packed space of the crematorium's hall where the service was to be held. Hundreds of people were gathered and more still were arriving. The murder of the twins had been headline news. Everyone was there. A soft murmur of conversation could be heard but a voice broke through it.

'Tara, come over here,' Aunty Marie-Ann said, beckoning Tara to sit in the front seat next to her.

She ignored her aunt and instead looked for a familiar face. A friendlier face. She searched for Gabe but he wasn't sitting in the front row, nor the second.

Her aunty got up and came and took her forcefully by the arm. 'Your mother wants you to sit in the front row with us,' she said.

When they arrived at the bench, she pushed Tara down to sit next to Dela. 'Talking of your mum, where is she?'

'Still saying goodbye to Dad. We saw Uncle Jacob first,' Tara said. She shifted towards the aisle on the hard wooden bench, further away from her aunt.

She tried to shut out the fact that the police had said that the third shot she'd heard had been fired when her uncle had been crawling along the road. He'd been executed, shot in the back of the head. His closed coffin was proof of the execution. The mortician couldn't repair his face for the funeral. If he'd been dragged along further by Ziona, he might have come through the gate with her and survived.

She took a deep breath. She couldn't tell who helped her through the gate. Nothing could bring her uncle or her dad back, but another person didn't need to die because she couldn't keep a secret.

Aunty Marie-Ann tapped her on the arm. 'We still have a few minutes before they start. Do you want anything? A tissue? A drink of water?'

'Not unless you can bring Dad and Uncle Jacob back to life,' Tara said.

Aunty Marie-Ann reached for Tara and pulled her closer, sliding her back up the bench. 'I can't do that, but I can give you a hug.'

Tara grimaced. As soon as she could, she moved away from her aunt.

She didn't want anyone to hold her and make her weak.

She had to be strong. For her dad, her uncle and for Shilo, who had saved her from the same fate.

'You know for some people, learning to cry is harder than conquering Mount Everest,' Aunt Marie-Ann said.

Tara just stared ahead and ground her teeth. The minister entering the chapel saved her the daily lecture from her mother's sister about the body being a pressure cooker and the fluid needing to come out to release pressure. That crying was good for your soul. But Tara couldn't ask her aunt what was good for the body when one was withholding the truth.

The minister came out of the viewing room with her mum walking in front of him. The murmur grew louder, then settled into a strange quietness that wrapped Tara in a blanket of silence for the whole service. At the end, the minister gave each of the family members a single white carnation and a red ribbon from the flowers on her father's and uncle's coffins, then the coffins slid, one after another, into the room behind the curtain, on their last journey together.

Tara could not comprehend or control the rage that ran through her body. They were going to burn her dad and her uncle, and the killer was still out there.

She shook with blind anger. She was born in Africa and she knew the traditional codes and those of the land far surpassed her understanding. There were factors at work she did not understand – yet. But one day she would know, and when that day came, she'd put this whole wrong right.

She followed her mother to stand outside the hall, in the courtyard area. Here white roses bloomed on tall bushes, and neat borders of fragrant flowers shared their space with low green shrubs. Tara stood next to her sister as people came up and hugged her mum and then them. Their lament of 'they were *so* sorry' was like listening to a stuck record.

Tara began to get hot. There was no air and too many people. She swayed, staggered and then stood tall again.

'How much longer?' she asked her mother.

'A while, just keep moving your feet.'

But no matter how much she moved her feet, the darkness at the sides of her vision closed in on her.

'Tara!' Gabe jumped to catch his young cousin before she fell on the hard cement. He picked her up in his arms as if she weighed nothing.

'Please put her inside on one of the benches,' Maggie said.

'You stay here, Maggie. I'll look after her,' Aunty Marie-Ann instructed.

'*Imbodla*,' Gabe said as he put Tara on the bench at the back of the crematorium hall and smoothed her skirt down, covering her legs.

'Hey Gabe,' Tara said, seeing his large familiar smile.

'*Imbodla*, you okay?'

'Why didn't you sit down before you fainted?' Aunty Marie-Ann interrupted. 'What am I to do with you, Tara? You have caused your mother even more stress on a day she really didn't need it.'

'I'm sorry,' Tara said automatically. Already she'd learnt that her mother's sister wasn't someone who suffered fools. She was strict, and she expected to be listened to, no arguments. Tara had only met her once before in her life, and she hadn't liked her then, and she sure as hell hated her aunt now for her unkind words.

Tara looked at Gabe. Gabriel, with his kind, gentle soul, had always been in her life. He was as close to a brother as she was ever going to get. He understood her. Always.

'Marie-Ann, why don't you go grab Tara something cool to drink? I'll make sure she doesn't fall of this bench, it's quite narrow,' Gabe said.

'Oh very well,' Aunty Marie-Ann said as she went off to get the beverage.

'Stuck up old biddy. How her and your mum could be related amazes me,' Gabe said. 'Come on, let's see if you can sit up.'

'Gabriel,' Tara said, 'what's going to happen now?'

'We're going to munch our way through that spread of cakes and drink lots of cups of tea in the room over there, and then home.'

'No, not now. I mean what's going to happen now that my dad and Uncle Jacob aren't there to run their businesses? Who's going to run Whispering Winds?'

'Ah, your mum will most likely sell it. I know Mr Potgieter has approached her already.'

'He can't have our farm! It's not right!' Tara said. 'He's horrid. Whenever I have seen him he always has on the same grass-green suit that looks like he'd split the seams at any moment. Gabe, it's the same colour as baby poop when they get diarrhoea. And his thick legs always in his green knee-high socks, and his safari shorts always ending just above his hairy knees.'

'Don't be nasty about his lack of clothes sense. That look was in vogue a few years back.' Gabe smiled.

Tara grinned. 'Did you see how his bushy beard sticks out at all angles, and he strokes it like it might be a cat. But it doesn't smooth down, it bounces up and curls around his hand as if it were snakes. Like Medusa from my Greek mythology book, except the hair is on his face, not his head. And did you notice that his beady grey eyes are the same as his pit-bull terrier? Like those of a pig, slit and untrustworthy.'

'Now you are just being nasty, Tara. You can have a problem with him, but you can't go around saying things like that—'

'Only to you. I wouldn't dare to anyone one else, Gabe. But I don't want him to have our farm. I don't want anyone to have Whispering Winds, or anything that is ours, except us.'

Gabe smoothed a stray hair off her forehead. 'Sometimes in life it's not what's right that happens, it's more like dumb blind luck. Come on, here comes your aunt and before she gets up at you again, let's get you on your feet and back with your mum.'

'Thanks, Gabe,' Tara said. 'I'm so glad I have a cousin like you.'

'Me too,' he said.

Three weeks after the funeral, Gabe strode through the door of the house Maggie and the girls were renting in Bulawayo. It was so much smaller than the farmhouse that their furniture dominated the rooms. But Maggie had insisted that the girls complete their year of school, and she had moved the family to the city where the girls could continue as day scholars for the rest of the year.

'Maggie, I'm here to take Tara to say goodbye to the horses. I'll bring her back on Sunday night.'

'I still think it's a bad idea. I just wish she didn't need to go back there and that the two of you weren't so adamant to do this without me.'

'It's not that we don't want you there, it's just that it's Tara's goodbye. You've had yours. The girls were still at boarding school when we packed up the farmhouse and moved you into the city. And when you left, you said you'd seen the last of Whispering Winds.'

'I did. And I signed the papers to sell it to Buffel Potgieter last Monday. We don't own it anymore. The bank and everything has been dealt with. I told Mauve this when she called.'

'I know, Mum did tell me. So I called Buffel, and I told him that we wanted to say goodbye, that we need closure. I've already let him know we're there till Sunday, and he said it was fine. Just that we were not to shoot any of the animals.' He turned to Tara. 'You packed?'

'She packed on Tuesday,' Maggie said.

Tara was already standing next to Gabriel with her suitcase.

Together they walked out the door.

Gabe opened the door of his mother's car and made sure Tara was inside. He put her small suitcase in at her feet.

'It's *chockers* in the back, this will have to travel here,' he said before he closed her door, walked around and climbed into the driver seat.

'It's almost like being collected on a Friday from boarding school,' Tara said. 'Going home for the weekend.'

'Almost, except this will be the last time we drive out to Whispering Winds.'

'I know …' Tara said as her voice cracked. 'And thank you for this, Gabe.'

He grinned at her as he started the car. 'Don't thank me until we've survived the weekend's cooking duties together. You know, without a cookboy employed in the farm house anymore, we are going to have to cook our own meals.'

'*Braai* every meal?' Tara asked.

'You bet. Except we can stop for a hot pie and warm bread at the station just as we get onto the Vic Falls road. And I did pack a crate of Coke.'

'We can't drink only Coke all weekend,' Tara said, settling back into the seat as Gabe stuck his head out the window to reverse out the driveway, the camping gear filling the back seat to the ceiling blocking his view.

Once he was out on the road and moving forwards again, he wound up his window with the handle. 'Who says? It's just us. We can do as we please.'

'Can't wait!' Tara said, grinning.

Still grinning after a night of sleeping on a roll-up mattress on the floor in her old bedroom, Tara was woken by Gabe bringing her tea in a tin mug. 'Come on, sleepy head. It's time to get moving.'

'Where we going?' she asked.

'Everywhere and nowhere. We can just ride around the farm, say goodbye and think of all the fun we've had all over this place.'

'Okay,' Tara said. 'I don't want to go near the river.'

'Oh, we're going there. You need to say goodbye to your dad.'

Tara stilled and looked at Gabe. 'I'm not sure I want to go there ...'

'You must, Tara. It's just a place. You need to see that your dad isn't there any longer. Now it's just bush, like everywhere else. Besides, I already asked Buffel Potgieter if he was okay with us visiting there. I told him that I'd spoken to the Member In Charge at the police station, and that he had said it was a good idea that we were coming out to say goodbye.'

'You went to the police?'

'No. I lied. I just told Buffel that so he wouldn't try to stop us going down there. We might never know who shot your dad and Jacob, but we can go say our own goodbye.' Gabe looked at Tara intently. 'I don't know what happened that day. You have been really quiet with the details, and I haven't pushed you to tell me anything. But you can, when the time is right. I know the police tracked the shooter to where he climbed into a *bakkie,* and tracked the spoor of the *bakkie* all the way to the tar road. Then they lost it.'

'Gabe, can I trust you?'

'You know you can. Spill ...'

'It's so hard ... I don't know who killed them, but if I tell about it all, someone who might know, they may die too. I'm not a killer, Gabe, and neither is he. He saved me, he opened the gate. So I made a promise not to tell.'

'You know that could mean your father and uncle's murderer will always be out there?'

She nodded. 'They will get justice when I'm older. Dad always said that justice comes in many different ways, and at many different times.'

'Oh Tara, how is that you're only twelve and yet you understand so much in that head of yours?'

'Maybe because I've got smarts!' She laughed at her cousin and knew that he'd never tell her secret. It was safe.

'So much has changed so fast, Gabe,' she whispered. 'It's all happening too fast.'

'Changes aren't all bad.'

'So far they are. Mum selling the farm, us moving into the city, and then us moving countries so fast. Going to South Africa will be horrid.'

'Hey, South Africa isn't that bad. I'm twenty, and until I started university there two years ago, I had never even been out of Zimbabwe! Treat it as an adventure. Something new. Something different. I felt like that when I started at university. It was so big, so different.'

'That doesn't count. You come home for holidays, and then we see you. Your university is in Stellenbosch and my mum's family is in Durban. When will we ever see you? I don't want to go live anywhere else, I want to live here, Gabe. I just want to stay here.'

'I know, but your mum can't manage this farm alone. That's why she sold it.'

'She *chose* not to manage it. She did most of the work when Dad was working in the city every day, and when he was in the army. I don't understand why she suddenly can't do it anymore.'

'I don't know. Sometimes adults do these weird things.'

'She sold everything without even talking to me and Dela. She never even asked if I wanted to keep anything from here. I have nothing, Gabe. Nothing that belonged to Dad or to Uncle Jacob. She took it all and sold it. My dad wasn't dead for two weeks and she'd sold everything. She couldn't wait to wash her hands of Whispering Winds. To get rid of every memory of Dad.'

Gabe gently placed his hand on the back of her head. 'There are so many things here that I want to take home too, but they don't belong to your family anymore. They are Potgieter's now.'

'My horse – she sold my Elliana and Dad's Apache without even seeing if we could keep them in the city somewhere, like at the showgrounds, or on someone else's place. Or take them to South

Africa with us. What am I supposed to do in South Africa, Gabe? I can't even speak Afrikaans!'

'There are people there who speak English too. I don't know her reasons for not asking you about what you wanted. I think this weekend is her way of saying sorry, that she was wrong. At least she let you come out here with me. It's our weekend to say goodbye to your dad and Uncle Jacob, to the farm and the horses, and also to each other, because I don't know when next I'll see you in South Africa. I promise that we can stay in touch by letters and by phone.'

'Promise me you'll never turn weird like my mum, Gabe!'

'Oh *Imbodla*, I promise,' he said, and he hugged her to him.

She wrapped her arms around his strong shoulders and hugged him back.

'You know what, Gabe? Life without my dad is so not fair. It's crap.'

'I agree with you, but we have to go on living and make it better. Come on, I'm going to get the weapons out of the wall safe. At least your mum didn't sell them with the farm so I could bring them with us this weekend. I know you were unarmed on the day your dad died, but you won't be today. As much as I hate guns, we'll carry them just in case. You need to feel safe while saying goodbye.'

'Gabriel,' Tara said. 'Thank you for understanding me.'

'Sure, kid,' he said as he walked out of the room.

Bomani had saddled Apache and Ziona for them.

'Saddle Elliana as well, Bomani,' Gabe said. 'You can ride with us today.'

Apache stood ready, his coat glossy from brushing and his hooves shining from their recent brushing with linseed oil. His eyes followed Tara's every move. She noticed that Bomani had put her saddle on the stallion.

'But he's Dad's,' Tara said as she turned to Gabe.

'Your dad would want you to take him to say goodbye. Bomani is taking Elliana, so she'll be there too. You can ride both horses.' Gabe looked at Elliana and Apache, standing saddled side by side, as they had been so many times before. 'Let their last ride together be a memorable one with us.' Gabe smiled. 'But Bomani will have to walk Apache if you ride Elee, or he'll be thrown.'

'I guess,' she said, lost in thought about how her father's horse wouldn't let anyone else on him, only her dad, and now her, as she led him over to the corral-style fence so she could climb up on onto the saddle. She remembered when they'd built the horse corral. They had cut down the huge gum trees. And, so that no horse would get hurt, they cleared the stumps from the area. Now the ground was smooth and compacted with just soft sand on the top. Her dad. Her uncle. Gabe. Bomani and the farmboys and her. She ran her hand over the railing where it showed wear from her stepping on it to get onto the horses.

'I don't know why we never got a step of any sort here, you know that? I've seen you clamber up that fence for so many years, getting on horses that were too big for you, yet we never got a block of wood or anything.'

'That's okay, me and the fence are old friends,' Tara said as she slipped her leg over Apache's back and put her feet into her stirrups. They were perfect, no one had changed her saddle. She smiled at that thought, and then frowned.

'She didn't keep my tack, Gabe. I don't even get to keep my saddle Dad gave me for Christmas. It was mine and she sold it.'

'You know, I think if we snuck it into the city Potgieter wouldn't notice. We can hide it at my house, so your mum doesn't know, then when the removal people come to pack your house, we can put it in your garage so it moves with you to South Africa. I know we can't take it all, but we can take your saddle and your dad's if you want. Just because those were special.'

'I'd like that. But Potgieter might come looking for it and I really don't want to see him, Gabe.'

'I bet he hasn't been here yet. Bomani, has *Baas* Potgieter been to look at the horse shed?'

'No. He hasn't been through the gate at all,' Bomani said as he tightened Elliana's girth.

'See, he won't know.'

Tara grinned.

'I won't tell,' Bomani said. 'I will rearrange the tack room so you can't see it's missing.'

'Oh thank you, Bomani!' Tara said. 'Thank you!'

Bomani's white teeth showed in his wide grin. She knew she was going to miss that smile, his gentle touch with the horses, the hours he'd ride with her searching for and picking the sweet donkeyberries when they were in season. Finding the Kaffir oranges that she loved so much, the sweet juicy insides a reward for breaking into the thick yellow exterior. Even when she wasn't out with him, he'd bring some back to her as a gift, because he knew she liked the wild fruit, almost as much as the wild figs that he would bring home too. She smiled as she remembered the amount of times Bomani had ridden with her to collect the ripe prickly pears at the top end of the farm, and would ensure the bucket didn't fall on the way home so they could have the fruit, icy cold from the fridge, with thick cream from the dairy as dessert after dinner. Bomani had always been with her. He wasn't just her horse boy, he was her friend. She just had never realised it before.

She shook her head to dislodge the thought of how much she was going to miss him.

'Come on,' Gabe said and the three of them set out at a walk that soon turned into a canter along the straight stretch of road.

'Race you to the velvet beans,' Tara said, and she kicked Apache in the ribs. The big horse's muscles rippled underneath her as he surged forward.

The canter soon turned into a full-blown gallop towards the field. Tara could feel Apache labour under her and stretch for his next stride. She rocked comfortably in the saddle, crouching low and feeling the breeze stroke its fingers through her hair. The velvet bean field was on their left, and as she raced towards the gate at the far end, she thought about how recently the beans had been flattened by their neighbour's cattle when they had broken through the fence on the far end of Whispering Winds, and eventually ended up in the planted lands. She thought about how, now he owned the farm, it no long mattered that his cattle ate the crops that had been sown to feed the people on the farm that she'd never again sit in the kraal eating *sadza* and beans with *mfino* with Bomani and James, or with Kela or Inacio.

She saw the gap in the fence line where the thick branch of the camel thorn tree had fallen, making a natural steeplechase jump. She slowed Apache to a canter and lined him up then gave him his head. He strode over without even touching the thatching grasses that grew tall and brown on the other side. She slowed him to a walk, and waited for Gabriel to come alongside her.

'*Balla Balla*,' Bomani said, and she turned in her saddle to look where he pointed. A big kudu bull with its twisted horns stood on the edge of the clearing. When Tara clapped her hands once loudly in his direction, he bounded away through the thick bush and was quickly gone.

'That wasn't nice,' Gabriel said. 'He was just minding his own business.'

'Well I don't want Mr Potgieter to see him here. He hunts all the time, you know. You heard him shooting last night,' she said.

Gabe smiled at her. He didn't remind her that her father had hunted too on the very same farm they now rode on. Instead he let her drift away through the forest of trees at the far end of the farm.

When they reached the shallow dam they unsaddled the horses and led them into the water. Soon it was too deep for Tara to stand and she simply held onto Apache's mane as he swam. Ensuring his reins were knotted over his neck, she slid along his body and held onto his tail, floating behind him. When she noticed that he was no longer swimming but beginning to walk she slipped onto his back again. Reluctantly she turned him towards where they had left the saddles. A family of warthog arrived and foraged on the bank.

'I'm going to miss those,' Tara said. 'Every time we ride through here, I watch for them.'

'I know. If you didn't you might get thrown off your horse!' Gabe said as Ziona swam nearby.

Tara smiled.

Eventualy they clambered out the water. Without fear of the horses bolting for home, she watched as they rolled in the dry patch of sand, drying off. Soon they were back on their feet, their neatly brushed hair whorled in all directions as they sneaked the opportunity to snack on the green grass.

Tara, Gabe and Bomani lay on the bank, drying off in the sunshine, watching Egyptian geese squabble over some titbit of food they'd found in the shallow waters.

When Bomani had resaddled Apache, and Tara had strapped her holster back on, Gabe helped her mount into her saddle again.

She looked down at him. 'He's never going to see this again, is he? He'll never ride with us, never touch Apache. He's really dead. He's never coming home.' The tears began to flow.

And they wouldn't stop.

Gabe didn't try to comfort her. He didn't try to stem her tears as Tara howled into Apache's mane. He allowed her the space to grieve.

Bomani looked away.

One month after her father had been murdered, Tara at last cried real tears.

CHAPTER

5

New Beginnings

Hluhluwe, South Africa
January 1982

Hluhluwe in South Africa was small. It was what the Afrikaans people called a *dorp*. But Tara saw it as a new place to call home. Around the town was bush, and wide open spaces. She wound down her window and breathed in the country air.

'What are you doing?' Maggie asked.

'Just filling my lungs with freedom. Smell that air! No soot, no smelly fish sea air ... ah!' After the last three weeks in Durban with her mother's family, she was happy to be out of the city and back in the country, away from their relatives.

Tara knew that moving to Durban hadn't exactly worked out for her mum. The happy family reunion Maggie had hoped for was short-lived. Tara's grandmother and Aunty Marie–Ann had started badgering Maggie about getting a decent job, about her daughters' schooling, and how she was going to keep her 'wild farm girls' out of trouble almost from the first day they arrived.

Dela's voice broke into Tara's thoughts. 'The map says turn off the N2 at R22.'

Her mum made the turn where a huge sign said Hluhluwe Town, with an arrow to turn right, and Game Reserve, with an arrow to turn left.

They drove along, looking at the town they would now call home.

'We need to go through the town, then just before the railway line at the end of the town, we turn right, back towards Durban,' Dela said.

'There's lots of places that take tourists into the game reserve,' Dela pointed out, looking at the shopfronts.

'I'm just glad it's not tall buildings that crush you in and make you feel like you're just an ant,' Tara said, and Dela and Maggie laughed.

'Here, Mum, turn right,' Dela instructed as they reached the railway line.

They drove along the dirt roadway to the end of the houses, then turned left and stopped at a wide Z-style gate where a single house sat behind tall trees. Tara hopped out of the car and opened the gate, then followed behind as Maggie parked in the carport attached to the house.

The house was a whitewashed single storey with a green tin roof. Big trees ringed the property and the scent of freshly cut grass greeted them. A note was pinned to the back door, which Tara read out loud.

'"Welcome, Wright family. The door is open. I'll stop by later to see that you're comfortable." It's signed "Alice Cinco".'

'That's the lady who did the telephone interview with me and organised our accommodation,' Maggie said.

'So this is the lady who gave you the job despite the fact she knows you can't type?' Tara asked.

'Yes and you don't need to rub in the fact that I don't know how to be a railway secretary. I'll learn fast, it can't be too hard to do. I think she sensed my desperation to keep us guys together.'

'I know, Mum,' Tara said. 'I'm so proud of you for getting a real job. But mostly I'm just happy to be out of Durban.'

'I guess it's as good a place as any,' Dela said. 'Just as long as I get my own bed again, I'll be happy. But I'd rather be home in Zimbabwe.'

'We're not going back to Zimbabwe, ever. The financial sanctions in the new Zimbabwe were not real nice to me as a widow, all I could bring out was ten thousand dollars and our furniture. If it wasn't for the laws of the new Zimbabwe, we wouldn't be having to battle financially at all, and I wouldn't have to go to work. Despite your dad providing for us in his death, I couldn't get any of that money out of Zimbabwe. It's almost like walking out like a refugee, except they allowed us to bring our beds. Our days of having a nice house are a thousand kilometres or more behind us. So Dela, this is home now,' Maggie said.

Tara saw her mum dash away a tear.

'Dela, you idiot!' she said. 'You made Mum cry again!'

'I'm sorry, Mum. I didn't mean to upset you,' Dela said. 'It's a good job, and we'll learn how to fit in in Hluhluwe, even though we don't speak any Afrikaans and we'll be living in a railway house …'

'Dela, your days of being a "mistress of the manor" are over. Alice Cinco told me that people who work for the government get their children's schooling at a cheaper rate, and this way we can afford to rent this house and stay together. If I didn't get this type of job, we would be stuck in Durban with your grandmother. Do you think you might like that better than here? At least here we are in the bush again!' Maggie said as she pressed down on the large brass handle on the door and opened it inwards. For a moment there was silence between them, then Maggie gasped as they stepped into the house. 'And we have our own kitchen, look at that old *Esse* stove!'

A big anthracite-burning stove sat in one corner with an electric stove opposite it. The kitchen was functional, but old. The built-in cupboards were made of what looked like plain wood, sanded and hung, unpainted, with no handles. The floor was an ugly red lino. A huge fridge stood on the other side of the room, next to the door that led into the main house.

'It's not a five-star hotel, but it's ours,' Maggie said.

They walked into the next room, Tara leading the way. There was minimal furniture in the dining room, just a fold-up table and four chairs. A brown carpet that had seen better days covered the parquet floor.

'At least we have a table to eat at until our furniture arrives,' Maggie said. 'Come on, let's look at the rest.'

They toured the house together, surprised to find that it had two bathrooms and four bedrooms, more than enough space for the three of them.

'Wow, it's big,' Tara said.

Three mattresses had been piled together in the main bedroom, with neatly folded sheets, pillows and blankets.

'It's nice of Alice to lend us those and the linen,' Maggie said.

'I bags the room that looks over the front lawn,' Dela said as she tugged one mattress off the pile and carried it through to the room she'd chosen.

Tara took hers to the room that was closest to a bathroom. It was the only room with a picture on the wall. A huge old painting of a baby giraffe, a mother giraffe gently pushing it onwards, dominated the small space. Its calming effect appealed to Tara. She ran her fingers over the intricately patterned gold frame.

She walked to the window and looked through the thick metal burglar bars embedded in the plaster on the inside of the wall. Her new room faced onto the back garden, where a washing line was strung between two uprights. She opened the old sash window and breathed in the scent of lavender. She noticed movement in the bush to her left, and a fat warthog trotted out, its grey skin bristling. Tara held her breath.

It stopped at the washing line and scratched its butt on one of the uprights, shaking the lines and the pole as it got to a spot that was obviously itchy. She let out the breath slowly. After nearly four months away from the bush, she couldn't help but gaze at the ugly animal. The warthog foraged on the lawn under the lines, obviously used to there being nobody in the house.

Tara smiled.

Their house.

It was a bit of a fixer-upper, but it was theirs, for now.

No granny.

No Aunty Marie-Ann.

Just the three of them: her mum, Dela and her.

She walked through the house to the car to fetch her suitcase, which she dragged into her room. The first thing she unpacked was the picture of her dad, a present from Gabe. She thought of when her mum had handed the gift to her at Christmas, how she'd slowly opened the wrapping paper and found the simply framed photograph, taken on the day her dad had died. It was of her and her father together. He'd just helped her onto Apache and she was looking down at him while he looked up at her. Apache's ears were forward and alert, showing how proud he was to have her ride him. At the bottom of the photo Gabe had written: 'Remember moments like this and everything will be okay'.

She set it on the windowsill.

'We're here, Dad. It's not Whispering Winds, but at least there are dirt and animals outside,' she said.

Then she unpacked her writing pad, and began to write: 'Dear Gabe ...'

That night, after Alice Cinco had visited and they had eaten a takeaway meal from the Indian shop in Hluhluwe, Maggie called the girls into her room. 'Come, sit.'

They sat down on the mattress and snuggled in next to her.

She took her hands out from where they were hiding under the blanket. In each palm she held a small sparkly box.

'Mum!' they said together.

'I wanted to give you these today because it's our first day in our own home in South Africa,' Maggie said.

Dela ripped hers open at the same time Tara opened hers. 'Thank you, Mum,' Tara said.

She lifted the silver bracelet out of its box. Inscribed on the back were the words: 'Three's a family too – always.'

'Aw, Mum, it's so delicate,' Tara said as she turned the bracelet over and ran it through her fingers.

'Neat!' Dela said.

'Look,' Maggie said as she showed them her wrist. 'I've got one too, because now that we're three, we need to be reminded that we're still a family and we need to stick together.'

Tara looked at her mother and snorted. As if she needed to be reminded that they were now just three.

Her father was gone.

Her farm was gone.

Her horse and everything else that was her life was gone, taken away and sold.

She didn't understand what her mother had done by uprooting them and moving them to South Africa, taking her and Dela away from everyone and everything they knew. Changing their lifestyle so drastically.

A few years ago she had been trusted to carry a weapon with live ammunition, to sleep with claymores in her cupboard and crates of weapons under her bed. But now her father was dead and her mother treated her and Dela like children, incapable of helping her to make any important decisions. Yet she was reminding them that they were the remnants of a family. Just the three of them.

Tara shoved the anger and resentment deep inside.

'You okay?' Maggie asked.

'Will be,' Tara said as she put the bracelet around her wrist. 'Thanks.'

She took a deep breath. And she looked at her mum and sister. They were still together, not scattered across different countries like Gabe was from his family. They had a place they could call home again. That was enough for now. There were new roots beginning to be put down. And for the first time since her father was shot, Tara felt the first stirring of hope that she might not lose her whole family along with him.

That maybe they might not get taken away from her too.

CHAPTER

6

The Butterfly Theory

Piet Retief Farm, Zimbabwe
July 1982

Buffel rocked backwards and forwards in his armchair. Sleep eluded him, despite his exhausted body. Sleeping in his chair was becoming a necessity. He found it easier to wake up from his nightmares in his chair than in his bed, and even if he couldn't sleep, not sleeping at all was better than the nightmares.

He knew that peace was coming eventually. The butterfly dream had shown him that so many months ago.

Peace for Impendla.

Peace for his own conscience.

He just needed to be patient.

Mwari had showed her plan to him.

She hadn't sent a Karoi to tell him, instead she'd entered his nightmare and shown him the way to peace.

In his dream, the angel had taken Impendla's hand and walked with him, crossed over to the other side, and helped him on his journey to his ancestors. And all the butterflies had come from the bush from miles around and flown around them like confetti, to celebrate the release of the children's souls from their cocoons.

If Impendla's soul could be saved like the *Karoi* had saved those people who cast a stone in the deep blue water of Sinoia caves, then his dream of the angel in the cocoon was the path he needed to take.

The angel's blonde hair was so white it shone like a halo. He'd seen it in the dreams that started the very night after she visited him with her mother.

She was the key to helping Impendla's soul cross over.

She was the perfect age to be the sacrifice for Impendla.

Perfect.

The perfect angelic cocoon.

But he'd missed the shot.

He rubbed his hand, fisted it and looked again at where his fingers should have been.

For so long he'd learnt to compensate for the loss of them, and yet just a slight wind, a little excitement at once more taking a human life, and he'd missed the girl.

His dream had shown him that he needed the angel to be part of the ritual. But the beautiful butterfly-in-training from next door had got away.

Shooting the overprotective father and uncle had been a small compensation.

He remembered how the police had crawled over everything at the farm next door and the road on his property near the river bed where the killings of the brothers took place. They had asked everyone about what they had seen. He'd told the police he had been in the house, having a sleep.

Shilo had backed him up, saying that he was in the house snoring.

His *kaffir*-boy hadn't let him down. They had been together during the Rhodesian Bush war, and were bound together by the blood spilled during their time in the PSYOPS unit.

He smiled. It was good to have someone you could trust working for you. It allowed you to pursue alternate interests.

Buffel looked down at his own disfigured hand. Before the war started, he had sacrificed his fingers, saving four other men from certain death during a routine blasting that had gone wrong at his quarry. Those same men had recognised not only his above-average strength, his tenacity and sheer stubborness not to give up, but also his temper that had ultimately given him the physical power to cut his own fingers off to free his hand, and give him time to clear the blast area, and survive. But they had also been privy to his irrational insistence that they try to find the pieces of his fingers. They had spent hours searching, but to no avail. His fingers were gone, and all that the hospital could do was neaten the amputation up, offer condolences, and praise him for saving his workers, one of whom was an ex-South African. From then on they all referred to him as Buffel.

He looked at the two fingers he'd taken from the men who had protected the angel that day. And he remembered the sight. In death the brothers had looked like he did, incomplete.

Collecting tokens from them had been an unplanned bonus.

He'd pinned them with dress pins to a piece of kaylite to dry, then he'd put them with the other trinkets he collected to decorate his cocoons. He'd get to use them one day. He'd have that butterfly moment in real life, not just in his dreams. But sometimes, like tonight, he would dig them out from their hiding place, and he would touch them, as if touching the father would bring him knowledge of where the daughter now was. As if perhaps he could lead him to her in South Africa somewhere.

One day he would get to decorate the angel with their bones, hang them around her neck as a decoration to take with her into the spirit world. She would appreciate having her father and uncle there to guide her, to be with her, as she guided Impendla and the other boys towards the light.

He tipped his head backwards and rocked again.

Perhaps one day, *Mwari* would reward him for his sacrifices, and his dedication, and he would allow Impendla's soul to be saved, as it had been in his dream. Allow his friend's spirit to fly like the butterflies they used to watch down at the dam when they were just kids.

Allow him to fly free and join his ancestors in the light, instead of remaining an eternal child in a cocoon state.

Where they had been. Never to hatch. Never to know the sense of freedom and the gift of flight.

He still knew that his friend rested in a dark place.

Only now he understood he needed to appease *Mwari*, to allow Impendla into the light. To cross over and go to his ancestors.

His minister father had always claimed that Impendla was an innocent child and God forgave and welcomed the innocent into his heaven, but Buffel wasn't so sure about that. He believed Impendla had paid incorrectly.

It was he who should have been taken.

It was he who had disturbed the *Karoi*'s magic and invaded her area. It was he who had angered the *Tokoloshe* and yet it was Impendla, who had warned him of the dangers, who had paid the ultimate price.

For a moment, he shuddered at the thought that he'd already sold his own soul to try to save Impendla's. The concept didn't rest easy within him, even all these years later, his Christian upbringing and the expected morals that came with it like a megaphone in the back of his head.

But in reality, this was his punishment to bear.

He'd done nothing at the time to save his friend.

And that rested heavy like molten lead in his conscience.

The feeling of sadness lifted, and he knew that *Mwari* was giving him guidance. He closed his eyes, holding his trophies in his hand as the TV flickered. Its black and white images broadcast out to no one as Buffel fell asleep, still in his armchair.

He moved slightly in his sleep, grunted, and plunged into his dark recurring nightmare. The one that he had stopped having for a while, but had lately returned. The one he avoided sleep to escape from.

* * *

The bald-headed vultures circled, riding the hot air currents, gathering like dark clouds above the mission station. Soaring on the wind, they eyed something way below them, waiting for the opportune moment to drop from the sky and devour whatever carrion they could. Human or animal, they didn't care, meat was meat and death meant a meal.

It was their way of life.

They glided lower, then rose in height again, as if they knew that although there was food they were as yet unable to gather it.

Buffel peered upwards at them through the thick green bush, knowing he was almost as invisible as his horse, Benga, who was decorated in the same green and brown foliage that surrounded them, even though his black fur already provided natural camouflage in the dense bush. 'Scavengers. Never a good sign,' he whispered.

Slowly he edged his horse forward, trying to glimpse the mission they knew had come under attack as recently as two hours before. The team was uncertain if they would be able to approach, if it had been abandoned or if there were still survivors they could rescue. A weight sat in his stomach, a dread.

Death had visited, that he knew.

'Check for trip wires,' Corporal Mike Mitchells instructed.

Together they dismounted and signalled for the four men with them to do the same.

Buffel handed Mike his reins. 'I'll go.'

He edged out from their position, methodically checking the ground for signs of landmines, or trip wires that would set off concealed claymores tied to trees. Those built to maim, with explosives that drove fragments of metal with maximum impact ripping through human flesh.

He held his breath, expecting the explosion that could end his life at any moment. He studied the leaves on the trees to see if anything had been tampered with, and his eyes darted to the ground beneath. Nothing appeared out of place. His trained eyes returned to the trees, his trained eyes searching deeper into the shadows to check if anything looked suspicious.

Nothing. It looked just as the African bush should.

Slowly, he walked the final fifteen metres to the clearing around the mission. Ahead of him was the mission's eight-foot security fence. Without the modern wire fence, the property could have been the mission he had grown up on. The architecture of the whitewashed building might be different, but it looked similar in that it invited those inside to find peace within its walls. The unit of six Grey's Scouts had already navigated through the orchard and fields where food was grown to feed the hungry that came to worship here, and the familiarity squeezed his heart.

A different time. A different mission.

It had been many years since he'd thought of the mission where he'd grown up. He'd been happy to leave there when he was just sixteen to forge his own way in life. Away from the tyrannical rule of any God.

He needed to concentrate on his surroundings. He needed his wits about him to stay alive. His whole focus. Once more, he looked at the ground for any signs of traps or anti-personnel mines laid there.

It looked clear.

He dropped to his stomach and used his binoculars to search the buildings.

Once whitewashed and proud, the Dutch gabled building was scarred black from mortar fire, and red brick showed through where the building had taken a direct hit, crumbling under the modern explosives. The old mission walls had fallen in, despite being made of solid local grey stone and double bricked. The cross that had once stood proudly lay face down on the ground in pieces. It now looked more like a peace sign than something you would crucify someone on.

'Two friendlies deceased on the mission steps,' he relayed the information to Mike behind him. 'Two more against the wall of the church to the right.' He could see the splatter of red against the whiteness, and he knew they had been executed.

He'd seen this exact scene before. Almost duplicated.

This was the second mission to be attacked in a month. But it never stopped hurting his heart to see the death, the destruction. The barbaric cruelty.

'I doubt we have any survivors here.'

Mike nodded and handed him back his reins as he remounted, and signalled into the bush for the other scouts to join them.

They rode in silence into the mission, gathered together in a defensive knot, weapons aimed in all directions. The horses packed tightly together, noses flared as if they knew the danger they were heading into.

A lone white goat with a brown head and long ears bayed as it ran out past them, its tail clamped between its legs.

They let it run.

'Something's still here to spook that goat,' Zack said.

'You bet,' Mike replied, 'let's flush them out. We don't ride these demon horses for nothing.'

Henny sniggered.

'It's not a joke, Henny,' Mike said, 'the reputation of our horses being able to run through fire and enter any building is legendary, and one day fear of these horses will be the only thing that stands between you and certain death. The superstitious tales of our horses with glowing red eyes will save you from that death as some *ter* craps in his *broekies* when he sees them. Don't underestimate the black mind that believes in magic.'

'I know, Corporal, but to me, it's still silly that they believe in demons—'

'You are young. You'll learn there is more to life than what you know at nineteen. Now you and Zack stay here,' Mike instructed the two youngest of the group. 'If anything happens to us, get the hell out of here, and keep riding until you get back to the trucks. Don't look back!'

'Yes, sir,' the two youngsters said.

Buffel shook his head. 'Ah, to be young and indestructible—'

'Problem is, they haven't leant yet that bullets don't bounce off you, they hurt. Let's try keep it that way!' Mike said, then he clicked his tongue, and the four older men's horses broke into a canter together. They thundered down on the building before splitting up. Mike took point, riding up the steps of the church and in through the once humble doors now hanging on their hinges.

Buffel took the left flank to circle around the outside of the back of the church and funnel anything there towards the church. Nick rode hard to the right and behind the missionaries' houses, while Enoch rode further right to come around the back of the school rooms.

Buffel could hear Benga's laboured breathing as she jumped nimbly over another body. He didn't need to stop to check for life signs. Anyone with eyes could see half the *piccaninny*'s head was blown off. There was no way he was alive.

He continued his search. He entered the back of the chuch building through an archway in the rear side. He rode towards the back of the altar.

He stopped Benga and stared at the sight in front of him.

There were twenty-five children, ranging in age from about three to fifteen. Every one had been executed by a single shot to the head, then laid out next to each other. He stared at them as he dismounted.

A blinding rage tore at his heart.

The orphans.

They had killed the orphans.

Innocent children, who had no one but the priest and nuns to care for them, had been executed.

Slowly he checked each one was dead, then he joined their hands together, so that they were no longer alone in death.

His mind thought back to when he was just ten years old and how the children who died had been laid out next to each other. Each body had been so small, including Impendla's. Someone had joined their hands.

He racked his memory to remember who.

But he couldn't remember. It was a dark time. A time when his father said Satan was winning and he needed to believe more in God to banish the devil from their mission, their home.

Buffel shook his head, trying to dislodge the sudden memory.

He didn't normally remember anything about that day, other than Impendla being dead. His mind had blanked it out. His father had said God's angels had touched his head and helped him to forget so that he could live a normal, healthy life in the service of God.

The mission worker had said *Mwari* had spared him, but now he owed *Mwari*.

He didn't believe either.

Looking at the massacre of the children, he knew that as an adult, he still didn't.

Having grown up under the strict rod of the Christian God with the influence of the Shona peoples' gods and superstitions, he thought perhaps he was closer to agnostic. He did believe in souls and an afterlife. He believed in *something*, just not what was being preached at that time.

He remounted and looked around. Mike was still sweeping for terrorists, pew by pew from the back towards the front. He saw a second door behind the altar was closed and tapped Benga's flank, giving her permission to open it. With a splintering whack, her iron-clad hooves shattered the bolt, as she smacked it in quick succession with first her right, then left front hoof.

They entered the room.

Nothing.

It was empty, a storeroom or something, with no place for anyone to be hiding from them.

They backed out together and headed for another closed door to the right.

Only this time, as they approached, the door opened and a gook ran out, shooting wildly at them with an AK-47.

Benga stayed true.

She knocked into the gook's chest with her head, tossing him a few feet in the air. He landed on his backside, eyes wide. He rolled over onto his knees and attempted to crawl away. Benga didn't waver when her iron-hooves bit into the flesh of his back as she trampled him underneath. The immediate danger disabled, she pranced to the side to allow Buffel to complete his task. He jumped off, kicked the AK-47 away and knelt on the enemy's back, binding his wrists quickly and firmly with rope.

He could feel the man beneath his knee breathe and knew he still lived. At least they had one for information.

Benga's nostrils flared.

Danger.

He'd been with her long enough to trust her reactions in any combat situation. Alert, he looked around. Mike was now standing near the dead children. He looked further, through the doors of the front of the church, just as the clearly marked mission Land Rover drove past.

Leaving the captured gook secured, he remounted Benga and ran towards the door, past Mike, who was mounting up.

Once out of the church Benga jumped down the stairs, her body supple beneath his, her hooves gripping true as they bit into the rough concrete. Buffel watched as the vehicle headed directly for Zack and Henny. Now he had a better view he could confirm that the man at the wheel was no missionary. It was clearly another gook, spraying bullets liberally towards the young ones. Instead of running, Zack and Henny were keeping their horses under control and aiming at the driver. Henny was shooting at him. Buffel saw a shot hit the seat behind the driver as Henny reloaded and tried again. Taking careful aim. Zack had frozen.

He dug his heels into Benga's side and raced towards his fellow scouts.

Slowly he adjusted himself to lie over Benga's neck, putting his barrel between her ears, and at her next stride he lined up the hairs on his scope on the man driving the Land Rover. He knew if he missed he could shoot one of the youngsters, or their horses, but if he didn't, the gunman would mow down the two youngest members of their unit.

He and Mike would never forgive themselves. So far, they had lost no one from their platoon. And he didn't want to start today ... He blacked out the noise of the wind.

Henny took another shot, the sound loud breaking Buffel's concentration.

The vehicle veered left, and slammed into a blue gum tree, the horn blowing loudly as the driver slumped against the steering wheel.

Zack and Henny were still mounted. They had kept their post. They hadn't run as instructed by Mike. Zack's gun was still at his shoulder.

'You okay?' Buffel called, as he looked at the young boys. Henny nodded. He patted his horse and drew the strap of his rifle over his shoulder, automatically adjusting his weight in the saddle to compensate for the shift in his posture.

'Am now,' Zack replied as he too slowly lowered his FN and flicked his safety back on, but his face said otherwise. He wore the stark expression of terror.

He was pretty sure Zack had lied about his age to join the scouts, but he was a good rider. His rapport with the horses was already legendary, and he had come into the Grey's Scouts knowing how to track, and how to shoot. A farm kid used to the bush, animals, and weapons. All he needed was experience behind him and the kid would be one of the finest scouts in the whole battalion. He didn't drink, didn't appear to flirt with the girls, and was well liked. A sergeant major in the makings ... if Buffel and Mike could keep him alive long enough.

'Just take deep breaths. The fear will subside,' he said quickly, 'Settle your horse, she's prancing.'

'Thank you,' Zack said as he patted his horse reassuringly. 'I couldn't shoot him.'

'Because he was moving?'

'No,' said Zack, 'because I knew him. He used to be one of the tobacco shed packers on our farm up in Mashonaland. I couldn't kill him. And he just kept coming.'

'It's shoot to kill or be killed. You were lucky Henny had your back today. Better yet, do as you were instructed and run next time!'

'Yeah right, and be labelled a chicken?' Zack said.

'Better a live chicken than a dead one,' Buffel said. 'Henny, you did good. Zack, we are going to need more practice once we get back to base.'

'I second that,' Mike said from behind him.

But as he turned Benga towards Mike, he heard two shots, each shot followed by a sickening fleshy thunk. And then another two.

Time stood still.

He whirled Benga around to the youngsters. Henny was lying on the ground. His face had been blown away. Zack clutched at his chest, slowly slumping forward to topple off his horse. Buffel threw himself to the ground, just as a bullet whizzed closely past him. He could hear its hollow sound.

'Down!' he instructed Benga. She immediately listened and collapsed her legs, lying flat next to him, her head against the ground. The whites of her eyes were large, showing her fear, but she knew to trust her master. Mike and his horse were already on the ground, but they were unharmed.

Buffel drew his trusty FN into position and crawled on his stomach closer to his horse. All the while he searched the bush for where the shots had come from. Another flash from a barrel as the gook took a shot at him and Mike, giving away his position, and Buffel and Mike opened fire together with automatic setting, mowing anything in the vicinity down.

Buffel heard his bullets hit true, but crawled closer to check the gook was dead.

He was.

Buffel pumped the rest of the clip of bullets into him just in case.

Then he turned and looked at the boys lying on the hard ground.

He'd lost them. Two boys down.

They had trusted him.

Just like Impendla all those years ago.

Now they were dead.

Rage bubbled up like lava inside him, while an inhuman noise came out of his mouth.

He took his rope from behind his saddle, and tied the gook's feet together. Then he hung him upside-down from a branch in the tree just inside the security fence of the mission. He stripped his clothes off, then he carved the dead man's already bleeding body with the same cuts that the *Karoi* had made to the children's bodies, so many years ago.

It was as if Impendla and his *Mwari* were now in charge of his actions. As if *Nyamhika Nehanda* herself guided his moves. Once that first gook was strung up in the tree, he fetched the other one from the Land Rover. He searched in the back and found more rope. Then he hoisted him up on his shoulder and easily carried him to the tree. Performing the same ritual, he made sure he bound the gook's rifle to his side, just as the *Karoi* had done with Impendla so many years before.

This area was cursed.

No one must ever come here again. The mission was never to be resettled.

He went in search of more bodies.

'Buffel, snap out if it! Now! That's an order!' A voice commanded from a distance, but then he felt someone slapped him hard across the face. His cheek stung. *Not so much of a distance ...*

Buffel's eyes took a moment to focus on the camo-clad assailant in front of him. Then he charged like a bull out of a chute with cows in the paddock, right at his assailant.

But the assailant was smaller, quicker than him as he stepped aside, and Buffel passed by. The assailant quickly disarmed him of his bush knife with one clean sweep against his body. Shaking his head at the loss, Buffel turned back for another pass at his assailant, but he heard the distinctive sound of a rifle being loaded.

'Don't take another step, soldier!'

Buffel stepped forward slowly.

The assailant shot at the ground just in front of Buffel's feet. Sand scattered up his shins and over his shoes, and then Buffel felt a sensation wash over him as if a million Matabele ants had climbed over his skin. Buffel looked at his attacker.

'Fuck Mike, why are you shooting at me?' he asked.

'You don't know? Look around you. Look in the tree!' Mike demanded.

Buffel looked around.

Buffel saw the six bodies hung like cocoons in a jungle, and he saw the fresh blood as it congealed on the black bodies hanging in the tree. Each dangled by their feet by rope, with their weapons tied at their sides.

Six dead bodies.

'What the fuck!' Buffel said. 'When did a *sangoma* visit here?'

Mike was staring at him. 'No fucking *sangoma*. This was you!'

Buffel sank to his knees. The memories flooded back into his conscious brain.

The smell.

The tree.

The Karoi killing his dog.

Him dropping his father's rifle.

Impendla swinging by his feet in the tree like a cocoon, suspended between death and the other side.

Death. Impendla was dead.

It was as if he was ten years old again, and he was reliving the execution of his best friend.

Now he knew why his brain had locked the memories away.

Now he knew what was inside of him.

'Impendla. Oh my God. It's like Impendla said, the *Nyamhika Nehanda* is inside of me.'

* * *

With a start Buffel woke. Sweat dripped from his forehead and ran down his chest. His hands were clammy as if he'd had them clenched for too long. His breathing was hard and ragged.

The dream had been so real.

He had been back there, reliving it once again.

He sniffed the air and couldn't smell horses.

He listened.

Silence.

He took a moment to move from his nightmare back into reality as he looked around. He was in his chair, the TV station had ended for the night and black and white snow filled the screen. There was no sound. Not even static came from the small box in the corner. No champagne frogs croaked in the dam. No jackals called in the distance.

Something else had woken him.

It was too quiet.

He stood up, and his forgotten trophies fell to the floor. He walked to the window. It was dark outside when he moved the curtain. He ran his hands over his face and down his chest, patting his pocket to look for his tobacco pouch.

He took a little and slipped it into his mouth.

The familiar action of chewing his tobacco calmed him, slowed his racing blood. He moved his head from side to side, stretching it out. His neck made an unhealthy clicking sound, loud in the stillness of the night.

It had been a few years since he'd had that particular nightmare, although his sleep was constantly plagued with vivid nightmares of other times.

At first when he was transferred from the Grey's Scouts to the PSYOPS unit, he'd had that day replay itself in his head every night. Followed by the bitter disappointment he'd seen in Mike's eyes. The total horror in Nick's and Enoch's eyes at what he'd done to the dead *ters*.

But PSYOPS had sorted all that out, and made him feel special.

Different.

Needed.

Gradually, the day that forced the memories to return, his last day as a Grey's Scout, faded into oblivion, and was replaced with a recurring nightmare of the day they had found Impendla cocooned in the tree. Only in his nightmare it was the voice of the dead and bloodied Impendla who called out to him. Begged him for help. Some nights it would be other faces, others he'd killed and tortured during the bush war who called out to him, but he never woke up startled from those dreams. He felt nothing for those people. They were just black *kaffirs* whose path of death and destruction had crossed over with his.

They were not his friends. He cared about his dreams when he dreamed of Impendla.

The others were just a waste of a peaceful night's rest.

The power the *sangoma* had over the minds of the majority of the black population was incredible. Just a short time ago, before the new Zimbabwe, he'd preyed on that fear, duplicating the ritual, the *sangoma*'s dark magic to ensure the black population were scared, were controllable.

Once he'd remembered the ritual.

Now that he remembered, he never wanted to forget again.

He needed to make up for his memory blank, for the time he did forget and for not helping Impendla earlier.

But none of his sacrifices had helped Impendla.

Sure, they had kept the black population from misbehaving at the time, but it hadn't eased the sorrow of the dead children from his childhood.

He needed to silence the children in his head, who still called to him for help alongside Impendla.

Only when he'd got the ritual perfect would Impendla's soul be saved. Only when he found Tara Wright would it be completed.

He knew it wasn't perfect yet, despite all the practice he'd had during his PSYOPS years.

The butterfly held the secret to unlocking Impendla's cocoon … she could help him.

One butterfly.

He needed one butterfly on the edge of maturity to complete the ritual …

He frowned.

Tara Wright was out of his reach for the moment.

Perhaps he could find another girl with blonde hair and deep blue eyes.

For some reason, there were no children who lived on his farm. The workers all chose not to live with their children. It was a strange set-up, but he thought it was just as well, because if too many children were taken in one area, suspicions might begin to turn to why the *sangoma* was doing so many ritual killings, and the real *sangoma* might come looking for who was really responsible. He shuddered at he thought of a real *Karoi* visiting him. As an adult he was more afraid than he'd been as an innocent child.

He knew that in most tribal trust lands where he had once been active as a PSYOPS operative, the people now kept their children watched closely. No child herded the goats and cattle alone anymore. No child went unaccompanied, and even the newer white-influenced practice of having the children sleep in their own bedroom had quickly stopped. People had gone back to their traditional sleeping arrangement of the family group in one large room. Everyone under the same roof.

Because of that, he would need to go further if he was to collect his butterflies.

Hunt in new territory.

But the trust lands didn't hold angels with blonde hair. Those were few and far between on the farmlands, too. He'd need to look in the cities.

He was due to go to South Africa to fetch his new Dorper rams for his breeding sheep. Perhaps he could kill two birds with one stone.

Once he had a blonde-haired, blue-eyed replacement for Tara, he'd see if his ritual would help Impendla's soul.

He peered into the darkness.

'Shilo,' he called out. 'You walking around out there?'

No answer.

Then he remembered he'd fired Shilo.

He had driven him away.

Anger burnt deep down in his stomach at the betrayal he'd felt.

Panic rose in his throat that he was now alone and would have to deal with many things that Shilo had said. And it was all starting again with the return of his nightmares.

He still couldn't quite believe what had happened. He'd trusted Shilo, and Shilo had let him down.

He shook his head as the darkness threatened to crush in on him.

It was Shilo's fault that his butterfly had got away. He had blamed himself, yet it turned out Shilo had been there and saved Tara from his trap against the fence line.

The gate had been opened and closed. Someone had let her and her herd of horses free.

It could only have been Shilo. Yet, when confronted, Shilo had never denied that he had been there. Instead he had started yelling at him that that he was in the wrong, not Shilo.

He was a monster.

He was *penga*.

He thought of the tracks again. No other African on his farm had the skills or the strength and stamina to run in the bush, and to almost perfectly cover his tracks. When he'd happened upon the old footprints, deeply embedded into the mud near the river, Buffel had known.

Had known that those footprints belonged to Shilo. Known when they were made.

He remembered the first time he'd seen footprints like these, years ago, on their first mission together into Mozambique. Three sets of prints doubling back and stopping to watch him at the school. But only Riley had confronted him. He knew then that two other men had witnessed what he'd done.

He hadn't had to wait long to find out who.

From the five men left in the paratroopers, Shilo and Kwazi had been unable to look at him the next day when everyone was called together to tell the company that Sergeant Riley had died. He knew then that they had been the ones. They couldn't stand to be near the PSYOPS maniac.

So he'd insisted on having them with him constantly, arranged for them to become PSYOPS so he could keep an eye on them and keep them bound to him. They had learnt to serve their Captain above all else. They became part of 1st PSYOPS. They learnt that their motto of '*Tiri Tose*' – 'we are together' – was forever. The acknowledgement that they were all responsible for what happened within the unit ran strongly within them. It was likely that 'there is no escape' became more of their motto than 'we are together'. No one within PSYOPS would ever tell a soul about their work, as bringing shame to someone within your own company would bring shame to the whole unit.

They were brothers in arms.

You never spoke of what you had to do in the name of protecting your country. If you ever spoke about it, the others in the unit would hunt you down, and silence you.

The war had ended soon afterwards, only two and a bit years later, but by then Buffel knew that Kwazi was never going to be a problem to him and would never talk. He'd built up too much wealth that he didn't want to lose. He was a strong man mentally, clever, but his weakness was his wealth. Threaten that, and Kwazi would do whatever he was told.

But Shilo was different.

Silent. With no family, no wealth. He knew with certainty that Shilo had to be kept close to him, because Shilo possessed a moral compass bigger than that on a Portuguese exploring vessel, and he'd always shown compassion in the end. He was a natural born hero.

If there was ever a war commission for reconciliation, Buffel suspected that Shilo would be the troopie talking and helping to ease the masses. Calming the people, making things seem right when they were wrong.

Shilo was now a loose cannon, because Buffel had tossed him out into the world in a temper tantrum that even a two-year-old would find it hard to rival.

He'd made a huge mistake making Shilo leave.

But Shilo had wanted to leave.

Buffel shook his head at his own confusion, not sure where the truth was. He walked to his television and turned the knob slowly to the off position. The loud click in the quiet night was foreign and intrusive. In the dark he made his way to his bedroom.

He dragged an old rucksack and his duffel bag out the cupboard and began packing.

He had work to do if was going to save Impendla's soul.

But first he needed to track down Shilo, and silence him forever, because unlike the military massacres that were forgiven under the new regime that now ran Zimbabwe, leaving a credible witness to his shooting of two civilians was a different kettle of fish.

Only after that could he again search for the butterfly Tara Wright, with the white hair, whose mother had taken her from Zimbabwe, and moved her into South Africa.

He would find her.

He would save Impendla.

CHAPTER

7

Shilo's Freedom

**Nyamandhlovu, Zimbabwe
1982**

Shilo walked into the train station. Self-consciously he patted the dust from his tatty blue overalls, and curled his toes inwards in an attempt to hide that he wore no shoes. He carried no luggage, and sported a bruised eye that bulged slightly outwards, but he was smiling.

He was emerging after hiding in the bush for three weeks, since the day *Baas* Buffel Kirchman Potgieter had fired him. Thrown him his wages on the dry *goosie* sand and turned his back on him. The PSYOPS Captain had had enough of his black paratrooper being underfoot.

When the unit was being disbanded, it had been his idea to stick to Buffel for a while, to make sure that he didn't continue his killings in his civilian life. He thought that perhaps when they returned to his farm and continued with a normal life that the killings would be over. Kwazi had disagreed, his thoughts were that Buffel had gone *penga* and would continue the killings and the ritual.

Kwazi had been right.

But it had only started after almost a year, with the shooting of the brothers.

Only after Buffel's fated tea with his neighbour's wife Maggie and the child Tara. *Imbodla*. The child with the golden hair.

It was as if having the youngster so near him had rekindled a deep violent urge. Only luck had allowed Shilo to save the girl that first day. Keeping Buffel away a second time, when Gabe had called to say they would be at the farm paying their respects and their goodbyes, had been torture.

He'd sabotaged Buffel twice before he was found out.

He was lucky he was just fired, and not dead.

Buffel had concealed his rage and anger well from the police who visited, and from the community as he attended the funerals of those same men he'd killed.

From everyone except Shilo.

Shilo had seen the beast re-emerging, and had been terrified he wouldn't be able to help the next time he decided to kill a child.

Getting away was a bittersweet freedom.

Now that he was fired, there was no reason to hang around Buffel.

Now that he was fired, there was no way for him to stop Buffel going after more children.

Now that he was fired, he was free.

He cursed that he hadn't covered his face when he'd had to reveal himself to Tara Wright. He realised afterwards how much the promise he'd asked the young Tara to make would plague her and how hard the secret would be to keep.

Being around Buffel put Shilo in more danger than not being around him for the time being, so he'd been trying to leave ever since. He had tried.

He'd resigned.

Buffel had not accepted it.

They had quarrelled.

He had left in the night. Gone into the bush, and only emerging once he hit the tarmac of the main road that could be walked on with very little sign of his presence. He had almost reached the town siding, where he had hoped to catch a train and leave.

But Buffel had driven up next to him in his *bakkie*, and told him to get in the back. His home was with Buffel.

He'd told Buffel that his mother had died and he needed to go to her funeral. Buffel said she'd died during the attack on Shilo Mission at the start of the war. Buffel's memory was longer than the wiry hair on his beard. Buffel had seen through his excuses, pressing him as to why he suddenly wanted to leave.

Shilo closed his eyes at the torment when he realised that Buffel genuinely didn't want him to go, but he couldn't work out why.

Buffel lacked the basic emotions of someone who could be a friend. Shilo wondered if in some small way, Buffel didn't want to be alone with what he'd become. Perhaps deep down he couldn't live with what he'd done, and having Shilo around helped him. Perhaps he felt that, still being with someone from his PSYOPS unit who shared the guilt of war crimes, he could live with what he had done.

'*Tiri Tose*. We are together.'

A burden shared was a less heavy one.

He thought of their final argument and what he had said to Buffel.

He remembered the pain as Buffel had hit him in the face, but he hadn't struck him back. Buffel thrived on violence, and Shilo now knew that to feed the monster made him worse. So he had talked to him instead.

'You can't go around killing children.'

Buffel had laughed. 'It will save Impendla's soul, I have to do it this. *Nyamhika Nehanda* herself guides me on this mission.'

'No, Buffel, sickness guides you. You began to enjoy the killing too much, and when the war stopped you needed to stop too. You didn't.'

'But she can save him, she can save him, Shilo! And you helped her! You helped her escape so that the voices now cry in my head, and I can't silence them.'

'You are sick, Buffel. You are sick. You need to go to *Ingutchini*. I cannot help you anymore. I cannot stand by and watch this. I almost shot you by the dam the other day. I am a black man in a country that still has a lot of white rules, and I would have gladly died in prison for shooting a white man, because what you are doing is wrong. She is just a child. Buffel, you have to see that.'

'No, it is what *Mwari* wants. It will save Impendla,' Buffel shouted.

'You know that I was brought up in the Shilo Mission. I believe in God the Father, God the Son and God the Holy Spirit. The one God. I can't help you if you choose to believe in the Shona God, Buffel, I can't stay here anymore.'

'If that is what you must do, then go. Leave me. You are fired. Never darken my doorstep again. I'll get your pay drawn up.'

It was still hard to remember that just moments later, Buffel had thrown his pay in the dirt, and then he had beaten him some more in his rage. And when Shilo had walked away down the farm road towards his *ikhaya*, Buffel had got into his *bakkie* to get past him. He had thrown petrol on his *ikhaya* and burnt his humble home down.

'Still leaving, Shilo? Now you have nothing.'

'Yes, still leaving,' Shilo said as he had walked away again.

This time Buffel didn't follow and didn't do anything but stand on the spot for a long time.

Shilo soon melted into the bush, determined that this time, he was gone for good.

This time Buffel wouldn't find him and bring him home like a stray dog.

The price was high, but he was happy to pay it. He had covered his tracks. He had doubled back, he had watched Buffel try to track him, and slept in antbear holes to smother his scent and to lose Buffel. And after a week, Buffel had given up. He wasn't at his farmhouse, but he hadn't tried to track him anymore.

At last he had earned his freedom.

Freedom from a monster.

He lifted his head at the ticket vendor behind the small barred window. 'One ticket to Umtali.'

'You have to go to Bulawayo, then to Salisbury, then to Umtali.'

Shilo handed over the money from his wages.

The ticket master held out his tickets. 'This one takes you to Bulawayo. When the conductor checks your tickets, give him this one only.' He put the second ticket next to the first. 'This one, it goes to Salisbury. Don't give the wrong ticket to the conductor. This last one,' he put the third part of the ticket down, 'this takes you to Umtali. Get something warmer to wear before you get there.'

Shilo grinned at him.

'You keep those somewhere safe, make sure there is no hole in the pocket you put them in, understand?' The old ticket vendor had probably been doing his job for many years, sweeping the station, and now in the new Zimbabwe, he'd been promoted and was in charge of the ticketing. He was proud of his job.

Shilo looked down at his own clothes. The blue overalls were damaged at the knee and had seen tidier times. Anyone would mistake him for a vagrant farm worker.

He took the paper ticket in his right hand. '*Siyabonga kakulu Madala*,' he said to the older ticket vendor as a sign of respect. 'I will look after them.'

'Travel well.'

Shilo looked at the man sitting in the cubicle. His face was lined deeply by the sun and years of living. He had the look of old age, but the dark eyes that sat in that bald head still looked at him with intelligence and understanding, but more, with compassion.

He was early, the train wasn't for another hour, but Shilo hadn't known how long it would take to walk from his hiding place in the bush to the train station. He hadn't seen any sign of Buffel following him so he'd decided that today, he'd catch the train.

He sat on the bench and waited, closing his eyes. He'd hear the train coming from miles away and feel it when it got close, so for the moment he rested.

He saw white sands and an ocean so blue and clear that the silver fish darted from seagrass clump to seagrass clump to avoid being seen. He could almost feel the wind on his face as the dhow cut through the water, skimming towards the island.

The sound of a soft step nearby startled him and he jumped up, pulling back a fist ready to strike. But it wasn't Buffel, just the old man from the ticket office who stood in front of him. He quickly dropped his arm, and his fighting stance.

The old man smiled at him. 'I had this in my office.' He handed Shilo a hand-knitted woollen jersey that had seen better days. 'Just in case. You will need it more than me in Umtali. It is cold up in those mountains.'

'Thank you, *Madala*. Thank you.'

The old ticket vendor nodded and shuffled back to his little booth that sat on the edge of the concrete platform, back into his little work place, with a ceiling fan that defied its age and continued to swirl the already hot air around the small room, as the sun beat down on the red corrugated iron roof.

Shilo stared after him and wrapped the jersey around his hands. That single item of clothing was now his only possession, other than what he wore. Buffel had burnt down his *ikhaya* and all his possessions in it. He'd nothing now to show of their days together. Snorting, he corrected his thinking.

He'd nothing to show for his thirty years on the earth. Well, except a bank account, that he no longer had a bankbook to access.

But he was alive.

At first, keeping an eye on the war torn PSYOPS Captain hadn't been that hard. Ensuring no children lived on the farm had been easy. Accompanying him everywhere he went had not been difficult. But since the Tara visit, when he'd begun to kill again, it had become a living nightmare. Such an innocent catalyst to bring the monster out again. Such an insignificant event, yet the results were horrific.

Almost a month after her father's funeral, Tara had visited Whispering Winds for the last time. Buffel had informed him they were going hunting, which was nothing new. But Shilo had known the moment they went to cross through the strands of barbed wire, and onto the neighbouring farm, that this wasn't a normal hunt.

They were hunting humans.

With a sickness in his stomach, Shilo knew he just couldn't live this life anymore. Couldn't continue to put his own life on hold while he watched over a monster who could emerge at any time. He had dreams of his own. For a year he had protected the children on Piet Retief from the monster by ensuring they were moved away. There had been no killings. Then a single child had come into Buffel's orbit, and the monster inside Buffel had awoken and wouldn't be pacified again. They were out hunting the girl.

They had concealed themselves well in the bush, and even the kudu that passed them had not flinched, nor even scented their presence.

But Shilo wasn't a killer. Although at that moment he had wanted to kill Buffel before he unleashed his wickedness into the world again, his conscience wouldn't let him. His Christian upbringing was strong, and murder condemned a man to hell.

Killing during war was different, that was kill or be killed, and Sergeant Riley had said to them that they would be absolved from those sins by God. He had believed his sergeant.

But murder of a unit member. His soul would belong to the devil. Eternal damnation.

Instead he'd attempted to stop the killing. Yet he was mindful that if Buffel suspected him, he would show no such mercy and would cut his throat without a second thought.

Shilo had removed the firing bolt from Buffel's .303 that night while Buffel slept. He wanted desperately to throw the bolt as far into the bush as he could, so Buffel would never be able to use his rifle again. If he did that then Buffel would know that he had tampered with it, but if when they got back to Piet Retief homestead, he could drop it on the floor where Buffel always cleaned his weapons, or lay it on the bench, Buffel would find it, and think that he had messed up while cleaning his weapon the last time before putting it away, and hadn't reassembled it completely before he stored it in its soft case. An easy enough mistake to make. Carefully, Shilo had put the bolt into his sock in case Buffel patted him down. It was a risk, but it was one worth taking to save the girl's life.

Buffel continued to snore, unaware that a unit member was betraying him by sabotage.

In the morning Tara had ridden towards their hiding place on her horse, her blonde hair shining in the bright African sun. She'd swum in her clothes in the dam on Whispering Winds. The young white man, Gabe, had been with her and the horse boy, Bomani.

But Buffel had surprised him.

When the girl came out of the water, and began weeping, he hadn't even reached for his weapon to line her up in his crosshairs of his sights and kill her. Instead he'd continued to watch her through his binoculars in fascination as she cried.

'She's not ready yet. She's still too young. She needs to blossom. She's still like a boy when you look closely. She's yet to become a woman,' Buffel said.

Shilo had hung his head in relief, silently sliding his own .9mm back into its holster. Having had no sleep the night before, worried about what was about to occur, he had eventually come to the decision that he would not allow the murder to happen. Surely the God who was all forgiving would forgive him if he shot Buffel if he shifted the rifle from its open carrier to line her up. Because he knew that if Buffel didn't get to shoot her with his rifle, he would take Shilo's and use that. And Shilo hadn't sabotaged his own weapon in the bush.

Enough was enough.

Like a sick dog, he had been about to put Buffel out of his misery before he hurt another child. He had decided that in this case, murder was justified.

He would save the child.

Tara, Gabe and Bomani had remounted their horses, and ridden off, not knowing that Tara had dodged death from Buffel's hands a second time.

But it was just as Shilo was beginning to breathe normally again, and his heartbeat had begun to slow as they walked back to Piet Retief, that Buffel had knelt in the riverbed, next to a set of deep old prints.

Buffel had fingered the prints as if trying to assess them, and then he had looked at Shilo's feet.

He'd known that Buffel knew – they were his prints.

When he'd covered up his tracks from saving Tara the first time, he'd laid false trails and used the leaves to cover up his run through the bush when he realised what Buffel was about to do. In a hurry to return to the house, he'd neglected to cover those in the riverbed. And there had been no rain to wash them away since that fateful day.

His secret was out.

Now Shilo needed to save his own life.

He couldn't go to the police as men from the once feared PSYOPS unit had been integrated into normal life and were everywhere. He knew one was a judge. He knew one was in the police force. They had been elite once, now they hid in clear sight of everyone, but each held their tongues and kept their secrets. Kept the unspoken vow never to reveal the atrocities they committed in the name of freedom and national security.

A few of their unit had fled south and been absorbed into the Recces in the South African Defence Force, knowing that there they would be untraceable and safe from any prosecution.

Buffel had simply returned to his farm, Shilo with him.

No one, except Shilo, really knew the monster that had been unleashed during the bush war years and who now lived within their community.

And Shilo was leaving that monster in the community, unguarded.

Even as he sat on the railway bench, he fought a war within his own conscience. Should he go back to Buffel, or continue walking away, saving his own soul?

He jerked upwards and alert as he heard the train whistle at a siding further up the track. Soon Shilo could feel the train as it approached. It vibrated through his feet and up into his heart. He smiled as the train driver blew the whistle and the train slowly came to a stop.

No one got off the train. Shilo opened a carriage door and climbed inside.

Slowly the train pulled out the station, gaining momentum as it laboured on the steel tracks with its heavy carriages dragging behind.

Shilo sat down in a spare seat. He let out a deep breath and turned his head to watch the siding slide by and silently prayed that he'd never again have Buffel's face darken his life.

* * *

The train stopped at Umtali station. Shilo climbed out and breathed the fresh mountain air. He'd missed this place.

His regiment had come this way many times on their way to Mozambique to attack terrorist camps, and as always, it was cold. He looked at his overall bottoms, and lack of shoes, but he felt warm inside the jersey that the old man had given him. He walked proudly out of the station and turned south down the street. He didn't need direction to know where he was going.

The Blue Lady Shebeen was at the far end of the township of Sakubva, almost seven kilometres from the real city centre. Shilo walked past the *Musika Wahuku*, or as the people liked to call it, the chicken market, around which all life in the area now centred. The huge outdoor food and free trade market was bustling with colourfully clad vendors hawking their goods. White chickens clucked loudly, and those that had cages to enclose them fluffed up as they challenged the diamond-spotted guinea fowl in the cages next door. Goats bleated, children ran about squealing in happiness chasing after a car made of wire with polish tins for wheels. Smells of different spices on offer, of curry, cumin and *achaar*, swirled with the different cooking smells of *boerewors* and *braaivleis*, and mingled with the tart smell of cooked *sadza* to create amazing aromas.

Sakubva, on the outskirts of Umtali, had been the first black township settlement. The once male-only accommodation had long since been crowded with family groups, and the excess had spilled out into surrounding areas. Now it held more than half the town's population, in the smallest area.

He walked down the street he knew so well until he saw the familiar sign. The faded hand-painted sign had seen better days, but the ground outside was swept clean of leaves and any rubbish. The large sign on the door claimed in Shona that the place was 'under new management'.

He laughed at that as he pushed the door open.

The Blue Lady Shebeen had always had just one owner.

Behind the bar area, a black man sat on a high stool. In his hand he held a hunting knife that he was using to pick at the dirt underneath his nails. His hair was done up in dreadlocks, if you looked carefully you could see cowrie shells braided intricately into them. Care had been taken to drill the holes into the shells, and braid them. Bits of his braids were bleached to an almost yellow blond and made the dreadlocks look like a fancy multicoloured mop. His fringe was short, but also braided, and stopped directly in line with his eyes, as if he couldn't stand not to have 20/20 vision. Although his feet were propped up on a second chair, his counter was spotless. No dust sat on the varnished mahogany wood, no water marks marred the perfect surface. Even with his elaborate hair, Kwazi was unmistakable.

Shilo smiled. 'An old friend told me once, that if I ever walked away from a monster, that I would always find a bed to sleep in and food for my belly in his home.'

Kwazi looked up and dropped his feet to the floor. Standing to his full six-foot-three height, he asked, 'And did this *old* friend tell you that if you called him *old* he'd throw a knife through your heart?'

'No, *Madala*!'

Kwazi put the knife down on the counter and laughed. He walked around the bar to meet Shilo halfway across the room. They hugged like the good friends they were, friends who had shared adventure, terror and tears together.

'It is good to see you,' Kwazi said at last. 'I must admit that I thought I never would.'

'A long time in the making, but a short trip here once I was free.'

'The monster already came by two weeks ago looking for you. I could truthfully tell him then, I hadn't seen you. Now, come sit at my bar, tell me what has been happening. But first, let me get you some shoes, it won't do for customers to think that I run a shabby shebeen. This establishment has class – yes?' He laughed and walked through some tacky beaded strings that marked the end of the bar and the beginning of his home section of the building.

Shilo followed.

The lounge room behind the bar didn't belong in a black man's house. The leather lounge suite and the smoky glass tables were smart. The parquet flooring peeking out from under the throw rug was shining and buffed, and as Shilo stood on the rug, his toes sank in as if it were made of lambs' wool. In one corner stood a big television.

'You're this rich now?' he asked Kwazi.

'I was always rich, it was just that we were at war and I couldn't show it, but now, in the new Zimbabwe, I can dig up my money and spend it on nice, comfortable things. I am never sleeping on the ground again. My army days are over. It's just me and my shebeen, and maybe a few of the ladies …'

'You and the ladies, they have always been your weakness and they will be the death of you.'

'Here,' Kwazi said, 'through there is a bathroom, with running water, the towels are in the cupboard by the door. Have a nice hot shower, and take these clothes to change into. Then we can talk.' He handed Shilo some faded blue denim jeans and a black T-shirt.

'Thank you,' Shilo said as he took the clothes and heard Kwazi say, 'Don't lock the door, the lock sticks.'

Shilo smiled. It was so typical of the new Zimbabwe, the black people everywhere were prospering, showing off their wealth, and yet they were not fixing small things like the locks on the bathroom door. He closed the door but didn't lock it. Shilo stepped in to the shower and cranked the hot water to blast off all the dirt and memories of the last few weeks.

Drying his hair after his shower, Shilo sat on the bar stool opposite Kwazi. Kwazi's voice was rising, slowly getting louder in volume as he disagreed with him.

'Shilo Khumalo, you're mad,' Kwazi said. 'There is a war on in Mozambique still. Zimbabwe, we're at peace at last. But you want to go into Mozambique and fight again?'

'No, I want peace and quiet too, but Buffel will continue to look for me. He'll come again, looking to silence me. Like you said, he's already checking each person in the unit, and eventually he'll come back to you again, and he'll ask you if I was here. And we both know you're not a good liar when it's Buffel who's asking the questions.'

'I could have been interrogated by anyone but him. Just knowing what he is and what he's capable of … You're right, I would speak. Quickly. I like my tongue, my teeth and my balls, thank you. I don't want to hang upside down in a meat locker with dead pigs.'

'I know. That's why I can't stay, that's why I just stopped here to get some supplies, and a few good nights' sleep. Soon, I'll head out, go past the old Addam's Barracks, and across the minefield, by Freddie's Ridge, into Mozambique. I only hope that they haven't changed all the mines' positions.'

'I hope so too. Are you sure you want to go that way, and not up further north and into Mozambique instead?'

'This is the area I know, so I cross here. Then I head wherever there is the least fighting.'

'North?'

'You saw the ocean there, the clear water. There doesn't seem to be any fighting on their islands, just the mainland. I'm looking for an island to live on one day, but there is talk of establishing "safe" corridors in Mozambique by the Zimbabwe government. Maybe I can get work on one of those corridors, keeping the people safe. I'm good at that. As a white man, Buffel will not follow me into Mozambique. It's not safe for him there, but I can be a civilian, I can hide, mingle with the locals, learn Portuguese and French, and he won't find me.'

'No, but the people in Mozambique will, and give you up as a *Komeredes*, a new Zimbabwe soldier, and you will be butchered. You're going to walk in to a FRELIMO and RENAMO wasp's nest. Why not just go underground here, at least here you have contacts, and people will hide you from Buffel.'

'And do what? Go where?'

'If you go east, go live with the Batonka tribes in the Kariba area. They are my people. I will come with you and you can hide there, work the land. Catch kapenta for a living on Kariba. He won't find you there. Or you could go and work on those tobacco farms in Karoi. They are always looking for workers, you can hide there. Even in the lowvelt. You can get work in the *Thuli-makwe* irrigation scheme, or even in Triangle, safari camps and hunting safaris are springing up everywhere. Go to Botswana. You're a good tracker, and you can shoot straight, get your professional guide licence or your hunter's licence and join a safari. Just don't go near Buffel, and if you see him, hide. I have spoken to people from all these places, all over and they are looking for hardworking men to farm and you know how to do that. I can give you some names—'

'No names. They can't know I came via you or they too could be hurt by Buffel.'

'I don't suppose you want to go to the police and have him put in jail?'

'You know our rule. You were there, you said the oath alongside me. My best bet to stay alive is to keep quiet. Besides, if the unit turned a blind eye to what Buffel has become, it would be a white man against a black man's word, and our Zimbabwe hasn't changed that much yet. Just remember who is it that sits as a judge now in the Supreme Court? I would be killed, no matter what, for turning on my own unit. Besides, who's to say there wouldn't be another amnesty and Buffel would be let out of jail. He would get me then. I'm not talking about it to anyone. I just want to get away from him. Make a fresh start and who knows, maybe meet a girl, have a life of my own.'

Shilo looked at Kwazi, who was nodding.

'I will go somewhere, but you can't know where I go. You have a life here, you can't go with me, not even to introduce me to people to help make my life easier. He knows that you are my best friend. Buffel will come back again, looking for me. The less you know the better.'

'I agree. Just do me a favour and go anywhere in Zimbabwe, or Botswana, not to Mozambique,' Kwazi said.

'Maybe for now, it's better. But one day I am going to swim in that ocean again, with the silver fish, and feel that warm sand slip through my fingers. I'm going to eat fresh crayfish and calamari steaks around a bonfire as the sun sets.'

'You're a dreamer. You always were, my friend,' Kwazi said. 'Come, time for you and I to have a beer.'

'No beer, I won't drink in case he comes …'

'Fine, Coke for you and a beer for me. You stay a few days, we get your some clothes that fit properly, some new overalls, and boots. Like a worker. Then you go, change your name, and one day when it's safe again, you know that in the Blue Lady Shebeen you will always find a bed to sleep in and food for your belly. You will always be welcome in my home.'

'Thank you, brother,' Shilo said and shook Kwazi's hand.

CHAPTER

8

Getting To Know You

Margate Beach, Natal, South Africa
July 1984

The drive to Margate, where they were heading to house-sit a beach cottage for one of the families in Hluhluwe, was uneventful. The old car chugged along, the radio blaring as always, the four women singing songs to pass the journey. Their excitement in the car heightened as they drove out of the dreary-looking Port Shepstone, and on the other side, they could see the sea sparkling blue against a backdrop of clouds, the white horses of the waves dancing on the water. They rolled down their windows and breathed the salt air.

'This is so cool,' Dela said.

Tara looked at her sister and laughed. It was the first time in ages Dela had been excited about anything. She'd become withdrawn and moody.

'Ah, the seaside,' Lucretia, their maid, said.

'Make sure you take your bottle home, you know, the one with the sea sand in the bottom and filled with the ocean water.' Tara teased. Lucretia was a fat Zulu lady, with beaded hair, and an attitude that didn't fit into the South African population. She was as outspoken as the Zimbabwe people that the family were used to.

'I have to, it's my tradition,' Lucretia said, but she was smiling.

'What do you do with the sea water anyway?' Tara asked.

Lucretia smiled. 'Muti. It fixes the stomach ache.'

Tara giggled. 'Oh Lucretia, that's sad. It's just salt water, it doesn't fix stomach ache.'

Maggie interrupted. 'Everyone has traditional beliefs, Tara. Don't laugh at Lucretia just because hers are different to yours. Respect different beliefs too.'

'But Mum, it's just salt water—'

'To you, but to a believer, it could cure a stomach ache. Like a placebo. I used to give you chalk when you were a little girl when you said you had a headache, and it would disappear.'

'Fine,' Tara said. 'I'll even help you get some bottles, Lucretia, and I can find you some nice shells on the beach to put in there too. Make it look like decent ocean water at least.'

'Thank you, Miss Tara,' Lucretia said.

Tara smiled. Lucretia had appeared outside their house within a week of them moving to Hluhluwe. She never asked, but rather had told Maggie she was now working for her and living in the small *ikhaya* at the back of their property. She had said it wasn't good that they didn't have a maid to look after them.

She hadn't been a maid asking for a job, she'd been a woman telling a family that they needed her as much as she needed them. She didn't want money, only food and board to start with. And she'd assured Maggie that she wasn't a prostitute so there would be no men visiting her *ikhaya*.

Suddenly life had gone from difficult to liveable. Lucretia was a godsend and she'd taught the girls how to do things, in her kindly manner. They could now cook, and even Maggie, who was the worst cook of all of them, no longer incinerated their meals. Their house was neat, mainly because Lucretia still tidied up after them, but she'd insist on the girls helping too, and she'd taught them to iron even though she still ironed their clothes so that they no longer had to go to school looking like second-class '*Rooinekke*' as Tara had been called on her first day back in Standard 6. That had been her first year of high school and first year at school in South Africa.

Lucretia had been with them now for two and a half years, and to Maggie, Tara and Dela, she was part of their family. Wherever they went, Lucretia went, except to their granny's house. They spared Lucretia the racist attitude of Maggie's mother. Although there had been a few sparks when she'd visited with them in Hluhluwe.

They turned right at the intersection and followed the coastal road which snaked its way along until they came to a 'Welcome to Margate' sign covered in huge painted flowers declaring they were on the Hibiscus Coast. They turned again, and with Dela reading the map, they eventually drove into a tar driveway.

The beach cottage was built from bricks, and although it was serviceable and neat, it didn't have any of the luxuries one would expect at a beach house. There was no ocean view for starters.

It was across the road from the ocean-view homes, which dwarfed it and made it look like the poor relative. The garden was overrun with jungle vines and brown grass as high as Tara's hip.

'The Biscoffs said it was a bit rundown, but I'm sure we can make it liveable,' Maggie said.

After depositing their cases inside, Tara rummaged for a pair of shorts and an older T-shirt. Finding them, she left her mess on the bed, and wandered into the garage, looking for a lawn mower. Finding an old hand push one, she checked it over to make sure it worked. Apart for an annoying squeak every now and again, the blades rotated just fine. She smiled to herself. There was a time she hadn't even known how to drive a broom, and now she could do household chores. Now she knew not only how to run a household, but how to be part of one too. Before she would have been waited on, and had everything done for her by the staff. Now she would go out and do what was necessary to make the family more comfortable. They were an unconventional family, but it worked for them.

Their small garden back in Hluhluwe was fragrant with bushes and shrubs, and sweet peas grew in the winter to blossom in spring. They had a veggie garden that had a few mielie plants and cabbages, gem squash and lettuces. The girls had learnt to look after the garden, and cut their own lawn, as Lucretia had told them that the Zulu men were lazy and not worth paying when they could do it themselves. The warthog, Frederica, wasn't the best lawnmower, leaving forage holes in the grass rather than clipped lawn. Lucretia had shown Tara how to push the lawnmower and how to make the grass look good.

After an hour, Tara hadn't made much progress on the front yard of the beach house. A small pile of grass lay flattened, but the yard was large and the going was tough. Blisters were already forming on her hands. She lifted the bottom of her T-shirt and wiped the sweat off her face.

'Hey, Tara,' a deep voice said. 'I knew it was you.'

Quickly she straightened her shirt. Dang ... she should have known better than to lift her shirt and show her stomach to the world! She could feel the heat radiating up her chest and up her neck, knowing any second the blush would reach her face. She stared at the boy in defiance.

'We have a petrol mower I know how to use if you want me to help you?'

'Wayne Botha,' she said in greeting. Of all the boys in her class at school to see her with her top up, wiping her sweaty face, did it have to be Wayne?

'Seriously, I know you're a great athlete and all that, but that garden needs a machine or you're going to spend the whole holiday attempting to get that grass under control. I don't know why the Biscoffs don't have a garden boy down here to look after their place. You renting it for the whole holidays?'

'No, we're just house-sitting for a week.'

'Well then, you definitely need our mower. Come, that's our cottage over there.' He pointed across the road. 'We can grab the mower and the grass will be cut quick as.'

The house he pointed to was no cottage. A modern monstrosity that dominated the ground around, it towered three storeys high and was surrounded by a pristine white security wall six feet tall, topped with razor wire and a strand of electric fencing.

Wayne had been in her class since Standard 6. At first, he wasn't in her social circle, but recently she'd been playing squash with him, and it was debatable who was the higher ranked player, although his strength had got the better of her in their last match.

She'd had him as a science lab partner once or twice. He was quiet in school, always top of the class. He played every boys sport, just like she did the girls sports, and they were even in the shooting team together.

'What are the odds?' Tara asked. 'Your house is next to the one we get for a week's holiday at the beach. Weird as!'

'I have no idea of the odds. If the gardenboy was working this holidays I would send him around to mow your lawn, but his mother died, so he isn't here. At least I can help you mow your grass and you can come enjoy the beach. Perhaps you can even come with me to the beach party tonight, instead of sleeping in exhaustion after you finish pushing that old thing around.'

'You know, I won't say no to that mower. I'm not into self-destruction, seriously. If it will make my life easier, I'm all for it. It would be nice to spend the week at the beach and not trying to cut the grass.'

'Great. We can grab my folks' mower and then hit the beach when it's done.'

'I have to tell my mum where I'm going,' she said.

'Sure, I'll be right here,' Wayne said and Tara rushed into the cottage.

Nothing had prepared Tara for the sight of Wayne with his shirt off, in his tiny rugby shorts, and his *takkies* with no socks, manoeuvring the mower around both the front and the back yards.

She could not stop staring.

He paused and powered down the mower when she brought him a cold drink. 'Thanks. It's hot work,' Wayne said.

'I can do it, if you just start it for me. I know how to cut the grass,' she said. Yet her eyes were not on the mower but mesmerised watching him drink. Watching the bob of his Adam's apple as he swallowed every drop, and turned the tumbler upside down as he threw his head far backwards. He looked forward again, wiped his mouth with the back of his hand and passed her the glass. His fingers brushed against hers.

'I know, I've seen you cutting yours. But it'll go faster if I do it for you, then we can hit the beach together.'

'With Dela, too. I can't leave her here with Maggie and Lucretia, she needs to get out as well.'

'Of course with Dela too, I like your older sister.'

Tara remained silent.

Wayne smiled. '*Like* as in I'm happy for her to tag along with you and me, so I can show you the beach, and maybe get you to surf a bit with me. Spend time with you.'

Was Wayne flirting with her? Her heart skipped a beat. How did that happen? Uncertain what to say next, she pulled a face, then asked, 'There is a you and me?'

'Sure, I just cut your lawn, so you owe me. You can spend time with me as payment.'

Tara started realising that the flirting was crossing over into territory she knew nothing about. 'Maybe that's not such a hot idea. Thank you for—'

He cut her off. Shaking his head.

'Why do you always push every boy in the class away when they want to be anything more than friends? You have this barrier that you put out there, and I used to believe you didn't even know you put it there. Now you're doing it to me.' He smiled. 'Come on, we're at the beach, almost four hundred kilometres from school. Besides, this has to be the first time I have ever been able to do anything for you. First time I have ever had your full attention since day one when you arrived in Standard 6.'

Tara stared at him. 'You remember me from two and a half years ago?'

'First day, you walked into Miss LeRoux's class room, your hair was in two high pigtails, and it bounced when you walked. I had never seen anyone's hair do that before.'

Tara stood still, not knowing what to say.

He rubbed the back of his neck with his hand and Tara found herself watching the movement of his chest as it lifted with the motion of his hand. She felt another blush start in her neck, and quickly turned away.

Tara glanced back at Wayne's face. She looked at his deep blue eyes and saw that he wasn't laughing. He chewed the inside of his lip, like he did when he was doing a hard maths sum. He was serious.

'It—t—' she stumbled. How to put the emotions she felt into words? She wasn't good at that, and didn't know what to say, but she tried again. 'It's not that I push anyone away on purpose. I've just never been interested in any of them, their antics and their silliness.'

'What if I gave you more of a chance to get to know the real me ... the one you play squash with, not the boy in the classroom?' he asked.

Tara swallowed hard, staring at the mower, uncertain what to say. This awareness of Wayne was very new. She'd been in on conversations at school with the other girls talking about the boys but had never experienced ever wanting to have someone else touch her, and be in her personal space, like the other girls did. She'd always chalked it up to just being different, and channelled her energy into her sports instead.

She'd already become closer to Wayne than any other boy in her class. Thinking back, it was he who had challenged her to those squash matches, and not the teacher who had organised them. His father's sugarcane farm was further down the road from Tara's home, so Wayne would drive the farm *bakkie* along the back roads to her place, and they would walk the two and a half kilometres from her house to the courts, play their game, then walk all the way back. Talking. Laughing. Spending time together. He always had an extra drink bottle for her for afterwards, something nice, not just water. Now that she thought about it.

She'd been blindsided.

She thought he was just being friendly, wanting to play squash with her. She took a deep breath in when she realised that he'd been courting her in his own gentle way. Then she began to breathe shallowly and her head became light. She grabbed for the mower to help her stand upright.

Wayne noticed her distress and quickly added, 'Hey, it's okay. Don't freak out. I'm not rushing you or anything. I thought you knew that I was kind of into you already.' He reached out and ran his hand up her arm to her shoulder to help support her.

Such a small gesture of support and understanding, but now that he'd made her aware of the situation, it felt like his hand was made of molten lava and he'd burnt her arm the whole way up.

She looked at him then, and could feel the colour rush back into her face.

'See, not so bad. Just think of me as big mouth Wayne, blurting it all out and hanging it all out to dry at once because I was so excited to see you here and know that we have a week at the beach together. Maybe we can just start as we always have been, just being better friends. How's that?'

Relief shuddered through her body. Friends she could do. Love and all that stuff she couldn't.

Except for Maggie and Dela, everyone and everything she'd ever loved had either died or been ripped away from her. Her mind flashed back to her father's and uncle's murders, to being taken away from her farm, and the horses, and leaving Gabe behind.

She liked Wayne. She didn't want to lose him too. He'd probably become her closest friend at school over the last term. She just hadn't noticed until today.

Panic gripped at her throat. If she crossed that line with him, history said she'd lose him, and right now she really liked having him in her life.

'Okay,' she said and looked up at his chest. She didn't remember when Wayne had grown taller that she was, but at sixteen he was almost six foot two. She'd never noticed the hair on his chest, or the way it scattered across his pecs, then downwards over his muscular stomach and pointed further, drawing her gaze downwards.

She quickly looked up at his face.

'Beach ... fun ... friends sounds good. Do you know if anyone else from school is here?'

'Sure, Tracey and Michelle Sinclair, they're staying in the Colemans' place for the whole holidays. And Graham Davidson and his sister Rose are here in their house too. I don't know if you know Craig Streydom, he's in Standard 10. Him and his girlfriend Marci are here too, and Paul and Ben Timbal.'

'Great, a whole gang.' She stepped back. Distancing herself a little. Hoping it would give her space to breathe, space to recover her composure which was still lacking.

'Every holiday there are a heap of us here. It's always like that. Makes the beach fun!'

'Well, I'm not going to let the crowd from school spoil my first ever holiday at a beach other than Durban.'

'You go to Durban?'

'Yeah, we stay at my gran's house when we have to. It's a horrible area and we hate it. Its only redeeming quality is that the beach there is nice. And the beach gets us out the house, so that's always great.'

'Come on, let me finish here, you grab the rubbish bags that I've filled and haul them over to the curb.'

'Sure,' she said, and turned away from him, but not before sneaking one last look at his stomach muscles and the way they rippled when he moved. She let out a small sigh.

The beach party was in full swing when Wayne led Tara and Dela onto the sand. There were teenagers everywhere and a few adults supervising things. Blue cooler boxes were dotted around the beach, and towels lay discarded on the soft sand warming in the winter sun, or draped over coolers to dry.

'Oh my,' Dela said. 'Look at that.'

The sea was azure blue, with white waves lapping at the golden sand that heated the underside of her feet as Tara walked barefoot across to where the sand turned moist from the waves, and hard from the moisture held in it.

'Last one in is a rotten egg!' Wayne called as he ran until he was about waist deep, then dived head first into the water. He disappeared for a few moments before reappearing beyond the white breakers, in the swirling blue. He tossed his hair to the side and smiled, gesturing for Tara to join him.

She dropped her towel and flip-flops next to the cooler box Wayne had carried down, and grabbing Dela by the hand, she dragged her with her into the sea.

'Cold,' Tara said as she ran in, and she stopped where the waves broke on the sand, only at waist height.

'Told ya it was great!' he said as he struck out, swimming strongly for deeper water.

'Hey Tara, Dela!' Tracey and Michelle both waved in greeting, before ducking under a wave then swimming after Wayne.

'Come on, Tara,' Dela said.

Tara hesitated.

She could stand where they were, yet if she went deeper, she wouldn't be able to see the bottom, and she would need to tread water to keep afloat.

Dela swam off without her.

'Don't swim where you can't see the bottom.' The words haunted her. Even though the man who had said them to her had been gunned down three years earlier, she still heard them clearly in her head. Wayne was out there beckoning, and Dela had reached him and looked like she was fine. Tara swallowed. She swam with a bit more caution than Dela as she didn't feel she was such a great swimmer. She was better than most her classmates at sport, but she knew that swimming was her one weakness. She heard her father's

voice in her head again: *'That's what you would expect from a land lover in a landlocked country.'*

She took a deep breath and finally followed the others in.

'Hey you,' Wayne said as she reached him. 'Glad you decided to join us. Look!' He pointed.

Just a few metres from where they all trod water, a school of dolphin dived through the waves. She watched as they surfaced, and she heard as they exhaled and then disappeared under the water. She could hear the clicking sounds they made as communications passed between them. She smiled as she watched a mother nudge her wayward calf to bring it back into the group.

The dolphin came closer, surfing along a wave towards them, then suddenly they were all around. Tara held her breath as the baby surfaced almost within touching distance and exhaled, its beautiful grey-blue body glistening in the sun. It appeared to her as if it was curious what she was doing in its ocean. Then it dived back under. She had wanted so much to reach out and try touch it.

Still treading water, she turned her body to follow the dolphin.

'Come on,' Wayne said and she didn't need more urging as they swam, attempting to stay with the dolphin pod for as long as they could.

Just before sundown, everyone's mothers brought down food, and trestle tables were set up. Then, as the sun sank behind the trees to slide away in the west and the seawater turned pink in the fading light, someone set a match at the bottom of the fire. The small orange flame slowly crept towards the dry kindling of grass and newspaper, and took hold. It hungrily consumed the kindling and grew upwards from the bottom, edged in blue and green as it burnt through the driftwood piled high to make a bonfire. As the flames leapt upwards in a joyous dance, everyone cheered.

Maggie came down with their Hepcooler from the house, and sat with Wayne's dad in the circle watching the bonfire. Dela flopped on the sand next to her, and lay on her back with her eyes closed.

'Would you like a walk, Tara?' Wayne asked, his hand already waiting for hers to help her up from her cross-legged position. He'd gone up to his house and pulled on some dry clothes, and a lightweight tracksuit top. The cool ocean breeze was picking up now that the sun was gone.

'Sure,' she said putting her hand into his. It felt strange having her hand held by Wayne's bigger one.

'Don't go too far, Wayne,' his father warned.

'We won't, Dad, just to the other side of the rocks and back.'

'Fine.'

'Be safe,' Maggie added.

'Will do, Mum,' Tara reassured her.

Wayne kept Tara's hand in his, threading his fingers through hers, as they started their walk away from the bonfire and the crowd. Tara tried to pull away, but he held tight.

'Just let me hold your hand, Tara. That's all.'

'Okay,' she said, suddenly unsure why she'd agreed to the moonlight walk in the first place, but her heart did a small flip all the same. 'Your dad is as protective as my mum. I thought that maybe with a son, it would be different.'

Wayne nodded. 'He worries. The war is being fought far away, on our borders, but there is still plenty of petty crime too. Always pays to be vigilant.'

Tara's heart thumped as she walked next to Wayne, only now her hand felt comfortable, with her fingers lightly entwined in his. He walked next to her on the rough path.

'So, quite a day, huh?' he said.

'Yeah, brilliant. Those dolphin, they were so great. I have never been so close before, they were amazing!'

'You must come surfing in the morning, they surf right next to the board.'

'Seriously?'

'Yes, I'll come by your place and fetch you. It's really something. I love our beach cottage because I can just kick back and surf.'

'Might I remind you that your beach cottage is bigger than your home on your farm.'

Wayne smiled. 'Kujana will always be home, but this shack is a close second,' he said then lifted her hand and kissed it. 'But the cottage and the beach are now so much better because you are here.'

Tara felt the blush rise up into her face.

'Where is your mum, Wayne?'

He shifted his weight on his feet. 'She hates the beach, the cottage is my dad's and my get away castle!'

For a while they navigated the rocks in silence. Then they reached the point, and they stood close together.

'Wow, just look at that,' Tara said as she looked out into the ocean where the lights of a vessel out in the shipping channel twinkled brighter than the stars that had just started to appear in the sky. Then she looked to the right, along the coastline there was the darkened area of another beach with not many houses hugging it, but on the left, she could see the lights of so many buildings clinging onto the edge of the ocean, as if trying to be as close as possible to the magical waters.

'It's so beautiful,' she said.

'It's the beach,' Wayne said and he hugged her closer to him, and tightened his arms around her. He kissed the top of her hair.

She shivered.

'You're cold!' he said and he took his tracksuit top off and helped her into it.

He touched her breast with the back of his fingers as he shimmied the top down into place, and she felt a frisson of pleasure, as if her body wanted him to touch her more. She was scared of the feeling, yet intrigued by her own body.

'Thanks,' she said, choosing not to mention that he had touched her, because if it was just a mistake, she didn't want to embarrass him, not now. She rolled up the sleeves so that her hands didn't look like sock puppets. Then she leant back into his warmth, as she burrowed her nose into his top and inhaled his masculine scent.

'Is it like this when you visit Durban?' he asked.

'No, I hate Durban, I hate visiting there,' she said.

'Why? It's a great city, so much to do. They have an ice-skating rink, and the aquarium, and their beachfront is beautiful. Except in the silly season, no white person goes there at Christmas and New Year – too many black people swamp the beach.'

'I know, my granny wouldn't let us anywhere near the beach when we first got to South Africa for Christmas.'

'She was right,' Wayne said, 'they lose their own children, they swim in their underwear and many drown because they can't swim. It's sad really. The life guards can't keep up because there are just so many people.'

'It is sad, because they are people too. Despite what the Apartheid government says, the colour of our skin doesn't make a difference, it's how someone conducts themselves and behaves that makes a person into what they are, and if they are worth knowing or not.'

'I agree. My dad thinks that too. He says that Apartheid is in its last days, soon it will be gone and we'll have a black government. And he says that when the change comes he hopes that it's peaceful. Not like some of the other countries in Africa.'

Tara opened her mouth to speak, then closed it, thinking better about voicing her opinion outright. She kept silent for a few moments as they stood together, then Tara said, 'You know what, there might have been a war in Zimbabwe, but at least our blacks were treated like people. They were fighting too, alongside the white people. We were a nation united together.'

'I'm not judging you, or your views, I'm agreeing with you,' Wayne said as he ran his hand up her arm and back down, reassuringly.

'Thank you,' she said and she smiled.

'So, back to Durban. Why do you hate it so much?'

'My aunty Marie-Ann and my grandmother live there.'

'And that's bad?'

'It's better to have them living there, than in Hluhluwe with us. When we first got to South Africa, my aunt was so bossy and my gran was so mean to Dela and I.'

'Bossy? You have just one bossy aunty?' Wayne asked, his arms adjusting a little to settle around her waist.

'Oh yes. My mum's only sister, Marie-Ann. When she used to visit us in Zimbabwe, she would shout at us and smack us, and Dela and I still have no idea why when my mum and dad never smacked us. And then when we moved here, and we drove Mum's car down from Pietermaritzburg into Durban, she insisted on driving, when my mum was quite capable of completing the journey. At least in South Africa she didn't have to avoid all the donkey carts like Mum always does … did. Aunty Marie-Ann flew down the pass at one hundred and twenty kilometres an hour, and spent the whole trip telling us that it had been many years since my mum was in South Africa, there had been a lot of changes, and Durban was a really busy city now. As if Bulawayo wasn't busy too. She tries to lord it over my mum the whole time.'

'Really?' Wayne said.

'Yes, and at one point she told me that I had to learn that in South Africa my attitude wouldn't be tolerated.'

'What attitude? You don't have an attitude!' Wayne defended her.

'Exactly. Just because I stand up to her she says I have an attitude,' Tara said, and it was as if a floodgate inside her had burst and she began to tell Wayne more. Things she would normally keep to herself.

'Once she called my mother a "brick", and when I told her my mother wasn't some piece of building equipment that will be broken down and thrown away she hit the steering wheel so hard, I thought she would break it.'

'Oh I bet that went down well.'

'No.'

'I don't think I like your bossy aunty much.'

'Me neither,' Tara said. 'Do you have one like that?'

'No, my dad was an only child, and my mum doesn't talk to her family. If I have them, I don't have contact with them.'

'That's sad. He was an only child, and now you are too. Don't you get lonely? When we were younger, Dela and I would play together for ages. I know I was never lonely.'

'No, I can't remember being lonely. I was usually with my dad on the farm, playing with the *piccaninnies*. There were always other kids to play with.'

'We used do that too. Guess a Zimbabwe farm upbringing and a South African one have their similarities.'

'So where exactly in Durban does your gran live? Durban is pretty big.'

'Off Point Road.'

'You kidding? Point Road is known for its hookers and being a rough dock area with lots of whorehouses.'

'Very funny,' Tara said. Even though she knew of its reputation, the people she had met there hadn't seemed so bad. Like her family, they were just trying to make a living and get by. 'She lives in a terrace house, and it shares walls with neighbours on two sides,' Tara said. 'It's railway housing. Apparently my gran used to work for the railways, and she got to keep her house when she retired, because Aunty Marie-Ann's husband still works for them, so they say he and Aunty Marie-Ann live there with her, so it's technically his railway house now. But my uncle and aunty really live in Marie-Ann's flat on the Berea. And my gran lives alone at the Point.'

'Wow, I never even knew there was housing down there. I thought it was all docks,' Wayne said.

'When I first landed up there, I wondered what had happened to my life. I'd lived on a beautiful farm with horses, and wide open spaces, and friendly workers. Then in a decent enough town house in Bulawayo, with a pool, in a lovely neighbourhood, and suddenly there I was in that terraced house, in a slum. I didn't know life could get so bad.'

He hugged her tight again. 'Hey, you got out of there, and now you have a nice house in Hluhluwe.'

'And a nice warthog in the garden. But when I first got to South Africa, it was scary. My mother's family was scary. My gran took great pleasure in seeing exactly how much we couldn't do around the house.'

'Meaning? Like what, make your bed?'

'Yes, and more. We'd always had maids, and at boarding school you don't do a thing either, the school staff do everything. I had never washed clothes before. Or peeled potatoes, or washed and dried dishes. My gran seemed to take great delight in torturing Dela and I by introducing us to all those things in the first few days of us living in South Africa.'

'Wait a minute, you'd never washed a dish?'

'No, our maid Emilie did that or our cook boy Yedwa. I never washed dishes!'

Wayne laughed. 'I don't think I have either, but I think I could, it can't be that hard.'

'It's not, once you are shown how to, and how to rinse them.' She shifted on her feet.

'That's not the point, the point is that my gran seemed to take great pleasure in seeing how much we didn't know how to do around the house. Grans are supposed to be for loving and spoiling you. My dad's mum, my granny on his side, she was a real granny.' Tara smiled as she thought of her granny. She relaxed a little more into Wayne, pressing into his chest. 'I don't remember her being the most demonstrative of people when she was alive, yet she always had a sweetie in her pocket for me and Dela, or a small present with a trinket of some sort, a new pencil for school, an eraser that had a smell. When she visited, she would always come into our room and tuck us into our beds tight so that you couldn't move.' Tara scowled, and she could feel her body tense. 'My mother's mum is a slave driver.'

'At least you got to know your dad's mum. She sounds so nice. I don't know my grandparents.'

'If they are like my mother's family, then you are better off,' Tara said. 'Although, I have to say, now I think my gran is just like any other bully.'

'A bully?'

'Yes. When we had been there a day or so, my gran told me that her hand was itching, and she raised her hand to hit me across the face. I caught her wrist and squeezed her – hard. I told her that I was too old to have her try and hit me now. And if she did try, even though I was still shorter than her, I was younger and probably stronger and I would hit back.' Tara's voice was fierce, and she pulled away from Wayne slightly. 'I reminded her our dad trained Dela and I in unarmed combat just in case something happened on the farm, so she could forget hitting Dela too, because I'd come after her if she ever touched her. I told her that her days of smacking us were over.'

Wayne hugged her closer to him again. 'Tara, that is awesome. You stood up to her!'

'I did. But it was sad too. She looked so defeated when she realised that she could no longer control us by force. I pitied her that she believed that that was the only way to control us granddaughters. And I told her that grandmothers were supposed to be for loving, and spoiling, and extra hugs, not hurting their grandkids.'

'You are incredible. Such strength in such a small body.'

'Hey who you calling small? I'm petite, don't you know.' Tara smiled then giggled.

'No, you are not. You are perfect,' Wayne said and he brushed his hand flat across her belly.

She turned around in his arms to face him. 'You know, I'm not so strong. Standing up to her wasn't my idea. I told Gabe, my cousin, before we left that the one thing I was dreading was more smacks from her for no reason, and he said, "Then don't let her. Stand up for yourself and for your sister." So I give the credit to Gabe, that she hasn't even attempted to hit either of us again. And she obviously told my aunty because she never tried it again either.'

'I'm so sorry you have had such a hard time, Tara. Really. It's unfair,' Wayne said, pressing his forehead to hers. 'And I'm so happy to hear they don't hit you anymore. That is how it should be. My parents have never hit me. Despite my dad being so much older than my mum, from almost a different generation, he doesn't believe that stupid saying "spare the rod spoil the child". I think he would go *berserk* if he ever found someone had hit me.'

Tara turned back face the sea and they lapsed into silence for a while, just watching as the huge boat in the Aliwal shoal shipping channel continued northwards to Durban or Richards Bay to dump its cargo.

'Just so you know, I can't cook or do washing either,' Wayne said, and Tara began to laugh.

Wayne smiled. 'Come on, it's time we got back. My dad will send out a search party for us soon.' He let go of her reluctantly and then once again held her hand as they negotiated the path back to the beach party, and the bonfire they could see burning brightly, causing a warm orange glow above the beach area.

CHAPTER

9

Love's First Touch

Margate Beach, Natal, South Africa
July 1984

A strange sound against the window woke Tara.

'Pssst, Tara, wake up, it's time to surf,' Wayne called out under her windowsill as he threw beach sand against the panel again.

She opened her eyes and groaned. Last night, when her mum had agreed to letting her have a surfing lesson, Tara hadn't taken into account the late night–early morning timing. Her eyes still felt like grit, her body heavy from lack of sleep. Yet somehow, she jumped out of bed smiling. Opening the window she said, 'Hi. I'll let you in through the kitchen door.' She closed the window and rested her head on the security bars for a moment, then rushed to the kitchen.

'Come on, sleepyhead, the surf's great at this time,' he said, as he walked through the doorway, then he stopped and simply stared at her.

'What?' she asked, self-consciously patting her pyjamas down, making sure she wasn't showing too much skin.

'You look ...' he said, and he smiled. Her heart melted at his grin as it lit his whole face with a joy she hadn't often seen there.

'Come on, get ready. The surf doesn't wait for anyone. Make sure you bring a long sleeve top to surf in, it's turned cool.'

She almost skipped out the room in happiness, rushing to pull on her costume. As she quickly brushed her teeth she stared at herself in the mirror. She looked just the same on the outside. Her ash blonde hair was turning darker as she grew older, and at the moment she wore it in a bob cut, blunted just below her jawline. Her body was the same as ever, she didn't have lots of boob, as they, like everything else, had taken their time to even start growing. She wondered what Wayne saw when he looked at her.

Down on the beach the sea breeze was cool, the clouds had blown in overnight. Dressed in her costume and a tracksuit top, she was enjoying the clean salt air and the company. Mostly she sat on the board Wayne had strapped to her with her feet just dangling in the water as she watched him catch wave after wave, and surf in, only to fall off and have to swim out to her again. She'd tried to catch one, and was about to try her next one.

'This one, get ready. Go.'

She lay flat on her board, and paddled with her hands, then when she could feel the sea was carrying her board under her, she held on to the side, and tentatively raised her knees off the board.

The board continued forwards.

She stood up, put her arms out and came crashing down off the board into the sea.

Spluttering, she came back up, laughing at the sensation. Wayne was already near her.

'You okay?'

'Fine. It's harder than you make it look.'

'You stood,' he said as she clambered back onto her board and sat up.

'I did.' She grinned in happiness.

He swam his board closer to hers and then laid his hand on her board so they were joined together. 'You were great,' he said, 'so great!' He leant over to her, putting both hands on her shoulders, pulled her to him, and kissed her.

It was a short kiss.

It was her first kiss.

'Mmm,' he said as he then pulled her slowly towards him again, this time taking time to rain little kisses from her cheek to her mouth. Eventually his soft lips captured hers, and his tongue ran the length of her mouth, which she opened for him, and then couldn't help but sigh as she tasted Wayne.

Waves of pleasure ran through her at his kiss, and she pulled away, startled and shocked that she'd participated.

'Wow,' said Wayne.

She brought her hand up to her lips and touched them. They still tingled with sensations that she didn't quite understand, and she could still taste a minty freshness, the masculine difference of Wayne.

At fifteen she'd just experienced her first real kiss.

Her heart sang, her body felt like it was so light that she could fling her arms out and turn circles ... then reality struck as she lost her balance on the board and, after almost toppling into the water, she quickly righted herself.

'Wow,' she said out loud.

But there was no one to hear her. Wayne had just caught another wave in and she could see him as he balanced on his board, moving as one with the water.

He paddled back to her. He pointed. She looked behind and could see a big swell coming. She got ready.

This time she stood up for longer, and she was dumped harder into the water when she fell. The cord on her ankle yanked as her board was thrown one way and she another. She surfaced through the foaming water, coughing up water.

Wayne was surfing another wave already, coming towards her at speed. She watched him until she realised that he was going to go right over her. But he'd seen her and instead he jumped off and swam the small distance to her, towing his board behind him.

'You good?' he asked.

'Fine. But I think I swallowed half the ocean that time.'

'Let's go in, the sea is turning rough. Do you want to have hot chocolate at my place and warm up?'

'Sure,' she said and together they got back on their boards, and paddled to shore.

When they got to the beach Wayne held her ankle in place as he removed the ripcord. Once he took it off, he stroked the area with his thumb. 'Hey, it chafed you a bit.'

'It's not sore,' she said.

'Might be later. I'll put some antiseptic on when we get into the kitchen, so it doesn't get infected.'

'Thanks,' she said, tugging her leg back, not because she didn't like his touch, but because she liked the feeling of him touching her too much.

She tried to think back to every conversation she'd had with Dela. As sisters they talked all the time, about everything, and nothing was off limits. She thought about the conversations she'd listened into between the other girls at school, about boys, how they felt when they were touched, and how they acted with their boyfriends. She couldn't remember a single one of them saying they liked having a guy touching them. Being curious, and letting him touch, sure. Actually wanting him to carry on touching them further? Have their hands explore them? No. Not even the girls who were in the next standard up, with boyfriends, had ever said anything like that.

She shivered.

'You cold?' Wayne asked. 'Here, take your wet tracksuit off and wrap up in a towel, you'll be warmer soon.'

'Thanks,' she said pulling her top off and wrapping the large towel around herself. Although it cocooned her, hiding her from the outside world, it didn't help stop the shaking.

'Hey, you really did get too cold,' Wayne said. He stepped towards her, put his arms around her and ran them over the outside of the towel, up and down her body, helping transfer heat to her. Where his hands touched her she was on fire, but her body couldn't process the heat, and she shook more.

'You're not alright,' he said after a while. Hugging her to him and just standing still. Holding her.

After a while, Tara found her voice. 'I'm fine. Just scared.'

Immediately he dropped his hands away from her and stepped back.

'I'm not about to hurt you,' he said, his voice strained and in a pitch that she'd never heard, as if he was pained by what she'd said.

'I know that, Wayne. It's not you. It's me. I can't do this. I'm not made like you,' she protested.

'I scare you?'

'No, I scare me. I liked your kiss. I liked your hand touching my leg, and that's what scares me. I have never had a boyfriend before, you know that. I don't know what to do, what to say, what to think of these new feelings. I don't know what will happen to you if you love me because everything I love is always taken from me. I loved my dad, and my uncle, yet they were taken away. I loved our farm and my horse and they were sold off. Everything I really love is taken from me, and I'm too scared to love anything in case that gets taken away too. I stopped having any feelings for anyone, because if I do, it hurts too much to have them ripped away, so I just don't. I can't. It hurts too much.'

She looked at him as he slowly took the step back towards her. Once again he drew her into him. Still wrapped in the towel she couldn't protest and he hugged her close. Squeezing her lightly, trailing his hands slowly over her back.

'I'm here now. And when we get back to Hluhluwe, I'll still be there beside you. I'm not going anywhere. I really like you. It's not something sudden, and it's worth us working on. We can take it slow, you and me. I haven't had a girlfriend either, so we can explore these feelings together. I'm not too proud to tell you that.'

She felt herself begin to melt into him as her shakes subsided, and a new heat started where his body touched hers.

'So many feelings, Wayne. I just don't know how to take them all in.'

He laughed and smiled at her. He lowered his forehead onto hers. 'Me too,' he said. 'We'll work it out. Just talk to me, tell me what's going on in that pixie head of yours, and I can try to understand.'

'I'll try,' she said.

'Cool, so does that mean we are going steady now? I can call you my girlfriend?' he asked.

'I guess,' she said and she snuggled closer.

'Wear this dry tracksuit top until we get to the house. I make the best hot chocolates, even my dad thinks so,' he said.

He helped her drop her towel, and shimmy into the tracksuit top.

'This is getting to be a habit, me wearing your clothes,' she said.

'I like you in my clothes,' he said as he rolled up her sleeves for her. It was far too big on Tara, and came down her thighs like a mini dress. It was fleece lined and warm, and it smelled of Wayne. Spicy and salty and Wayne. She inhaled the scent deeply before helping him pick up their gear and head to his house.

Wayne held Tara's hand as they walked back to his cottage from their last morning of surfing. It was Saturday again, this was going to be her last day at the beach before heading home.

She hadn't ever known time to pass so fast. She was trying so hard to comprehend where the week had gone. She knew that she had spent almost all of it with Wayne.

'My dad had to go to Port Shepstone early so we have the place to ourselves. I'll make the hot chocolate once we've showered.'

'Great because I'm cold,' she said.

'Tara, you are always cold. Give me a second to wash these boards and I'll come cuddle with you and warm you up,' he said, standing the boards up under the outside shower, first rinsing them, then his own body. Tara watched as he removed his wet suit, and stood just in his jocks, under the water.

Her mouth went dry.

'Grab the towels won't you? I left them by the kitchen door,' he said.

She reluctantly turned around to get them. In the last week she had not gotten so used to seeing him almost naked that she was immune to it. She liked seeing him like that, and walking away was hard.

She liked to run her hands over his golden body and feel as each of the muscles twitched at her touch. She didn't think that her hands would ever get used to that, or that she would ever have enough of him.

Grabbing the towels she walked back to where he had stepped out the shower and was gesturing for her to get in. She took off her warm clothes and went into the hot shower, still in her cossie. but instead of stepping away, Wayne put his towel down, and joined her.

'Wayne!' she squeaked as he stepped behind her and kissed her neck. 'You're in my shower.'

'Our shower now,' he murmured as slowly he began to run his hands down her body under the hot water.

She turned to face him, and his lips met hers as she leant into him, and surrendered to the burn that started deep in her body.

Hours later they were seated in the lounge, watching movies on his television. 'Here,' Wayne said as he passed her a glass of Coke.

She reached up and took it from his hands. 'Thank you.'

His fingers lingered against hers. 'I still can't believe we have the cottage to ourselves.'

'Amazing, that your dad left you at home alone.'

'I'm not alone, I have you here,' he said.

'You know what I mean. When mum had to go do some training in Richards Bay for the railways, Lucretia moved in and slept on a mattress in the lounge to be nearer us, we're never left alone.'

'I'm older, and a boy, so I guess my dad thinks it's okay. Besides, it's just for the day, he'll be in later tonight.'

'You're only one year older than me, Wayne!' she pointed out as she took a sip and put her glass on the coffee table.

'A whole year. Three hundred and sixty-five days,' he said as he leant in and kissed her. She put her arms around his shoulders and he pulled her closer.

After a while she pulled her head away.

'This is the first day since we got together at the beach that we're totally alone. There's always someone around us.'

'Guess we're lucky today,' he said, and he pulled her on the couch and pulled her into his lap. 'And I'm lucky to have you here alone with me.'

'My mum expects me home by eight tonight so that we can be ready to leave in the morning by seven o'clock,' she said as she let her hand wander over his chin and down his neck, tugging at the shirt he had thrown on after their outdoor shower, demanding entry.

'Ah, but there is plenty we can do before then,' Wayne said as he nuzzled into her collarbone, and kissed from there up her neck. She shivered.

'You are mine. For now and forever,' he said. 'I love you, Tara.'

'I think I'm in love with you too,' she said.

'Only think?' he asked, and then he kissed her again. 'I think I might need to change that "think" into a definite "I love you Wayne",' he said, as he quickly shed his T-shirt and lifted hers up more slowly, kissing each strip of exposed flesh as he went.

'Hurry,' she said, 'we might not have all day, your dad could come home …'

She could feel him chuckle as he laughed against her stomach and nipped lower …

Tara watched Wayne disappear from view from the back seat of the car. He was staying at the beach, while they were driving home. After a week together she didn't want to be apart from him. She'd talked more to him in that week than to anyone, except perhaps Gabe, ever.

'He's a good boy that one,' Lucretia said to her. 'I see him around town, he's respectful.'

'Thanks, I like him, and I'm sure he'll behave at the beach after I have left,' Tara said.

But she wasn't sure who she was reassuring, Lucretia or herself, as every kilometre they drove north towards Hluhluwe, Tara felt more pain at having left Wayne behind.

Everything was so new.

Her feelings for Wayne had crept up on her gradually as their friendship deepened. She couldn't stop smiling every time she thought of what they had done, and how much she knew that she loved him with all her heart. She was in new territory, and it made her a little uneasy within herself. She didn't want to lose him now that she had him in her life, and that scared her.

The heat from the winter's day warmed the car, and soon Tara was nodding, almost going to sleep. She opened her window and a refreshing blast of cooler air came in.

'There is snow on the Drakensberg,' Lucretia said. 'You can feel it in the wind.'

Tara smiled. 'I won't challenge you on the weather, you always have it right.'

'I lived in that area for too many years, Miss Tara. This year there will be deep snow and come spring the plum trees will be pretty with their pink confetti all over the roads, and the plums in December will be big and juicy. It is a good year for the stone fruits. And where we are now, the sugarcane will be lush and thick. The animals will get fat in the National Park.'

'How come you know so much about farming and weather Lucretia?' Tara asked.

'I grew up on farms, and spent a lot of time in the Transkei homeland. I learnt things from the women, from the mothers of the land, who teach the girls in the Xhosa homelands and those in Zululand.'

'I thought those homeland areas were just full of faction-fighting males having territorial disputes over nothing,' Tara said.

'No, Miss Tara, you have it all wrong. Mostly they are peaceful, and the children are free to play outside and learn how to live on their land. Sometimes there is violence, and much of it is caused by outsiders, coming into those areas, causing trouble.'

'Well, I'm glad that you came to us. No matter where you came from,' Tara said.

'I'm happy too because I found your family. Now I can see a young family grow up, and see you do things that an older black woman never can. And I know that you will treat me well, because you have no man in your house. Maybe one day, pay me a pension to stay at home when I get old too.'

'What if we can't afford to pay a special pension when you're old, and we just keep paying your normal wages, what then?'

'Then you look after me like your own granny,' she said, and smiled.

'You don't want to be our granny, Lucretia. You have heard us talk about that old bat, she isn't kind or nice. Not at all like you.'

'Aww, Miss Tara, you must respect your elders, I always tell you that.'

'But she's all bitterness, she doesn't let the sunshine in anytime. How are you supposed to respect that?'

'Be patient with her. One day, maybe she might be your friend if you let her.'

'No way, not her, and not Aunty Marie-Ann either. Those two uptight ladies deserve each other.'

Lucretia just smiled at her.

Time passed slowly as they drove through rich farmlands where the sugarcane grew as high as Tara's shoulders, and still they continued north. Eventually, they could tell the start of the Hluhluwe area where the fences became higher and the fat cows changed to fat impala, zebra and other game, and they neared the turn off to their town.

Tara watched as the telephone poles and electric wires on the side of the road had crows sitting on them, waiting for their next meal as the hawks flew around above their car. She saw a barn owl as it hovered over a patch of brown grass, then dip lower and catch a field mouse. It flew off to a grove of taller trees and was lost in the landscape before it even reached the tree, blending with its environment.

Just on midday, they drove into Hluhluwe, and into their own driveway.

Tara jumped out and opened the gate, and her mum drove through and to the carport. Tara closed the gate and walked along the small road. She looked at her home after their first real holiday away.

The back lawn was covered in divots where Frederica had been foraging, and the grass was going to need a cut. But Tara just smiled at the mess, her mind instead thinking of Wayne with his shirt off, cutting the lawn at the beach.

Tara looked around her room.

It was decorated in browns and blues with purple trimmings. The same decorations she'd always had, that the removalist company had delivered along with their household of furniture that first month they were in Huhluwe. On one shelf were all her trophies from her various sports, hung next to ribbons for achievements. She'd added to them in the last two years so now the assortment were from both Junior school in Zimbabwe and Senior school in South Africa, blended together like a blur.

Next to her bed was the picture Gabe had given her of her dad, and she smoothed over the corner where the cheap silver frame was now discoloured to more of a bronze colour underneath the thin coating.

'Hey, Dad,' she said. 'I really like him. I think you would like him too. He's funny, and strong, and patient,' she told the photo. 'And being his friend just kind of crept up on me, and now I'm not sure that I want him to creep out of my life again. I kind of really like him.'

She smiled at the photograph then put it back next to the light that was on her bedside table. Her room wasn't a girly room at all, but then she'd never been a girlie-girl, so it suited her. She had her saddle and bridle sitting on a mount in one corner. Her mother had freaked big time when she'd seen them come out of the packing, but eventually she'd settled down, and even gone to the *Xhostas* Store and picked up the stand they now rested on.

The walls of Tara's room were blank, painted pearl white by her, after her mum had been able to purchase their small house when their money had eventually been transferred from Zimbabwe. As a widow, her mum had been able to bring with her only a household of furniture and $10,000. She knew that many more families had done the chicken-run out of Zimbabwe with a lot less, and that because of the sanctions they had not been allowed through customs with anything except their suitcases.

It was now their house, and this was her room, and she loved it. She snuggled deeper into her duvet, needing sleep after having late nights and early mornings at the beach. But it had been so good to spend precious time with Wayne. She closed her eyes again, clutching his tracksuit top that she hadn't returned to him. It still had a faint hint of him.

Later, Lucretia gently shook Tara's shoulder. 'Miss Tara, you need to wake up.'

'What time is it?' Tara asked.

'Almost three o'clock in the afternoon. Master Wayne is here.'

'Very funny. He's still at the beach.'

'He's waiting for you in the lounge. Get out of bed,' Lucretia said, as she walked to the windows and drew the curtains, letting the white light from outside flood the room.

Tara jumped out of bed, and pulling on her tracksuit, she rushed out of her room. Anticipation zinging through her body at the thought of seeing him. Ignoring her reflection, she ran into the lounge and right into Wayne's arms.

'Hi to you too,' he said, kissing her lightly on the mouth, then deepening the kiss.

Tara melted, even her toes melted as he held her close, then he squeezed her tightly and lifted her off the floor and twirled around with her for a moment before putting her back down.

Gasping for breath, she inhaled much needed oxygen and he grinned.

'What are you doing here, I thought you still had another two weeks at the beach?'

'My dad told me this morning that he had to come home for business, so I came with. I didn't see the point of staying at the beach without you.'

She grinned at him as he held her close.

'Let's go walk around town.'

'Okay,' she said and bounded out of the room. 'Dela,' she hollered as she went down the passage. 'I'm going out.'

'Enjoy,' Dela's muffled voice called from her room.

Tara and Wayne walked out the house, hand in hand, ready to show Hluhluwe she had her first boyfriend. They were now a couple.

CHAPTER

10

Malabar Farm

Karoi, Zimbabwe
1985

It was the end of September. The transplanted tobacco seedlings' first vital four weeks were up, and the daily wilt of the tobacco leaves that needed to be rehydrated at night in the cooler and moist air was over. Now the new plants would begin to drink deeply, and grow. Their roots sank far into the primed earth below.

'*Mvura*,' shouted Jamison Shilo Khumalo, signalling with a helicopter gesture above his head so that the huge overhead irrigation sprinklers were turned on by his co-worker Maidza. Jamison stood under the sprinkler as the water splashed down over his hat, and dripped onto his body, cooling him under the hot sun. For three years he'd learnt how to grow the tobacco. Now he'd taken over as bossboy of Malabar, one of the biggest commercial tobacco farms in the area, and he couldn't have his first crop transfer fail.

He looked at the line of sprinklers pumping the water above. The distances were perfect, with the metal piping perfectly spaced in its six-metre lengths, the riser out the piping up to the sprinkler head jutted towards the blue African sky. His spacing was square, to ensure that his crop didn't show watering circles. He knew that differences in the water pressures and winds blowing the water were just two of the factors he needed to compensate for to ensure there were no patterns in the crop.

The cool water splashed down on the rich soil, and into the channels dug between the rows of the plants. The water quickly disappeared into the sand, but was replaced by more, and as it fell on the seedlings, Jamison smiled.

This would be a good crop. The seedlings were strong, healthy and eager to grow. He knew that he wasn't too late with the water. He'd been taught well by the old man Kitwelle before he retired to his kraal. The white manager of the farm had gone away within a few months of Jamison being employed on Malabar, threatening the farm workers, saying that without him the farm would fall into disrepair and their jobs would disappear. He'd left the old Widow Crosby with only her 'black boys' to help her.

Jamison remembered well that once the white manager had gone in his *bakkie*, and his dust had yet to settle, old Kitwelle had explained that he'd been caught stealing tobacco bales from Widow Crosby, and she'd sacked him.

The workers had remained on the farm.

They didn't want to leave Widow Rose Crosby.

True, she was very colonial in her ways – the workers were still referred to as *kaffirs*, and her house servants wore gloves, but she was a fair *baas* and a strong farmer's wife. She had inherited the farm when her husband was killed during the War of Independence.

She was still hands on, working her farm despite her advancing years. Jamison could see her riding her horse towards him now, mindful that she rode in the ditches between the tobacco plants, so as to not damage the young seedlings in any way.

'Jamison,' she called. '*Huya pano!*'

He jogged towards her to the end of the row, and out of the cool spray. Immediately his overalls began to dry as the hot sun sucked all the moisture from them.

'Good morning, madam,' he nodded in respect.

'I listened to the wireless last night, and the weatherman is predicting the rain to be late again this year. More drought … but we have deep boreholes on Malabar and they can pump the water we need to grow both the tobacco and the wheat. The people on the farm will not go hungry, despite this drought.'

'Madam,' Jamison said and nodded.

'Come,' Widow Crosby said and turned her horse towards the tobacco barn nearest the field. Jamison walked slowly behind her horse, looking all the time at the tobacco, checking for insects, and checking for signs of stress that might indicate their crop was in danger of failure. He couldn't see any.

Soon they came to the barn and Widow Crosby dismounted. She wrapped the reins into a knot and just left them on her horse.

'I've seen those new seedlings, they look healthy. We'll have a good crop this year,' she said.

'Yes,' Jamison agreed. 'But the rest of the area are feeling the drought. In the TTL there are cattle dying from no water, and no food. It is too soon after the last one. The land, she's not recovered fast enough. Already their reservoir is empty.'

'Already?' Widow Crosby asked as she waited while Jamison pushed the door open. She went inside.

'Yes,' Jamison said. 'We could take a tanker of Malabar water to fill their reservoir again. The people would appreciate the help.'

'You can do that. Take that new *piccaninny* with you and make him work. That one has shifty eyes, and if he wasn't related to Jossie, I wouldn't have hired him. He's going to steal us blind.'

'No, he's a good boy, madam. He won't steal. He's a Matabele, and his eyes look shifty because he's squinting all the time. Maybe we can get him to the hospital for some glasses. I saw when he was planting a few weeks back, he uses his hands to guide his plants to the holes already dug deep into the earth. He can't see properly.'

'You serious. I hired a blind boy to work? Why didn't you tell me that when we hired him?'

'He'll be a good worker when he has glasses and can see, madam.'

'Fine, take the tanker of water and take him with you, and then get him into the clinic and sort his eyes out. I don't want anyone stealing, understood?'

'Yes, madam,' Jamison said.

'Make sure you check this barn early, Jamison, I don't want any trouble this year. A good crop means a good pay cheque for everyone. Understood.'

'Yes, madam,' Jamison replied. He'd heard the lecture from her before, but he didn't mind hearing it all again. Twice a week she'd come out onto the property and discuss the running of it with him. The rest of the time, if he needed anything, he'd go up to the farmhouse to speak with her.

They had finished checking the flumes in the barn. He held the door open for her as Widow Crosby walked out. Her horse was near where she had left him, too well trained to try to nibble on the tobacco crop. She walked him to where Jamison had placed an upturned sawn in half 44-gallon drum. Stepping onto it, she mounted her horse.

Jamison smiled that she always used the drums, but had never commented that he had noticed she needed them as the years passed. He stood quietly by her side.

'Right, to the house now, I have some old clothes that you can distribute when you go into the TTL.'

Jamison nodded, and walked alongside her towards the farmhouse.

The farmhouse was a sprawling brick structure. It still had impact shields about a metre and a half away from the windows, protecting the glass from any mortar or grenade attacks. Even though the war was over, Widow Crosby had never wanted them removed. They had seen her through the Rhodesian Bush War, and were extra security for her now, making sure no one could see into her home. She said that one day the fighting would come back to Mashonaland, and the dissident wars that were happening in Matabeleland would spread all over Zimbabwe again. But she had Felix, the garden boy, cover them with creepers. She called them wisterias. The vines trailed across the shields creating a green screen for most of the year, but when it was their time to flower in the spring, the blooms gave off a heavy perfume that he could breathe in forever. In lilac and white, the flowers intertwined on the screens looking like bunches of flower grapes, and softened the hard red brick of the house behind.

Madam Crosby had modernised the house, and although she still had a wood stove in the kitchen and a donkey boiler outside, just in case, she also had an electric hot water geyser and an electric stove for her cook to prepare meals on.

When he visited with her they would sit on the veranda at the back of the kitchen, she'd have her tea in tiny bone china cups decorated with pink roses, and he'd have his in a big enamel cup. Sometimes, she'd give him a biscuit on an enamel plate, or share some sandwiches with him while hers were white and had the crusts removed, his were thick brown bread spread thickly with butter and peanut butter with syrup dripping from the sides.

Shilo – now Jamison – thought on how he'd been able so far to avoid Buffel finding out where he was. He had a warning system in place. His cousin Gibson had gone to Buffel's farm and taken a job as a builder and tracker. If Buffel was gone from his farm for longer than a day or two, he would let Shilo know. In the past, Gibson would leave a phone message with Widow Crosby's maid for him, in case Buffel was coming for him. But now that he was head boy, he had his own house and his own phone that Gibson could call him on. Gibson had been a policeman, but had been retired when he was shot. He had no immediate family, and Shilo had warned him about the children, that he must keep them away or else they would be 'taken' at that farm.

No one on Malabar knew him by his true name. He was bossboy and earning decent money, and the Widow Crosby had all her workers working for her on a profit-share basis so that they worked harder, and their bonus was directly related to their crop. If their yield was big, so was their *bonsella,* their *chipo*, and if they didn't look after the crop, then they got no gift. He liked the system that rewarded the people as well as the tough old white farmer.

And best of all, he had met Ebony.

He had never intended to have a relationship with anyone. Despite telling Kwazi he wanted a family, he knew that actually having one was always going to be out of his reach. No woman could love a man who kept such dark secrets as he did. No woman would want a life that she couldn't publicise with pictures of their wedding in the paper, because he would always need to stay inconspicuous, laying low in case Buffel was still looking for him.

But then he'd met Ebony, and all the reasoning in the world went flying away like Egyptian geese migrating north in winter.

Although it was in the past, he remembered the time, as if it was a video playing in his head. Just the year before he had been attending a tobacco auction with old man Kitwelle, before he retired, making sure that no one stole any of their bales, and also to ensure that Kitwelle didn't do any of the heavy lifting which he shouldn't do anymore. They had driven to the loading area of the tobacco warehouse and had helped the staff there to unload the truck. One by one the bales were weighed and marked, then reloaded onto a collection of wheelbarrows and hand trolleys, and taken to the sales floor where they were put in neat lines. Jamison began loosening the twine on the bales so they could be inspected by the officer from the Tobacco Industry Marketing Board for undesirable foreign matter. The buyers would walk the same steps as the officer, offering a price on the bales. As the farm's head boy, it was Kitwelle's job to listen to Widow Crosby, and remove the bales from sale for the time being, if the price given was too low.

As he was getting the bales ready for their inspection, Jamison couldn't help but notice the woman in the next aisle. She was tall with a traditional figure, and she wore a long white and blue dress, with a matching '*doek*' as Widow Crosby like to call it, or head scarf, as the ladies on the farm referred to it. Her smart fitted dress, that showed a hint of bosom when she bent over, would have been better in an office job, because it wouldn't stay very clean working with the tobacco. He could see her muscles flex in her shoulders as she moved because the neckline was low and wide on her shoulders that glowed like rich Jamaican chocolate. She wore no jewellery that could be dislodged and fall into a bale, contaminating it.

Jamison was impressed by her as she seemed unaware of the magnificent sight she made as she worked. She was performing the same duty that he was, and obviously was proud of the product she displayed. Her face captivated him.

An older man, dressed in blue overalls, hobbled in her area using a carved knobkerrie as a walking stick. He ambled behind where she'd worked, as if checking up on her. At one stage she stopped, and it seemed as though she was checking on the older man, as she motioned to the back of the warehouse where other workers were taking a break. He shook his head, and gestured with his stick, to look at the whole tobacco sales floor. She nodded, reached out and rubbed his shoulder in the affectionate way a child would to her father, before continuing her work.

After a while, she looked up, and smiled at him.

Jamison looked back over his shoulder to ensure that no one stood behind him who she was greeting, but there was no one, just bale upon bale of brown tobacco.

Her smile was for him, and his heart was stolen forever.

Jamison had asked Ebony to marry him the first day he met her at the auction warehouse in Harare. After speaking with her for most of the day while they worked and watched the buyers, then watched the auction take place. They had talked until both Kitwelle and her father had fallen asleep while they waited for the younger ones in the small market place outside, sitting at a table made from an electrical power wire spindle, on seats that were upturned milk crates.

He had blurted it out. 'Marry me. Stay with me always.'

Ebony's face hadn't shown horror at his frankness, or at his unromantic proposal. 'I will keep that proposal in my heart, and when I know you better I will let you know when the answer turns to a yes.'

He had seen her every Sunday after that for a month before Kitwelle had suggested that she come for an interview with the Widow

Crosby to come and work at Malabar farm. Ebony was well educated, and she knew tobacco.

When he had told her about the interview, her brown eyes had shone with unshed tears.

'Now I can see more of you. We can be together,' she said. A month after that, she had moved to Malabar Farm, and into the quarters for single females.

Sometimes he saw her during the day when his path and hers crossed over at the farm.

But at night time, they got to spend more time together, before returning to their single quarters to start the next day with another early morning.

When he was told by Kitwelle what they were doing, he had smiled knowing he would definitely see her in the sorting shed.

He followed behind at a respectful distance as Widow Crosby crossed to the next building. Once inside, she made a beeline for their new worker.

'Ebony, how are you finding it here? After a month working in a new shed, a new farm, away from your father?' Widow Crosby asked.

Ebony nodded her head in respect, then looked at her employer. 'It is a little different, but it is good. It is honest work.'

'I like this one,' Widow Crosby said to Kitwelle who walked alongside her. 'Jamison, make sure that you never give her cause to leave. Marry her and keep her here.'

Jamison looked down, trying to hide the heat that entered his face, but he couldn't help smiling. 'Yes, madam. I hope that she will not be leaving any time.'

'Good, we could do with a party for a wedding,' Widow Crosby said as he turned away. 'We haven't had a wedding on Malabar for a few years now ...'

Kitwelle and Madam Crosby continued on their rounds, and Jamison caught a moment with Ebony before catching up with them.

'She likes you,' Jamison said.

'That's why she hired me?' Ebony said. 'I thought it was because she knew that you were hopelessly in love with me?'

'I don't have that much power with the Widow Crosby. She has her own mind and thinks her own way, does her own thing.'

'No. She listens to Kitwelle, and to you. She relies on you both to help her to run this farm, and to make it work. I had spoken with many people about her before I came to work here. She treats people well. That was why my father supported my moving here.'

Jamison smiled as he reached out his hand to her. 'Eb, I like that you moved here too,' he said.

'I hope it's more like *love* that I moved here, because now that you have me, I'm staying.'

'You're right, I love having you here,' he said softly.

'I'm happy to have a party, and invite her,' Ebony said. 'I can wear white and you can pay *roora* to my father, because you respect me enough.'

Jamison looked at her. His heart raced.

Every day since she had moved to the farm, they would walk together, talk after work. Eat supper together. Ebony was a good cook. She made traditional foods like *sadza neNyama*. But also white man's foods, like spaghetti bolognese and shepherd's pie, two of his favourite meals. And never during their time had she ever brought up his marriage proposal. He had feared she had forgotten it.

Apparently not.

Hesitantly, he asked, 'So is that a yes, you will marry me?'

'Yes, I'll marry you!' Ebony said.

He threw his arms around her, and the other women in the tobacco shed clapped and began to sing for them, dancing where they worked.

PART TWO

The Butterfly

CHAPTER

11

Recce Life

Fort Doppies, Caprivi Strip, South West Africa
1990

Wayne dropped his pack on the hard ground. Bevin and two of the other Recces flopped down alongside him under the tarpaulin that shaded the area during the heat of the day.

'Home sweet home,' Bevin said.

Wayne looked around their home of the last few years, Fort Doppies, a base in the Caprivi Strip on the Cuando River, in South West Africa. It was here that much of the Special Forces training was conducted, because of the area's similarity to the bush in Angola, and its isolated location. This base trained with live rounds. This was one of the last stops before the real combat zone on the Angolan border. This was his base camp.

He'd accomplished so much in the last six years. He'd left Hilton top of his class and had been offered bursaries and scholarships for several of the top universities, which he'd deferred so that he could enter the army and become financially independent from his family sooner. He'd completed his initial basic training, as every man in South Africa who was called to National Service had. Then it had been suggested to him that he try out for the Special Forces Unit. The Recces.

The week-long selection test had been a bitch, but after training, he'd passed their tests and he was one of the few elite people who could call themselves a Special Forces Operator.

He'd been presented with his red beret, and his Special Forces Operators badge, with its distinctive commando knife within a laurel wreath. He was now so used to doing the legendary 'Gunston 500s', that he was no longer in awe of the feat. Mockingly nicknamed after the real-life surfing event by the men, the 500-kilometre walk inside the Angolan border was totally completed without air support, with only your pack and your unit for company. A far cry from the glamorous event where hot babes in bikinis lined the beach, covered in coconut oil, while surf pros from around the world competed for a rich prize pool in the cool ocean in Durban.

His unit had just returned from yet another of those epic journeys, but this time their mission had been more than reconnaissance. They had focused on the wildlife trade, not the war that raged on the Angolan border. They had gathered intel on the illegal trade in ivory and live animals, and on the drug trade. Not on rivers, and water supplies, not on suspected terrorist bases. And for the first time in a long time, Wayne had found an area of interest that he could become ultra passionate about. The desperate need for the preservation of Africa's wild animals.

Together with his Recce team, they'd tracked ammunition boxes filled with ivory from Angola, through Namibia and into South Africa. They followed the carnage by the poachers from the bush, through the kraals and into the big city where the fat cats in Johannesburg sat within a society that hid behind high walls and fences, trying to keep out the same drug addicts that they supplied the drugs to.

Wayne was sickened by the corruption he'd seen and by the trade in drugs that was happening. Mandrax was using the same pipeline to get into South Africa, and the SADF were denying that their trucks were being used in the illegal trafficking.

But as yet they still couldn't prove that it was someone high up in the army who was involved. Every time they came close, every time someone asked questions, they came across the same line, blocking their inquiries.

'It's none of your business, and you will be sorted out if you continue to stick you nose in where it doesn't belong.'

The SADF had 'lost' intelligence staff who asked too many questions, and it was now the Recces who were trying to uncover the mastermind behind the drug and animal trade.

Someone was profiteering in the illegal trade, and it wasn't the SADF.

Wayne's heart hurt thinking of all the wildlife that was being decimated for profit. He snorted as he shook his head, trying to dislodge the disappointment he felt just thinking of their last mission, of their losses and their inability to nail the son-of-a-bitch responsible for the desecration of the wild animals across Africa.

He dragged himself upright and moved to the edge of the shade area, looking out over the river that meandered below. The sun was setting. They had pushed hard to make Doppies by sundown.

Terry, the resident lion, wandered into the camp. He chose to sit quietly next to Wayne as they gazed out at the view of the river together.

Unlike many other parts of Africa, the fighting here had been going on for so long, most of the animals had become gun shy and had fled or been hunted by soldiers for fresh meat. Those animals that had once fled to the Caprivi Strip to escape the fighting in the north in Angola had been savagely poached. There were stories told among the older men, about finding elephant ivory stashes of fifty to two hundred tusks. About caches of hippo teeth in tea chests. And the men who had served for many years remembered when game had roamed so thick that you could sight elephant daily.

But now, no one remembered seeing an elephant in the area for at least ten years, and those that were reported were said to limp from bullets embedded deep into their flesh from attacks in the north. Sometimes when they were crossing through the bush, they would come across an old carcass, its white bones scattered about by scavengers, signs that the tusks had been chopped out clearly visible in the once mighty skull.

Yet Terry the lion remained fat. His diet was often supplemented by the men in the camp who regarded him as part of their operation. Terry had been just a cub when he'd stumbled into their camp, and had chosen to claim the human world of their camp within his territory. The men had never tried to harness him and tame him. He was still a wild lion, he'd just chosen the men as his pride.

Terry licked Wayne's fingers as he reached out to give him a rub in his huge mane.

'So Terry, how was your day at the office?' Wayne asked, then laughed.

'One day that lion is going to talk back to you, and then what?' asked Bevin.

'Then I'll know I've finally lost it,' Wayne said as Terry moved his position so that his large body pressed fully against Wayne's leg, and his belly was accessible for a rub.

Bevin sat in the dirt on the opposite side of Wayne to where Terry was lying. It wasn't that he was frightened of Terry, just cautious. 'That lion seriously is just a giant pussy cat with you, do you know that.'

Wayne smiled. 'It's just a shame that one-hundred-and-eighty kilos of kitty-cat is hard to share a regulation army bed with.'

Bevin laughed at Wayne's complaint. Many had experienced the delight of having Terry decide theirs was the bed he was going to sleep on that night. After jumping up onto the bed, and pinning down the occupant, he usually licked their faces with his sandpaper tongue before trying to settle horizontally on top of the person to sleep. Since Wayne had entered the camp four years previously, mostly he'd chosen to sleep alongside Wayne.

He also chose to patrol with Wayne when he was outside of the camp, and would walk the perimeter check with him when he was on duty.

Bevin dug his toes into the sand. 'It was great having him with us for the first part of that mission.'

'Yup. I still think we crossed out of his territory on day five and that's why he turned back. That or he smelled a female.'

'Actually it was quite comforting having him with us while we were out there. I mean, come on, what gook is going to attack someone in the bush with a lion hanging around them? They are too superstitious for that,' Bevin admitted.

Terry rolled back over, and the ever-present flies hummed around him, then settled again.

'Have you always been good with animals?' Bevin asked.

'Never really been around them. I guess I like my dog at home, and the barn cats brush up and say hello, but I never thought of it as an affinity with animals.'

'Perhaps when we get out this shithole of a war, you can do something with them.'

'Perhaps,' Wayne said, but he thought of Tara and how he needed to find her.

'Are you thinking of taking Terry with you when you check out?'

'He's a free lion. This is his territory. I couldn't relocate him without good cause. Even if we suddenly stopped this war by some miracle, he'd still be a wild animal. No one should remove him.'

'But he's domesticated.'

'Lions can't be domesticated. He'll want to take on a pride soon, now that he's fully mature. Apparently when he came into camp he was just small, and the guys who encouraged him in with milk and meat and attention, they never realised he'd stay around. But it's eight years since he came here, almost time for him to find a real pride of his own. He's strong, he'll fight for his own harem soon.'

'You see any other lions on patrol here? He's been left behind. They all moved out long ago. The area is too hot, even for the lions.'

'Bevin, seriously I think you underestimate the instinct that lions have to survive. If they can't eat the wild animals, they will turn on unsuspecting humans and eat them.'

'Maybe, but that survival-driven pussy cat is eating your bush hat.'

'Terry, drop!' Wayne commanded. Terry just looked at him with eyes of molten gold, with his eyebrows up in a questioning position, and continued to tear the hat apart. 'What will we do with you?'

Bevin laughed.

One of the support staff walked over to the tarp area. 'Wayne, the lieutenant is looking for you.'

'What did you do this time?' asked Bevin. 'You only just got back to camp.'

'Dunno,' Wayne said as he stood up. Terry stood next to him. He came up to halfway between Wayne's knees and his hip. The lion put his front feet forward and stretched backwards, just as a domestic cat would do. 'Come on, let's go see what he wants,' Wayne said to Terry.

He heard Bevin as he left. 'I think you and that lion look like George Adamson in *Born Free*.'

Wayne showed him the middle finger and continued walking. He followed the staffer to the lieutenant's office and knocked on the door. Terry sat outside, waiting.

'Enter,' Lieutenant Upton shouted.

Wayne opened the door. 'You wanted to see me, sir?'

'Sit.' He motioned to the visitor's chair the other side of his desk.

Being summoned to the lieutenant's office was almost as bad as being called into the principal's office at school. It wasn't something he had to do often. Mostly their lieutenant would speak with them as a group, or under the tarp while having a beer.

The lieutenant stood and retrieved two glasses and a bottle of brandy from the top of a filing cabinet. He put them on the front of his desk and poured a shot of about two inches into each glass, careful not to spill the golden liquid. He screwed the lid back on the bottle, and lifted a glass, passing it to Wayne.

'Drink this, you are going to need it.'

Wayne downed the brandy and felt the burn all the way from his mouth into his stomach. 'What?' he asked, putting the glass next to the lieutenant's empty one.

'You need to pack for condolence leave. I received this yesterday.' He passed Wayne a message that had obviously been written by someone in the comms office.

'Regret to inform Special Forces Operator Wayne Simon Botha of the death of his father, passed on 10 January 1990. Mother requesting only son to return to civilian life to take over the responsibility of the family farm.'

Wayne sat at the breakfast table at Kujana Farm.

He shovelled another spoon of banana ProNutro into his mouth. His father, who should have sat opposite him, reading the newspaper and grunting every now and again, or chuckling, was gone. Never again would he share a joke at the table from his morning papers.

His mother would always come in and turn the conversation to the bad articles in the paper. But his father had liked to share the jokes. How they had stayed together all these years, Wayne still didn't understand.

He stared at the milk carton on the breakfast table. The pictures of the blonde children who were going missing in South Africa stared back. He turned the carton so he couldn't see the black and white pictures. They reminded him too much of the young Tara who'd walked into his classroom in Standard 6. The younger Tara with the worried eyes, and the touch-me-not attitude.

He hated to admit that he was no closer to finding Tara than he had been after they had been forced apart all those years before.

She had left so quickly that week. And her family had refused to talk with him. Then while his life was still in turmoil, and he was sent to boarding school, her mother and sister had moved away from Hluhluwe too, and no one knew where they had gone. He'd asked everyone in their old school, had even asked the staff at the railway station.

He knew that she had family in Durban and had looked in the phone book for her there, with no success. He'd looked in the phone book of every major city and found nothing.

The following year he'd tried again.

And the next.

He'd spent almost every R&R he got walking the streets of Durban, trying to track her down. Always starting in the Point Road area where he knew her gran had once lived. He never used the time to relax at all.

He'd put adverts in the papers and in magazines. Even in the *Farmers' Weekly*. Asking anyone who knew any news of her to please contact him via his own post office box in Hluhluwe as he didn't trust his mother not to destroy mail sent to Kujana.

'Good morning, Wayne,' Isabeth said as she walked in.

He looked up at his mother. Her dark hair perfectly in place, her make-up already painted on her white face. Her clothes pressed and neat. For a forty-eight-year-old woman, she looked much younger, but he was only sorry that underneath the pretty façade lay a heart of stone. He'd learnt that lessons years ago.

First with Tara, then with boarding school.

He remembered the scene at that very table where his father had tried to defend him, and she'd laid down her law. He'd gone to boarding school just like she wanted. She had manipulated him into being sent away to school, away from Hluhluwe, and away from Tara. He hated her for that. Hated that she had forced Tara to abort their child. But mostly he hated her for not supporting him, for not believing that his love for Tara, no matter that they were so young, was real. And the hate of a teenage boy had burnt into the contempt of the man he now was, and coming home for his father's funeral was as a duty to his father, not as support for his manuipulative mother. He no longer had to put up with her self-centred nature. Their lives had parted ways when she had forced Tara from him.

Ironically, it was the boarding school she insisted on sending him to that had freed him up the most from his own guilt over being forced to abandon Tara and the loss of their baby. His time away at boarding school had also cemented his bubbling anger and resentment with his mother.

It had taught him to focus on what was important and ignore what was incidental. In his life, she'd given birth to him, and that was all.

'Morning, Isabeth,' he said, and continued his breakfast, a polite coolness between them.

'Samuel will bring the car around at ten o'clock for us to travel to your father's funeral.'

'Sure,' he said. There was no need for Samuel to have to play chauffeur, he could attend the funeral as the driver from the farm, instead of working that day. She knew that Wayne was perfectly capable of driving them to the funeral. Hell, he could drive more than just a car. With his training, he could fly her there in a plane too if he wanted to, about the only thing he couldn't drive was a nuclear submarine. Yet, he was past the point of rising to his mother's bait. Gone were his days of being manipulated by her. He knew she liked to fight, that was her thing, and he no longer indulged her.

'Wayne, this is nonsense!' Isabeth said. 'You can still call me Mum, you know.'

'I could,' he said, 'but I choose not too. You lost the privilege of being called Mum a few years back. You might be the woman who birthed me, but it was Dad who was the parent. It was Dad who constantly supported me, guided me in the direction that was good for me, not good for you. Now that Dad has gone, I see no point in keeping up the pretence. You can't hurt him anymore with your threats of divorce and of leaving him alone, like you did any time things didn't go your way. You manipulated him every opportunity you had, threatened him into doing what you wanted whenever he defied you. Just like you did to me and Tara. But you will no longer dictate what happens in my life. Those days are long gone, Isabeth. You are not part of my life. I will not be coming home to run Kujana as you instructed in your letter to the army either, but will be remaining in the Recces.'

'You're just like him!' she said.

'Good. Because as a person my father was kind, compassionate and a decent human being. I'm not saying he was perfect.

He indulged you constantly. That was his biggest character flaw, because mostly he tried to be the best man he could.'

'Oh that he did, he was always the better man. The better person. Everyone had to see him as that. Even when he was young, before we were even dating. He was the perfect gentleman! Now he's done the gentlemanly thing and gone and died on me. Leaving me alone. I'm not even fifty yet. And he left me.'

'Oh for God's sake, he can't help having a heart attack, Isabeth. It's not like he chose that!' Wayne pushed his plate away and rose from the table. 'I'll get ready. See you at the car at ten.'

The lawyer's office was starkly decorated. Wayne tugged at the collar on his shirt and tie. Damn, he didn't miss these when he was in the bush. His camo was so much more comfortable.

The receptionist answered her phone. Then she stood up and crossed over to Wayne and his mother. 'Mr Bezuidenhout will see you now.' She led them through to a boardroom.

Mr Bezuidenhout opened the large glass door from the inside. 'Come on in,' he said as he shook first Isabeth's hand, then Wayne's. 'Please have a seat.' He motioned to the chairs around a large oval table, and held out a chair for Isabeth. 'Maree, hold my calls.'

The receptionist nodded, closed the door and walked back to her desk. Wayne watched her go. He recognised her as one of the girls who used to be friends with Dela at school. He wondered if afterwards he could ask her for a drink and see if she knew anything about Tara's whereabouts. After all, Hluhluwe was such a small place, it was uncharacteristic that no one knew anything about where the Wright family had gone.

Mr Bezuidenhout sat in the chair opposite Wayne and Isabeth. 'Thank you for coming. And again, I'm so sorry for your loss.'

Wayne nodded. Isabeth sniffed into a tissue.

Mr Bezuidenhout continued. 'This is a formality. I have to say that I'm conducting this meeting at the wish of the late Johnny Bird Botha. Johnny asked that you both be present at the reading of his will.'

Isabeth shifted in her chair. 'Ben, I'm not so sure why we're having such a formal meeting. Johnny and I came in here often enough to sort out everything for the farm with you.'

'Death is never easy, Isabeth, and so often estates are left in a state of unorganised chaos. But not with Johnny. You have been spared that.' He opened the file in front of him. 'Johnny was my friend as well as client. It's still hard to believe he is dead.'

Isabeth crossed her arms and sat back in her chair. Wayne stared at Ben Bezuidenhout, wondering what was so important that they had needed to come into town to do the reading, and why Ben hadn't just come to the house, and visit like he always did.

'Johnny was meticulous with keeping his will up to date.' He looked at Isabeth. 'I have often updated both your wills on separate occasions. So this was his last will and testament.' He handed both Wayne and Isabeth a copy.

Wayne began to read it, the legal jargon flowery at the beginning. Then he got to the part where it said that there was to be a lump sum payment to Isabeth, so she could buy a house in the city, and which would keep her for her years, until either she passed or she spent it all. She wasn't entitled to more. Wayne inherited Kujana, the farm, along with a substantial working capital. Although John wrote that he assumed that at the time of writing, he knew Wayne wasn't interested in continuing being a sugarcane farmer, and there was an instruction that the farm should be sold if Wayne chose, with all the proceeds go to Wayne.

The third legacy was a lump-sum payment, held in trust, with a monthly annuity to continue being paid to his grandchild, Josha Wright.

Wayne sat numbly.

He had a son.

He had a son, and his name was Josha.

'Continued? Continued? Johnny paid that bitch and never told me!' Isabeth was shouting. 'How much money has already gone to that little bastard? Has she been blackmailing my Johnny all this time? Ben, how could you let this happen?'

'No, Isabeth,' Ben said. 'Johnny was clear on this when we set the trust up almost six years ago. Tara Wright was supported while she finished school, and expenses were paid to cover her costs in having to relocate to have the baby. The baby was to be kept in the fashion that he would have been if he were within the Botha household.'

Wayne turned to his mother. The look on her face was one of total contempt, and hatred.

He couldn't breathe. He wanted to smash something.

'Another lie, Isabeth. You told me that Tara had aborted our baby. You told me Tara had it killed!'

She darted a look at Ben and she put her hand on her throat. 'Wayne, perhaps this isn't the place and time—'

'It's the perfect place. In front of our lawyer. Our *family* lawyer.' Wayne flexed his fist. Anger like he'd only experienced once in his life bubbled to the surface. 'Did you know that Tara had kept our child?'

'That little bitch disappeared before I got to take care of that business. So the child was as good as dead anyway,' she said.

'You kept this from me ...' Wayne said quietly, and Ben stood up, as if realising how short the fuse was that Wayne kept tightly under control.

'No,' his mother said. 'I didn't know about this.' She burst into tears and slammed her hands on the table. 'He paid her off, he went behind my back after all and paid her off. And you helped,' she rounded on Ben, poking him in the chest. 'That's why she could disappear. I had the appointment made, I was going to drive her to the doctor in Johannesburg myself to ensure she had the abortion and she couldn't ruin Wayne's life.'

Ben pushed her hand away slowly. 'Please sit down, Isabeth,' he said in a calm voice.

Isabeth collapsed into the chair.

Wayne asked Ben. 'Where is she? Where is my son?'

'I don't know. My company pays the money into an account every month. We haven't had direct contact with her since 1984 when the initial paperwork was organised with our sister firm in Durban.' Ben shuffled his papers. 'Wayne, there is this envelope for you too. From your father. He kept it updated after he found out about his angina.'

Ben handed him an A3 envelope.

Wayne opened it and pulled out the contents. A handwritten letter on thick paper, and a second envelope that had instruction on it. *Do not bend.* He read the letter.

My son

You were a lucky token, coming so late into my life. I never thought I would get to have a child, let alone a beautiful son. I am so proud to have been your father.

There are so many conversations I wish we could have had ... but if you are reading this, time has run out for me.

Your mother was pregnant when she married me. The first time, she had an abortion, without telling me. The next time around I wasn't letting her have another one. I was with her twenty-four hours a day to ensure she didn't, I couldn't let her destroy another life. I was already forty and she was only nineteen. At first I thought she'd give birth to you, and just leave, and I would have you to myself, but life didn't turn out that way. She stayed because you became her weapon against me.

Make no mistake, I love your mother, but as you know she's my Achilles' heel. I guess this is what happens when love is one sided. I got a trophy wife and a son to love, and she got an old man and his money. Our age gap was large, but I always thought that my love could overcome that.

I was wrong.

But I can say with a clear conscience that I never gave up or that my commitment to love and cherish her always ever strayed. I hope you won't be too hard on her.

I have enclosed three pictures of your son Josha. One from when he was born, one from a few years ago, and the final one Tara sent to me through the lawyers last year, of them in a park together.

Of all the things in life I am proud of, I am proudest that I could help you, and help your Tara to escape Isabeth's jealousy and acidic nature and have your baby. I wish I could have been the grandfather that Josha needed, active in his life. Not the unknown man he will never know.

Tara looks like she is a good mum. I only ever asked for one photograph, and she has sent three.

Josha is a beautiful boy.

I knew that day after I sent you to boarding school that I had made the second biggest mistake in my life by agreeing with Isabeth and sending you away from me. I lost you then.

I also know that you're too proud to ask for help a second time. I understand that you're now a man, no longer a boy, and you want to do things in your own time, and with your own money.

You once came to me for help, and I couldn't openly show it to you for fear of your mother divorcing me, and taking you away from me. I can think of not one case when my friends have got divorced that the father has been granted custody in South Africa, even when the children were over sixteen. As you know, the mother always gets the children.

I told you that day you asked for my help that I don't believe in abortion. I believe that every life is precious, and family is important. I just wish I could have told you then that I would protect your baby no matter what Isabeth said.

I have a grandchild. You have a son.

Know that the farm now gives you total financial independence, and moving your mother into town will give you the space and peace and quiet you need when you bring your family back together.

You can sell it if you wish, but I have had many happy moments watching you grow up there, and I hope that this way, you get to experience those same memories, with your own son.

Come back to civilisation.

I love you my son. I have always loved you.

Dad.

Wayne opened the next envelope and looked at the pictures. The first was of Tara and Josha right after his birth. She was sitting in a wheelchair, in a pink hospital gown, her hair tied back, and he could see how she'd been sweating. In her arms she held a baby wrapped in blue, and she looked down at it with a love that radiated from the picture.

His son. So tiny.

He turned the photo over, and on the back was written: *Josha – 11 April 1985.*

He took in a deep breath, and pulled the next picture to the top of the small pile.

It was just Josha by himself, his hair blonde and curly around his head, his big beautiful blue eyes large in the close-up. Eyes shaped like Tara's, but the same colour as his own. The photo was sharp and clear, as if it had been done professionally. The third photo was the most recent. Josha was a lot taller. He was standing in front of Tara, giving her a kiss as she sat on a picnic bench. His blond head was only millimetres away from hers. She still wore her hair in its blunt bob as she had when he had last seen her the day they had parted on such bad terms, only now her hair was blonder. She was highlighting it. She had her arm around Josha's middle, and she looked like she was laughing. Josha wore a uniform, of a white short-sleeved shirt, with grey socks, and black shoes. He couldn't see the insignia on the shirt, and it could have been from almost any school in South Africa.

He flicked through the photos again. There was nothing in the pictures to see where they had been taken.

'Ben, as my lawyer, do you know where she is?' Wayne asked.

'No. But we can initiate a search for you. There are people who specialise in finding those who don't want to be found. But it will cost a fair amount.'

'You know my financial situation better than anyone, having worked so close to my dad. With his money that I have just inherited, can I afford those services?' Wayne asked.

'Yes.'

'Then, do it.'

* * *

Wayne sat on a plastic chair under the tarp at Doppies Base Camp. Terry sat near his feet as always, his head resting on his front paws.

Bevin coughed to get Wayne's attention. 'You know the Lieutenant suggested when we wrap up here at the end of the month, we get away, clear our heads. Travel, get in to city life again.'

'Yeah,' Wayne said. 'Would be in July, the coldest month. We couldn't wrap up in September when the temperatures are decent, before the heat and the rain arrive.'

Bevin smiled. 'So, I have arranged to visit my great aunt in Karoi, in Zimbabwe. She's sold her farm at last and is coming to live with my folks. She asked me to come for one last visit, help her pack her things, make sure she leaves nothing behind. You'll like her. She used to be a tobacco farmer, but she's now diversified and put in game too. For an old lady she's one hell of a farmer.'

'She's the farmer?'

'Yeah. For years she was just keeping afloat until she got her new bossboy, Jamison. He's the one who's basically been running the farm for her. Although my mother tells me my aunt is in no way acting like an old woman yet.'

'Sounds good. Hope you have a great time.'

'After that, a week on her houseboat in Kariba. That is going to be a party! But I wanted you to come with me, you know, travel together.'

'Does she know you're bringing a guest?'

'Yes, I wrote and told her two people would be visiting.'

'You assumed I would go with you? Why?'

'Because you need the break. You're coming with me, my friend. Time for you to live a little and to give yourself a rest from looking at that photo of your child and your girl all the time.'

Wayne smiled. 'It's become a bit of an obsession. I still can't quite believe that it's real. I have proof that I have a son, not just a feeling. Remember when I once told you that it was possible Tara hadn't had that abortion, that she had lost things in her life that she loved, that I thought she would fight with everything she had to keep our child. Well, I was right. I guess having my dad on her side helped her to win the battle.'

'You have your fancy lawyer trying to track her down. There's nothing you can do while you wait. So now that you're not squirrelling away your money like you used to, and have moola to travel, we're travelling, *boet*. It's already arranged by yours truly. You can thank me after we get back,' Bevin said.

Wayne put his hand on Terry and looked around. In a week they would be leaving the camp. Closing it totally. The Recces would leave, and then operations personnel would clear everything out. Strip the camp down and leave it empty.

Since the release of Mandela in February, the SADF had begun getting ready for a transition to a black government. Only this time there was nowhere left for the white minority to run south too. They were as far south in South Africa as you could get.

So they needed to protect those who couldn't run.

Protect those who would remain in the society for years to come, and whose families would continue to live in South Africa.

Documents had been burnt.

Files had been destroyed so that no trace of what was happening would ever fall into the wrong hands. So that every soldier who fought during the Apartheid war would be protected from a guerrilla government should the transition become a bloodbath. Should anyone seek justice for acts to protect their country be misconstrued as crimes committed during a war time.

Since 1948 South Africans had been fighting Soviet, Korean, Chinese and Cuban forces on the front line, as well as all the black factions, yet now it was over. They were being sold down the drain into black empowerment. South Africa could either change without mass violence, as F.W. de Klerk was trying to achieve, or there could be full-scale mass murder and genocide, as had happened in almost every other African country.

The SADF were doing their part to stop the mass murders, and continued to burn all their files.

He'd watched as his files on the poachers in Angola and those within the SADF that he'd linked to them had been burnt. All the evidence was now gone and no one would ever know what had happened to make a few people so rich while working under the protection of the SADF. White gold. Ivory. White powder in Mandrax. Diamonds. All commodities that had been traded, and syndicated from Johannesburg, and then distributed to the world from there. The blood that had been spilt, the huge price paid by the wild animals of Africa for a few greedy men, had been buried forever.

He shook his head as he looked at the fire in the middle of Camp Doppies. He smiled as he thought about the camp's name. Only a SADF camp could be called after a spent bullet. The camp had been called 'Doppies' because of a vervet monkey who used to come in and steal the doppies after the live ammunition practices. Apparently he'd run into camp, pick up the doppies then run out again with his treasure hoard. Twenty years later and Terry the lion was now its resident mascot, a far cry from that original monkey.

Soon, they were going to abandon the camp that had been home for the last few years, and he knew he was going to miss it. Soon it would be overgrown with African bush, the small brown mice would find refuge in the stone and brick foundations that remained. Seeds from the forests would grow into strong trees in the cracks in the concrete, breaking it further and reclaiming it into the wild. Buffalo weavers would build huge nests in the trees, and their droppings would fertilise the leaf litter underneath and more plants would grip their roots into the tough African soil, and grow. Grasses would cover over the mounds used for target practice. The scarring done by humans would be healed.

So many men had walked there over those last twenty years, yet once they cleared out, nothing would remain to tell the history of the place that had been home, a refuge to them. Only memories and stories would survive, around a campfire at a reunion somewhere.

People who had not been there would listen in disbelief to that oral history, and when all those who shared that history died, their stories would pass into obscurity.

But Wayne's melancholy mood was for something more.

He had arrived at Doppies young, naive and determined. But he was leaving jaded about the future of the defence force that he had once believed in. His one hope was that with the extra time on his hands and a civilian life, he might soon find Tara and his son, Josha.

He knew that he'd miss Terry more than the camp itself. He knew he was going to have to leave Terry behind. He was still a wild lion, he could fend for himself, but he was worried for him.

One of the first changes he'd made to his farm since January was to instruct the new manager to begin regenerating the bush on his farm. The sugarcane was to be slowly phased out, and as it did, planting of native trees and grasses was taking place. He was transforming his land into a game farm. He knew that logistically, he couldn't take Terry there now, but he could provide a home for the other lion, elephant, rhino and hippo that were being hunted to extinction. His closeness to the Hluhluwe Game Reserve made it a perfect spot to transform into a safari operation. He'd seen *Mala Mala* and the international trade that they did, being situated so close to Kruger – and yet providing five-star accommodation and service.

His manager had been employed because when Wayne interviewed him, he found the man had the same vision for a safari farm that offered photographic safaris and was built around the preservation of game – not hunting. The new manager had been working on it for six months already and Wayne was looking forward to seeing his progress when he went home.

'Earth to Wayne. I asked you to come to Zimababwe on holiday with me. Say yes,' Bevin said.

'Yes,' he said. He knew that Tara had once lived in Zimbabwe. He wanted to visit as something other than an operative to see what was happening in her former country. See if he could dig up any news on Tara. You never knew who would know something about the family. Perhaps he'd find something there, as so far, the investigator had got nowhere with his search.

It was as if Tara had disappeared, or moved overseas.

Now he was going to Zimbabwe, and he'd start looking there.

CHAPTER

12

The Pioneers

***Amarose Lodge – Private Game Reserve, Karoi, Zimbabwe
August 1990***

Wayne gritted his teeth as they drove over the abnormally large cattle grid. His gaze was drawn by the green crop of tobacco growing to either side of the driveway leading into Bevin's great aunt Rose's farm. In the distance, where the bright green ended, he could see a eight-foot-tall electrified fence.

'So this is where you spent your holidays when you were at school?'

'Yip. Loved it up here.'

'Why didn't you stay here, instead of doing your national service, and becoming a Recce?'

'I wanted to serve my country. I wanted to be that Special Ops man. Visiting my aunt was what drove me to want to fight. I have seen so much happen here, and I didn't want that to happen to my own country. In a way, as long as I was up in Angola fighting, I knew that she was safer here on her farm. I was last here in 1985, just before my aunt fired her white manager and Jamison took over the position.'

'He's the one who got her to diversify?'

Bevin nodded. 'He doesn't seem to be your average bossboy. Apparently the manager before him was stealing from her big time, syphoning off her best tobacco to another friend in the auctions so she looked like she wasn't doing as well as she was. Jamison came to the farm to learn about tobacco. When she fired the manager, the old bossboy was about to leave her too. Jamison talked him into staying and teaching him before retiring, and the old bossboy passed the reins to him. By then it was with her blessing of course. But in a time when she needed help, this Jamison had rallied everyone around her, and they stood together.'

'Sounds like a good man.'

'I always hoped so. Once he had the position, he began to instigate changes. She's always supported the poorer blacks in the TTL down the road, but he ensured that those living in that tribal trust land were looked after with basic necessities, like having clean water. He made sure they knew it was her who was looking after them, and that it could stop if they poached on her land, and suddenly the theft that she was experiencing from her sheds stopped, and there were no more snares on her property either.'

'That's a practical way to get rid of the problem. Wish more people would look at a sustainable culture like that,' Wayne said. 'I've got poaching happening on my farm. I think every farmer in Africa does. It's just the scale that differs from place to place.'

'You're right.' Bevin was still talking about his aunt's employee. 'Jamison was the one who encouraged her to look to diversify, because tobacco prices fluctuate so much. With the farm on a profit-share scheme, she needed to make sure that she could always look after her workers. I think she likes that they look to her as the Mama of the land. She took this man Jamison's advice and let him go with her *bakkie*, for three months during the off-season, to the lowveld to learn about how to recreate a bush environment. First he went to Gonarezhou National Park, and he visited farms in that area. He visited with the fenceless Mana Pools National Park up the road from there, and somewhere along the line, he became a licenced professional hunter, although the details of how he got that so quickly were a bit sketchy when she corresponded with me.'

'A licenced hunter, not a tracker?' Wayne said.

'Hunter, as in he knows his stuff with the flora and fauna, and he's taken down an elephant with one shot. Only then do you get your licence.'

Wayne looked at Bevin, but there was no expression on his face. Just a man relating a story. 'Sounds like a real businessman and a good marksman.'

'He came back to her and rolled out the plans for her farm that he'd worked on, with those he had visited, and they began building their fence. Next they ploughed in a huge section of tobacco, once it was done for the season, and they planted velvet beans to attract the natural game in the region.'

'That was smart. Why buy game if it's for free roaming around the place,' Wayne said. 'I think I like him before I even meet him.'

'You do realise that this is just a black guy, right?' Bevin said.

'So?'

'Black is still black,' Bevin said.

Wayne shook his head. The hatred was so conditioned in some people that they would never see past the colour of a person's skin. It would take generations to get rid of the unnecessary hostility drummed into them from when they were young. Wayne smiled. He thought of how his dad had been so much before his time, how as a farmer he carried none of the prejudice against blacks. He'd always treated his workers properly, built them decent-sized housing for their families. They had a small but decent compound with running water and electricity. The tractor collected the 44-gallon rubbish drums and emptied them twice a week into their dump on the farm. There were so many things that Wayne had to be grateful to his dad for, yet living by example was probably the most precious gift he could have passed on to Wayne. And he had saved Tara, found a path through for her when Wayne had been unable.

He loved his dad even more for that, even if he had kept it a secret from him.

'You need to get over that prejudice, Bev, South Africa will soon be ruled by a black government. Then what are you going to do? There's nowhere further south for white people to run. Except go overseas, if you want to do that.'

Bevin was shaking his head vigorously. 'Hey, Wayne, I don't hate the blacks. Not at all. It's just this man, Jamison, he's different to all the rest. I keep wanting to know what his ulterior motive is. I know my aunty Rose has ... had,' he corrected himself, 'a profit-share scheme, but I keep thinking that surely he wants more than that. Like if he loved the farm so much and she put it up for sale, why didn't he try and buy it?'

'You don't know if he tried to or not.'

'True, but there is just something about him. I keep wondering why would he do these things to help an old white woman.'

'Perhaps he likes your great aunt. Perhaps it's just a friendship that is different to what you've experienced. I think it's wonderful. What else did they do to the farm?'

Bevin harrumphed, blowing air through his teeth and lips. 'Aunt Rose paid some hot shot conservationist to come to the farm and help them to create natural bush as quickly as possible. They regenerated huge tracts of land with natural bush plants, and spread grass seeds so that when their fence was finished they could close the gates. They began to travel together, the old white lady and the black man, to collect wild animals, attend auctions, and buy in game. Zebra, giraffe, eland and wildebeest. She even organised him a passport so they could go down to South Africa on buying trips.'

'They sure wanted game. Weren't there like, restrictions bringing it through the border?'

'Sure, but they got permits and things, and drove on through Beit Bridge and came on up to Mashonaland. Jamison driving the big cattle truck they bought and modified, and my aunt Rose sitting next to him.'

'Bet the border post on the South African side just loved that.'

'Oh she's a firecracker, my aunt. My dad didn't want Jamison sleeping in the second bedroom of the cottage at the bottom of our garden, insisted that Jamison should sleep in the *ikhaya* the maid uses when she's there. But Aunt Rose read him the riot act about his bad behaviour and how Jamison was their guest too and she'd leave if he left. Guess who won?'

'Aunt Rose.'

'You bet. And after they had visited the first time, there were many more, and Jamison always used the second bedroom.'

'That's quite telling …'

'No, telling is that just two years after those two began their project, they opened their first safari camp. They worked like Trojans to get this place into what it is today. It wasn't only the money, it was the raw ambition behind getting it done quickly. I take my hat off to Jamison, I just don't understand where the drive to succeed comes from within a black guy, as I've hardly ever seen it so strong as with that man.'

'That's not true. What about Isaac, and Majoda? Those trackers practically lived with us, and although they weren't Recces, how many times did one of them save our necks?'

'That's different. They weren't in it for money, they did that to survive.'

'What makes you think that Jamison isn't doing just that?' Wayne asked.

Bevin shrugged.

'So if they are doing so well, why sell up? Why's she moving to your folks' house permanently?'

'Aunt Rose fell off her horse. Something spooked the animal and she fell badly. Although she's alive, she was pretty broken up, ribs broken, lungs punctured, legs both broken, and a hip had to be replaced. She's slower than she used to be. The doctors said she needed more than a maid with her twenty-four-seven, she needed to be in a frail care home. She refused, but Jamison managed to convince her that it was the right thing to do to sell most of the farm, because it was time and she needed to enjoy her retirement. He's crafty though. He told her to split the farmhouse and a small tract of land around it from the title of the farm so she had a home after the sale. I tell you, he's one clever black man. He thinks like a white man, seriously.'

'That's a compliment, coming from you.'

'I do admire him. I just want to know his reasons, that's all,' Bevin conceded. 'So a few months back, she put the farm on the market. She sold the tobacco side and the safari camps with all the game.'

'But not her home?'

Bevin shook his head. 'That's about it. When she sold, she still refused to move into frail care, saying she was going to die on her farm. But she hasn't healed as well as she should have. She's become more frail. The fall seems to have taken a lot out of her. When she had the accident, Jamison helped her upgrade from a maid to two full-time qualified nurses, and he insists that they stay. My mother has been on the phone with her constantly, asking her to come live with them, and after another fall, this time in her living room, she's at last agreed to move in with my folks. She'll still have nursing staff, but being with relatives will be so much better for her than out here in the bush with only the blacks to keep her company.'

'What an amazing old woman!' Wayne said.

'They breed them tough here in Zimbabwe.'

Wayne smiled. That was true.

His Tara was a born and bred Zimbabwean, and he was hoping that tough spirit had been passed on to their son. When they found each other again, then he was betting that it would be that toughness that would help them to create a real family.

They stopped at a huge security gate.

'This is it,' Bevin said, 'I hope she remembered to switch the electricity off in her fence.' He got out to open the gate.

The old woman standing at the top of the stairs was dressed for church on a Sunday. Her clothes were neat and pressed, a matching long cotton skirt and jacket of a natural linen colour, complete with white court shoes. She wore a small pill-box hat with a little veil that she hadn't bothered to pull down, and she rested heavily to the right-hand side on a walking stick.

Bevin wrapped her in a bear hug, then her gently lifted her off her feet in both his arms, holding her under her knees and around her shoulder. Spinning her around a few times, he set her back down.

Tears brimmed in her eyes, which she dashed away quickly. 'Now, Bevin, I'm getting too old for you to do that to me,' and she giggled like a schoolgirl.

Wayne couldn't help but smile at the reunion. Despite the generation gap between them, they were so obviously close friends, and for a moment Wayne hated that the SADF had kept these two apart. There was love and affection there, and he could now better understand Bevin's concern for her bossboy having such a huge part in her life. Bevin was jealous that it had been Jamison who got to spend the time with his aunt.

'Mrs Crosby, lovely to meet you,' Wayne said as he shook her hand.

'Just call me Rose, honey,' she said. 'Any friend of Bevin's is a friend of mine.'

Wayne grinned.

'You keep flashing those dimples at me, I'll die a happy woman,' she said.

Wayne laughed.

'Come, sit, Elise will take care of your bags and put them in the guest rooms. It's been too long since your last visit, Bevin. You have grown. My boy is now a man,' she said as she smiled with affection at her great nephew.

'How are your folks?' she asked as she limped back into her house. Bevin was immediately by her side, holding onto the arm that didn't wield her cane.

'They send their love and said to tell you that they are looking forward to you coming down. The renovation of the cottage is almost done. So by the time you get there, everything will be ready for you.'

'Your mother has always been a good person, the best thing my nephew ever did was marry her. I've always thought that she has a heart as big as Kariba. She's behind them asking me to stay,' Rose said as she sat back down in her rocking chair. She rested her walking stick next to her against the small table.

Wayne noticed that a groove had been cut into the table to stop the stick from falling over. He wondered who would have done such a thing for her if her family were sparse on visits, and then it dawned on him.

Probably Jamison.

From what Bevin had told him, the man was as close to the old girl as a good friend could be. He was no longer just the bossboy.

Bevin sat close to her, pulling another old but functional chair closer. Wayne sat opposite on the couch. He looked around.

The room was old world, with overstuffed furniture that didn't look like it would break when a man sat down. There were no trophy heads hung on the wall, and no skins on the floor. Instead there was a large round reed mat, and on the walls were paintings in heavy frames of pioneer days. Teams of horned oxen pulled heavy covered wagons through bushlands. Black overseers cracked whips, and dogs ran alongside. He stood up to get a closer look.

'My great grandfather's trek here, into Southern Rhodesia,' she said to him. 'His brother painted those, he was in his teens at the time. My grandfather was a *laat-lammetjie*. He was born under that wagon while they laagered during an assault by the Zulus. His mother was killed. You see the black woman in that picture.' She pointed to another one next in the frieze. 'That was his wet nurse, and the woman who raised him until he was sent back to England to attend high school and university. My great grandfather never remarried.'

Next to the painting was a beautiful certificate: Rhodesian Pioneer Society. The name Rose Crosby (nee Wilde) was on it, and a number.

He wondered if Bevin realised how lucky he was having proof of such close links to his ancestory.

'Such a rich history,' Wayne said aloud.

'Progress and colonisation, that was the motto then. It's a time gone by …'

The maid walked in with a tray of tea, complete with a knitted tea-cosy on the teapot. The fine bone china cups looked too delicate for him to use. The maid put the tray on the table.

'Should I pour the tea, madam?' she asked.

'Thank you, Elise,' Rose said, 'these days even the weight of a teapot is too much.'

Elise was obviously used to the routine of pouring tea, as she put milk into one cup, then added the tea, and finally she used tongs to drop in two lumps of sugar from a silver dish. She added the teaspoon to one side of the saucer, then she placed it carefully down next to Rose.

'Milk? Sugar?' she asked Bevin.

'Both, thank you,' Bevin said.

'Me too,' Wayne volunteered before he was asked and watched as Elise drew two more cups of tea and placed them on the little tables near each of the men.

Then she drew another, and placed it next to the spare chair near Rose. 'Jamison will be here soon,' she said to Rose in explanation.

'That's good, it's time he met Bevin and his friend Wayne. He'll help us pack.'

Elise had pre-cut huge slices of vanilla cake with a sweet icing, and these she put on plates which she set out, again making sure that one was put aside for Jamison.

'Thank you Elise, that will be all for now,' Rose said. 'We can serve ourselves if we need more.'

Wayne watched as Elise did a small curtsey and left the room.

He looked at Bevin, who was tucking into his cake.

The dogs barked outside, but in a happy greeting, not in warning, and Wayne heard someone stamping their feet on the veranda to remove the dirt.

'That will be Jamison,' Rose said.

A black man wearing green overalls filled the doorway and both Bevin and Wayne stood up. Jamison looked much younger than

Wayne had expected, although his closely cropped hair was showing small flecks of grey at his temples. He was also taller than Wayne had imagined him. He wasn't as tall as Wayne's six-foot-three but he had to be only a smidgen off six foot. He was well built and would have been an equal match for Wayne if they were to be in a fight. The muscles in his arms bulged as stuck his hand out to shake Bevin's. 'Good to meet you, Bevin,' he said. 'Your aunty talks about you constantly.'

'Same about you,' Bevin said. 'Meet my friend Wayne.'

Jamison's grip was firm, but he didn't try to crush Wayne's hand.

'So lovely that you could get time to visit with me today Jamison,' Rose said and he immediately gave all his attention to the old lady sitting behind him.

'Madam,' he said, and he nodded his head in respect.

'Have a seat, your tea is about to get cold,' Rose said.

'Thank you,' Jamison replied, and Wayne noticed that Elise had quietly entered behind Jamison and had laid an old towel on the seat. Jamison looked to the seat, as though to ensure he didn't sit down without it.

'Thank you, Elise,' he said as she swished out the room again.

'Well now that you have all met, I guess it's time to talk about how we can fill a few days of your holiday time, and then you can help me decide what is staying and what is being packed up to take to South Africa with me,' Rose began, and the men all looked to her to hear what she'd decided. 'Bevin, in your letters you asked if you could use my houseboat in Kariba, and you asked me along. As you can see,' she indicated to her body, and its frail state, and she shook her head. 'I can no longer do that, although that is still one of my most favourite places to holiday, so I have asked Jamison to take you. He's a good driver. For the last few years he's been with me every chance we get to go fishing for vundu and tiger fish. He is also very good with the wild game. He always manages to show me something interesting happening on the bank.'

Wayne watched Jamison. He drank about half his tea, then he picked up his cake, and he ate it with the little fork that was sitting on the side of his cake plate. As if he was so used to having high tea with the old lady, that her old-fashioned etiquette came naturally to him. Once his cake was done, he lifted the dainty teacup and sipped the rest of his tea.

Wayne picked up his tea and drank it too, and he used his little fork as Jamison had done. Bevin picked up his cake with his hand again. Wayne gave him a kick, and he quickly put it down, and lifted the fork.

Wayne noticed that Rose smiled, and he winked at her.

'That sounds wonderful, Aunt Rose. Now Mum and Dad said that you are to bring as much of your things as you want, there is no need for you to throw anything away. They want you to be as comfortable as you are here, just with them where they can help you.'

'That's sweet of them, but there is too much stuff that I will never use again, it belongs on a farm, not in a house in Sandton in the middle of Johannesburg.'

Bevin smiled.

Wayne kept quiet, and he noticed that Jamison did too.

'Jamison can show you the safari camps we made too. He's still managing that part of the farm even with the sale to the new owners. They are coming up to live here next month, so then things might change. Jamison and I put a clause in the contract that they would leave the safari camp and operations as is for at least ten years, but their lawyers changed it to two. We both worry that those people are going to try and operate hunting concessions here one day as they seem short-sighted and money hungry. But for now, there are still clients in the camps who are happy to take only photographs, and there are still tobacco seeds to germinate. Although of course I don't do any of that anymore.'

Wayne frowned at the news, but quickly covered it by asking Aunt Rose, 'Perhaps you would like to accompany us to the camps that you made? Bevin told me about them, and about how much you and Jamison have achieved there. We can go slowly, it's not like we're in a rush.'

She looked at him. 'I can walk quite fast now compared to a few months ago.'

Wayne grinned.

Bevin laughed and said, 'Not quite up to taking on a marathon just yet, Aunt Rose, but you're doing amazing.'

'That's because those nurses Jamison insisted on hiring do torture to me twice a day. Poor Elise has to listen to them yabba-yabba when they are changing shifts everyday.'

'Now, Mrs Crosby,' Jamison said, 'you know that they have to pass on the information about how well you're doing, you can't blame them for having to communicate.'

'Bah,' she said and screwed her face up. 'They eat too much too, Jamison.'

Jamison grinned at her. 'Them? No surely not. They eat like birds, trying to keep a new Zimbabwe figure, slim. Not like the traditional women with curves and good child-bearing hips.'

Aunt Rose laughed. 'No, not like your Ebony. One day she'll have a child and put those hips to good use.'

Jamison smiled.

There was obvious affection between the old lady and her bossboy, yet they still seemed to try and adhere to many of the older colonial ways. Jamison still referred to her in a formal manner. The towel the maid had put on his chair. Small things that pointed to an invisible barrier still between the black and white people in the house.

Jamison stood up. 'I need to get back to the camp to check how the afternoon game drive went. You are welcome to join me. I'll bring the *bakkie* to the front of the house, Madam Crosby.'

'I think that today, I'll accompany you, Jamison, thank you. I would like to be there to show young Bevin and his friend about. Even if I don't own it anymore, I still love this farm.'

Jamison was faster than Bevin in helping Rose up when she went to stand. He already had her walking stick ready, obviously a move they performed often. Jamison passed her strong arm to Bevin and said, 'I'll be right outside.'

He strode out the room towards the kitchen. 'Elise ...' they heard him call.

They walked slowly to the front door and by the time they were down the three front steps and on the pathway, Jamison had driven the *bakkie* to the end of the driveway, and parked behind their 4x4. His vehicle was fitted out for safari viewing, with seats in the back and a canopy to protect those inside a little from the harsh African sun and any unexpected showers. Wayne looked at the versatile Toyota. It had hidden safety roll bars, designed to look like canopy struts, in case the vehicle was turned over by elephant or something else.

Jamison waited near the *bakkie* for Bevin to bring Rose to the front. He had steps waiting for her and he'd put extra cushions on the passenger seat.,

'You spoil me, Jamison,' Rose said.

'You're worth spoiling, madam,' Jamison said as he quickly lifted her up, and placed her in the *bakkie*.

Bevin frowned.

Wayne punched him in the arm. 'Come on, let's get in the back.' He realised that Bevin was distracted by the fact that his aunt relied so heavily on Jamison, and obviously allowed him to do so much more than a farm boy had ever done in Bevin's eyes.

They drove through the gate and when Jamison stopped to close it behind them, Wayne hopped out and did the honours.

'Thank you,' Jamison said as Wayne jumped back onto the *bakkie*.

The drive across the tobacco fields to the safari gates was long, and the whole time Bevin and his aunt kept up a steady dialogue about how the tobacco plants were doing that year, and how the tobacco drying sheds would soon be in full use. The heavy smell of drying leaves clung to the breeze.

'We still grow Virginia tobacco and flume cure it, but now we rotate the fields with wheat and maize too. The irrigation system is used all the time, but we were in the process of swapping from overhead to drip irrigation. Perhaps Jamison will see the end of that, but I won't. I still find the tick-tick sound of the overhead systems soothing, but you hear nothing with the drip system.' She paused as if remembering another time. 'The new nursery plots where the young tobacco seeds are planted are off to the right there, behind that tobacco barn,' she said as they stopped at the gate.

A huge white sign was attached to the gate.

Amarose Lodge – Private Game Reserve
Trespassers Will Be Shot
BEWARE – Live Electric Fence

A ranger sat on the ground outside the gates as if waiting for Jamison to return. He quickly jumped up and opened the first gate. They drove through, and he closed the gate and then opened the second one.

'We brought in more big cats, so the double fence with the bonnox mesh is to keep them in or they could go and eat all the goats in the TTL,' Aunt Rose said.

The gate closed, the ranger ran to the front of the vehicle and climbed into the seat on the bonnet. He tapped the bonnet lightly to indicate he was ready, and Jamison drove on. Slowly they made their way into the thicker bush.

'This part is still rejuvenating, it was tobacco until two years ago, now it's planted as a Mopani forest. The grasses have grown fast, and we have been fortunate with them,' Rose said.

'It's amazing what you have done since I was last here,' Bevin commented. He leant forward and laid his hand on her shoulder, and she put her gnarled old one on top of his.

'If you want to be idle, live in a city. If you want to work, live on a farm,' she said.

Wayne laughed. 'How true.'

'Look at me, prattling on about everything that we have done, where are my manners. Wayne, Bevin told me that you recently inherited your family farm. So sorry to hear about your loss.'

'Thank you, I miss my father. I inherited his sugarcane farm in Hluhluwe. I employed a manager to keep it ticking over for the last six months, but now that I'm out of the SADF, I'll be taking on the challenge of farming full time.'

The ranger on the front tapped the bonnet.

Jamison stopped.

Wayne had been focused on the conversation. When he looked up he held his breath. Having been a Recce in South West Africa and Angola, he'd seen lots of game, and yet nothing prepared him for seeing an elephant on its hind legs, balanced precariously while it reached further up to pull on the branches of the marula tree in front of him.

The massive beast had the tusks of an older adult, and yet the agility he portrayed defied the forces of nature.

'Raviro is such a show off,' Rose said, and he heard low laughter from Jamison.

The elephant completed shaking the branch with its trunk. Happy that no more fruit was about to fall, he let the tree branch go. It snapped back upwards. He balanced on his haunches for a little while longer, then slowly lowered his front legs, so that first one front foot, then the other touched the earth.

Leisurely he began to eat the fruit that he had shaken loose. A baboon close by rushed in and stole a few of the ripe but not rotten fruits that had just fallen, then ran in the opposite direction when the elephant trumpeted at it.

'And he's still not learnt to share,' commented Rose. 'We brought in just five elephant. The rest, like Raviro over there, just arrived. Hence his name, it means "Gift from God" in Shona.'

The ranger on the front tapped the bonnet again and pointed to the right. Walking out towards the elephant as if he wasn't many times their size was a lioness and her two juvenile cubs. The one at the back of the line, playing attack the sibling in front, bowled the other one over, and there was a rough and tumble fight between the cubs. The tawny yellow of their coats flashed as they pounced on each other, until the mother turned around, and chastised them. Then they quickly lined up again and continued to walk with heads held as high as if they had been good all along.

The elephant ignored them as they passed him by.

'That is Xolile. We bought her in South Africa. She was already pregnant.'

'Who did she Make Happy?' Wayne asked.

'You speak Ndebele?' Jamison asked.

'Zulu, but the similarities are enough to get by. Most farm kids in South Africa will speak at least one native language,' Wayne admitted.

Jamison laughed. 'I think she made the farmer who was breeding them happy. She cost Mrs Crosby a small fortune.'

'But just look at her, already she's had two beautiful babies. And she's so pretty. Such a beautiful cat,' Rose said.

Wayne looked. He could see why the lioness was a much loved addition. She'd have been a perfect match to Terry, with her lighter golden colour, her head held like a regal queen, her huge paws purposely treading on the African dirt that she ruled.

This was her bush.

This was her domain.

This was her territory.

'The new owners said that they didn't want anything to change until they moved here permenantly, after their first visit to the safari camp, but I'm not sure that they truly understand that things in the bush change all the time. The fruit from the trees ripens and falls. The lion hunts the impala and then there is one less impala inside the gates. Life continues, even when the older ones go,' she sniffed. 'I'm going to miss this place when I move.'

Bevin put his hand on her shoulder again, and Jamison slowly eased the *bakkie* to move down the dirt strip road.

They were almost in the camp by the time Wayne realised it was there. Apart from one huge building with a steep thatched roof and what was obviously the kitchen and stores area built of bricks to the left, he had to look carefully for the sleeping quarters for the guests.

They were tree houses. Eight in total. They were built into the large forest that had never been cleared for tobacco, one of the few areas that had been left wild on the farm. The tree houses blended into their environment totally. They were elevated, built of wood, and instead of windows, there were clear all-weather blinds to pull down should it rain, that would also allow fresh air to circulate through the house, keeping it cooler. Nothing marred the view in front of each tree house towards the waterhole.

Each roof had a different animal motif cut into the thatch grass on its roof. Giraffe, buffalo, lion, rhino, zebra, kudu, monkey and warthog. Wayne looked over and saw that the main eating area had a large elephant on its roof.

Wayne smiled as Jamison stopped and everyone climbed out the *bakkie*.

'Come,' Jamison said as he once again picked up Aunt Rose, making sure she was steady on her feet and that she'd her walking stick before letting her go. Bevin stepped up to walk next to her down the path.

'I really appreciate all that you do for my aunt,' Bevin said. 'I know she can be a handful.'

Jamison smiled. 'It is my pleasure. She's a very special person in her heart.'

Wayne smiled, because he'd seen how she could be written off as nasty with her comments, like those she'd made about her nurses when they were having tea. Yet Bevin had told him a little about her help in the TTL. He thought that perhaps she wasn't so much bitter, but more like fresh white bread. Baked hard and crusty on the outside, but once you got inside, through that hard shell, the white soft centre was fluffy, a delight.

The staff at the camp all came out to greet their madam, and Wayne could see genuine affection for her shown from each of them. He wondered if Bevin's family appreciated how much this was her home, where she was a much loved matriarch.

It didn't matter to them that they had a new owner of the land, the people there still considered her their madam and their friend. They were part of her family that she'd been with all the years that Bevin had been in South Africa. She was leaving her family behind when she moved. These people would miss her.

He looked out at the large waterhole in front of the camp. He could see where fresh water pumped from deep in the earth to spill into the cement reservoir that then overflowed and fed the dam with its wall made from natural rocks and sand.

There were elephants bathing in the water and a herd of zebra grazed under the trees. A baby zebra, asleep flat on the ground, could have been mistaken for dead had its tail not periodically swished flies away. Wildebeest dug at the roots of the already short cropped grass. Ducks swam in the dam and dived for food, pointing their bottoms upwards before bobbing back up.

Wayne thought of the time he'd stolen off in the weekend and Samuel, their driver, had driven him and Tara into Hluhluwe National Park where they had watched the animals. How she'd loved the giraffe walking along the road, their slow uneven gallop as Samuel banged the side of the *bakkie* to move them along so they could get out the reserve in time and not be in trouble with the authorities for being late out. How the family of three giraffe had run down the centre of the road instead of off it, blocking them for longer, and Tara had laughed at them, the sound forever etched in his heart. He thought of his trips as a Recce that he'd taken with Bevin and the others into the Etosha National Park. The giant ghost elephants covered in white sand. The vastness of the sands and the herds of oryx with their long javelin horns as they trudged through the orange sands heading further west.

He had always felt unusually at peace during those times, despite the war that raged around them. He felt it again now within this fence line. The same feeling he'd had when Terry the lion was taking up more than half his bunk, or when Terry was with him in the bush.

Leaving Bevin to sit with his aunt in the shade of the communal area, Wayne slowly walked towards the viewing hide at the end of the path. This also had elephant motifs cut into the thatch. Inside was cool after the hot sun. There were benches in the front near the half cut wall under the thatch and a large comfortable looking three-seater couch at the back. He chose to sit on the bench and rest his arms on the wall. The elephant at the waterhole were moving off, coming towards the hide, ambling in a disorganised mass. One young bull elephant came up to the hide and rubbed his butt against one of the corner posts of the roof, which caused the whole structure to shake.

Wayne stayed still, not wanting to disturb the beautiful youngster.

Once he'd completed the scratch, he ran his head along the edge of the thatch, his trunk inside, touching the wall, as if looking for something. When he touched Wayne, he stilled. His trunk tested Wayne's arm, and the rough elephant hair felt strange on his skin but he didn't move.

'Hey buddy, nothing to eat here,' he said softly, as he raised his hand and stroked the trunk. 'A friendly pat, but no food.'

The elephant exhaled and stilled as he patted him, leaving his trunk to be gently scratched by Wayne. 'You're a beauty.'

'He likes you,' Jamison said from behind him. 'Most people pull away when the elephant want to interact, but you didn't. You're used to large animals?'

'No. We had a lion in our camp, but not lots of experience with elephants.'

'*Eish*, a lion. You know they never tame down totally?' Jamison said.

Wayne smiled, he'd lost count of the number of people who had told him that about lions. The elephant attempted to feel his chest, still looking for food. His trunk travelled over his chest, and then lower towards his stomach.

Jamison passed him an apple, and motioned for him to put it in his top pocket.

'Sneaky!' Wayne said.

The elephant, now smelling the apple, touched its trunk upwards again, and nudged it out the pocket. With the apple fully secured in his trunk, he pulled it out, and put it in his mouth. Within moments, his trunk was back, looking for another snack.

'You're a greedy guts,' Wayne said as he stroked the trunk.

Jamison laughed. 'Come on, Jumbo, out, you had a snack, someone else's turn now.' He pushed at the trunk and it reluctantly left

Wayne, sliding back over the wall and the young elephant walked away.

Another took its place.

'As long as they find someone in here willing to give them apples, they will hang around the hide,' Jamison explained.

'So you cheat. You give them fresh water to bathe in, and apples so that the tourists can see them up close and personal,' Wayne said.

'I guess you could say that, but I call it giving them incentive to keep calling around.'

Wayne fed another elephant, and another after that. Sitting in silence the two men simply passed the time together.

Wayne looked at the waterhole, at the giraffe who'd just come down to drink. They bent their necks so elegantly with their bodies looking so awkward, yet he knew that their agility when neck fighting was amazing. He saw guinea fowl run at the edge of the security fence that protected the camp, and heard a loud ker-bek-ker-bek-ker-bek, krrrrr. He felt purpose grow inside him.

He'd been right in beginning the regeneration of his Kujana. This was definitely the direction he wanted to take his farm in. He looked to the heavens to thank his father for his foresight in gifting it to him, and felt a sadness that it had taken the death of his father for him to realise exactly which direction he wanted to take his life in.

'This is a magnificent camp you have built here, you should be proud of it.' Wayne indicated all around with his hands.

'I am. It's everything that Widow Crosby and I set out to make and the tourists come in from everywhere to stay at Amarose Lodge.'

'So now that she's sold it, will you stay here or will you move on?'

'That depends on a lot of factors,' Jamison said.

'This was all your idea. Until you arrived at the farm Mrs Crosby was content just doing what her husband had done before her, growing tobacco.'

'She liked my ideas, and to be honest it revitalised her. She came alive while we were building Amarose. She was far from her family, she needed to have something to believe in – and someone to believe in her.'

'I can imagine.'

'And the new owners have taken you on. You happy to stay?' Wayne asked.

'At the moment, yes. I have a wife, and we are settled.'

'If you ever have cause to leave, I could use a man like you on my farm Kujana in Hluhluwe,' Wayne said.

'Is it a fair distance away from anywhere?'

Wayne laughed. 'Guess in the old days it was. But not anymore.'

Jamison shook his head. 'Thank you, but for now I will say no. Until Madam Crosby goes to her new home South Africa, and the new owners move to Amarose full time, I am needed here—' But he never continued, as Bevin stuck his head into the hide. 'Hey, Aunt Rose says she's ready to go home.'

Reluctantly, Wayne got up to leave. As he did so, his wallet fell from his pocket and open on the floor.

Jamison picked it up but instead of handing it to Wayne right away, he stood staring at the photographs that were inside. One was the picture of Tara holding Josha when he was first born.

Wayne put his hand out.

Jamison quickly passed it over to him. 'Sorry, but your wife and baby are very beautiful. I didn't realise that you were married and had a family.'

'I have a family, but I have to find her again before I can marry her,' Wayne admitted reluctantly as he put the wallet back in his pocket.

CHAPTER 13

Finding Shilo

Piet Retief Farm, Zimbabwe
1992

Buffel rocked backwards in his new leather recliner. As he cranked the handle on his right the footrest popped out to support his feet, still in their *velskoene*. He looked around his lounge room at his trophies.

A large grey kudu with three distinct twists in its horns was hung next to an eland with long thick horns that had a single twist to them. He remembered that that eland had made him walk for hours. But he was so worth the wait. The perfect trophy on his wall, unmarred by a headshot, as he had waited patiently for the eland to expose his heart.

He put his own hand over his heart to feel the beat of life, just as his doctor had shown him years before. To feel the life inside himself, and to listen to his body.

When his body was happy, he could sleep, with no drugs and no nightmares.

When his body was restless, he needed to take the drugs, to stop the nightmares. To stop the darkness that threatened to pull him under. The new drugs helped his sleep, and they had slowed the frequency of the nightmares. They kept the voices of the children in his head hushed, but they never silenced them totally. He knew that only the butterfly would do that, one day, when he found her again. When he saved Impendla's soul. The doctor had said that he had a chemical imbalance, that the drugs would help make it right.

It was Gibson who had called in the doctor, one morning when he thought Buffel was dead. After a period of a few weeks of repeating nightmares, night sweats and hardly any sleep, Buffel had in desperation taken a full container of headache pills to try and stop the nightmares that plagued him. To quieten the voices of the children, and Impendla's cry for help. But the pills had made him sleep for too long. Gibson had entered his house to check on him when he hadn't come out in the morning as usual, and was still asleep in bed at ten o'clock.

Buffel had woken in hospital after they had pumped his stomach free of all the painkillers. The doctor had listened to what had happened, and he had prescribed medicines. He had explained to Buffel that he didn't need to stay on the medication all the time, if he didn't want to, as long as he listened to his body.

He had followed the doctor's advice, and soon he found that the voices would quieten down naturally when he was outside hunting, that was when his body felt the best. He had started hiring himself out as a professional hunter and guide, along with Gibson, and they had been contracted with different safari operators since.

He looked at his bull hippo. Its mouth set wide open, as if ready to fight. Its sharp tusks polished to perfection, the ivory shining as it caught the specialist lighting he'd had installed in the room and positioned to highlight the head. And every other head in the room.

He smiled at the hippo. Just the year before he'd shot that bull, the hippo had been added to some of the South African and Zimbabwean lists of dangerous game. It was a place well deserved. He knew that the river horse killed more people in Africa than all the other members of the Big Five put together. They were extremely aggressive. And when the hippo made their way back to the water after grazing on the banks and encountered a human, the meeting often resulted in a fatality.

But that didn't make the hippo easier to kill.

It made it harder.

A challenge that Buffel enjoyed.

The bull hippo was hard to recognise within his water environment. You could hunt him on land, but the chances of him charging you were high, and invariably, you would end up ruining your trophy with a brain shot. The only option was to put the one and a half tonne beast down before he put you down. Permanently. And every hunter knew that anything smaller than a 40 calibre might not stop him.

Or perhaps you could be patient, recognise the bull from the cow in the water and shoot him with pin-point accuracy. The bull's head was only a little larger than the cow, but his tell was he had two tiny humps on either side of his nose where his lower tusks fit into his upper jaw.

The bull needed to be shot through the eye, or the not so clean alternative was a shot just below his ear. Although the hippo would sink down into the water and disappear, within the hour, his carcass would then float up to the surface again, and you could send in the trackers to recover the body.

His bull had taken fourteen men to pull him from the river. He'd used his trusty 416 Rigby with a soft nose up the spout, and he had no damage on the head from the bullet's exit.

His bull hippo was a trophy worth hunting.

All around the room, every trophy had been both shot and then mounted with patience, and skill. First his own, then the taxidermist's, who had painstakingly recreated the animal's size and bulk, with the synthetic materials for the inside, and then they tanned the leather outside. Lastly, they added in the glass eyes. The best quality eyes that didn't look dull, but made you want to reach out to the animal hanging on the wall, and touch it to see if it breathed, as the animal appeared to watch you everywhere in the room, their expressions so real within the glass.

His trophies would last forever.

A hunter was judged on his trophies, and they proved his patience and his accuracy.

Both things Buffel prided himself on.

He felt the easy beat of his heart and he knew that the medicines that sat in the mirrored cabinet in his bathroom could stay there for another while.

He had another hunting client coming in a week's time, and he was looking for a new concession to take him to. The client had requested a trophy elephant, but his special request was that he wanted to shoot it with a crossbow.

Buffel had at first been reluctant to take a man who hunted like that into the bush. A wounded elephant could kill you real fast if you got it wrong. But the client had sent him, via fax, pictures of other kills he had made, of American bison that had been taken down with a single shot with his new fancy carbon fibre arrows from a compound crossbow that looked nothing like anything Buffel had ever seen before.

Buffel had begun research into bow hunting and found that it had become legal in South Africa in 1983. Yet the most important information he had learnt was that just this year, the South Africa Executive ruling had come down, the hunt was to be done under a professional hunter's supervision, and if competence could be proven, then bow hunting could be used to hunt all animals. It opened up a whole new opportunity to new hunters to bring new foreign currency into the country.

His interest was piqued.

The gentleman was arriving soon to show his skill with that crossbow, with first an impala hunt, then a kudu, and on his list for this trip he had added a giraffe to prove that he could take on an elephant.

Buffel had changed the hunt from a giraffe to a buffalo bull. Perhaps if this hunter could take down an African buffalo in one shot, he would consider the elephant hunt. Not before.

The client was happy with those terms.

He lifted the new bunch of brochures he had sourced at the last Travel Expo he had attended in South Africa. He picked up his coffee that sat on the table next to him, and took a sip, then he lifted the top brochure and began reading.

Buffel spat his coffee onto the paper. Then he wiped it quickly with his sleeve.

'Shilo!' he said as he stared at the colour picture in the advert for the Amarose Private Hunting Ranch. Shilo hadn't aged much. He looked just as fit as he had the day he left Piet Retief. Perhaps a little grey had snuck in on his temples in the last few years, but otherwise his smile was just as big as always.

He looked happier than Buffel had ever seen him. It seemed to be an inner glow, rather than an exterior expression. Buffel frowned and ran his finger over the image.

It didn't look like he was posing for the photograph as he drove the Toyota with its tracker on the front. Three big elephant bulls with their large tusks stood in the left of the picture.

Just what a trophy hunter wanted.

He continued to read the animal listings and costs of the newest ranch to publicise its hunting quota for buffalo, lion and leopard. The Amarose Private Hunting Ranch held four of the big five up, and was advertising concessions for hunting within their fences.

But Buffel only saw Shilo.

Shilo, who had deserted him.

Shilo, who had information that could destroy him now that he had built up a new business and a reputation.

Shilo, who knew too much, and needed to be silenced.

Shilo who had helped the butterfly escape, and might know where she was now.

He put his hand over his heart as the voices rushed back into his head.

It raced.

His body was unhappy that after these years, when he has been so settled, he had found Shilo again.

But he wouldn't get up to take his meds waiting in his bathroom. He was stronger than those meds, he didn't need them.

Soon he would be hunting and then calmness would return.

Patience.

Buffel knew that patience was the secret to checking in on Shilo, making sure he'd remembered their PSYOPS code and never talked.

Patience.

He looked at his fireplace where two huge ivory tusks arched towards each other. Set in elephant feet, and weighted, he compared the size of his last trophy to those in the picture. About forty centimetres still remained inside the elephant, but he thought that the elephant he had shot in the Zambezi valley was bigger than what was on offer from the private ranch.

But he wasn't going be visiting Amarose for the animal quota this time.

CHAPTER 14

The Phoenix

***Amarose Lodge – Private Game Reserve, Karoi, Zimbabwe
1992***

'Happy anniversary, my darling,' Ebony said to Jamison as he walked through the door. He looked at the room.

It was magical. Ebony had brought every candle in the house and put them in the dining room, and she had a table laid out as if they were in a five-star restaurant.

'Eb,' Jamison said. 'Look at this place. Wow. You did this for us? For me?' Jamison walked around the flickering room. Shadows danced across his pathway, and the candles flickered and light leapt and soared with the changes of the air swirling through the room.

'I thought that I could spoil us for our fifth anniversary,' she said.

He walked up to her and took her in his arms. 'Ebony, my heart, you spoil me.'

He dipped his head and kissed his wife thoroughly.

Breathless, she eventually pushed him away. 'Let's eat, I'll grab the dinner and put it on the table while you have a quick shower.'

'Deal, I'll be two minutes,' he said as he walked away towards the bathroom. She flicked his butt with a tea towel, laughing.

Jamison headed into the shower. He stepped in without waiting for the water to run warm, and washed so quickly, he was just rinsing off as the water was heating up. He switched the water off and grabbed his towel.

Humming, he quickly drew on a pair of tracksuit pants, and a button-up cotton shirt so that he would at least have clothes on for their dinner. After digging around at the back of his underpants drawer, he took out a small gift box that he put in his pocket, and hurried out to join his wife.

Ebony sat at the table, their dinner in front of her, and he paused for a moment to take in the sight.

'I still can't quite believe that you are here, and that you agreed to marry me,' he said to her from the door.

'I'm here, and I'm not going anywhere,' she said.

He grinned.

'Now, come on over and eat,' she said and she gestured to his place.

He sat down and looked at her. She glowed with an inner beauty. Her mahogany skin shone in the candle light. His beautiful wife.

'Happy anniversary, Eb,' he said as he passed her the box.

She opened it.

'*My wena*,' she said. 'Jamison, I can't wear this on a farm, it's too beautiful.' She looked at the dainty square-cut sapphire sitting in a channel of diamonds, and set in a platinum band, with separate gold bands on both sides. 'It's too beautiful!'

'I know that they say one year or on the birth of a child, but when I saw this, I knew you would love it, and I had to buy it for you.' Jamison grinned. 'I'm glad you like it.'

He reached over and took it from the box, then he stood up, and went and knelt next to her chair. 'Ebony, you are the love of my life.' He took her left hand and added the ring to her plain wedding band that was already there, and the band of eight small diamond chips he had given to her for their engagement. The gold colours matched perfectly. But the ring was a little tight to get on.

'Ebony, I'm sorry it doesn't fit, I traced one of your other rings, the jeweller must have made a mistake with the size,' he began protesting.

'No, there is no mistake. It's perfect timing. That is my present to you tonight. My hands are already changing. I'm putting on weight and in seven months I'll be fat like a hippopotamus, and as cantankerous as your buffalo you love to watch in the early hours of the morning.'

'We are having a baby?' he asked.

'We are!' she said and she reached for his face as he knelt there and kissed him.

After a long while, he got up off his knees, and he picked her up.

'I'm too heavy, put me down, you idiot!' she said as she hung on tight with both arms around his neck.

'No way, Eb. Even when you are huge with our child, I'll still be able to pick you up. You and I, we just fit right.' He kissed her on the forehead, then, cradling her to his chest, he walked towards their bedroom. 'That is the best anniversary present you could ever give me,' he said, 'we are having a baby. I never thought I would see that day I got to have a family, a wife and a child. You have made me the happiest man in Zimbabwe, in Africa, in the whole world!'

Jamison heard the shouts of people before he smelled the smoke, and was instantly alert.

'Jamison, wake up, wake up,' someone yelled and banged on his front door.

He jumped out of bed, and pulled his tracksuit pants on.

'What is it?' Ebony asked.

'There is a fire, I have to find out where,' he said. 'Stay there, I'll come back.'

Jamison briskly strode to the front door and opened it, stopping the incessant knocking.

Moeketsi, one of the farm's best trackers, who was nearly qualified as a professional hunter, stood outside. 'There is a fire, Jamison, in the tobacco drying shed number 35.'

'Get my *bakkie*,' Jamison said as he turned and ran to his room. 'Ebony, one of the tobacco sheds is on fire. I have to go!' He hurried into the walk-in wardrobe and pulled on clothes that he could fight a fire in, a long sleeved shirt and long pants. He dragged on cotton socks. 'Damn, this season was going so well too,' he cursed.

'It will be okay, Jamison.' Ebony said from the bedroom. 'You will get the fire out, you will keep it from spreading and everyone will be safe. You always look after everyone, they know it. They rely on you to keep them safe.'

'I know, Eb, but a barn fire, we have never had one since I took over for Widow Crosby. They burn hot, Eb, someone could be hurt badly.'

'Then hurry up and go,' Ebony said, but she softened the command with a smile. 'I love you, now go do you job,' she said as she kissed him as he ran past. 'Stay safe.'

'Love you!' he replied as he fled from the room, his mind focused on the fire.

Moeketsi waited outside his front door, the *bakkie* already running. Jamison jumped into the driver's seat, the soft sand spraying backwards from his tyres as he sped off.

He slowed and stopped for the workmen from the safari camp, who flagged him down for a lift as they ran towards him, eager to help him with the farm fire. Fully loaded, with men standing in the back, hanging on, he drove through the reserve's double gates, and towards the glow in the distance.

Jamison arrived at the burning tobacco shed. For a second, he just sat there looking at the inferno that used to be shed 35. Not believing what his eyes saw. Then he sprang into action.

'Hoses, get the irrigation pipes,' he called as men scrambled at his command. 'Stop the fire spreading to the other sheds!'

He jumped back in his *bakkie* and drove for the main control valve for the irrigation. It was about halfway down the tobacco field, in the middle of the planted land. He checked that the couplings were in place, and then he turned on the power, and spun the handle so that water would pump into the hard pipes.

The pump gargled and spluttered before it came to life and it churned out fresh water from deep in the earth. He could see his workers as they put the last section of pipe into place, and then held the pipe tightly, knowing the velocity of water that was rushing up the pipe.

Once he could see the water at the shed he relaxed a little, and wiped the sweat that gathered from his forehead. Running back to his *bakkie*, he gunned the engine until he got almost to the fire, then he brought it to a dead stop, about two hundred metres from the fire. He got out, and reassessed the situation.

The tobacco barn would probably burn out, but they needed to continue fighting the fire, because if it spread, or embers from that fire spread to one of the other drying sheds, they could have more than one fire on their hands.

'That's it, well done, Moeketsi,' he said as he saw the young man turn the water on to yet another patch of the exterior of the barn that was now on fire.

The fire continued to consume the building. Its huge orange and red flames licked out the top as if trying to escape. The roof would be gone soon, and then the building was sure to collapse.

'Maidza, you sure no one is in there?' Jamison asked as he passed the worker who was rostered on duty that night for the barn.

'No one, I was outside when I saw the fire,' Maidza said.

'More *mvura*,' Jamison said as the next team of men brought more irrigation hoses closer to the structure. The couplings were holding despite the angle the men were bending the pipes in, and the water rushed from the pipe, and into the fire at high pressure.

There was no fire truck in the bush that could help them. They were on their own unless a neighbour saw the smoke and glow, and came to help.

The interior structure gave way, and the whole barn leant to the left, then collapsed in on itself. Embers were pushed upwards, high into the night, burning orange, illuminating the dark sky as if a million fireflies had been released simultaneously. They glowed then slowly faded. There was no re-glow. The embers were no longer alive.

The surrounds seemed to darken as the fire, no longer reaching upwards, burnt in a heap, yet it had no less ferocity. Its orange flames consumed everything, the tobacco, and the structure. There was a roar as oxygen reached a place previously inaccessible, and the fire found a new angle to burn, then the sound of the irrigation pump throbbing in the distance, and the water as it hissed and popped when the men sprayed it onto the glowing embers.

A *bakkie* load of people arrived from the TTL to help, having seen the orange light in the sky and the smoke that rose up into the darkness. They came armed with hessian sacks and a 44-gallon drum of water on the back of their *bakkie* to help fight the fire. Old Widow Crosby had been gone two years already, but memories ran deep, and many still remembered her help during the droughts, and her support of the people within the boundary of the TTL.

They gathered in a close group when they saw that nothing could be done for the barn, and murmurs could be heard as people watched the last of the barn burn black.

'Moeketsi, take my *bakkie* and turn off the irrigation pump, there is no more we can do here,' Jamison said eventually. He dreaded having to call the owners and tell them that there had been a fire. They still didn't live on the property, allowing him to manage both what was left of the tobacco fields, and the newer safari reserve.

But things were changing.

They were after a higher income than the fledgling safari camp could raise from tourism alone, and had expressed an interest to venture into big game hunting.

Jamison had expressed his dismay.

But they were unmoving.

For the first time in ten years, Jamison felt uneasy. He was now keeping his eye out for another manager's job. He didn't want to be manager of a hunting safari, that had never been his intention or Widow Crosby's when they set up Amarose.

But in his heart he knew that his reluctance to stay was about more than simply the hunting safaris. He couldn't shake the thought that Buffel was a hunter, and he might now visit the ranch looking for trophies. He had managed to stay hidden from Buffel for so long. He had flown under the radar, and he had found a life worth living. He didn't want to put his life on hold once more, and especially not now he had Ebony, and a baby coming.

He looked at the black charcoal and twisted metal roofing that remained of the shed and thought of the tobacco crop destroyed, that was now just ash. Embers still glowed in the dark, but the majority of the fire had subsided. Its fuel depleted, the fire was fast losing its life, and would soon be totally out.

Maidza came and stood next to him.

'What happened?' Jamison asked, his voice thick from the smoke he had breathed in.

'I don't know, Jamison. I swear it,' he said. 'You were with me last night, we checked this shed together, and the fire was good. I stoked the fire at one o'clock. There were no leaves on the flume pipe.'

'Maidza, tell me honestly. Did you go to sleep?'

'No, Jamison, I was awake. I heard a noise, like a baboon barking, behind the shed, and I went to see what it was, but when I got back, I saw the orange glowing under the shed door, and then I could see that there was a fire.'

'Did you find the *gudo*?' Jamison asked, alarmed.

'No, there was nothing there.'

'Did you see anyone running away when you returned?' Jamison asked. In the ten years he had been on the farm, they had never had a barn fire. He was careful with the fires, he checked the barns about four times during the day, and he scheduled mature men to stoke the fire during the night. Everyone knew that the vents in the bottom of the barn picked up the heat from the fires lit in the furnace, and they took the hot air from the flume pipes up to the vent in the top of the roof so that the moisture in the barn was removed. The heat dried the leaves, not lit them on fire, unless there was an accident or an untidy shed where the leaves were allowed to fall onto the flume pipes and stay there. Their farm was run neatly and with pride by all the men and women who worked there. They were still on a profit share basis for now.

Jamison shook his head, trying to dislodge an uneasy feeling that they were being watched, just as his *bakkie* returned.

'Moeketsi, did you see any footprints of a baboon in the water around the pump?' Jamison asked.

'No. Not that I noticed,' Moeketsi said. But he had a look on his face, that of a tracker now wanting to look again.

'I tell you, it sounded like a baboon, Jamison,' Maidza said.

'First light, we meet back here, we fan out and look for spoor from this baboon. I want to make sure that he's a wild one and not a human. This shed shouldn't have gone up in flames.' He looked all around in a circle. 'It makes no sense. Oh no—' he said as he saw an orange glow in the sky, from the direction of the safari camp. 'Ebony!' he said. 'Quickly, everyone in the *bakkies*. Fire at the safari camp.'

His heart raced. He knew that it wasn't a coincidence.

They had controlled the embers from the barn fire as best they could, and they had put out spot fires around when they saw them happening. The spot fires were few, the grass was green, the bottom leaves from the tobacco field closest had only just been harvested, so there wasn't lots of dry foliage around. The men from the TTL had spread out with their sacks and made sure that there was no fires on the outskirts of the tobacco field in the bush. The fire in the safari camp couldn't possibly be related.

Unless both had been deliberately lit.

He gunned the engine just as someone tapped on the roof that they were ready to go on the back. He raced as fast as he dared along the dirt road that ran down the centre of the tobacco and past the irrigation pump. He turned at the bottom onto the main road that lead through to the game reserve. The game guard on duty at the gate was nowhere to be seen, and both the gates were open.

Jamison's heart sank. He was unarmed, having run out into the night to fight a fire, not deal with wildlife.

He stopped his *bakkie*.

Moeketsi jumped off the back, and after the TTL *bakkie* had followed them through, he closed the outside gate, then the inside one, all the time cautiously looking around for lion. Jamison pushed towards the camp, leaving Moeketsi to jump onto the back of the already crowded TTL *bakkie*.

Jamison rounded the last bend in the road, and the scene in front of him was a nightmare. Thankfully, the main camp was untouched, but tourists were milling about, many had cameras and were running in the direction of the glow that came from the where his own house was tucked into the back of the camp.

His house.

'Hold on there, Eb, I'm coming,' he said quietly.

He drove through the main camp, and headed towards his home.

He could see pieces of his furniture on the lawn area outside his house, the lounge suite, the dining room table, some things from the kitchen, Eb's prized chef mixer, and a toaster. His game guards were hurrying in and out carrying the furniture, trying to shift it as quickly as they could, pulling his personal possessions from the clutches of the fire, trying to save as much as they could.

Two men had the garden hose switched onto full, and they attempted to spray the burning thatch. As much water as they put on the roof, it was never going to be enough to stop the fire, but they didn't give up, hoping perhaps it might just maybe slow it.

'Ebony!' he called as he stopped the *bakkie* and jumped out at the same time. 'Eb!'

He could see the back end of the house was already well alight, the fire's grip on the thatch making billows of white smoke rise into the sky.

'Ebony!' he called again, running towards the house.

'She's over there,' Felix said as he quickly set down the television set. He motioned with his head, and Jamison looked over to where Felix had indicated.

'Go, I got it this end,' Felix said.

Ebony lay on the grass, Joss kneeling next to her. Jamison couldn't run fast enough.

'Eb, I'm here,' Jamison called as he ran, and soon he skidded down next to her. 'Are you okay?'

She held her hand up to him, and he took it. Her other hand lay possessively on her stomach. 'I'm sore, Jamison, but I'm alive. When the fire started I couldn't get out the room. I tried to push the door, but something was blocking it. I tried to climb out the window instead, but I couldn't get it open. I had to break the French windows, the glass panels with the chair, and then I had to break a hole in the timber frames. But climbing out, it was too high and I slipped, and hit my stomach on the windowsill. I got out though—I got out.'

Jamison put his hand over hers resting on her stomach, and he could see her wince.

Joss interrupted. 'Felix and I were doing a perimeter check. We saw the fire. We thought that Ebony was still inside. But when we got to the bedroom, an old kist was blocking the door.'

'Inside the house?' Jamison asked.

'Someone had blocked her inside the bedroom,' Joss said. 'But we heard her screaming still, and we went through the door and out the window after her. She was still too close to the fire, and she has breathed in lots of smoke.'

Jamison looked at his wife properly for the first time. She was dressed in her night gown, but it was torn, and she had lost the sash that closed it somewhere. He could see the ugly purple bruising across her stomach, and he quickly closed her gown as best he could. She would hate to know that she was indecently dressed.

She wore no shoes, and her legs were bloody. She had taken the skin off her shins and her knees, and there was dirt in the wounds. She still held her stomach with the hand that he didn't hold, and he could tell that pain had just ripped into her as her body tensed. She gripped his hand tightly.

'My stomach hurts. It hurts to breathe,' she said, and tears ran freely down from her eyes, into her hair.

Jamison's heart broke.

'Eb, I will get you to a hospital, you need help, but you are going to be okay. You have to be okay!' He squeezed her hand back. 'Joss, go call the ambulance.'

'Bennett went to the office already, they are on their way.'

He held onto Ebony's hand, stroking his thumb gently against her skin. Reassuring her he was there.

Deep down inside, this was his fault.

Because of him, she was hurt.

It could only be Buffel who had attempted to kill him, and hurt Ebony instead. Even though he hadn't talked, he had kept to the code.

But he had no proof. He'd had no call from his cousin to warn him of Buffel's extended absence either. Not that their warning system was infallible. Gibson often accompanied Buffel to places, but they had thought that as long as he travelled with him, they could know that he wasn't looking for Shilo.

The first fire had probably been a decoy for the workers, and Buffel hadn't counted on him getting out of his house to organise the fire fighting. Buffel had gone in to his house, and instead of trapping Shilo in his house to burn to death, it was his pregnant Ebony who had been trapped.

But Ebony was strong. She was a farm worker. She wasn't a town princess who was afraid to break a fingernail. She had found a way to save herself despite the fire, and she had got out.

He heard Felix commanding, 'That's it, everyone stay outside.'

He looked at his home.

Felix was right, in the short time since he had arrived, it had become unsafe for anyone to go inside anymore. Everything that they hadn't got out needed to stay. It would simply burn. He was suddenly aware of the heat that came from the house. The whole roof was now on fire, and the flames played tag through the windows. The noise of the fire as it celebrated its victory in consuming the house was loud and triumphant as the level of the flames rose for a moment.

The game guards were watching for embers, and the TTL *bakkie* men were once again putting out any embers that landed with their wet sacks.

Jamison realised that in his hurry to get to Ebony, he had not instructed everyone on what to do, but somehow they had all managed to find a way to help, to work together, to be a team, even without his instructions.

The thatch on the roof slid down, off the steep pitched rafters, and suddenly the house looked like it was ringed in fire. Its black skeleton poked out from the top as if a pyre was burning.

The heat continued to push those with the hose further away from it, and the men with the bags were still unable to get in close enough to fight the real fire, as the inferno that burnt the house was still too new.

'Go, sort out your farm,' Ebony said. 'Joss can stay with me, then when the fire is out, we can go to the hospital together.'

'No, Eb, there is nothing more I can do there.' He kissed and gently hugged his wife. 'It can just burn out now.'

Together they surveying the fire from a safe distance,

Frazzled embers rained down on them, but Jamison brushed them aside. Black and grey ash streaked their clothes.

'It is mostly gone. They saved what they could,' Ebony said as she looked at the pitiful pile of their possessions.

'Posessions don't matter, Eb. I'm just thankful that they went in after you. You are the most precious item in that house, and nothing else really matters in this fire, except for you.'

Ebony reached up and put her hand against Jamison's cheek. He put his hand overs hers and moved it to where his heart beat in his chest.

In silence they watched the fire, as the last of the flames turned to smouldering embers, and as the sky turned from black to grey then brilliant red and orange as the sun rose, and with the smoke particles in the air, the stunning day began for the rest of Africa.

'Red sky in the morning, shepherd's warning,' Jamison commented.

* * *

An hour later, the police arrived, their arrival sparking an excited hum of conversation. People shouted to one another as they came to stand near to hear what was being said, shattering the quietness of the African bush. The birds stopped singing. Even the crickets hushed for a moment as the sound of loud human activity invaded the normally tranquil ranch. An ambulance had arrived first, and the paramedics who had stabilised Ebony were still working on her. They had put in a drip and given her pain medication.

Jamison glanced over to where Ebony was, with the paramedics working constantly, but the police were keeping him busy and they wanted him to remain at the farm.

Too soon, and not soon enough, he stood watching the ambulance take the love of his life away from him.

She was hurt. She needed medical attention, and the sooner the better, even if it meant he couldn't be with her.

He had seen the way the bruising showed on the top of her stomach area. She was being brave for him, and for everyone else, but he was certain that the internal bleeding was bad. He hoped that the baby was still safe, and not affected.

He felt selfish because for the first time ever, he wanted to put his family before the people he managed. All he wanted was for Ebony to be alright.

'Jamison.' The police constable redirected his attention onto their ongoing conversation. 'We have looked at the first fire site, my colleagues said that they couldn't find baboon prints, but one of your trackers, he found boot prints, and they were going in a different direction to everyone else. Those same prints are nearby your house.'

'Did you find the man in the boots?' Jamison asked.

'No, it's like he disappeared. Your tracker is going over the site again and there is a reservist with him.'

'If anyone can find him, Moeketsi will,' Jamison said. But he wondered if Moeketsi's skills were good enough to find Buffel, the master of concealment.

They continued their walk around the site of the burnt-out house. The policeman looked at the smouldering rubble.

'You were lucky your wife got out, that she was strong enough to break the wood on those fancy windows you had.'

'I know. And I'm blessed that she managed.'

'So if you didn't put the kist blocking the doorway, who did?'

'I have no idea. But if I ever find out, I'll kill him!' Jamison said.

'No, Jamison, you won't, that is just the adrenaline talking, you need to leave him to the law to sort out. You will do that, won't you?' The policeman looked at Jamison, as if to say he mustn't say things like that in front of him.

'Yes, of course,' Jamison said.

'You sure you don't know who could have started these fires? Someone you fired? Someone not happy with the change from a reserve into a hunting ranch?'

'No one has been fired in the last six years since I took over control. Everyone who has gone has either died of the thinning disease or they left on their own. This ranch is profitable. We all share in those profits, and I make sure I employ the right person for the job. My work force isn't transient, they stay. This is their home too, they don't leave.'

'So there is no inside reason? No fighting internally going on?' the policeman asked.

'No.'

'So it has to be personal. Against you or against the owners.'

'I don't know of anyone who would want me dead, or my family dead,' he said, and silently he crossed his fingers to cover up his lie.

It had to be Buffel, but he couldn't report him. If the code was broken, he would die. Of that he had no doubt.

'—we will look into the new owners,' the policeman was saying.

But both men knew that the police force was stretched to its limit in the countryside, and no more investigation would take place.

This was Africa.

No one had died in the fire, so the priority on the case wouldn't be very high.

'Thank you, Jamison.' They shook hands, and Jamison watched as the police climbed in their *bakkies* and vans and left the farm.

Felix had organised that the tourists were to still go on their morning game drive, and they were about to leave. He regretted that they had been subject to the interrogation and questioning by the police, but they all seemed happy enough to help, realizing how lucky they were that the fire had not spread into the main section of the camp.

He waved down Felix as he passed.

'Felix, I have to go away, Ebony is in hospital. I'm putting you in charge of Amarose. Maidza will watch over Malabar and the tobacco. You will need to work together to run everything.'

'Thank you, Jamison,' Felix said. 'And I will look after everything until you return.'

Jamison shook his head as he reached out his hand. Felix took it.

'I am sorry, Jamison. I have worked with you for many years, you are a good man. You take care, and good luck,' Felix said. 'Look after Ebony.'

'I will,' Jamison said as Felix let his clutch out and glided away.

Jamison knew that the game reserve would be in good hands. He had trained Felix well. Once just Widow Crosby's gardener, he had been able to expand his education and become a game guide. At the moment he was still studying for his professional hunter's licence, but he would get there, he was keen and he loved the bush and the animals, and had respect for it. Unlike the new owners who did not share that respect.

But there was one person left to say a personal goodbye to before he left Amarose for ever. He went in search of Moeketsi.

Once again, his home had been destroyed with fire by Buffel. Only this time he cared about what had been in the house. Ebony.

He longed to dig his heels in and make a stand against Buffel, but he knew he couldn't, not on the farm he was on. If Buffel had found him, and hadn't immediately killed him, then Buffel wanted information from him. Once again there was another he would need to protect. One he had saved before, one he knew was in danger, because if he was dead, Buffel would track her to the end of the earth to use as a sacrifice.

Jamison knew there was another farm that was being reforested, planted with green trees and transformed, and it would soon be a game ranch, a huge bonus was that the owner was special ops, like him. He prayed that perhaps, united, the two men standing together, they could take on Buffel and win the next time he came at Jamison and his family. He prayed that if Wayne had found Tara Wright since their last meeting together, they could protect her too.

He knew that if Buffel had come after him, he would try again.

He had no choice but to move on. He had to leave Amarose. This time it was not only him, he had Ebony and their unborn child, but he knew how to keep moving, to double back, to cover their tracks. He knew how to hide from Buffel, he had done it before.

Already he knew where he could find a place for a fresh start, only getting there would take time. Ebony was in hospital, and his first priority was her and the baby's health. He needed to get them, then they would disappear.

He would take Ebony and their baby to the end of the world to ensure they was safe.

He looked around.

He would miss Amarose.

He had dirtied his hands as he had got into the mud and planted trees, he had spilt blood as he found and transported animals with Widow Crosby. He had seen it built from nothing into the game ranch that it was. He had shared in the profits of the tobacco harvest. He would miss the green tobacco fields of Malabar, but he could easily be replaced as the manager.

He could never replace Ebony.

There was no contest.

Jamison knew that covering his tracks when they involved hospitals and doctors was never going to be easy. Ebony was a striking woman, and the type of injuries she had sustained were easily recognisable, especially in rural Africa. A few questions here and there, and money changing hands, and they would be found.

He couldn't afford to let Buffel find them, because next time they wouldn't escape. Buffel had made an uncharacteristic mistake with the fires, and Jamison was not going to let him try again. Moving so fast, reacting right away, would be his first advantage over Buffel, who would have expected them to remain in Karoi hospital. To not move Ebony. To be sitting ducks to be finished off at Buffel's leisure. But Jamison had other plans to ensure his family would survive.

He drove along the tar road towards Francistown, Botswana. Ebony lay flat in the back of his *bakkie* on a mattress. It was the only way to transport her, without access to an ambulance, and he needed to move her to the next hospital that night. After one day in hospital, the doctors had said she was stable, and he and Ebony had made the decision to run then.

Years before, they had discussed this very scenario together, hoping it would never play out. But it had, and now they had reacted.

They were on the move.

Somewhere that Buffel wouldn't expect.

Jamison had thought of going to Widow Crosby for help in Johannesburg, but then he would be putting her at risk, and besides, getting through the Beit Bridge border post always took an excessive amount of time. He couldn't take the chance that Ebony might collapse there, and be taken into another Zimbabwe hospital, not after he had practically had to kidnap his own wife from the hospital in Karoi.

His closest border post was into Zambia, but if Buffel decided to come after him, that would be the first place that he would begin looking. It was logical.

He slowed for a donkey in the road, before continuing.

They had passed through Plumtree border post as they opened, Ebony usually so strong, having to lean heavily on him for support as they cleared through the customs building with their passports. Putting her back to lie flat again, and leaving her there while he drove had been one of the hardest acts he had ever had to perform.

'Drive, just get me to another hospital,' Ebony said. 'I love you, Jamison, know that always.'

'And I you, with my whole life,' he said and kissed her. 'Just tap the window if you need me to stop,' he reminded her.

Luckily, their passports had been in a fireproof safe in the Amarose lodge office, and not at the house.

For a while he had to concentrate on the light traffic on the road, then he saw the turning from the A1 towards the University of Botswana, and the Nyangabwe Referral Hospital, and he turned towards people who could help his Ebony and their unborn child.

CHAPTER
15

Reunion

Kujana Farm, Hluhluwe, South Africa
1992

Wayne cursed again as the Turf Master hole digger attached to his tractor hit rock, and he had to bring it back to the surface. He shut off his tractor and jumped nimbly down to the ground.

He'd already built three-quarters of the new fence line, having chosen a stronger sixteen strand electric fence with bonnox which incorporated solar panels to ensure that it was more energy efficient and reduce the running cost of the fence, rather than the older style used by Hluhluwe National Park. Now he was concentrating on reforestation of his property while he waited for the solar panels to arrive.

Everything took so long to do. Africa time. That's how he was building his dream, on Africa time …

The fence line had to be of a high enough standard to accommodate the animals that he planned on reintroducing to his land. The gentle impala, the shy *inyala*, and the more common animals such zebras and wildebeest, and the bigger safari pleasers, the buffalo and the giraffe, but also the big cats that he wanted to bring in, especially lions. He wasn't taking the chance that a lion would get out and attack a human on a farm next door.

Tall Natal yellow wood trees sat nearby in thick black plastic bags, waiting to be planted. He had brought them in to the far section of his farm by tractor and trailer. Surprisingly they looked really good considering their journey up from Durban in the cattle truck, along with tamboti trees, with their leaves that turned red in autumn, stinkwoods, red-stem corkwoods, cape ash that attracted the butterflies, different types of acacia trees, fever trees that giraffe liked so much, and that weavers nested in, and the common cabbage trees. Arranged in between the taller trees were redbush willows that attracted parrots to feed on their seeds, common coral trees, and beautiful sugar bush shrubs. Every plant had been hand selected by him.

Lastly he had row upon row of grasses, and bags of grass seeds to disperse. Apparently native trees in urban gardens were the new rage, and he'd no trouble sourcing quite established samples to put in the ground. Buying them already established would save him a few years in waiting for his forest to re-establish itself, and give him an edge in an industry that in his opinion was about to boom even more.

His attention was momentarily taken by a flock of noisy hadadas that called overhead as they baulked at something unseen to the naked eye. Now aware of animal sounds around him, he listened as a dove cooed nearby, the sound almost went unheard as he was so used to its serenade.

The large group of workers behind him halted when he shut down his machine.

'Lunch,' he called.

He walked to his *bakkie* parked near the edge of the planting quadrant. He snatched his water bottle out the Hepcooler in the back, watching as the tell-tale dust trail signalled another vehicle was approaching, bouncing along the road towards them. His border collie, Storm, began to bark, signalling a visitor. He called her to heel.

He didn't recognise the *bakkie*.

It stopped just outside of the planted quadrant, and a tall black man got out. He put a Stetson on his head, and walked to the passenger side and opened the door. A buxom figure got out. She held a Japanese-style fan and fanned the hot air as if hoping to cool herself. When she turned sideways, Wayne could see that she was like a ship in full sail, almost at the end of her pregnancy.

The man put the tailgate on the *bakkie* down, and ensured that the woman was seated on the ledge, before he turned and strode towards Wayne.

Wayne's eyes were drawn to the familiarity of the approaching man.

'I'll be damned!' he said as he smiled. He'd know that figure anywhere. Having spent two weeks with the man in Zimbabwe walking all over Amarose, talking about how to go about recreating the African bush, and then having a week of cruising around the waters and walking over the shores of Kariba with him, Wayne was unlikely to have forgotten the man who had taught him so much. He remembered them dodging buffalo, safeguarding against crocodiles so they didn't eat their vundu and tiger fish catches as they dried on the banks. He had shown Wayne how to make the elephant hair bracelets that he still wore, and produced silver wire to use as knots on the one he'd made for Tara. The bracelets still sat in his cupboard, waiting to go on the arms of both Tara and Josha, when he found them.

Wayne shook his head as the man approached. In their time together at the Kariba, they had watched the huge hippopotamus as they dragged themselves from the water in the evening, waddling onto the land to eat the sweet grasses on the banks. The man knew the bush as well as he did, and he knew how to read the wild animals that inhabited it.

Jamison.

'Friend,' he told Storm, who stayed by his side but dropped the aggressive hackles that she was showing towards the newcomer.

'So, you were being honest when you said you were a hands-on farmer,' Jamison said as he stuck his hand out.

Wayne clasped it and shook it.

Storm whined, and he made the introduction, she smelt Jamison, then rolled over for a belly scratch.

'Some guard dog you have there,' Jamison said.

'She does her job, but she's young still. 'It's good to see you. Is this a social visit or are you coming to work with me?'

'My life is packed up and in my *bakkie*. I figured you were doing the exciting part and I didn't want to miss that.'

Wayne smiled. 'Congratulations, I see you are expecting.'

'Thank you. It was touch and go if she would be able to even keep our child after she was in an accident at the beginning of her pregnancy, but we have been blessed. Still another month to the due date, and Ebony is determined to carry to full term.'

Wayne smiled. 'I wish you all the luck with your family.'

'Thank you—'

'You know, I could sure use your expertise. I might have been a good Recce but my farming skills need work,' Wayne admitted.

'You have done a lot in just under two years from what I've seen as I drove in.'

Wayne said, 'I have, but I could still use more help.'

Wayne stamped the dirt from his boots. 'Come sit,' he said drawing out a white steel wire chair from the table and motioning to Jamison and Ebony to sit on the veranda, in the shade. Jamison crossed to where Wayne had gestured to the chair, and, pulling the chair out even further, he signalled for Ebony to sit, and made sure she was comfortable before pulling another one out for himself.

Wayne gazed out at the lawn, trying to view his redface brick home through Jamison's eyes. He saw his lawn was immaculately mowed, and rose petals fluttered across it like lazy moths from a garden of white flowers. Strategically placed trees shaded the garden in places and he could see reeds growing dark green and tall from a pond. Bulrushes speared the skyline, and some had burst, shedding their fairy-like seeds to float on the small breeze. It was a typical farm house, modest in size and functional.

'Ella,' he called behind him, 'I'm home for lunch and we have visitors.'

A moment later an older black woman, dressed in a traditional South African maid's uniform covered in green flowers, came through the door. 'Master Wayne, I was just cleaning—' she said.

'Jamison, Ebony, meet Ella, the best cook in South Africa.' Wayne made the introductions and Jamison sat back down. Ella bustled about, quickly laying a lunch on the table in front of them. She put a jug of orange juice next to the food platter, then three chilled glasses.

'Thank you,' Wayne said.

She nodded and silently left them on the veranda.

'The manager's cottage is free at the moment, but there is a lot of other stuff in there. If you can put up with the mess for a day or so, I can arrange to hire a container and it can be packed into that.'

'Thank you, that is more than I expected,' Jamison said.

'Don't thank me yet, you haven't seen how much is packed into that space. When I inherited Kujana from my father, my mother was still living in my house. So when I employed a white manager to run the place, with plans that I would still be in the SADF, I had a new house built for him to move in to. It's a little away from the main buildings so that he had space, and wasn't under her feet.'

'So where is your manager now?' asked Ebony, her fan still slowly moving the air around to help cool her.

'Gone. He was already converting it towards a game ranch at my instruction, but the progress was slow. When I came back from Zimbabwe and told him my new plans, and how I was going to accelerate the process and achieve it, he was out of here so fast. Told me he wanted nothing to do with game farming anymore, and he was more interested in growing sugar cane. It was less work.'

Jamison nodded. 'You are lucky. Men who do not understand that the wealth of Africa is in its wildlife are idiots and best not to have around.'

'Agreed. I lived in his house until my mother found her new home. Then I hired an interior decorator to refurbish the old homestead, while I began building my dream outside. So, the manager's house has been storing all my mother's old junk. She at last moved down to Umhlanga, but she left lots of furniture and crap behind. I didn't want her things around, so I put them there. I'll have to check if she wants any of it or if she wants me to get rid of it.'

'We'll be happy to use it, rather than give it to someone. I have no furniture to fill a house with,' Ebony said.

Wayne smiled. 'You say that now, but you have no idea what it looks like.'

'We'll be happy with it, believe me. It's better than an *ikhaya* and an outhouse, which is what most of the black people in South Africa have on farms,' Ebony replied.

'Not here, they have proper housing,' Wayne said.

'Good to know,' Jamison said as he bit into the ham, cheese and tomato sandwich that Ebony had made for him from the assortment of food that Ella had put in front of them.

They ate in silence for a while, and when they were full, Wayne cleared his throat. 'So you are really going to take the job?'

'I am. Thank you. But don't you want to know why we left Zimbabwe?'

'Not important, unless it will interfere with you performing your job here?' Wayne said, then looked at his wristwatch. Jamison exchanged a look with his wife.

'No, it won't interfere with my work.'

'Good, then I can show you your cottage. You start first thing in the morning.' Wayne stood and held out his hand, and once Jamison shook it, he turned to Ebony. 'Ebony, I hope you will be very happy here at Kujana.'

CHAPTER 16

Mhondoro

Piet Retief Farm, Zimbabwe
1992

Buffel knew he'd had to take action.

He couldn't stop himself once he had seen Shilo Jamison Khumalo in Amarose Private Hunting Ranch's advert. Since then his fragile peace had been shattered by the re-haunting of the nightmares that began again the very night he had seen Shilo's picture.

He'd had to try to silence Shilo. He was the only one who could connect him to the Wright brothers' murders. Only once Shilo was silenced would he would be free to track down the butterfly, to pursue her in earnest, to save Impendla's soul.

He might have failed in seeing Shilo die, but the fires that had lit the night sky had made Buffel remember what power he did possess. He had grown old and weak on the medication that suppressed the nightmares. On the synthetic drugs his doctor had prescribed him, to sleep and to wake.

Weak.

He put his hand over his heart and then pulled it away. It was all a heap of shit. His body told him only one thing. Impendla was dead. He had survived.

Impendla called to him for help, for peace, and he had to deliver that.

Being back near the mission where he'd been brought up, and visiting the Chinoya caves that he and Impendla had spoken of had stirred more memories and feelings from his childhood he thought were long forgotten. He had purposely thrown a stone into the blue water and challenged those ancient spirits to come and take him. He had felt power again, possession, as if he was *Mwari*'s vessel himself, like Impendla used to say. He was the *mhondoro*. The lion spirit.

He wiped the back of his hand across his forehead. The spirits of Chinoya hadn't come for him, and he was thankful because instead of being taken by the spirits, he had returned to Malabar a few days later, late at night, and captured a game guard who would provide him with Shilo's new whereabouts. Then he could finish the job, and this time, he would use his knife. At least that way he wouldn't fail.

'That bastard had better talk today!' he cursed and pulled his shorts and shirt on. Walking with purpose, he made for his mushroom shed. He knew the way in the darkness of night, but he lit it with a torch anyway, conscious of the spitting cobras that could be active at night.

He opened the door to the shed and as the smell of drying skins and heads washed over him, he detected the scent of fear too. A scent he had smelt years before, when torture was just part of his life in PSYOPS.

'You ready to talk yet?' he asked the man hanging by his arms from one of the rafters that held the corrugated iron roof in place.

'I don't know where Jamison has gone. I don't know. After the fire was out, and he had spoken to the police, he left, and he didn't come back.'

Buffel picked up a long dressage riding crop. He had found it in the tack room of Whispering Winds years ago.

He flexed the crop. Then he flicked it with his wrist. The split leather at the end bit deep into the naked flesh of the anti-poaching guard he had kidnapped from the Amarose. The man screamed, the sound sweet to Buffel's ears. Many years had passed since he had heard that sound. He once thought he hated it, the sob of a grown man in such pain that he would begin to cry like a child. But after the last two days, he realised he had missed it. The sound of a broken man whose spirit he owned.

In the dim yellow light of his torch, the body of the guard glistened black, but the welts from the lashing to his body marred the shimmer, making it appear mottled. Imperfect.

'Where did he go?' Buffel repeated.

'I don't know. Please, I don't know.' The man began to sob. 'No more, I can't take it, no more. I beg you.'

Buffel drew back his arm and whipped him.

'One,' he counted aloud. 'Two ... three ... where is he?'

The screaming had intensified as the man sobbed at the same time. 'No, I don't know, I don't know,' he sobbed.

'Four ... five ... six ... seven. You ready to go to heaven yet, you useless trash?' he asked the man.

'No, I don't know,' the man sobbed again.

'What? You don't know if you want to die?'

'I don't want to die. Please stop. Please,' he begged.

Buffel stuck the end of the riding crop against the man's exposed penis. He slammed it down with precision, and the man passed out from the pain. Still hanging by his hands, his shoulder made a loud popping sound, dislocating to allow the limp body to sink further into the bloodied ground, which was covered in faeces and urine of a man soiled in his terror.

'*Eish*, you gooks have no stamina anymore,' Buffel said as he drew his .9mm from its holster. He slowly screwed on the home-made silencer.

Originally the blacks on his farm had become restless when Shilo had left as bossboy. He went down to only three staff after their exodus, and he was pleased that he hadn't replaced any. Those three who stayed were his tracker, Gibson Ncube, who had arrived after Shilo left, and two men who had always looked after his few cattle and his Dorper stud sheep.

Gibson was a good *kaffir*, he had saved Buffel's life more than once, first with the doctor, and later in the field while hunting. He was sure that the other two men sold their generous rations on the bush-meat market for extra money. But meat wouldn't buy their silence like his bond with Shilo had once done, ensuring he didn't talk. But now Buffel wasn't so sure anymore.

He had to be more careful now that the war was over. Their *ikhayas* were situated too far away to hear a scream in the night, but they would hear a shot.

He was getting nothing from this man. He knew nothing.

Buffel put the gun to the man's head and shot him.

His body jerked once.

'Useless waste of time,' Buffel muttered as he sat on a pile of skins. He wiped the blood splatter from his gun on his cotton handkerchief. He waited for the heat to leave the metal before he unscrewed his silencer, and put it back in his pocket, and the gun in its leather holster at his hip.

He walked to the far back corner of the shed where the roof was lower and he needed to stoop to fit. He lifted the large spade that waited there, ready to bite the earth floor, and he began to dig a shallow grave.

The smell would mingle with the rotting aroma of newly harvested kudu horns that dried in the shed and the huge skins laid flat with salt on them, drying in the heat on the inside of the shed. He returned to the body. With his hunting knife he cut the rope that held the man's hands, and dragged the corpse along by one arm. When it fell into the grave at an angle, he kicked at it with his foot to ensure it crumpled totally into the hole. Taking the spade again, he moved back the disturbed dirt until it covered him. Finally, he shifted an old pallet over the grave, and covered the uneven ground with a stash of dried skins waiting to go to the taxidermist in Bulawayo.

'So, Shilo, you are in the wind again,' he said.

He would revisit Kwazi, Shilo's best friend for so many years, and see if the man of the Blue Lady Shebeen knew anything about Jamison's whereabouts. Later. Later when he woke, because a wave of tiredness swept over him, and as he closed the corrugated iron doors to the old mushroom shed, a calmness overcame him, and he had to concentrate on putting one foot in front of the other one to get back inside his house. Throwing himself on his bed, he went back to sleep.

Buffel jerked awake, sitting upright in his bed, reaching for nothingness. The sun wasn't up yet.

'Ugh,' he said.

Now that he was awake, he could shut his mind to the nightmare, to the sound of Impendla calling out to him. Demanding that he bring the butterfly to help him cross over into the afterlife. Telling Buffel that he was still trapped at the tree, that his spirit was still suffering.

Buffel hung his head.

So soon. Impendla was calling for new blood already.

He pulled his body from his bed, and walked naked into his modern ensuite bathroom. When he had first started on the pills from the doctor, renovating his farmhouse had helped him sleep. The hard work as he had physically demolished and then rebuilt parts of his home had left him exhausted each night. He had completed the renovations with the help of his tracker Gibson, who had surprised him by being able to build.

Still raw from Shilo's betrayal, he had been suspicious of Gibson when he first appeared at his farm looking for work a few weeks after Shilo had left. But Gibson had proved to be a useful all-rounder on the farm, and a bladdy good tracker for hunting. Patient, and knowledgeable of the bush, he was older than the other workers on the farm, but he was hard working.

Buffel cursed as he looked at the stranger staring back at him from the mirror.

He looked into the bloodshot eyes of a madman he thought he had laid to rest with the pills from his doctor. He was still tall. Still lean, he hadn't developed the beer gut that seemed to plague men his age. There was no outward sign that the man in the mirror didn't belong in society. He knew that he was still stronger than most men half his age, but he also knew that something was wrong inside his head.

It had been wrong for so many years.

He had tried using the doctor's sleeping medication to stop the nightmares, but they continued to play like a stuck record in his mind.

Impendla hanging in his tree.

The destruction of the tree when his father had reported it to the police force.

The dead children holding hands.

Impendla's own mother not looking at him, not wanting to claim his body as her son's.

Her subsequent disappearance.

The dead boys in the Grey's Scouts, and the recreation of the details of the ritual he performed over and over during the war.

The butterfly dream.

The best dream, where Tara Wright saved Impendla and walked him over to the other side. Where she saved his tormented soul. Where she gave Buffel peace.

And finally, the newest, most frightening and disturbing of the nightmares, in which Impendla cried out to him because he had been forgotten. Cried aloud that his friend Kirk had forgotten him, and no longer cared about him.

In the silence of that dream after the screaming stopped, all the butterflies in the bush lost their wings and fell to the ground, dead. Tara fell dead to the ground before she reached Impendla.

There was no one left who could help Impendla to cross over.

It was already too late.

He looked into his own brown eyes staring back at him. Trying to ignore the blood vessels that streaked over the whites of his eyes.

The lines around his eyes looked deeper than when he'd last looked, like the dried claws from a wedge tail eagle he had once kept to decorate one of the warriors with.

He hated the face that stared back at him.

He turned away and climbed into the shower, letting the cold water pound his skin and punish him for being the survivor.

The one who should have died but didn't.

The one who after all these years still wasn't doing enough to save Impendla's soul.

He needed to visit his tree.

An hour later, dawn had only just turned pink in the African sky. A thin mist hung low on the bushveld, but no moisture brushed off the brown grass as Buffel made his way through the early morning. Go-away-birds serenaded his passing, and vervet monkeys scampered away from his direct path, but stopped close by to watch his progress. His silent step faltered as he noticed the spoor in the sand.

The fat pad of the cat print looked like a sub-adult lion. The print was nearly ten centimetres in total, and the smaller imprints of the toes were more rounded. No claws extended. There had been no lion in that area for many years, so that left just one animal to claim the print.

A leopard, and from the size of the print, a big male.

Sure, its claws were retracted now, but when it took down a kudu with skill and strength alone, they would extend in all their glory. One of nature's best engineered killing machines, the leopard wasn't too proud to go scavenging when it needed to survive. He had long held the mighty *ingwe* in high esteem.

The spoor was fresh, not much wind to blow any sand over the print or distort it in any way. Still clear. No other tracks criss-crossing over it either. A perfect imprint. He would have been surprised to see any human prints this far inside the *sangoma* zone he'd created. Most of the black populations still respected the boundaries of the muti. Even muti that had been placed in the bush many years before. The ground became known as sacred, and the population learnt to avoid it, rather than anger the *sangoma*.

Buffel slid the strap of his .303 off his shoulder, and repositioned his rifle. He pushed the rubber-padded butt into his shoulder and slid the safety off, then slowly he pulled the bolt back and loaded a bullet. He was ready to defend himself should the need arise. Only an idiot saw spoor like that and didn't prepare for a charge, even from a usually elusive nocturnal animal.

He looked up into the canopy of the trees that were scattered around him. Leopards were famous for their strength and ability to haul their prey up into trees to avoid losing it to the hyenas. He searched with practised eyes above him and in the grass.

Nothing.

He continued forwards, slowly picking his way towards his destination. Alert.

Then he saw him.

In the large tree, the leopard paced along the branch. Its yellow eyes focused, keeping its balance. Its tail acted as a counter balance behind him as he hopped nimbly from one branch to another. The spotted coat shone golden in the rising light of early dawn. He approached a large V in the tree and wrapped his supple body up into a ball, using the space to secure himself. He yawned, and Buffel could see his large yellow teeth and pink tongue as he slowly closed his mouth, took one last brief look around his perimeter, and tucked his head down into his body. He closed his eyes.

Moments later, the leopard was asleep.

Buffel looked to the lower branches of the tree. Where six bodies should have hung, preserved and mummified into skeletons, decorated as warriors and tombis, now only bleached bone fragments were scattered around the tree. The skeletons were once wrapped in skins. Rope had bound around then, ensuring that their weapons could shield them in death and into the afterlife, did not fall off when hung in the tree. He could see where the nylon ropes had been shredded as hyena or jackal gnawed on them.

He looked at the leopard. At least he knew what had dislodged them from the tree in the first place for the other animals to scavange over.

He watched the leopard as it slept, unaware that he'd intruded on its territory.

No wonder Impendla was crying out to him. His butterfly escorts and warriors had been destroyed.

With meticulous slowness he sat cross-legged on the ground, and began to plan how he was going to replicate the sacrifice.

He damned Shilo to hell for bringing him to this place again.

If he had not seen him in the brochure, he would have been taking his client crossbow hunting right at that moment. Instead, he had cancelled with him, postponed indefinitely.

He couldn't have anyone around him for what he needed to do.

For waking the spirits of the dead.

For waking the nightmares, so that they could communicate again with him, and show him once more that *Mwari*'s work was not completed.

Impendla's soul was still unsaved.

He watched the leopard through eyes that closed into slits. His breathing was soft and heavy, he was ready to sleep himself as he relaxed in the presence of the majestic beast who slept, aware that he would bark or growl should there be danger. A calmness overcame him.

He would not kill the *ingwe* that had adopted his tree into his territory, but he would ensure that the next time when he hung the sacrifices up, they would not be so easily dislodged. Leopard's fur was soft and beautiful and for years had been used for ceremonial robes and coats, but Buffel wanted the leopard to remain in the tree's territory. He wasn't about to sell the creature's valuable parts, the tail, claws and whiskers, as medicine to a muti-man or into the taxidermy trade for overseas fetishes. He wanted the leopard alive. Protecting his tree.

A lone emperor swallowtail butterfly flew into his view and rested on his knee. The huge butterfly, as big as his hand, closed its wings, then quickly opened them again. The six eyes on the back of the butterfly all looked at him from their camouflage of yellow and dark brown. The wavy edges soothed him, as he watched the fragile butterfly with its strange hind wings that sported tails. The top of its body was black. Yet when it snapped closed again, he could see that underneath, the wings were more yellow, as was the body. He remembered a time when the sky had been filled with white butterflies, like raindrops all around them. He had collected the butterflies with Impendla, and they had pinned them to boards, so proud of their collection of dead animals that once flew free in the bush, but Impendla's mother had thrown them away. She said that the white butterflies were their ancestors, those that were pure in heart, and they were now the angels of the bush, bringing blessings to those who struggled along their own path of life. They were the saviours.

The butterfly flew away, up towards the tree, and rested near the sleeping leopard.

It was a sign.

He needed to complete another ritual, only this time he needed more than one blonde-haired sacrifice to help Impendla cross over. Perhaps if he changed the ritual again and collected all six white girls, all those butterflies would guide Impendla's spirit home to rest.

They would be the butterflies to help set his own soul free.

CHAPTER 17

Gabriel

Cape Town, South Africa
1992–1993

Gabriel looked over the copy of the police report on his desk. He blocked out the sounds from the busy *Cape Argus* newspaper office outside his door, and concentrated on the papers that had been assigned to him when his editor Stephen casually tossed them on his desk.

'More of your black voodoo going on,' Stephen said.

'Thanks, I'll take a look at it,' Gabe said, but his boss had already walked out and into the next office.

He opened the envelope. Another group of bodies had been found on the outskirts of District 6. As usual, there was to be no report in the paper about the ritual killings of the black children. There were so many kids who were killed for traditional muti. Most of them were chopped up. All the black children so far were unclaimed, as were many of those they found in a traditional ritual. Their parents too scared to come forward and claim those children who had been taken and mutilated.

He looked at the photographs of the bodies. A shallow grave had been dug and the bodies had been dumped into one mass grave, as if the parts that they didn't need for their ritual had no value.

He grasped the edge of the table with both hands as he fought the anger that boiled inside and threatened to burst out.

They were just children.

Even after all these years, he still didn't fully understand why these ritual killings still occurred in today's society. What type of person still believed that human body parts would help to cure an ailment, or increase the potency of a cure? Or bring wealth to someone who wasn't prepared to work hard to get it?

He looked at the pictures. The hands, tongues, lips, genitals and hearts, essential items to the muti trade, were often removed, and in some cases even the head was missing. That was a newer occurrence that was happening in South Africa, and it was a trend that was filtering downwards from Nigeria, as the people fled the genocide happening further north mingled with the accumulation of black people generally pushing south, and they brought with them their own versions of the muti trade. Human sacrifice was on the increase and it was a dangerous sign of the thriving muti trade that happened all over Africa.

Lately, he was seeing more and more of this style of killing cross his desk.

He dug in his drawer and pulled out another file.

The pictures were similar. The same parts removed. Only this time they had been performed in a more rural location, and the hyena had got into the grave. Only the fact that a game guard doing a patrol in the area had recognised some of the bones scattered around had led the police to that gruesome body cache.

He put the pictures side by side before pulling out his last file. It was a copy of an article taken from a microfiche in the archives, of an old ritual murder that he had stumbled across while working for the Bulawayo newspaper, and it had grabbed his attention. The case was from 1946. The sketch that had been done was an artist's impression.

What had fascinated him were the decorations adorning the murder victims. The dried animals, the skins, and the carefully assembled arsenal of weapons. The headline had caught his eye: 'Native Ritual Murder Hanging Tree Found'. Having majored in African Studies at university along with his journalism degree, his interest was immediate.

This was something that wasn't well documented at all. The traditions of ritual human sacrifice were kept silent in Africa. The black people would never dare write down such a thing, in fear of their lives from the retribution of a *sangoma*, and the white people were so repulsed by the facts that they wouldn't record them without a judgemental slant.

The writer of this article had gone into no detail about the ancient traditional ritual, and had focused instead on the missionary family who had reported the find.

He looked at the picture again and thought once more about how differently the lives of the black people and those of the white people were treated by the police. Second-class citizens back in 1948 and they still were treated as such in 1992.

In his eyes, the *sangoma* involved in this ritual should have been charged with murder. It was the brutality of the murders, and the traditions behind them that kept his attention. He laid the last file on his desk.

There was nothing in common between the newer murders and the older reports.

'Hey, Gabe, nice piece on the aid money for the Cairo earthquake not flowing through to those who needed it,' Andrew said as he flung himself into the visitor's chair, then wheeled it closer to Gabe's desk like a schoolboy would. 'You know that you're becoming the go-to journalist if you need anything in African affairs reported.'

'I know,' Gabe said. '*Mushi* hey!'

'*Mushi*? After all these years here, you need to get it right, say *baie lekker*. Get with the times, your Zimbo terms are outdated, you live in South Africa now.' Andrew laughed. 'I'm heading to Durban this weekend to cover the cricket. India vs South Africa, the joys of being a sports reporter.' He grinned.

'Enjoy,' Gabe said.

'You got plans?'

'Tara's already working on her master's thesis so I'll be at home. Taking turns with Lucretia to keep Josha entertained and out of her hair while I try to work on Monday's column.'

'Your cousin's so lucky to have you. When are you going to invite me around again so I can drool over her? She's one hot babe!'

Gabe laughed. 'Never. Last time you were there you proposed to her and then to my mother.'

'I was drunk. Surely she's forgiven me?'

'No, she hasn't. Besides, you know she won't date anyone. Her focus is on Josha and on her studies. Having her help on some of the profiles is a godsend, not long now and she will be a fully fledged clinical psychologist.'

'Best-looking widow I ever met, and brainy too. I'm begging you to take me home to spend some time with her,' Andrew said.

'Not going to happen any time soon,' Gabe said, but he softened the blow to Andrew's overinflated male ego a little by adding, 'It's not you, it's everyone. She just doesn't date.'

Andrew pushed up from the chair. 'Seriously, if you weren't such a *moffie*, I'd have to beat you up for living with her.'

'Hey, it's my house, she lives with me. Keep your mind out the gutter about my cousin! Or at least around me anyway,' Gabe said, and then he frowned. 'And who are you calling a *moffie*?' He reached across his desk to grab at fresh air as Andrew jumped out the way of his muscular arm.

'Yeah, you,' he said. 'See you on Monday.'

Gabe saluted his friend, and sat back down.

He tried to concentrate on the file on his desk. When he'd started at the Cape Town paper, he'd just been an intern, and it had taken two years to get his first real story, an exposé on the corruption of the supposed cleaning up of District 6. That first article had secured him a desk and a permanent telephone number on it. Luxuries any journo wanted. The assignments had continued to cross his desk and he wrote constantly. He had soon moved to a cubicle, then an office. Not that he needed an office much these days, it seemed that he was more often out on assignment than he was in it.

He'd just delivered his latest foreign report, having arrived home that week from a whirlwind two weeks in Cairo investigating how much of the foreign aid raised by the world for relief from the devastating earthquake was actually getting through to the 500,000 homeless there. Although he had seen a lot of the aid was getting to the people who needed it, he had heard rumours that a large portion was being diverted by corrupt officials, and that some of the aid was being intentionally delayed. People were sitting outside the rubble of their homes, waiting for the government to accept that they were destroyed before they got help. He had hated seeing those big brown eyes of the children, begging in the streets amongst the rubble that had once been their homes. He'd thought of Josha in Cape Town and been so thankful that he had been able to provide Tara and Josha a home to live in.

He smiled.

Well perhaps not him, but thanks to his mother's support he'd been able to. She had gifted him a house when he went to university in Stellenbosch, which he'd sold in 1984 to buy a place in Camps Bay, the year he and Tara had moved to Cape Town together so that he was closer to the city and the paper's offices, and Tara had a new start, for her and Josha.

He loved that kid, make no mistake about it.

He wasn't Josha's dad, but he knew that this was as close to his own child as he'd ever get. He carried his picture with him in his wallet, and had a picture of Tara and Josha on the corner of his desk. Those who knew him, knew who she was. His young widowed cousin, Tara Simon, who had married her childhood sweetheart who had then been killed in the SADF. So many men had died that their story had never been questioned. No one knew that she had taken Wayne's middle name, and used that instead of her own.

But he knew the truth, and he still protected Tara's secret for her, despite being unhappy with her for keeping Josha from his biological father.

He loved Tara as his own sister.

He could not remember a holiday that they hadn't spent time together. He was the older cousin pandering to her every wish, but still ensuring that she didn't get into trouble along the way. Until that fateful day when her father was murdered.

He should have been there. He should have been riding that day, not driving with Maggie in the *bakkie*.

That day had changed both their lives.

The man he kept on a pedestal as his mentor, who he most wanted to be like, had been murdered, and a cataclysmic ripple of effects had occurred because of it. He'd had his best friend ripped from his life, taken away to another country, and he had been powerless to do anything about it as Tara's place was with her mother and sister, and he had university to finish.

Soon after that day, his drunken father had raised his hand to his mother, and she hit back. His parents had at last divorced after all their years of bickering, and his mother had moved to Cape Town to be near him.

That day had also put Tara on a path so different to what she'd have been on if she had remained in Zimbabwe. Gabe knew she was studying clinical psychology so that she could understand her father's killer, and what had motivated him to kill the brothers. Her focus was on what made a killer tick. She was still wanting to go back to Zimbabwe one day, and find the murderer of her family, but she was going to do it with a full clip of ammunition, not rush in there half prepared.

Gabe knew that when she was younger, she had wanted to be a veterinarian, and help horses and other animals. She had such a soft heart, wanting to heal everything.

So much had changed that day for both of them.

* * *

December 10, 1993, and Gabe had never been more proud as he watched Tara graduate from Cape Town University. Standing in her black gown and cap with her sash telling the world that she now had an MA in Psychology. She glowed more than he had ever seen her before.

She was such a focused person.

She'd earned some income by tutoring other students at varsity who needed help in their social science classes. She always said that one day she'd pay Gabe back for all his help and for believing in her, and not letting her down. He always said that there was no need. She believed differently. It was a stand off. So Tara had started helping him research his articles. What had started as a way of paying him back with free labour had become a route to a profession.

Soon she had become an intern at the paper, and that had changed to employee status when they recognised that with Tara as a full-time clinical psychologist on their personal staff, they could ensure that their staff were looked after, evaluated and got the help needed to not burn out from some of the horrors they witnessed in their violent country on a daily basis.

The fact that she was good at research and could help on many of the stories was a big advantage too. If someone needed to talk to her about the angle they were targeting, she had an open-door policy.

She'd been the best intern he'd ever had, and it wasn't because they lived in the same house, it was more. They worked well together, she seemed to understand the angle he was looking at for his stories, and the human connection he needed. She still focused mainly on Gabe's stories, but she had also begun consulting more and more for the other reporters.

Yet she managed to always put Josha first, before her work.

Josha was a great kid. He had started school, and was doing well. He had got into his first fist fight with another boy about equality and treating people decently, so at seven years old, Josha was already a hero in training. Just like Tara described his dad.

Only last night Gabe had decided it was time to tackle her on the issue, after she had told Josha a story about how she met Wayne.

'Josha asleep?' he had asked.

'Yes, it's almost as if he's so busy during the day that at night he's exhausted and falls into a dead sleep.'

'I remember you doing that. I used to watch you sleep and wonder how it was that when you woke up you would have just as much energy as always, and yet when you slept you were a dead weight.'

Tara smiled.

'You talk to him of Wayne all the time. When are you going to contact him? Give Josha a chance at having a real father in his life, not a dead hero.'

'You know that's not going to happen.'

'You're being stubborn, like a donkey. *Ee-oor.*' He watched as she smiled, and nodded.

'I used to dream that one day he'd drive up to our home in his *bakkie* and declare his love for me. Tell me how wrong he was, that he should have chosen me. That he was ready to marry me—but now I dream that he'll never find me. That Josha and I are safe from the barbed claws of his demented mother and his father who only wanted to pay me off to get rid of me from his life.'

'Are you sure that's all he did? Don't you remember telling me you thought you saw an old man in the park and he looked familiar? You thought it was Wayne's dad.'

'If it was him, surely he'd have come and introduced himself again, made contact, not sat there like a paedophile watching us from the bench. Perhaps I was mistaken. I so wanted it to be him, checking on his grandchild, wanted to think that Josha was more in his life than just a trust fund and a lump-sum payment to me to keep out of Hluhluwe, and away from Wayne. He can justify it by saying it was all to keep me away from his wife's influence, who by the way was trying to have me kill my son. But we all know it was a payment to get out of Wayne's life.'

'For five years. He stipulated five years, that doesn't say don't come back, it says, come back when Josha is older and Wayne is over twenty-one.'

'Whatever. I did what had to be done. I have Josha, and I have you, I don't need Wayne.'

'Wayne'll be almost twenty-five years old now. He should have a relationship with his son,' Gabe said. 'At least give him the chance. The choice he didn't have when you were younger.'

'Why is this so important to you? Wayne is nothing in your life, just the sperm donor for Josha. He threw us away years ago. He has no rights. Josha is my son. He never wanted us, he chose his mother and father over me. He didn't stand up to his mother, he didn't tell her to back off, or that she was demented for wanting me to have an abortion, he never chose me and Josha. Remember, he asked me to leave, to go away. He never even gave us a chance.'

'I guess it's important because I see so much in Josha. You are doing a fantastic job, but he has a father. A real father. And I remember you with your dad. He was a good man, not a son-of-a-bitch like mine. I remember that special relationship you had with him, and I know that Josha would benefit from having that with his own dad.'

'But you are basically like his dad, Gabe. You are the special male in his life.'

'No, that is his dead dad. The man he hero-worships. The man who is still alive, but you are keeping him from knowing. Tara, Josha is going to hate you when he finds out you kept this from him. Think on that.'

'I have. And it's a chance I'm willing to take. If Wayne came back into our lives, he would try and take Josha away from me.'

'No, maybe he would share him, but the court would never allow him to be taken from you. You are a good mother. He could never prove you unfit. You might have needed help all those years ago when we made this plan to come to Cape Town and live here together, but you have proved yourself time and time again since then. You have matured, and are no longer that scared sixteen-year-old who gave birth to Josha.'

'I don't want to share Josha. Wayne hurt me, Gabe. I remember that hurt.' She crossed her arms over and hugged herself, in a protective stance.

'Ridiculous! It's not what you need, but what Josha needs. Josha needs to know his father is alive.'

'How am I going to tell a seven-year-old that his mother is a big fat liar?' she asked.

'I don't know, you're the psychologist. I'm just the journalist. You work out what you're doing to your son in the long run, what harm you are doing to him.'

'Gee, thanks, I needed to have that rubbed in my face. I can't, Gabe, I just can't break Josha's trust now. I never thought it through far enough when I told everyone that Wayne was dead, that Josha would also be told that story. By the time I realised, it was too late. I can't tell him now, he's too young. Maybe when he's older, maybe he'll understand why I lied to him.'

'And maybe pigs will fly. Come on, Tara, it's not that you can't tell him, it's that you won't because you don't want to share Josha.'

'I share Josha heaps, with you and your mum, and Lucretia. And my mum and Dela when they visit. He even likes Aunty Marie-Ann, and has her wrapped around his little finger.'

'But not with Wayne. Wayne, who you still hold a torch for.'

'I do not.'

'Yes, you do! If you didn't, you would date.'

'What, like your friend Andrew? That boy dressed in men's clothing. He's immature, unreasonable and rude!'

Gabe laughed. 'No, not like any of my work colleagues. Someone else.'

'No, I'm not free to date. I have Josha to think of, and you, and—'

'And plenty of excuses. But I'm not really with you, in that way, the whole kissing cousin thing, yuck …'

She pulled a face. 'That was not what I meant.'

'I know, but don't let your experience with Wayne spoil every other man out there for you.'

'But I don't want any other man!' Tara said.

'Ahh, got you!' Gabe said, and wagged his finger.

She frowned at him.

'Just give it some thought, maybe not now, or in a few days' time, but sometime, you're going to have to let Wayne back in. You created a child. Perhaps you can create a new life for you three.'

Tara laughed. 'You're such a romantic, Gabe!'

'I like to think so,' Gabe said, but while he didn't understand Tara's reasoning at all he planned to keep pushing her. He planned to wear her down, because what she was doing was unfair and cruel to Josha.

CHAPTER

18

Mr Brits

Cape Town, South Africa
1998

Tara sat at her desk at the *Cape Argus*. Her head throbbed as it always did lately, despite the larger number of codeine-based pills she had been told to take. Only today it was worse. Someone inside had a ten-pound hammer and was trying to break out the front of her forehead. The tablets she had taken for the pain had done nothing. She had never been one to have headaches, so the multiple and constant occurrence of them was a worry.

She looked at the clock. Her appointment with Mr Brits, the neurologist, was in an hour, and she was dreading it. She had been referred to him by her regular GP when conventional remedies and medications had not eased her headaches. Mr Brits had examined her and sent her for an MRI.

Today she was getting the results.

Acid burnt in her stomach. Something was wrong in her head, and it couldn't be good news.

She was scared. Her hands shook. She spent moments flexing them every time she saw her unsteadiness, trying to calm herself, but panic balled like a fist in her throat. She silently thanked her lucky stars that she was kept busy at work, because she knew that if she was sitting at home, stewing, her stress level would rise like a tick on a giraffe's head that climbed on at waterhole level, and suddenly found itself in the tree tops. She swallowed and made a determined effort to shut her mind off to all the scenarios of what could be wrong.

'Hey, Tara, quick word,' Gabe said as he walked into her office.

'Sure. I have twenty minutes and I'm counting them down.'

'You sure you don't want me to come and hold your hand?'

'I'm twenty-nine years old. You would think that by now I could manage to go to a doctor's appointment alone without relying on you as always, Gabe.'

'Neurologist, not doctor,' Gabe said. 'A little different to a simple snotty nose.'

'I know. Now, what's up? What interesting thing have you brought to me today?'

Gabe put a folder in front of her. 'These abductions. I think there is a pattern ... Look, at first, we had one girl go missing in 1982. Then in 1983, two girls, same age, same build, same MO. The girls were taken from the beach while on holidays. Cape Town and Durban. Both big cities, both small-town girls, not really savvy with strangers.

'Then we have a break. In 1992 it jumps to six girls, the next cluster spaced over a short few months. Six white children, all blue eyes, blonde hair, all just becoming adolescents, hitting puberty. Then it returns to just one at a time again. I think we either have a single serial killer, or a collector. Perhaps it's a paedophile like the police think, but I'm not so sure. I think it's someone else. I think it's something to do with the black tribal muti trade.'

'Gabe—'

'No, wait. Hear me out. They *are* specific, if you take these girls out of all the kids who go missing and look at them as a group. Their ages, they don't change, the physical characteristics, they are the same. It's just the demographics from around South Africa that vary. Interestingly enough, none of these girls are from a farming community, and other than the first two, all were taken from public places in northern cities, Pretoria, Johannesburg, Upington, Pietersburg, Kimberly and Bloemfontein. Always the girls were alone, except in this last case. The girl was abducted as they returned to their car after they had walked their dog and the father was left for dead in the parking lot of the shopping centre. And the father's ear was cut off. He lived, but has no recollection of even being hit on the head and knocked out.

'Which to me means that wherever this killer is from, he's shopping in a different territory. He's not from a city, he's in the country and doesn't want to draw attention to his area, so he is spreading the net outwards. And he is now collecting souvenirs, a change in behaviour—'

'Clever theory. Really clever, grouping those girls. But what is the significance of them, the police have never found any bodies?'

'That's why I think it's the muti trade, and I think that if they look in the right place, they will find pieces, but not whole bodies. There are too many girls now not too. I think we are about to have more abductions soon. Look at this line when I group them.

'One, then two, then six and then the rest are all singles, as if he's just ticking over. That, or we have a second case in here messing with my data. I think we are about to have more girls in serious trouble.'

'Good theory. But you need evidence, not just a hunch,' Tara reminded Gabe as she massaged her forehead.

'I know, and I was kind of hoping that you were feeling well enough to do me a profile. The type of person who would target just one type of victim.'

'You want a profile, just off the top of my head? You do know that my head isn't really well at the moment, Gabe,' she said and smiled at him.

'I know, and no pressure on this. I just saw the trend and thought I'd share. We have been working on this for so long.' He smiled at her and her heart melted.

He was always her rock. The cousin she treated like a brother. She was so lucky to work with him now, share his world. She knew that even if she was so busy that she had not a moment to spare, she would make time to compile his profile for him.

She would do anything for Gabe.

'Thanks. I know what you meant. So, right off the cuff? Number one scenario: a psychopath and there is no pattern and you are seeing one where there is just random chaos. Or the second scenario: someone focused who becomes manic. If it's the second, then we are in more trouble than you think, because he would be meticulous, planning everything, even the unexpected. But he has a trigger, something that sets him off on another spree, if you want to call it that. Something that accelerates his manic behaviour.'

'Alright. Psychopath is too random, going with the second there. A manic, like how? A trigger like what?' Gabe frowned. 'Talk English, not psycho-babble.'

'Like someone who has undiagnosed PTSD. You know post-traumatic-stress—'

'I know what that is, smarty-pants,' he interrupted her.

Tara stuck her tongue out at him. 'Or, someone who has been diagnosed PTSD and goes off their meds. Like someone who's seriously mentally ill, someone who is totally past reality enough to not recognise those children as humans, but as something else. Gabe, the big question I want to know here is why is it only girls? What about the boys? Where do they fit into your theory? Are there no boys with the same characteristics that are going missing?'

'I don't know why there are no boys. I have searched the missing children's reports but didn't find clusters of blue-eyed, blond-haired boys.'

Tara held her head in her hands. 'Gabe, have you considered that maybe you are searching those exact criteria, because you have a beautiful blond-haired, blue-eyed boy at home?'

'Maybe subconsciously. He's coming up to that age when these girls disappear, but it's more than that. It's a feeling I have. I can't explain it. But these feelings have kept me alive in war zones before, so I'm not ready to dismiss it just yet.'

'I'll go along with that. No scientific proof, but if that's what you feel. What's your next move?' She looked at him, her eyebrows raised.

'Reinterview the parents of these missing girls. There has to be something that links all these kids together, we just have to find it.'

Tara nodded, then held her head to try and keep it still. 'Okay. I'll work on a proper profile for you, when I get back. Right now I need to get out of here and to my appointment.'

She closed the file and handed it back to Gabe, then she gathered her bag up out of the drawer and walked to the door. She hesitated, and then turned back.

'You know what, Gabe? I think I will have that hand to hold onto. Come with me?'

She held Gabe's hand firmly in hers. Terrified of the results, she walked with him into the neurosurgeon's office.

Mr Brits sat on his side of the consulting desk. He was approximately forty years old, and had a killer smile. But he also wore a wedding band almost ten millimetres thick. Tall and slim, he spoke with a slight Afrikaans accent.

She made the introductions. 'Mr Brits, my cousin Gabe. Gabe, my neurosurgeon, Mr Brits.'

'Emile, please, good to meet you, Gabe.'

The men shook hands and Emile motioned for them to take a seat. She sat on the edge of her chair as Gabe moved his chair closer as if knowing that she needed him close, and he took her hand in his again.

'How have you been feeling, Tara?' Emile asked.

'My head still hurts, I still can't get rid of the headache. Those pills you prescribed to trial didn't help at all, so I only took the initial two, like you suggested.'

'That's understandable,' Emile said, as he leant forward and opened a file on his desk. He laid out two different films on the table in front of her, black and white images. 'Take a look here. I want to show you something. Do you see this area on this picture? You are looking at the pituitary gland.' He pointed to a place in the brain scan. 'Now look at this picture. Can you see the difference?'

He pointed again to a part in the picture, on one it was clear, on the next it had a small white mass showing.

'Which one is mine?' Tara asked.

He pointed to the one of the left. 'Tara, you have a tumour, what we call a pituitary adenoma. There is a mass growing near your pituitary gland. That is the "master gland" that controls all the hormones in the circulatory system.'

She felt Gabe squeeze her hand and she was so thankful that she had decided to bring him with her.

'Usually it presents with headaches, galactorrhea, where your breasts can suddenly excrete milk, and temporal hemianopia, like double vision, or partial vision loss. There are other symptoms too, but you appear to be lucky, as other than the headaches you are not displaying any of them, and from your blood test, it doesn't seem to be affecting your hormone levels so far. Most often, tumours found here are benign. But at this stage I can't tell if that is the case or not.'

Tara sat still. She had a thing growing in her head. She had a tumour.

She began to shake. Her breathing became restricted in her throat. She felt faint, as if someone was pulling a dark sheet over her head.

'It's a lot to take in, Tara. It's a shock. Hearing news like this is never easy.'

Emile put a small bottle of opened fruit juice on the desk in font of her. 'Drink, it will help the shock.'

She tried to drink the juice but after a sip or two she gave up, her throat was still feeling as if someone was trying to push two ping pong balls down it, and nothing could pass.

She could feel Gabe as he patted her back and rubbed it. Still holding her hand, he murmured to her. That she would be okay, that the doctor would look after her. That they would get through it, like always.

Yet she felt so alone.

So lost.

'Am I going to die?' she asked.

'Not if I can help it. Our best bet is to go in and remove it. The operation is called transsphenoidal surgery, basically we drill a little hole into your brain and remove the tumour through your nose. When we do that we will be able to tell if it's cancerous or not. As I said, most of these types of tumours are benign, so hopefully you won't have to worry about radiation or chemotherapy treatments. But I can only confirm that after we have it all out.'

She nodded. 'So what happens if I don't want to have the operation?'

'The tumour will grow. You could lose your sight, you could experience numbness or pain in your face. You will start feeling dizzy and you will have a loss of consciousness. From the tests that we've done so far you are clear in the secretion of hormones, but if it gets any larger, it will interfere with the production of those. If we leave it to develop further, you could get a condition called acromegaly, like gigantism in children. Your could develop growth in your skull, hands, and feet, you voice can go deeper, because of the facial bones growing again, your jaw can begin to protrude. You could have increased body hair growth. And you could be more susceptible to both heart and kidney diseases.'

'That's a grim picture,' Gabe said. 'So surgery is the only option here?'

'I believe so.' Emile looked at Tara to ensure she was still listening. 'Tara, you need to know that you won't just wake up one day being a giant, these changes can happen slowly. If we don't get in there to see if it's malignant and it is, the cancer could spread to the rest of your brain and you could potentially die.'

Tara sat in silence.

A brain tumour.

She could die.

Suddenly the tears began to flow uncontrollably down her cheeks, and they dripped off the bottom of her jaw and on to the white linen pencil skirt she wore. In all her daydreaming since she was a child, she had never envisaged herself dying young. No one did. Now she was glaring death in the face.

Tara wiped her tears with the back of her hand, and Emile leant over from sitting on the corner of his desk, and reached for a tissue box, which he put in front of her.

'How long do I have before I have to make a decision on the surgery?' she asked.

'No decision, Tara,' Gabe said. 'You are having the surgery.'

'Obviously the sooner the better, but I wouldn't leave it longer than a month at most. We don't know how aggressive your tumour is, it's no use taking chances with your life when you don't have to.'

She smiled weakly at Gabe through her tears. Then she turned to Emile.

'So is there anything else we can do while we wait for the surgery, to reduce the headaches?'

'Injections. We can begin to schedule drug dosages, morphine. But I would caution against any long-term use of those drugs. The chance of addiction is extremely high.'

'How soon can you book her in?' Gabe asked.

She looked at Gabe. He was everything that she should have in a man, caring, loving, and her best friend. She relied on him for everything, and she always had, but Gabe was not hers. Suddenly the realization hit. If she died, she would have such regrets in her life. Because she had such a rock in Gabe, she had been able to shut out the one person she still loved above anyone else in the world, Wayne.

Josha. If she died, Josha would be alone without anyone related to him by blood.

'If I die—' she croaked out.

Emile looked at her. 'Tara, let's talk about living, not dying. With the location of this tumour, we go in through the nose. I need to caution you that there are always risks, as with any operation. General complications like bleeding, blood clots, infection and even reactions to the anaesthesia. But I'm confident that I can get your tumour out, and you can continue to live a normal life again.'

'What type of risks are related directly to going in through her nose?' Gabe asked.

'Commonly, cerebrospinal fluid leak, when the fluid that surrounds your brain leaks through a hole in the lining of the skull. You could experience a watery discharge from your nose, or feel a postnasal drip. Sometimes, there is major swelling, and that could mean more surgery to patch the leak. And strokes sometimes occur.'

'I could end up a vegetable?' Tara said.

'We don't use that term professionally, but no, if a stroke happens while you are on the table, we can try to restore blood to that part of the brain that is starved of it, or at least minimise the damage.' He said, 'I know it's a lot to take, but getting it out is your best option.'

'Can I asked you something?' Tara said. 'If this was you, what would you do?'

'Hypothetically speaking, if it were me, I would find the best neurological surgeon to remove the tumour, and I would take all the chances of everything going well.'

'And if it didn't? If you had to plan to maybe die?'

Dr Brits smiled and shifted in his chair before answering. 'Then I would take my time before my surgery and live life to the fullest. Go watch that sunrise at the beach, make peace with everyone around me, and ensure that my wife and kids were provided for in my will, with the least amount of paperwork afterwards for them to worry about. Make my passing as complication free as it could be.'

'So get my house in order just in case, and celebrate being alive at the same time?' Tara said.

'Basically, yes. Don't go mortgage your house and sell your soul, because if you do live, you will need to pay it back. But have a holiday with your son, give him memories to hold onto in case he needs to. Make sure that he is provided for and that you know what will happen to him if you go. Make sure the people around you know you love them.'

'Right,' she said, and blew her nose.

Gabe still held his hand around her shoulder. 'Do you want to fly your mother down to be with you?'

'No, she has enough on her hands with my gran and her dementia. If she was here, Dela won't cope with gran alone.' She reached up and squeezed his hand.

Emile looked at his file. 'Statistically, you have a good chance of being one hundred percent afterwards, and I firmly believe that you will be.'

'Okay,' she said. 'I bet you say that to all your patients.'

'No, just a few lucky ones who I know will be alright. Sometimes the news I have to deliver isn't the best. There is no easy way to tell someone they are terminal,' Emile said.

Tara smiled weakly.

'So surgery it is then,' Tara said.

'Right. Now we can go through to see my secretary, make a date, and you can call your medical aid company, and discuss this with them. Know what costs you are looking at.'

She heard what he was saying but she felt numb. As if someone else listened into his conversation. All she could think of was all the years she had wasted in her life and how she wished, if she could have a do over, how much more she would have fought for the things she wanted.

Like Wayne.

CHAPTER 19

The Letter

Kujana Farm, Hluhluwe, South Africa
1998

Wayne walked into his farmhouse after yet another hard day working on Kujana.

He was ready for a shower, some dinner, then his bed and sleep. He headed straight into his bedroom, and through to his ensuite where he took his time under the hot water in the shower.

Slightly refreshed and feeling decidedly cleaner now that the grit and smell of the wildebeest they had been transporting was washed off, he ventured out and ambled into the kitchen.

When he opened the fridge he found his dinner, pre-cooked and waiting under a clear cover on a dinner plate. His new maid Nomusa had learnt fast from Ella, and he smiled as he remembered how Ella had made sure Nomusa could cook when she had trained her to take her place in the house. Ella had been promoted into his office assistant.

He took out his plate and put it into the microwave. While it spun around warming he looked at the piles of mail from that day.

Ella had already sorted it into baskets marked *Personal* and *Wild Translocation*, the name of their translocation game service that they ran together to supplement the income from the tourist trade while the farm came into its own. It was never supposed to become a full-time job, however they had soon found that Jamison and he were good at it because they worked so well as a team. The business had flourished and it gave Wayne a steady income to continue to develop the safari side of the farm.

Kujana was a bottomless pit for the money he earned. Fences, building lodges, bringing in Eskom to install the power cables for the underground electricity lines so that they didn't mar the landscape. It all cost money. Money they had to continue to generate if Wayne's dream of a private safari lodge to rival the best in the Kruger area was ever going to happen. It was a work in progress, and he loved it. He sorted through his personal mail pile.

Most of it looked like bills, but there was one in a crisp white envelope that was addressed by hand. He looked at the postage stamp. Cape Town. The date was the week before.

The microwave dinged and he took his plate out. He walked through to his lounge area, putting his plate down on the small coffee table.

Looking up at the mantlepiece, he smiled when he saw that Nomusa had rearranged his photographs again. She had a habit of doing that, she didn't quite put them back in their right places.

But he didn't mind, instead he stared at the picture closest to him, the one of Tara with Josha in the park. His family. He smiled as he remembered a day when Jamison had decided that he trusted him enough to tell him his ulterior motivation behind driving his truck down from Zimbabwe to accept Wayne's offer. He recalled the night almost word for word in his mind.

Jamison had walked over to the huge fireplace where he had his three large pictures of Tara and Josha on the mantlepiece. Jamison lifted his hand to the one where Tara had just given birth and was holding Josha.

'Do you remember in Zimbabwe when you asked me if I knew Tara Wright, and I told you no?'

'I remember,' Wayne said.

Jamison took the large frame off the mantle, carried it to an armchair and sat down. 'I lied. I knew *Inkosazana* Tara, with the blue eyes, and the white hair of an angel. We called her *Imbodla*.'

Wayne sat very still. Worried that if he spoke, the big Zimbabwean would clam up again. It had taken him years to begin opening up, to accept him as a friend more than a boss. To cross over the imaginary line that existed between the black and white men in South Africa. To be as comfortable with him as he had once been with Widow Crosby.

'I lived on the farm next door to Whispering Winds, her father's farm.'

Wayne nodded.

'From your pictures, she grew into a beautiful woman,' Jamison said as he passed the picture to Wayne.

Wayne touched the picture. 'That she did.'

'You two have a beautiful son. Josha, a nice name, much like Joshua, her father's name. She is a woman with traditional values.'

'I like to think so,' Wayne said.

'But still you have not found her, because she is not here at Kujana where she belongs.'

Wayne snorted. 'I don't think she knows this is where she belongs. Our last meeting was painful. We didn't part on the best terms.'

'When you find her, I'll be very happy to see her again,' Jamison said.

Wayne laughed. 'You and me both, Jamison. You and me both.'

Shaking his head, Wayne returned to the present. 'Well, Jamison, you and me are still waiting, aren't we.' He spoke out loud, even though he knew Jamison was in his own house, with his beautiful wife Ebony, their oldest daughter Sibusiso, who everyone called by her English name of Blessing, and their newborn child, Thabisa, which Jamison had already shortened to Joy.

He began to eat his *bobotie* with just a fork, the rich taste of curried minced meat and fat sultanas swirling around his mouth. He reached for the envelope, and opened it.

2001 Victoria Road,
Camps Bay
Cape Town
8040

23rd February 1998

Dear Wayne

After all these years, I hate to admit it – I need your help.

We have a son. I named him Josha.

I'm saddened to admit that only when I'm facing such a monumental issue, have I realised that I've made huge mistakes along the way in my life, and perhaps I might have only a short period of time to correct them. To put wrongs right.

I have been diagnosed with a brain tumour. At the moment everything is up in the air as to if it is benign or not. I have a month before I undergo surgery. There are risks involved, and although the neurosurgeon is being positive, he has also said that there is still a possibility there could be complications, and I have these four weeks to put my house in order, just in case.

Wayne, I know that after all these years, the last thing you expected was to hear from me, but I really want you to meet your son before it is too late. I always believed that I had more time. Time to explain about you to him. Time to get in touch with you again one day. I know I might be expecting miracles, but can I dare hope to get the two most important men in my life to meet and perhaps that you and Josha can at least be friends? If I don't make it through, there will already be a foundation for a friendship, and you will no longer be a stranger to him.

We both made decisions years ago that have affected our lives. Perhaps not as we thought they would at the time, but now we can make one right choice together. Please come and meet your son.

I'm sorry if this causes you upheaval and hurt, especially if you now have a family and are settled with someone else.

Enclosed is an open ticket on South African Airways to Cape Town. I have included my telephone numbers and our address too.

I will always love you,
Tara

The letter slipped from Wayne's hand and fell to the floor.

His chest hurt, he couldn't breathe, he saw black spots rush in front of his eyes. Forcing air into his lungs, he rapidly blinked his eyes to clear them, his breathing slowly returned to normal.

Tara.

After all these years, in which he had found no trace of her, Tara had reached out to him to make contact.

She had a brain tumour. She could be dying.

He glanced at the clock that hung above the arch in the lounge. 21:30. If he got his helicopter pilot Ryan Maskell up and ready at first light, he could catch the commercial plane out from Durban to Cape Town in the morning.

Now, there was someone else who needed to know. Someone else who had waited years for news of Tara.

He stood up, still holding the letter, and rushed out the door.

Just shy of twelve long hours later Wayne removed his leather wide-brimmed hat, and ran his hand through his short hair. He struggled to hide his frustration at the people in front who were taking their own sweet time getting off the plane. Choosing business class was supposed to speed up your departure off the plane, but there were some tourists just ahead of him who were in no hurry at all. He chomped at the bit, waiting to get off.

'I'm driving,' Jamison said right behind him. 'You can navigate.'

Wayne almost smiled. Ryan had flown them in their Squirrel helicopter to Virginia Airport. A car had taken them to Louis Botha Airport on the south side, where they had boarded the flight to Cape Town. Travelling light, his duffel bag slung over his shoulder, Jamison was right behind him.

He was almost on her doorstep.

Fourteen years he had waited for this moment.

Fourteen years he had dreamt that one day Tara and he would finally be together again. And Josha. His family. He'd never imagined their reunion to be like this.

Within moments they were at the check-in desk of the car rental company.

Wayne asked, 'Can I please have a map of the city?' and was given one. As the clerk behind the counter continued with the paperwork, he took his credit card from his wallet and laid it on the desk, and within minutes they were handed the keys to the car.

Wayne glanced at his watch. The plan was to go to Tara and Gabe's house before booking into the hotel. He had rung from the airport payphone before he caught the plane, to let Tara know they were on their way. At the time, Tara had been out walking on the beach with Josha, but Wayne had spoken on the phone to Gabriel. Gabe, the same cousin Tara had spoken of so fondly so many years ago.

He stared out the window at the buildings as they drove through the city. Lost in his own thoughts of when they had first been together. Always and forever they had pledged. To him it had meant the end of time.

Until he received her letter. Now he knew differently.

His heart squeezed in his chest just thinking about her, and a lump formed in his throat. There was a possibility that he was going to lose her, and there was nothing he could do about it, for the second time in his life.

The only silver lining to the gloom was that he was going to meet his son, Josha. He didn't even know if Josha knew about him or not. What if he detested him? His future was filled with doubt and uncertainty. Fourteen long years had passed since the last time Tara had thrown his world into turmoil, when his mother had been responsible for ripping the two of them apart, and he had allowed it.

He had pushed Tara away just as his father had told him, to stop his mother forcing Tara into having an abortion. Yet at sixteen years old, he had never imagined it would take him almost another lifetime before he saw her again.

Now he wasn't an impressionable youngster anymore.

This time he could make his own decisions.

He was a man and a father.

Realising that Jamison was asking for the next direction, he forced his mind back to the present, and found the road name to get them to Camps Bay.

CHAPTER
20

The Meeting

Cape Town, South Africa
3rd March 1998

Wayne drummed his fingers on the side of the car as Jamison pushed the intercom on the gate. Someone inside pressed the button to allow the gate to open, and Jamison drove up the driveway to park their car alongside a dark blue BMW under a carport in the front of the beachfront home. The front door was already opened when Wayne and Jamison strode up the steps.

Wayne looked Gabe over. He was the same height as him, and he looked as if he belonged on the cover of a fancy *GQ* magazine. Even his black shoes had a shine to them.

Gabe greeted them in a hushed tone. 'At long bladdy last we meet. I told her you would come!'

Wayne liked Gabe instantly. 'Nice to meet you too,' he said, keeping his voice quiet. 'This is Jamison,' Wayne said in introduction as he shook Gabe's hand, and Jamison did the same.

'I'll take you through. She's sleeping, but should wake soon. It's the pain drugs, they knock her for a six, but they lessen the headaches,' Gabe said.

They passed through an open-plan lounge that combined with a dayroom in the front of the house. Wayne's palms sweated, and he could feel his heart rate had elevated. The large room overlooked the sea, and was decorated to match the surroundings in whites and light blues, with a nautical darker blue flowing throughout. The white wicker chairs, with their overstuffed blue-striped cushions, seemed to invite you in, to enjoy the comfort and the view. He could see an antique chaise longue set up near the window, and Tara lay propped up on cushions, a light blanket covering her from feet to shoulders.

Tara.

Fourteen long years had passed since he had last seen her, and now she was there, in front of him. He snatched a quick intake of much needed oxygen, as his eyes travelled further into the room.

A willowy boy was sprawled in the chair next to Tara. His hairy right leg twitched as if he was keeping the beat to some music. Wayne noticed the set of headphones over his fair hair. He wore rugby shorts and no shoes, and was slouched at an unusual angle over the chair as only a teenager could manage and still be comfortable. His eyes were closed.

It had to be Josha.

He wanted desperately to rush up and hug him tightly. He had missed everything with Josha: his first smile, first step, and first day of school. He had a son who was a total stranger to him.

He took a deeper breath. Since receiving Tara's letter, the haunting question had been, did his son know about him?

He had assumed that his son would be in school, that he would have a chance to speak to Tara before meeting Josha, yet his son was there, an unexpected gift he wasn't sure he was ready to face just yet.

Jamison was right behind him, and had bumped into his back when he had stopped so suddenly.

For a moment more, Wayne simply drank in the sight, Josha's eyes closed and his large foot tapping haphazardly.

He walked slowly into the room.

Josha didn't notice the intrusion. He didn't move from his position in the chair, his foot still tapping.

Wayne couldn't stop his heart thumping in his chest.

Good God, when last had he been so nervous? He wiped his hands on his Wranglers.

Gabe tapped Josha on the foot.

The moment of truth had arrived.

Josha opened his eyes and jumped up. He stared at Wayne as he took the headphones off, leaving them dangling around his neck.

'Josha, this is Wayne,' Gabe said.

Wayne held out his hand as he looked at his son. He was tall, not quite the same height as himself, but he hadn't filled out yet. He was almost thirteen. He was at the stage where his arms and legs looked too long for his body. His baggy T-shirt top didn't hide the fact that his son stooped, as if conscious of his height and hating it. His thick blond hair was cut in a typical boy's school cut, blunt fringe and short back and sides. Eyes as blue as the African sky stared back at him.

Eyes he'd stared at in a photograph for years, now connected with his.

Josha looked like Tara, the shape of his full lips, his pixie nose. The freckles that touched his face as he had been kissed by the sun. But he could see his younger self in Josha's face too, the way he held his head, the cheekbones and dimples. There was no mistaking they were related.

'Hi,' Wayne said.

Silence could have shattered every glass pane in the room.

Wayne watched Josha opened his mouth to talk as realisation struck him, but no sound came out. Not even a voice-breaking squeak.

Josha stumbled backwards, the chair catching him in the back of his knees, and he thumped down into it.

Wayne put his hand back by his side.

'Woah, it's okay, easy, Josha. And that is Jamison,' Gabe said.

Jamison just waved from where he stood.

Wayne frowned. Damn, this wasn't how he'd dreamed of this moment happening. 'Pleased to meet you,' he said, his voice betraying emotions he tried desperately to keep in check.

Josha sat frozen in the chair. 'Um.'

'You scared the kid,' Jamison said looking at him.

'N—o,' squeaked Josha. 'Sur—surprised. Not scared. I aways thought I looked like Mum, but now I see some of you in me, just old!'

'Gee, thanks,' Wayne said.

Gabe chuckled at Josha's choice of words.

'That's okay. Give it time. Perhaps we both need time. It's a shock for both of us meeting today, I'm sure,' Wayne said. His mind reeling with the shock he'd seen on his son's face.

He didn't know who I was before he spoke to me.

Was it possible she never told him, or was it shock because he didn't want to see Wayne?

He had never anticipated that Tara would have poisoned their son against him ... panic swelled in his throat, and he swallowed it hard.

He needed a distraction to diffuse the situation. He needer to get his emotions back under control. Get the kid to talk to him. He stepped away, giving Josha physical space, hoping it would help. He switched tactics.

'Will Tara sleep for long?' Wayne asked, forcing Josha to focus on his mother instead.

'She's been sleeping a while already. She always sleeps when she comes back from the beach and her meds kick in. She should be awake in another fifteen minutes or so.'

'You obviously know her routine well,' Wayne said.

'It happens when you spend your days at home with her. If she's not at home she's having tests, scans and things,' Josha said, in a voice far too adult for a teenager.

Wayne wondered just how much Josha knew about his mother's tumour. He suspected far too much, but then what reference point did he have to make a judgement like that? He knew nothing of his son's abilities or his maturity, of how his life had been.

He was longing to ask Josha so many questions, but like a wild newborn colt, this long-legged teenager would bolt if pushed, of that he was sure, so he just played it cool instead. Buried the curiosity deep inside and attempted to make friends.

Wayne turned his attention to watching the gulls out the window as they rode the thermals and the winds. 'A beautiful view you guys have here, peaceful, and great weather,' he said.

'The weather? You are going to try get a teenager to discuss the weather?' Gabe said. 'You seriously don't have any clue with kids, do you?'

'No, I have no idea.' Wayne scratched the back of his head with his hand.

Jamison backed him up. 'Ebony and I have a five-year-old and a newborn. Wayne won't hold Joy because he says she's too tiny, but in his defence, I have seen him attending tea parties hosted by Blessing. He just hasn't had exposure yet to too many teenagers.'

Wayne laughed then, it was nervous and came out a bit loud, but suddenly Josha was laughing too.

'It's okay,' Josha said. 'Uncle Gabe warned me you were coming, but it's all still a bit of a surreal moment.'

Gabe reached over to him and ruffled his hair, the affection between them obvious.

'So-you-really-are-my-biological-father-as-in-Wayne-Simon-who-died-in-the-SADF?' Josha spoke as if the words were bursting inside him and needed to be said.

Wayne was taken aback, and had to process what Josha had said, then he worked it out, and replied, 'My full name is Wayne Simon Botha, I was in the SADF but I didn't die. And yes, I'm your father.'

Wayne stared at Josha. Damn, Josha didn't look like a clone from when he was that age, but he could hear a younger him talking. A teenage him, from a time before Tara got pregnant and took Josha from him. Clever, taking his middle name and using that and not his surname. No wonder no one could find her.

But Josha thought that his father was dead.

Eventually, he said, 'You know, I spent years looking for you, once I knew you were in the world. I searched for Tara before that too. I never stopped.'

Josha nodded.

Then every time the boy opened his mouth to talk, he shut it again, as if the words stuck in his throat, and wouldn't come out past his thick tongue. Wayne knew the feeling.

Josha suddenly asked Jamison, 'Are you Wayne's bodyguard?'

Wayne smiled at his blunt question.

'No. Does he look like he needs a bodyguard, kid?' Jamison said. 'I'm his business partner, but he was adamant that he would fly the chopper down to Durban at first light, and hop a plane to Cape Town. He was worried sick. So I did the only thing a friend could do, and came with him. He was in no state to do much, so I'm just here to make sure he's going to be alright. This is a moment we have waited a long time for.'

'Neat,' Josha said.

Wayne relaxed a little. 'And as Jamison mentioned, he has a newborn baby in the house who screams, constantly,' Wayne said. 'So Jamison was happy to take off for a few days.'

'That's not true, I don't hear her screaming. Ebony takes good care of the girls all the time. Besides, Joy is a colicky baby, they all sound like that,' Jamison defended his family.

Josha looked at Wayne. 'You really have your own helicopter?'

'Sure, we use it for game capture, mostly,' Wayne said. 'Do you like flying?'

'I've never flown anywhere, so I don't know,' Josha said, 'but I'd like to try it.'

'Perhaps ...' Wayne stopped himself from making the invitation.

He had no right to invite his son for a trip to his farm, to fly with him in his helicopter.

He still had no rights to Josha at all and until he had discussed that with Tara, he couldn't – wouldn't – make promises to his son that he couldn't keep. He wanted to be a better father than that.

Josha stood up to check on Tara. He tugged her blanket up a little, sat on the edge of the daybed and looked at Wayne again.

Wayne looked back at him. 'I suspected you were tall, but seeing you in real life is different from how I imagined. You grow much more and you'll be as tall as me.'

Josha straightened out his shoulders and seemed to uncurl from his stooped teenage position, sitting up taller. 'I never knew you were so tall,' he said at last.

Wayne smiled. 'Well, I don't know what your mum has told you about me, but I would like to get to know you and at the very least be your friend.'

'Mum always told me you'd died. When she found out that she had the tumour, and she was going to have her op, she told me that she lied to protect me ... you were not really dead.'

'I'm sorry.'

'Why are you sorry? It wasn't you who lied to me.'

Wayne could hear the hurt in his son's voice, and the betrayal he had faced, having to deal with his mother's lie.

'I'm sure she had her reasons,' Wayne volunteered.

'Humph.' Josha made the universal non-committal teenage answer.

'Guess we both have lots to adjust too. I assumed you would at least know who I was,' Wayne said, and he watched his son's body language closely. It said that he was angry, but it also said that he was agitated. 'That's okay, we can work on details later. We have time. Lots of it.'

Gabe stood up from the chair he was sitting in. 'You alright, Josha?'

Josha nodded, and he gave Gabe a thumbs up.

'Good, then I think I'll go ask Lucretia to make us some refreshments and bring through lunch for when Tara wakes up. Jamison, you want to come see the rest of the house?' Gabe asked, providing Jamison an excuse to leave Josha and Wayne to become acquainted.

'Do I have a half brother or sister?' Josha asked Wayne once the others had left the room.

'No. You don't have any siblings. You are my only child.'

'Are you married?'

'No. Never married. I was always waiting to marry your mother.' He looked over at Tara, then back at Josha.

Josha walked back to his chair. He flopped backwards into it, the wicker groaning under the impact. 'Adults, I don't understand them!'

'You and me both,' Wayne said.

Josha pulled a face, and Wayne smiled at him. It was easier talking to his son than he had expected.

Almost natural.

Silently he wished the last years hadn't happened, that he could have been here earlier. For Josha, for Tara, for himself. Hindsight was a luxury he couldn't afford, but he knew he should have fought for her right from the beginning.

'I wish things had been different,' Wayne said. 'That I wasn't meeting you under such awful circumstances. But know that I'm so happy to meet you. To get a chance to know you.'

'Um – okay,' Josha said.

Wayne moved into the other chair to face Josha. 'I love your mother. She's always been the love of my life but I wasn't strong enough to walk away from my roots. To stand up to my mother. I guess in the end, I didn't fight enough for what your mum and I needed.'

'So you abandoned her—' Josha said.

'It was complicated. She moved away—' Wayne sat quietly watching his son.

'Why are you staring at me?' Josha asked.

'I don't mean to stare, but frankly I've thought of not much else since I found out that you had been born. I still find it hard to believe that my son is almost thirteen years old. Your mother was lucky having you near her all these years.'

Josha's eyebrows went upwards. 'You didn't know about me?'

'No. I knew your mum was pregnant, but once she went away, I didn't know if she had you.' He thought a moment if he should censor the rest, then threw caution away. His son needed the truth. 'I was told that she had an abortion, but I hoped it wasn't true. Not until my own father, your grandfather Johnny, died, then I learned that you were alive and well, and that you have a birthday next month.'

Josha shook his head. 'I'm not leaving her to live with you now that you know where we are—'

'I don't expect you to. I'm not leaving her either.'

Wayne crossed over to the bed and looked at Tara sleeping. She was still as beautiful as ever. He took one of her hands in his and slowly he brought it up to his mouth, kissed it gently. 'I'm here, Tara.'

Her eyes flickered open.

'Hi, precious,' Wayne said, his voice coming out like a croak, his emotion raw and evident to anyone else.

'Wayne. You came,' she said. 'I didn't know if you would. I mean I wanted you to—, but I thought that you might not still be at the farm—' she managed.

'Mum, you got some visitors,' Josha said, stating the obvious.

Wayne smiled, hearing his son. 'I got your letter yesterday. And here I am.'

'So Mum, this is Wayne. My dad who isn't dead.' Josha pointed out.

Wayne saw her tense.

'You met already?'

Wayne nodded.

'*Ja*, Mum. Don't worry about me. Wayne and I are doing okay,' Josha said from his chair.

Wayne bent over and kissed her softly on the forehead. 'I'm with you for as long as you want me here, Tara.'

She slipped both her hands up onto Wayne's cheeks. Wayne saw tears well in Tara's eyes as she held his face. She touched his face as if trying to see if he was real, as if trying to understand the difference from the image of the boy she had in her mind, to the man he had become. 'My Wayne,' she whispered.

'I promised, now and forever,' he said, and kissed her. Then taking her hand in his, he reached out his other one, palm upwards to Josha.

Josha rose from his chair. He walked slowly towards his parents, and then he reached out and tentatively touched his father's hand.

'I love the both of you,' Wayne said. For a moment the family stood together for the first time, each touching the other, connected for a moment, then Josha pulled his hand from Wayne's.

Tara frowned. 'So are you okay with Wayne being here, Josha?'

'*Ja*. We're cool,' Josha said with a shrug of his shoulders.

'I'm glad.' Her eyes filled with tears again. 'I'm sorry, sweetheart. It's so much for you, all on top of each other.'

Josha smiled. 'You could have picked worse you know, he could have been a total loser …'

Wayne almost choked as he tried to swallow the laugh that wanted to burst from him.

Jamison, who had just come back into the room, wasn't so quick, and his laugh came out loud and clear.

'Mum, that's Jamison, Wayne's friend. Not his bodyguard.' Josha filled his mum in.

'Nice to meet you,' she said politely to Jamison, but her attention was on Josha, and she barely looked in his direction.

'I'm glad you're alright with him, give each other time, sweetie. Time …' A single tear slipped down her cheek, and slid down under her chin.

Wayne looked at Tara, still in awe that she was so beautiful. Time had improved her, her hair was now more golden than white, her nose had a few more freckles sprinkled over it, and her lips were fuller. Those of a woman.

Her body was still petite, and even in her day bed she had an air of confidence about her.

Gabe came back into the room, bearing a tray laden with food.

Lucretia bustled in after him. 'You forgot these, Gabe,' she said, holding out the condiments, the plates and the serviettes. She stopped when she saw Wayne.

Wayne looked at the old lady.

'You,' she said in a frosty manner.

'Hello, Lucretia,' he said politely.

'You try not hurt my Tara this time,' she said as a warning, as if she had a say in their relationship.

'Lucretia, *shoosh*!' Tara said.

'I'll be watching you,' Lucretia said, and Wayne smiled, glad to know that she was still with Tara. That Tara had a friend who had stood by her all these years.

Lucretia bustled out the room after placing the forgotten items next to the tray laden with sandwiches, cut into dainty fingers with their crusts cut off, that Gabe had set on the coffee table.

'So can I expect the same reaction from your mum and Dela?' Wayne asked.

'I doubt it. They're kept too busy. My gran developed Alzheimer's disease. Mum and Dela both live with her now. Dela is a really good artist, and she tutors advanced art students. She has her studio set up at home so that between them, they watch over gran, look after her, and they have managed to keep her with them at home where she is comfortable and recognises things sometimes.'

'Sorry to hear about your gran. That can't be easy, for any of them.'

'It's life,' Tara said.

Wayne looked at the sandwiches. It looked like ham, cheese and salad stuff, and something that resembled tuna and mayo with lettuce or bully beef and cheese. He dithered with his selection, but Tara helped herself to some.

'Bully beef, yum, I love this stuff. When I was pregnant I would eat it out of the tin, the whole tin … used to drive Lucretia mad,' she said. He stiffened. This was the first time she'd said anything to him about her pregnancy, and he wasn't sure just what to say.

'Because you were eating disgusting bully beef?' Wayne finally asked.

'No, because I wouldn't use a plate. She used to have this thing about leaving food in tins. She would go off about some sickness you could get from tins. So my solution was that if I ate the whole thing she wouldn't get mad. But as my pregnancy progressed, my tastes changed, and soon eating a whole tin of caramelised condensed milk just wasn't an option, too much sweet. I would eat half, and then put it in the fridge. Lucretia would always scold me about it when she found it, without fail.'

Gabe said, 'She still doesn't use a plate, and Lucretia still goes off at her.'

'Gabe, I so do!' she said.

'No you don't, Mum.' Josha backed up Gabe.

Wayne looked down to where she had a sandwich in her hand, without a plate, and battled to cover a smile.

'Oh, you siding with Gabe is just not fair,' she said to Josha. She glanced briefly at their other guest, but it was more a passing glance as she focused back on Wayne even before she spoke. 'Jamison. Do you have children?' Tara asked, in what was a blatant manipulation of the conversation away from her.

'Yes, Joy was born just last month on the fifth of February, and her sister Blessing is five.'

'What beautiful names,' Tara said and she frowned, turning her attention back to Wayne. 'And your family, Wayne?'

'You and Josha have always been the only family I wanted,' Wayne said.

Unshed tears shone in her eyes.

'Come on, Tara, don't cry, it's a happy time. I have got to meet my beautiful son, and see his beautiful mother,' Wayne said.

'I know, they are happy tears, but I was so sure you would have gotten married, had a family. Settled down.'

'No family. I did buckle down, got to work and made as much money as I could, but it didn't help me find you,' he said.

Tara smiled.

'So are you up to explaining more about your tumour?' Wayne asked. 'I did ask Gabe but he said you needed to tell me what you wanted to tell.'

'That's Gabe,' she said looking at her cousin with obvious affection. 'Always looking out for me. I don't know what I would have done without him all these years. He's my rock. I have just under three more weeks until I have the surgery.'

'So how did you know you had a – you know.' He pointed to his own head.

'A brain in my head? Or a tumour?' Tara smiled. 'It started a few months back. I began getting these headaches, almost migraines, they were so bad, and I'd never had headaches before. So I went to the doctor, who referred me to the specialist. I had the first MRI done and blood tests galore, and that's when they saw it, and Mr Brits broke the news and said that he wanted to operate. The date is set for the twenty-third of March.'

'So why a whole month from diagnosis to operation, why not right away?' Wayne asked.

'So I could get my life sorted.'

Wayne frowned. 'As in you could still die, even if he takes it out?'

'Yes. There could be complications—'

'Like having me come back into your life?' Wayne said.

'Like having to admit to Josha that I lied,' she said and she looked over at Josha, who had just stuffed a whole strip of sandwich in his mouth.

Wayne dropped his voice, knowing that he was talking about Josha and yet he was in the room. 'That must have been rough on him, he seems like a genuine kid, with a good moral compass.'

'He is, and shattering his trust in me—' She sniffed. 'I knew one day I was going to have to tell him, but the days just went so fast, and turned into years, and soon he was almost thirteen. He's a great kid,' she said. 'Not that I'm biased or anything as his mother—' She looked at her son, and she smiled.

Wayne had missed that smile. Whenever she smiled at him when they were younger, he thought that the world was made just for the two of them. It had been many years, but he had never forgotten her smile, and the happiness that came with it.

'Tara, how did we come to this?' he asked.

'I got pregnant, remember.'

'Like it was yesterday—'

'I can't do the hurt again, Wayne, I can't go over all the hurt. I don't want to rehash what has passed.'

'Then we don't. We wipe the slate clean, leave it behind. Maybe one day we can talk about it, maybe after your operation. I want us to have the happy ever after that we didn't have.'

'But you don't know anything about me now. I'm not who I was. I work here in Cape Town with Gabe at the paper. I consult with the other reporters—'

'I'm not asking you to change your life, but to give us a chance. Let us get to know each other as adults.'

'I can do that, because soon after this operation I'm going to return to a normal life,' she said. 'Perhaps it might help you and Josha to spend some time together, just in case. So he knows a little more about you, where you live—'

Wayne shook his head. 'I'm not taking Josha to Kujana without you. His time with you at the moment is just as precious as my time getting to know him. I don't see why they can't be done together. You are not dead yet, you can come and visit with Josha to Kujana, then you will both know where I live and what I do.'

'Hluhluwe is a long flight and a longer drive away. I'm not sure I can cope with that,' she said.

'You can cope with it, you just need the incentive,' Wayne said. He grabbed a plate, and dumping the sandwich she had abandoned on the small coffee table on it, he passed it to her. 'Eat, you need your strength.' He sat down at the end of the daybed again.

She glared at him.

'Wayne has a helicopter, Mum,' Josha said matter of factly from his chair.

'You seriously have a helicopter?' she asked.

Wayne nodded.

Jamison said, 'You won't need to drive to Hluhluwe. It's just under an hour in the Squirrel from Virginia Airfield to home.'

Wayne said, 'Piece of cake, you can manage that.'

'Will there be room for all of us? Uncle Gabe too?' Josha asked, all of a sudden paying lots of attention to what was being said.

'Yes,' Wayne said as he looked at Tara. She looked uncertain, but everyone could hear the excitement in Josha's voice.

'Come see the Kujana we have built. It's not the sugarcane fields that you knew. It's a game farm.'

'You own a game *farm?*' Josha said, extending the last word in the way that only a teenager could.

Wayne nodded, and Jamison smiled.

'I guess it's settled then, we are going for a visit. Gabe,' she said. 'You're coming with us, aren't you?'

'You couldn't leave me behind if you stuck concrete boots on me!' Gabe said.

'And Lucretia?' Josha asked.

'We can fit her in too. And all the luggage,' Wayne said.

'Where is everyone going?' asked an elderly woman who just at that moment walked into the lounge as if she belonged there in it.

'Mum,' Gabe said, getting up from his chair and hugging her. 'I didn't hear you come in.'

'Not surprising with all the excitement in this room,' she said.

'Mum, meet Tara's Wayne, and this is Jamison,' he said. 'Mauve, my mother.'

They all shook hands and Mauve crossed over to Tara and kissed her on the cheek. She spent a moment rearranging Tara's blanket.

Her affection for Tara showed as she touched Tara's cheek lightly. Then she turned to Josha, and opened her arms.

Josha got up off his chair and went and hugged her.

'How you holding up, kid?' Mauve asked.

'Good. But it's been a rollercoaster day.'

'I bet,' Mauve said. 'If you need breathing room, we can go shopping. I need some new potting mix and I thought you could help me to choose the new flowers for that front bed.'

'Nah, I'm cool. But I'll go with you tomorrow if you need me to—'

'We can cross that bridge tomorrow,' Mauve said, and then she sat in a chair that Gabe had fetched for her.

Lucretia came in and brought her a cup of tea. It was obvious that she was a welcome addition to the party.

Wayne felt emotion lodge in his throat. This woman had an obvious deep love for Tara and for Josha too, and they seemed like a tightly woven family unit.

He envied Gabe. His mother was so accepting, and so openly proud of her son and his extended family. It was a stark contrast to the relationship he had with his own mother. He shuddered just thinking of the last call she had made to him. He still tended to avoid her calls, not wanting the confrontations that she always attempted to embroil him in.

Despite his father now having been dead for eight years, his mother had not remarried.

She had, however, spent every rand she had, and was now about to come home to live on his farm with him again. He knew that she was family. He wouldn't abandon her, but he'd quickly started construction on a new cottage for her. Not near the safari camps, but closer to his home, in the grounds of the homestead area, but independent from him. He had ensured that she would have her own garage and driveway as part of the plan. Her cottage was almost finished, and there would be no happy mother–son time in his house. She would move directly into her own house, and he hoped to see as little of her as he could.

It wasn't that he didn't love his mother, she was just a hard woman to love. Besides, he held her directly responsible for ripping Tara from his life. That he had never been able to forgive or forget.

His mother was a cold fish.

Such a contrast to Gabe's situation.

Gabe looked like he loved having his mother around, and she was so good with Josha. Everyone was so great with Tara, he felt like the intruder.

He stood up and shook his head.

So many mistakes, that both he and Tara had made. But they had a second chance now.

She wasn't having her operation for just under three weeks, and there was a chance that she would be alright afterwards. He had time to get to know her again.

Now he had met Josha there was no way he wasn't going to be part of his son's life.

He looked at Tara.

She'd been the most selfish person he knew for keeping Josha from him, hiding away all those years.

He should hate her.

But he didn't.

He still loved her. A deep love that burnt in his chest, that made him feel ill just thinking about loosing her again. But he felt pity, and sadness too. Pity for who they once were, and how dominated and manipulated he had been by his parents at the time, without realising it. And sadness, for the fact that they had lost so many years when they could have been happy together.

He cleared his throat. Getting rid of the emotion, ensuring that he could talk.

'What day are we planning this trip to Kujana?' he asked.

'I'm happy for it to be this week. We don't have lots of time before the operation, so we might as well go there and see it. See how Josha gets on. He's the most important factor in all this,' Tara said.

Wayne nodded. 'Great.'

'I have a travel agent that does all our booking for the paper, I'll give her a call and she can arrange our side of it,' Gabe said, 'ensure we are all on the same flight into Durban together. I'll get her on the phone. Today is Tuesday the third, let's say Thursday morning, first flight out? Tara, does that work?'

'Yes!' said Josha, punching the air. 'My first time in a plane, and then a helicopter!'

Tara was frowning. 'It's fine. I might snore a bit on the plane when I'm dead to the world from the drugs, but hopefully Josha will close my mouth if it hangs open, won't you my son?'

'Mum! You are so funny!' Josha said and he got up and went and hugged her.

CHAPTER 21

Memories And Nightmares

Cape Town, South Africa
3rd March 1998

While everyone talked around her, Tara took the time to look at Jamison. When she had been introduced to him, she had a feeling that she knew him, he was familiar to her in a way that was unsettling. She knew that she knew him, she just had to rake through her drug-filled brain to find where. He was so familiar …

He looked at her, and he smiled, letting her know he had seen her observing him.

And suddenly she knew.

Last time she had seen him he had been in farm overalls, not dressed like a well-off businessman in a light blue checked shirt and denims. He had opened the gate on the day her father had been shot. He had saved her.

'I know you,' she said looking at him, and she lifted her hand and pointed her finger at him. 'I knew you before …'

'Yes, Miss Tara,' Jamison said and he got up off his chair and walked to her daybed and knelt next to it. 'You know me, Miss Tara, from years ago.'

Wayne stared at Jamison and Tara.

'What did you say your name was?' she asked, a frown creasing her forehead.

'Jamison, but you know me as Shilo. It's been many years, *Imbodla*,' Jamison said, and he dipped his head at her as a sign of respect.

'Oh my God,' she cried. 'It's you. It's really you!'

There was silence in the room as all eyes turned to Jamison and Tara.

'Why, Shilo—Jamison?' she asked. 'Why are you here? Why are you with Wayne?'

'To protect you again,' Jamison said. 'And this time you have two ex-special forces men working together to keep you safe.'

Tara looked at him, taken aback.

'Mum?' Josha asked, moving closer to where she was in her day bed.

Wayne still sat on the bed with her, holding her hand. 'What's going on?'

She looked at Jamison, and then at her son. So much time had passed since that fateful day. She had been just younger than Josha was now, and yet here Shilo was, popping back into her life, and warning her of danger once again.

She looked back at Shilo – Jamison. He nodded to her, as if telling her that now it was alright to talk. It was okay to tell people the truth.

'Josha, come, sit here with me,' she said as she patted her bed next to her. Wayne moved futher down and Josha sat where his mum indicated.

She looked at Jamison. 'All these years, I didn't tell.'

'But you need to now, *Imbodla*, the time has come when the truth needs to be told,' Jamison said.

She turned back to look at Josha. There were so many things in her life she had kept from him. Tried to protect him from. But this man, and what he had done, was heroic, and so she explained simply, 'Shilo saved my life when I was just twelve.'

'Son-of-a-bitch,' Gabe said. 'After all this time, finally we might get another piece in the puzzle.'

'Gabe!' Tara said, glaring at him.

'Well you have always been as tight as a duck's arse about what happened, then suddenly there is a man in my house saying he needs to protect you again. Sorry, Tara, I'm going to go off a little!'

'Calm down, everyone,' Mauve said. 'All this excitement can't be good for Tara's head. Josha come, we are going shopping!'

Tara shook her head. 'No. Mauve, Josha needs to hear this. It's just another secret that should never have been buried in my life.'

Jamison nodded, he adjusted his weight in the chair opposite Tara. 'We cannot face what is to come in this time without the past being known.'

'My son is old enough to hear this,' Tara said as she took one of his hands in hers.

A pregnant silence hovered over the room. All eyes were on Jamison.

'I swore the oath to the motto "*Tiri Tose*". It means "we are together" but it also means "there is no escape", in my native Shona. But I can help Wayne to protect you from him. The man who murdered Tara's father and uncle is obsessed with finding her again, and he still searches for me, and for her. He is coming for you, Miss Tara. He is cunning, and even after all these years he is still *penga*.'

'You know the man who killed Tara's father?' Gabe said.

'Yes, I know him. But he is one of the elite, and he cannot be judged by the law,' Jamison said.

'He's a diplomat?' Gabe asked.

'No,' Jamison said. 'What he is doesn't matter. But what he is capable of, and how we can protect Tara, that is what we need to focus on, now that Wayne has found her again.'

'Okay,' Tara said, but her voice was unsteady, as if thinking of that day so many years before was taking her back to a time in her childhood, a difficult time. A dark hour. 'Care to elaborate a bit on that?'

'He found me again after many years, and Ebony, my wife, was nearly killed. We almost lost our first unborn child that day.'

'I'm so sorry,' Tara said and she squeezed Josha's hand.

'Me too,' Jamison said. 'He is never going to give up on hunting for me. And he still looks for you, Miss Tara. I have someone who watches him – my cousin, Gibson, says he still talks about you. I met Wayne when he was finished at the Recces and he was just beginning building his farm. He became my link to you. A few years later, when the killer found me again, I moved to South Africa. I thought that if Wayne found you, then we should stand a better chance in protecting you, Tara. And now seeing the boy, perhaps the boy too.'

Tara stared, her eyes wide. 'He's after Josha?'

'Why me?' Josha asked.

Jamison tried to calm them with both his hands up in a stop-and-wait action. 'I don't know for sure. Josha looks a bit like Wayne, but he looks more like you when you were that age. This man, he wants you for a trophy, Tara, he needs you dead to help him put a demon to rest.' Jamison paused. He cleared his throat. 'Last time we saw you, Tara, you were swimming in the dam, on the day you said goodbye to Whispering Winds, and Gabe was there, too. But the man, he said you needed to mature a little, you were still too young.'

Gabe stood up.

Tara frowned.

'Jamison, what are you talking about?' Wayne said.

'Wait. You were with the killer. At our dam? Watching *me* swim. This is about me? My father and Uncle Jacob were shot because of me?' Tara asked, as she realised what Jamison was telling her. She took in ragged breaths.

'It was always about you, Miss Tara. From the first time you visited his farm.'

Gabe pulled the wicker chair closer to her bed. He sat down, letting her know that he was there for her, in this time too.

Wayne still sat on the bottom of the bed next to Josha.

Mauve sat next to Jamison on the couch, but she leant forward. Listening.

'Jamison, tell me that it wasn't Buffel,' Tara said quietly, rubbing her spare hand on her forehead.

'Wayne and I can keep you safe from him, and if he finds you again, we can kill him.'

She raised her voice. 'I had tea at his house! He lived right there next door to us!' Tara began to hyperventilate, her breathing erratic, and she clutched at her throat. 'I can't breathe. I can't breathe.'

Wayne was on his feet, standing in front of her, he held her shoulders. 'Breathe with me. Breathe in. Slowly. Breathe out. Slowly. Look at me. Focus on my mouth and breathe with me.'

'Calm down, Tara.' Gabe reached for her hand. He patted it. 'Come on, just breathe with Wayne.'

She took a moment, but soon she was breathing along with Wayne. The suddenly she moaned. 'I think I'm going to be sick!'

Gabe instructed, 'Josha, go fetch Lucretia, tell her to bring some Cyclimorph from the bathroom.' He got the sick bowl from next to her and held it near her mouth just in case, but she only dry heaved.

Josha ran out the room, and soon returned with Lucretia, who shooed everyone out.

Wayne stood in the doorway and watched as the maid stuck a needle into Tara's arm. Within moments, Tara's arm relaxed, and almost dropped off the side of day bed as if she was now passed out. Lucretia lifted her arm and tucked it under the light blanket she spread over her. She wiped her eyes, and stood watching over her charge for a while.

Wayne turned away, his own head imploding from the bombshell that Jamison had just dropped on them. Now not only was Tara in danger of dying, but some madman from her past was hunting her, and perhaps Josha as well.

And Wayne had brought Jamison right to Tara.

Perhaps Tara had been right when she'd hidden herself and Josha from him.

At least then she'd been safe.

He shook his head to dislodge that thought. He didn't believe it. Now that the threat on her life was out in the open, he and Jamison could plan to fortify the security around them.

Together they could protect her and Josha.

Because now that Tara was back in his life, there was no way that he was going to let some madman take her away. Their love had been strong enough to survive all these years apart, to beat all that they had been thrown against, and there was no way he was losing his soul mate now.

CHAPTER 22

The Net Narrows

Cape Town, South Africa
3rd March 1998

Gabe, Wayne and Jamison sat in Gabe's study. Mauve had taken Josha shopping with her to get him out the house while the adults talked. He had gone with her only reluctantly. Wayne would have liked to spend the afternoon with his son, but for the time being he needed to work out what their next move would be against the new threat in Tara's life.

Gabe was sitting behind his desk. It seemed old fashioned in the modern house, with its leather inlay in the top, and its large dark front panel. It dominated the room. The wood shone as if polished often. The desk obviously meant something to Gabe. He even had an antique-looking desk lamp for more light, despite the panoramic sea view one could see through the huge windows.

Jamison stood by the window. His feet apart, his arms crossed.

Wayne sat in one of the leather armchairs, his legs crossed with his foot up, resting on his opposite knee.

Jamison turned from the window. 'I'm sorry, this threat should have waited for your reunion day to be over at least, but I didn't expect her to recognise me after so many years. I thought she would just see me as Wayne's friend, and then, after her operation, when she came back with Josha to visit at the farm, then I could remind her. It wasn't my intention to add to her worry.'

Gabe pushed back in his chair. 'In all honesty, Jamison, I think it's a relief to her to know you are here. That day is like a noose around her neck, and it tightens every year that goes by with her father's killer still out there. She's good at her job as a consulting psychologist, but I think she would have been a better police investigator. She often helps me with research, and she's sharp. She's wanted to return to Zimbabwe so many times and look for you, and I have always talked her out of it. I'm glad now I did, hearing the little bit of what's happened, but I am dying to hear more of your side of the story.'

'Me too,' said Wayne.

'I'm sorry, Wayne,' Jamison said. 'I couldn't tell you and see you go through even more anguish while you looked for her, knowing that he might have got to her first. I couldn't do that to you.'

'I understand, sort of,' Wayne said. 'It's just been a hell of a twenty-four-hour ride. Find Tara. Meet Josha, then be told that not only could she still die after her operation, but there is a madman after her.'

'And perhaps Josha,' Jamison corrected. 'I wish he didn't look so like her. His age now is what she was when he first tried to kill her. But I don't think he's mad, I think he is mentally unstable. Sometimes he's in control, other times he is vacant.'

'Oh, whatever you do, don't use those words near Tara, she will think she can fix him!' Gabe said.

'No one can fix him,' Jamison said shaking his head. 'He is missing some pieces inside.'

'Pieces. My God! The girls. I might be right!' Gabe said suddenly as he began opening drawers in his desk, looking for something.

'What girls?' Wayne asked.

Gabe slammed another drawer closed. 'Buffel. He might be the same killer we have been looking for. I saw the pattern in the description of the girls, but dismissed it. We thought we were only seeing it because we were thinking of Josha!'

'I don't understand what you're talking about,' Wayne said.

'Me neither,' Jamison said.

Gabe looked around frantically, then he grabbed a file off the pile on his desk and opened it. 'Look,' he said. 'It's the pattern. They look the same as Tara looked when she was about twelve. They all have blue eyes, blonde hair. They are all slight in build.'

'What is that file?' Jamison asked.

'This is a story I have been working on for a few years,' Gabe said. 'This is Tara's and my file on a collection of disappearances here in South Africa. It's a personal file, not an official investigation by the paper yet, but something that I have had a gut feeling about for years, so I kept trying to find out more. These are the girls I was talking about. The lost white girls of South Africa.'

He took out a packet of smaller files from inside. He laid them on the desk. The pictures told the story. 'All these girls have been abducted and never found.'

Jamison sat on the couch. Guilt heavy on his shoulders. 'If this is his work, I should have stopped him.'

'No one can stop someone who is like him, Jamison, except himself,' Wayne said.

'I second that, you can't babysit a grown man,' Gabe said. 'Something has always drawn me to these girls, Tara and I discussed it and she thought it was because they looked like she did when she was younger.'

Wayne said, 'I remember seeing some of these on milk cartons years ago, and turning the carton around because I thought that too, but I always assumed I was just a lovesick boy, and that's why they looked like Tara to me.'

'This is just my theory, none of it is substantiated,' Gabe began, and he explained how he had grouped the girls, and how Tara had profiled the killer.

'We suspect he either has undiagnosed PTSD and is trying to control it himself, or he is a psychopath. Tara wants it to be the first theory because she thinks that the man needs help and compassion, not a lethal injection.'

'He's a killer and my biggest regret is that I never put him out of his misery that day when I realised he was hunting Tara a second time,' Jamison said. 'Tara was the real target on the day her father and uncle were murdered. She should have been killed. Only she didn't know that. I was too late to save her family, but because of her father's well-trained war horse she was taken away from the murder scene fast. I could help her when she became trapped like a rabbit at the gate, but I couldn't save her family. I didn't get there in time, I couldn't run fast enough through the bush to stop him.'

Wayne sat on the edge of his chair. 'Her father was murdered and she was there?'

'She never told you?' Gabe said.

'Once she said to me that she'd seen so many things that she should never have seen, but I didn't think it was anything like that. She said her father died, and that's why her family came to South Africa. At the time I never asked for more details. I was a teenager – details weren't important.'

'So,' Gabe said, 'Jamison, you need to fill in a few more details about this man, and if he is the killer then we need to get the authorities—'

'No police. No one can know that we are onto him, he is elite. The law doesn't touch him. The reach of PSYOPS is far and wide, it runs in Zimbabwe and South Africa, and spreads overseas like a disease. If one of us talk about our own, they will silence us, permanently.'

Gabe stared at Jamison. 'Tell me you were not from the 1st PSYOPS unit in the Rhodesian army.'

'I cannot,' Jamison said.

'Shit!' Gabe said.

'What the hell! Jamison, do I know you at all?' Wayne said. 'PSYOPS!'

'You know me better than any other man except my childhood friend Kwazi,' Jamison said. 'But I could not put you in danger and increase your worry for Tara for no reason. That is why you never knew my true background.'

Wayne hung his head. 'How did Tara get mixed up with PSYOPS?'

'By accident. What I tell you stays in this room. I put my life on the line here for breaking my oath.' Jamison checked with each of them as they nodded. 'And only to save Tara.'

'I was a paratrooper, but PSYOPS sort of adopted us into their unit after a mission, after we had seen things. Bad things.' He rubbed his eyes as if trying to scrub the memories away. 'After the war ended, we were integrated back into society. Some men, they went to South Africa, some went back to their normal jobs, or were put into other jobs in high places. No one knew that they had ever been part of such a unit. But I knew that one man in the unit wouldn't integrate and would keep killing. And he almost always killed the children, those on the edge of adulthood.

'So I looked out for the children in Nyanandhlovu, and kept them away, made sure I was constantly with him, and that he did not get close to any child. Except one day Madam Maggie came from next door, and she brought Tara with her. And then the killing started again. Only this time, he realised that I knew what he had done, and the crime was not covered by any war crimes pardon. In a moment of – I don't know what it was, he let me leave the farm. But he realised later his mistake, and he began to look for me. In 1992 he found me, and he hurt Ebony. He was trying to shut me up, but he needed to know first if I knew where Tara was. We ran, I took Ebony from the hospital, and I fled to somewhere he wouldn't find us. Then, when Ebony was better, we moved to Wayne's farm. I know he will find me again, it's just a matter of time. And now that Wayne has found Tara …'

'But why Tara?' Wayne asked. 'I don't understand, what did she do?'

'At first, she did nothing. It's not about her, it's about him and his demon. But it is also because she saw him, even if she can't remember it. She knows who killed her father. She can identify him. She is a witness.'

'Oh, I wish Tara was up to listening to this, she is going to be so angry when she hears it,' Gabe said.

'If she involves the police, if you try to use my word against his, I will be killed for breaking the PSYOPS oath. He is like a jackal, he is cunning, and patient, and he will disappear. Then we will never find him. At least for now I have a cousin who is with him most of the time. A tracker, he is also a little *penga* in the head, so he doesn't mind being there. He has lived with him for more years than I ever did. I mostly know where he is and when he leaves his farm.'

'If it is Buffel, then he is the best lead we have so far. Look at this timeline. If what you say is true, then it started after Tara left Zimbabwe and came to South Africa. He knew she was coming here, everyone knew. And he followed, only he couldn't find her, so he takes a substitute …'

'It's far-fetched,' Wayne said. 'Jamison, why does he still want to kill Tara, and why Josha?'

'My cousin says that he dreams a lot now, and he rants around his house and his mushroom shed about finding his light-haired angel Tara to save someone called Impendla. But Josha because he looks like a younger Tara, and because he is the right age now that he always used to kill.'

'Impendla. I know that name,' Gabe said, and he began looking through his files on his desk again, only this time he didn't find the file he was after. 'Dammit! The article I'm looking for is at work.'

'How can we protect them from him?' Wayne asked Jamison.

'If we do like I did for years, we just hide. Stay out of the paper. He doesn't know where she is, and now she has us to protect her in case he finds her, and just like Goronga and Moeketsi watch over Ebony while I'm away, we give Tara and Josha each an armed guard. Their own militia.'

'Who are Goronga and Moeketsi?' Gabe asked.

'Anti-poaching game guards, professional hunters. Part of our team at Kujana,' Wayne said.

'Ah,' Gabe said.

'Our problem is still if he finds Tara, then what?' Wayne asked.

'I shoot him between his eyes this time, put him out of his misery, so that he can never hurt another child, and never hurt my Ebony or your Tara again,' Jamison said.

CHAPTER 23

Stolen Moments At Kujana

Kujana Farm, Hluhluwe, South Africa
5th March 1998

Flying into the farm, Ryan buzzed the small airstrip, and the small herd of zebra grazing on the field scattered in all directions, a confusion of black and white as they trotted away, flicking their tails angrily at the disturbance.

The Squirrel touched down, and Wayne helped Tara with her harness.

A smiling black driver in khaki overalls leant against a green Land Rover. He pushed off as the rotor blades stopped.

'Moeketsi,' Wayne called to him, motioning with his hand out of the front door.

'*Baas*,' he greeted. Moeketsi opened the back door, and as he let the small steps down, Josha tumbled out the helicopter first in excitement. He turned to help his mum.

She stepped out and onto the grass.

It had been many years since she was in Hluhluwe, and the first thing that hit her was the heat. Already she could feel the sweat as it trickled down her back, and made her T-shirt stick to her. Wayne walked with her to the waiting vehicle and helped her into the front seat. Josha followed shortly, loaded down with two of their bags, and Moeketsi close behind him, similarly laden. Gabe was helping Lucretia out of the back, and then walking slowly with her towards the *bakkie*.

'It looks amazing, like we are in the National Park,' Tara said quietly. 'It's beautiful.'

'This is Kujana as I run it. Not my father's sugarcane farm anymore,' Wayne said.

'I think I like it so far,' she said.

Wayne stroked Tara's short hair. 'I'll be as fast as I can,' he said, 'I need to help Ryan tie down, then we can go to the house but we can go via the camps, they are worth seeing.'

Wayne, Ryan and Moeketsi moved the helicopter into the hangar and came back out, closed the door, and walked to the *bakkie*. Moeketsi got in the back of the modified safari Land Rover with its multiple rows of seats, sitting next to Josha, and Wayne climbed in the front. He started the engine and they drove towards the main camp.

'*Holy moley!*' Josha said.

The giraffe that was on the side of the road was practically in touching distance, and it turned towards the vehicle as if to see what was disturbing its afternoon snack on the acacia tree it chewed on.

Moeketsi laughed. 'That giraffe is *indlulamithi*, can you say that?'

'Inda— what?' asked Josha.

'*Indlulamithi*,' Moeketsi laughed again, 'you will learn fast, *Inkosana* Josha. You will learn.'

They drove further and then stopped as they came into the safari camp.

Tara held her breath. The camp looked like it was right out of a tourist brochure. The main building appeared to be built of stone, then timber, and was topped with a large thatch roof. The scattered chalets, all eight of them, were strategically placed so that they couldn't be seen into. They nestled among the large wild fig trees that dominated the site, all overlooking a large pan, filled with water.

Ducks swam on the glassy surface, but no game gathered around at midday, instead keeping to the trees and the shade to hide from the African sun.

They drove past the camp and up a road that said, *Private No Trespassing*. They went past a few small thatched cottages also neatly placed within the trees. Tara noticed that there was what looked like a new home being constructed nearby. Like the lodge, it was built of stone, roughly hewn trees and thatch, but it looked more like a home than a lodge. It had a large veranda running the whole way around it, and a red tricycle lay on the lawn next to a bright pink swing set.

'That's Jamison and Ebony's new home,' Wayne said. 'They have moved in, but the construction isn't totally finished. We wanted Ebony to have her own new home for the arrival of Joy.'

'It's beautiful,' Tara said.

'Don't be fooled by the rustic look, it's totally modern inside, and now I know why Jamison was so insistent on that top-of-the-range alarm system, and the extra electric fencing.'

'I still can't quite believe that that killer will still come for me,' Tara said.

'If Jamison is worried, so am I. We'll do everything to pump up security and keep him out.' Wayne's jaw set at a determined angle as he continued driving, knowing that Jamison wasn't too far behind them. He had gone on a shopping trip for Ebony, before driving home from Durban.

They came to a place that Tara recognised. The original sheds from the sugarcane farm still stood proudly, huge enough to hold a harvester, trucks and trailers. Then they rounded the bend and she could see Wayne's house.

Only this time, there was something different about it, two large Rhodesian Ridgeback dogs, bounding down the driveway towards them.

'Max and Sheba,' Wayne said as he stopped the *bakkie,* and opened his door. The dogs almost yelped with happiness, but not quite, their tails lashing the metal of the vehicle in their excitement of seeing their master. They licked Wayne's face, and then Sheba attempted to cross the seat to Tara.

'No. Down,' Wayne instructed. 'Out!' The dog listened and jumped nimbly back to the ground, but they both continued to stare at Wayne with amber eyes, and wagging tails that could have been declared lethal weapons they wagged so fast from side to side. Their paws didn't quite stay stationary on the floor, almost looking cat-like in their kneading of the ground as they moved in excitement.

On the steps to the building, along with an old border collie whose tail thumped excitedly, waited two black women. The older one was dressed in stylish clothes, like an office worker. She walked down to the *bakkie* as it stopped in front of the house. She was smiling.

'Welcome home, Wayne,' she said, and then she put her hand to her mouth. '*My wena*. He looks so like you—'

'Ella, meet my son, Josha. This is Ella, she was my nanny when I was just a boy, and she's still hanging around me,' he said with such adoration that Tara could tell these two people meant a lot to each other.

'And meet Nomusa, she looks after me now.' The younger woman, dressed in a black and white pressed maid's uniform, bobbed a customary Zulu curtsey.

'Ella, remember Tara?' Wayne asked.

'I remember you, many many years ago. You stole *khosan*-Wayne's heart,' Ella said with a smile on her face.

Tara smiled weakly. 'Would you forgive me if I told you I'm bringing it home today?'

Tears filled her old eyes.

'This is Gabe, and this is Lucretia.'

The introductions completed, Wayne led Tara through the front door and the lounge to a chair on the veranda. 'Have a seat.'

'Thanks. It's all so lovely.'

The border collie padded across and sat near her. 'Hello old girl,' Wayne said, 'Tara, meet Storm.'

Tara reached down and stroked the dog's soft muzzle.

He left her, and took their luggage from Moeketsi behind him.

'Lucretia, I'll show you where Tara's room is so you can get Nomusa to change anything that isn't as you need it.'

'*Yebo*,' Nomusa said as she followed him. Josha trailed behind him with his bags.

'Josha,' Wayne yelled.

'Right here,' he said from behind him.

'Sorry, I thought you were on the veranda still. This is your room.' He pointed to a closed door. 'Your mum is the next door down the corridor.'

'Thanks,' Josha said and turned the old-fashioned brass knob.

Josha walked into a time warp. Something from a hunting lodge of the 1800s he was sure. A mosquito net covered the bed. The room was decorated in mahogany and dark green, with a ducks and hunting dogs frieze. The wallpaper was distinctive broad vertical stripes from a picture rail downwards, and above the rail was a lighter teal colour. As rooms went, it was big. An old-fashioned writing bureau graced the corner, with its lid closed, a duck-shaped lamp sitting on a tall three-legged stool beside it.

The chair at the bureau was amazing. Josha walked over to it and ran his had over the wood. It arms and back was intricately carved with elephant heads, and the tusks that seemed made of real ivory were inlaid into the carvings. The cut out in the back and seat of the chair were made of some type of flat rope in a lattice pattern. The carvings carried on down the legs, and the feet of the elephant were carved at the base. The whole chair had a 3D effect as if it were the elephant.

'Man, what a chair!' he said.

Josha was too afraid it would break if he sat on it. He put his bag next to the bureau, and walked over to the old-fashioned wardrobe. It had a single oval mirror on the outside of the door, and didn't smell like mothballs as he'd expected it to.

Josha spent hours going around the antique markets with Mauve, and he knew quality antiques when he saw them. Wayne's house was loaded with them.

'So, what do you think?' Wayne asked from the door. 'Other than needing a new wardrobe to fit all your stuff, is it okay?'

'It's great, thanks.'

'Hey, you don't need to lie to me. First rule you and I need to make, no lying. Honesty always. We can redo it. It was the interior decorator who suggested this theme when she did the rest of the house years ago. I just went along with it as I didn't have anything better to suggest at the time. After seeing your room in Cape Town, I know we have work to do in here to make it yours. I want you to feel that you have a room at my house that you can call yours. That you will look at this as home one day too.'

Josha looked at Wayne. He hadn't pushed him into unwanted hugs or calling him Dad or anything, he had been amazing, despite Josha being a bit narky to him sometimes because he was uncomfortable with the notion of suddenly having a dad in his life.

'It's a nice room. Neat chair! Where did you get that?'

'That chair has been in my father's family for years. I remember him telling me about his grandad bargaining with a merchant from Zanzibar for it. I used it when I was at school, and I put it in your room. In case—'

'It's stunning. Mauve would do her nut for it.'

'It's not for sale. Some things are meant to stay within a family,' Wayne said.

'I get that. You should see this one bureau that she got, seventeenth century cherry wood, beautiful as—'

'You like antiques?'

'Sure. I love history and art, and they are just part of someone's past. Like your chair, every piece has a story for the family it belonged too,' Josha explained.

Wayne looked at his son. He was so much more than he could have ever hoped for. A surprise package to get to know.

'So where's your room?' Josha asked as he walked to the door.

'My room is up the hall on the left. Here is your bathroom across the hallway, there, and you will share it with your mum. Gabe has his own, and so does Lucretia.' Wayne pointed to other closed doors further up the way.

'Cool, thanks.'

Wayne ran his left hand through his hair. 'I hope you don't freak out at this gift, I wanted to give you this.' He held out his right hand and opened his palm. 'I made this bracelet in 1990, after I learned about you, and when I first met Jamison, he taught me how. I have always worn mine, to give me hope that one day I would be able to find you and hand over yours, and Tara's. To me they are a symbol of hope.'

Josha took the bracelet. 'Thanks. I have seen the basic elephant hair ones, but never with silver knots in them.'

Wayne watched as he put it on and adjusted the circles of hair to fit.

'Will you teach me?' Josha asked. 'To make one?'

'It would be my pleasure. We just need to go collect the strands of hair from the dam where they swim one day.'

'Seriously?'

'Yes.'

'Neat,' Josha said.

They walked back out to the veranda together.

Tara was asleep in a chair, her head at a strange angle. Wayne looked around for something to help make her more comfortable. Finding an ample supply of cushions embroidered with wildlife, he puffed one up, and then changed his mind. He lifted her up in his arms instead.

'You rest up, Tara, you're home,' Wayne said, as he felt tears swell up in his eyes. He kissed her forehead and felt the softness of her hair as it brushed his face as he carried her inside.

Home had never had such meaning before, and now they would only share it as a family for such a small time, it was even more important that he needed to do anything to protect both Tara and Josha, so that they could stay together.

Wayne lay Tara down on the sofa, then manoeuvred himself to hold her, cradle her head in his lap.

'She's exhausted,' Gabe said, as he came into the room and sat opposite Wayne. 'Can't believe she stayed awake so long. It's been awhile since she was able to do that.'

'She never even murmured when I moved her.' He stroked her hair.

'What are you guys going to do?' Gabe asked.

'Just get through the next two and a bit weeks. Jamison will get in touch with his cousin, see how things are going in Zimbabwe, and then we'll see after the operation.'

'Hey, Wayne, can I go out with the dogs?' Josha asked.

'Sure. Moeketsi is waiting for you outside, he'll be your guide while you are here when I can't be with you, and he'll show you around if you like,' Wayne said.

'Thanks, see ya,' Josha called as he was already racing out the front door.

'You have been amazing about your situation, do you know that?' Gabe said.

'Not so amazing. Moeketsi followed Jamison here from Zimbabwe, he's a PH, and as loyal as hell. He would die before he let any harm come to my son,' Wayne said in defence.

'PH?'

'Professional hunter,' Wayne said.

'Ah, but that wasn't what I meant. I was meaning more with the whole Josha and Tara thing.'

Wayne grinned. 'You have no idea how hard it's been. But having them in my life now makes it all worth it.'

'No, I can guess though. You are a good man, Wayne Botha. Just accepting Tara's extended family along with her.'

'You got that word right. Family. It's something I had lacked for a while,' he said. 'And if you are Tara's family now, then you are always welcome at my home. She and I still have unfinished business, but it can wait. It's waited so many years already.'

'Don't wait,' Gabe said, 'don't waste more time. You guys both deserve to be happy.'

'So easy to say, but so complicated. What about Josha?'

'You seriously think that Josha can't see the obvious love between you guys there? In the three days since you came back into her life, she has a glow in her that wasn't there before.'

Wayne smiled. He looked down at Tara sleeping in his lap. He bent down and kissed her softly on the mouth.

Tara woke in Wayne's arms.

'I've dreamt of this for years,' she said, as she tried to sit up.

'You can stay there if you want to,' Wayne said, 'I'm comfy with you on my lap.'

'Sweet Wayne, but what will Josha say?' She struggled to sit up and he helped her.

He threaded his fingers through hers and held her hand instead. Sitting close to her felt right. He felt as if he was complete.

'Josha left with Moeketsi to go exploring. He's a teenage boy on a game farm, with two protective dogs and time to explore. I let him go.'

'He's going to love it here. And your beautiful dogs, he'll love them, but Gabe, not so much. He isn't a fan of dogs.'

Wayne smiled.

'Talking about Gabe, where is he?'

'Upstairs in his room. He wanted to go over the file again. See if he missed anything, if he can put another piece in his puzzle, is what he said.'

Tara smiled.

'So it's just us. At last,' Wayne said.

'This room is different from when your parents lived here. I like it better.'

'I want you and Josha to be comfortable here,' Wayne said.

'But we have a home in Cape Town,' Tara said, and frowned.

Wayne traced the frown with his fingers and waited for her to relax a little. 'This can be a second home if you want it to. I told you I would love you always and forever and I meant it. I always dreamt one day, you would come home to me.' He took a deep shaky breath. 'And I can't believe you are really here.'

She snuggled into his side and she looked at the mantlepiece. 'You have the photos I sent the lawyer's firm.'

'My dad gave them to me in a letter when he died.'

'I was only supposed to send one when Josha was born,' she said, 'but then I couldn't not share a part of him with you, so I sent the others. I was never sure that your father got them, or if you would ever get them in the end.'

'When my father died, he told me in his will that he had set you and Josha up, and I got the photographs. He said he was sorry that he wasn't a grandfather who could be involved in Josha's life.'

'I'm sorry too. There were so many people affected, each so differently. I never imagined, at sixteen, that the fallout from our decisions then would have such far-reaching consequences. I thought I saw him once, your father, watching us in the park, but I wasn't sure,' Tara said.

'He never said if he saw Josha in real life in his letter. But if he did know where you were, he never told anyone. Not even his lawyers. They had a private investigator search for you for years.'

They sat in silence for a while, Wayne remembering the moment when he got his hands on the photos.

'You must have really hated me that you kept Josha from me too,' Wayne said.

She pushed herself away from him. Firmly but gently. She looked at him.

He combed his fingers through his hair. He couldn't control his tears any longer, they bubbled over the lump in his throat and into his eyes, and he didn't care. 'I loved you, and you broke off all contact. You didn't even let me know I was a father.'

He watched her as real pain crossed her face, and tears spilled over her cheeks. But he continued, he needed her to understand. 'My mother told me when they dropped me off at Hilton Boarding School that you had gone away and had the abortion anyway. I had no knowledge of Josha, not until my father died.'

He hated that he was hurting her by talking about something that happened so many years ago, when they had said that they wouldn't, but it had to be said.

'I'm so sorry,' she sobbed. 'I believed you when you first broke up with me, believed that I had to go away, but the longer I was away, the more I realised that you were being made to choose between your father and me by your mother. I wanted to contact you, let you know, but I couldn't do that to you. I couldn't make you choose. I couldn't be the one to destroy your family. I know how special your friendship with your dad was. And he had made sure that no one could take my baby from me. We were safe. Your dad had made sure of that. He'd made sure that I was so far away that she would never attempt to take my baby. Your mother used to be powerful in this community, if she chose to take our baby she could have, and not many people would have stood up to stop her. Your dad had me sign a contract not to contact you until I was twenty-one.' She took a ragged breath. 'I felt so guilty for taking his money and being paid off like a baby machine, but at the time, it gave me a financial freedom from dependency on my family, and Gabe and I were able to start a new life. He could be the male in the house, and I could finish school, still go to university and make a life for Josha and I. Lucretia looked after Josha, she watched him as if he were her own. The years just passed so fast. But as they passed, it was harder to contact you, harder to reach over the void that was between us.' She paused, but continued, her voice still thick with emotion. 'I couldn't forget that you hadn't had enough strength to stand up to your mother, that you had given up on us. You didn't fight for us then, you didn't want us.'

He couldn't see her in this type of pain. 'I was wrong. So wrong,' he said.

Wayne wanted to punch something. Someone. Emotion boiled, making his hands shake. But he knew that it wasn't anger, it was disappointment that they had wasted so much of their lives apart. Now they might be counting what was left of their hours together. 'I can only apologise that I was just a boy. You are right, I should have fought for us more, stood up to my mother for what I believed in, for what I wanted. In the end she packed me off to boarding school anyway, something my father had always been against, and drove a huge wedge in my friendship I once had with my dad. Our family fractured apart after you left. But I can't change the past. I don't know what you want me to do about that, because all I want to do is focus on us now that we have found each other again, and now that Josha is in my life.'

She reached a hand and laid it softly against his cheek. 'So much pain for both of us, and yet we found each other again eventually.'

'We did. And our son is happy and balanced. You did such a great job. I just saw my son run out the door to explore, so keen to have an adventure. This time, I chose to stay inside with you rather than to see his face as he explores. Yet it brings it home how I didn't see his first step, or hear his first word. I don't know my son from any other teenage boy. Yet I can never hate you for that.'

'Okay, But tell me one thing, Wayne. Do you honestly still really love me?'

'No, I travelled halfway around South Africa to argue with you because I have nothing better to do with my time. Of course I still love you, Tara. I already told you that in Cape Town.' He put his hand over hers, threading their fingers together, then he brought her hand over his heart.

Tara smiled. 'We're all going to stay here for the next fifteen days, we need to settle him in and spend time together as a family. If the worst happens and I don't make it out of this operation, as much as Gabe loves him, Josha needs to be with you.'

Wayne froze, stock-still as if he was a kudu caught in headlight. 'You sure?'

He saw her nod.

He sniffed. 'I've carried a torch for you for so long. I told you years ago, I would love you always and forever, and I meant it. Do you still love me?'

'I've never been with another man all these years. My heart has always belonged to you, so if you and I can have even one more chance, then I'm taking it. Maybe we'll get it right this time and I won't be stubborn and let my pride get in the way. Surely there is no time in the next two weeks to make a botch of it? And afterwards, if

I make it, we'll sort something out, because I'm not sure that I want you out my life now that you are back in it.'

He breathed deeply. Looked up at the ceiling.

They had both made so many mistakes. But they had another chance now. They were together, and now he had Josha. He looked at Tara.

He had always thought that he should hate her, yet now he realised that she probably was thinking she should hate him. He was glad that they were no longer stuck in their never-ending circle of regret and that now they could get on with reacquainting themselves with each other.

Now he had more to lose than ever.

Now the skill of the neurosurgeon mattered because he wasn't going to give her up so easily the second time.

And as for the man who hunted his family, he had to get past not only Wayne and Jamison, but Gabe, and all his workers too. He had already put his anti-poaching guards on high alert, and told them that a white man was trying to cause trouble with his family. Jamison wouldn't give them any more details, but Tara and Gabe had searched their childhood memories and Gabe had even done a sketch of the suspected killer that all the guards carried with them, just in case.

CHAPTER 24

The Eye Of The Storm

Kujana Farm, Huhluwe, South Africa
12th March 1998

Wayne's back ached from the long drive and his eyes felt like someone had thrown sand in them, having driven the last five hours from Gauteng back to Kujana while Jamison slept in the bunk in the truck, and Josha sat in the front seat, still staring out the window, looking at everything passing by.

'We are almost there,' Wayne said. 'We made good time, we're on Kujana and it's only four o'clock.'

'I can't believe we drove all those animals to Musina and then back in two days. Uncle Gabe hates driving out of Cape Town to Stellenbosch for a weekend, and we drove all that way,' Josha said.

It was Wayne's turn to drive. Jamison had driven from Musina to Gauteng, now he drove home to Hluhluwe. He avoided rubbing his eyes for relief, knowing that was never the intelligent option. It had been a hard overnight trip away from home.

'Its just part of the job,' Wayne said. But he grinned at his son, glad that he had impressed him.

He and Jamison had driven the largest and newest addition of their game relocation Mack trucks from a local game auction up to a farm outside Musina, near Zimbabwe. Four other relocation trucks had been in convoy with them, all belonging to Wild Translocation. Now his fleet were all home again. It had been a big delivery, but worth it.

He smiled when he saw the house.

'We're home, buddy,' he said.

'That was awesome,' Josha said.

'I'm glad you enjoyed yourself. And I'm glad your mother let you come with me to see what I do in my spare time.' He grinned as he let the exhaust brakes out, making an unnecessary noise, but knowing that Josha loved the sound.

Josha saw his mum standing on the veranda. He opened the door and all but fell out in his eagerness to tell her about his adventure, teenage excitement once again getting the better of his growing body.

Wayne smiled. His son had an infectious disposition, and was hardly ever sullen. He was easy to get on with and even though he ought to be near dead with tiredness, he was bursting with energy.

'Come on, old man,' he said to Jamison. 'You're home. Ebony and the girls just arrived in your *bakkie* to take you to your house. Goronga is on the back, he's doing a great job and sticking to her like glue.'

Jamison climbed out the back area, awake and rearing to go. 'Thanks, it has been a blast. I will see you tomorrow, I am taking the rest of the day off.'

Wayne smiled. Jamison hated spending time away from Ebony, and now that he understood why, he couldn't blame him. He remembered the nightmare the couple had gone through when they had almost lost their first unborn child, and he shook his head, trying to dislodge the imaginary smell of fire and sound of screaming from his brain.

'I wouldn't expect anything else,' he said as Jamison strode across to Ebony. He scooped up Blessing as she ran towards him, and then threw his other arm around Ebony and Joy and spun them around. His excitement in seeing them was evident to all.

And for the first time, Wayne knew that feeling of wanting to be home, and in the arms of someone you loved.

He looked out the windscreen at Tara.

Josha was standing next to her and Gabe, his arms wide open as he gestured about something. Tara was smiling, and Gabe was nodding. Lucretia stood a little off to the side and she was laughing. Ella was with her, the two of them seemed to have struck up a friendship since Lucretia had arrived.

His family.

Moeketsi nodded to him, as if he was changing over shifts, now that they were home, and he waved at him, glad that they had him and his game guards with them to help watch over his family day and night.

He saw Tara look behind him, down the farm road, and he checked in the mirror of his truck. His mother's car drove in behind him, and he remembered that despite the calm that had existed for a week at their home, his mother was about to blow a hole in it the size of the *groot gat* in Kimberly.

He scrambled to get out the truck and greet Tara, to be by her side before the hurricane from hell descended on them.

'Hello, Isabeth,' Wayne said as she walked up to them. 'You remember Tara, and this is my son, Josha.'

Isabeth was silent.

'Hello,' Tara said and she held out her hand to shake his mother's hand. Despite everything, Tara was not one to hold grudges or to be a snob, and she wasn't going to be rude.

'Yes, I remember,' Isabeth said, but she ignored Tara's hand.

Tara looked at Wayne, who just rolled his eyes. And she smiled at him, threading her fingers in his as they watched Isabeth turn her eyes to Josha.

Josha stared at her. He had been told about his biological grandmother, and Tara had explained to him that she was arriving, and prepped him for that arrival, but it was clear he had decided that he was not going to be the one who was nice to her, afterall this was the woman who had wanted him dead.

'I guess you are your father's son, you do look a bit like him,' she said.

'Isabeth,' Wayne cautioned in a voice cold like stone. 'You behave here, or you are out. I thought I made myself clear on the phone. There is no place for you here if you are rude, insulting or in anyway damaging to *my* family.'

'Oh Wayne, I thought you were just being unkind and mean to me as always,' Isabeth said.

'No. I laid it down straight. Now perhaps you want to try that again. Hello, Isabeth, remember Tara, and this is my son, Josha,' Wayne said, his voice hard as steel.

Tara had never heard him use that tone. They had talked at length about his mother's betrayal, about how she had used Wayne as a weapon against his father, and insisted Tara shouldn't be allowed to have their baby, about her betrayal of her own son, her lie to him, telling him that she knew that Tara had had an abortion. They had come to the conclusion that Isabeth had projected all her own guilt from her teenage abortion onto Tara and that she had sent her own son to boarding school purposely to destroy the relationship between him and his father. They had spoken about her consistently manipulative behaviour. And about the likelihood that her unreasonable behaviour towards Tara would continue, unless Wayne actively stood up to her and told her that her behaviour was unacceptable. He now needed to set some barriers, and put rules in place to ensure she didn't try and railroad their family in the present as she had in the past. But Tara hadn't expected the open animosity.

Isabeth put her hand out and shook Tara's hand. Then she turned to Josha. 'You are almost as tall as your father,' she said and she stuck out her hand to him.

Josha shook hers. But Tara noticed that her son looked uncomfortable. Unsure of the woman. His experience with grannies was Mauve and Maggie, both of whom were fun and compassionate and warm people. Even Aunty Marie-Ann had softened as she got older, and she spoilt Josha rotten. After levelling with the teenage Tara about being a teenage mum herself, and being the one to give Tara a place of refuge while she and Gabe took their time in relocating to Cape Town, Aunty Marie-Ann's and Tara's own relationship was now one of friendship, no longer any animosity between them.

But Isabeth was like a cold reptile.

Tara wondered how Wayne had turned out so great after having lived for so long with this woman while he was growing up.

Isabeth turned to Gabe, and Tara was astonished as she witnessed Isabeth's whole attitude change towards an attractive man. She might be getting on in years, but she was still predatory.

'I'm Isabeth,' she said and she put her hand out for Gabe to shake.

'Gabe,' he said, but he looked over at Wayne for help as she didn't let his hand go afterwards.

'And this is Lucretia, Tara's companion,' Wayne introduced her to Lucretia, who everyone could see bristled with contempt at the woman. 'Mother, your timing was impeccable as always. Nomusa will help you with your bags, in your house. Your driveway is past the shed. You won't miss it. Ella already filled your fridge and cupboards with necessary groceries, so you should be self-sufficient.'

She smiled, and then began to turn away.

'If you would like to join us for dinner at seven o'clock, you are most welcome,' Tara said.

'That would be nice, thank you,' Isabeth said, but the warmth didn't reach her eyes then she turned away again to move into her new home.

Josha walked away talking to Gabe, the two of them heading for the barn together, Josha calling out for Moeketsi. Wayne's young dogs were bounding around him. Happy to have him home.

Home.

Such a small word that in a few days had come to mean so much to her, and to Josha.

Tara rounded on Wayne the moment everyone was out of earshot. 'That was mean, dressing her down in front of us!'

'That was necessary. Tara, I don't know where you find it in your heart to be civil to her after what she put you through, but I have told you about my mother and my relationship with her. Yes, she's family, but my father was the one who taught me that you look after family. My mother is difficult, and I told you already, her lies hurt us, and I can't forgive her for that,' Wayne said. 'If I had allowed her to be rude to you and Josha now, it would have continued forever. I know my mother. She would try and walk all over you. But if she knows that she can't cross me on this issue, she will toe the line and behave. You don't need more stress while you are here, and my mother is the queen of creating stress.'

Tara nodded, giving Wayne the benefit of the doubt, and in fact she was too excited to have him home after his trip away to argue.

'You should forgive her, Wayne, because that unhealthy grudge hurts you more than her. She's obviously self-centred and oblivious to your feelings, so why waste energy on them? She isn't going to change, ever. People don't change as they get older, they get more set in their ways. You have taken a big step in the right direction with her, you have set down boundaries. Drawn the battleline in the sand, as you might say. She knows now where she stands, but also where she needs to tread more carefully,' Tara said.

'Is there a price to pay for your professional analysis?' he asked, but he was grinning, lightening the heavy mood as he teased her.

'A kiss,' she answered.

He gathered her to him, bent his head to her and kissed her. Slowly at first, he tested her lips with his, and then again, reacquainting himself with her. He breathed in her smell, so unique. Different from the girl he loved, the woman he was kissing now smelled of an exotic fragrance, and he inhaled it, and loved her even more.

'I think I need a lie down,' she said a little breathlessly a moment later. 'Come, Wayne, we can see everyone at dinner.' Her hand in his, she led him upstairs. She didn't stop at her room, but continued to his. Wayne hesitated at the door. But then she opened it and said, 'Surprise!'

She had moved her suitcase into the room, and left a few of her things on his dressing table, making sure that it looked more like a room that they shared than a masculine single man's room. She had moved in a lighter colour rug to the end of the bed, and she had piled the pillows from her guestroom on his bed.

Wayne could hardly breathe.

'Are you sure, Tara? This is a big step, this is a big statement to make to Josha,' Wayne said hesitantly.

'I'm sure. We could have just over a week left together, or we could be starting something that I want to last forever. I've never been surer of anything in my life, and I want you to hurry up in that shower. I have about another hour before I'm going to need more meds, and I want to make the most of this time we have together.'

Wayne stared at her.

'Are you one hundred percent on this, Tara? I can't go back to being just friends, to a platonic friendship like you have with Gabe. Once we cross over this line, I know I'm not going to ever want to go back. I don't think I'm strong enough to go back again.'

'I'm sure. I planned this all, remember, while you were gone for two days. I moved my things in, I have been thinking of nothing else for forty-eight hours. Now hurry,' she said, 'you are wasting precious time!'

Wayne dashed into the shower in the ensuite, and couldn't clean up fast enough. When he got out, he rubbed his body quickly with a towel before brushing his teeth, and just before he stepped into the bedroom, he paused. He had waited so many years to find her again. He didn't want to blow it all on a quick afternoon liaison in bed, he wanted more. He wanted her to be his everything, his friend, his wife, his lover and the mother of his children.

He wrapped the towel around his hips and slowly he opened the door. He walked to where she waited in the bed, with the sheet pulled up to her neck.

'Tara,' Wayne said. 'Before this, before we ... I wanted to ask you something. You don't need to answer right now but I want you to know. In fact, don't answer now because I never want it thrown back at me that I asked you under duress, and that you couldn't say no.'

Tara sat up, and he noticed a see-through negligee hiding under a longer dressing gown belted loosely around her waist before disappearing under the sheet.

He took a gulp of air.

'What?' she asked.

He crossed to his walk-in cupboard, and dug in the pocket of his jacket with a zip pocket that he had worn in Cape Town. He crossed back to the bed and knelt next to her.

'Marry me, Tara. Wear a white dress and tell everyone that you want to spend the rest of your life with me. Have more babies with me, or not, I don't care, we have Josha and he's just beautiful. Wear my ring, and tell the world that we beat the odds, that we found each other, and spend the rest of your life with me, and I promise every day to try my best to make you happy. To protect you, to be your friend and your lover.'

'Yes,' she said, 'I will.'

'You can't answer now. I'm not holding you to that answer. You have too many other things going on. Your tumour—'

'Nothing is going to change my mind. But if you want to, we can ice it, and I can answer again at another time.'

'Think about it, Tara, think really hard. I don't believe in divorce. I believe in working things out, and adapting as we need to. There is no out, once my ring is on your finger we are married and as far as I'm concerned, you are stuck with me for eternity.'

She dragged the sheet back and moved so that she was sitting on the edge of the bed. Her nightgown still covered most of her body.

She wrapped her legs around him as he knelt before her. Putting her arms around his neck, she put her forehead to his.

'Eternity with you is what I wanted when I was fifteen, and at twenty-nine, it is still what I want, Wayne. I love you, now and forever,' she said.

'Now and forever,' he murmured against her lips, as he lifted her up and then lightly put her back on the bed.

Tara's head swam with lightness in the best way, Wayne was kissing her, and sensations she thought long forgotten rushed upwards, setting her body on fire.

He ran his finger along her collarbone and downwards, and she could feel the blood rush to where he touched, a tingle that rippled a millisecond behind. She smiled.

'What?' he said. 'I can feel you smiling.'

'You, I so want you,' she said.

He smiled and followed the path that his finger had just taken with his lips.

Tara threw her head back and groaned, the sensation was so strong.

He nibbled at the top of the dressing gown where it gaped and didn't cover the swell of her breasts.

'Can I take this off?' he asked her as he reached for the gown's belt.

She nodded as she stood up. He stood up too and she pressed herself up close to him. He got the knot loose, and eased the silky fabric off her shoulders, and it dropped freely to the floor.

She stood in front of him in the see-through lacy negligee he had glimpsed before.

'Wow, Tara,' he said and he reached for the hemline that barely covered her bottom, seeing she hadn't bothered with panties. The negligee was pulled up and off in one clean motion.

For a moment he stared at her. She was totally naked.

'You are so beautiful,' he murmured as he came back to her mouth. Framing her face with both his hands, he lifted her chin slightly to kiss her.

Breathless, she grabbed for his towel and pulled the tucked-in end out. The towel loosened but didn't unravel.

'Impatient, are we?' he said, and he lifted her up and put her onto the bed, before climbing on beside her. Quickly he lowered his head to her breasts, and, taking one nipple into his mouth, he rolled the other one in his strong fingers. Slowly he moved his body, nudging her leg with his until he could lie comfortably between her legs.

Tara looked down. His darkly tanned hands on her white body added to the erotic moment, the sensation so familiar and yet so new. Her body ached for his.

This was Wayne, they had spent many hours together like this, but it had been years ago when he was a boy. Now she had the mature man worshipping her body, and it was even better. The coarse stubble of his beard rasped at the tender skin of her breast. He shifted his weight, and she moved her legs to accommodate him again. His flat muscular stomach touched her, and she gasped for breath.

He moved again, and reached for her with one hand, slowly parting her folds with his fingers.

She pressed up into his hand. Knowing what was coming, and wanting it so desperately.

He moved lower and worshipped her with his mouth.

He stilled for a moment, his breathing matching hers, ragged and uneven. 'So wet for me,' he said. 'You are so—'

Not finishing the word, he flipped them over, so that she was on top, and his towel unravelled totally. She sat on his hips and leaning forward, began her own exploration of his mature body.

She rained feather kisses over his face, kissing the laughter lines near his eyes. She leisurely explored down his neck, over his Adam's apple, and into the area where his neck met his body and created a valley of velvet softness, that she kissed.

She felt his fingers dig into her buttocks as she continued over his chest, the hair tickling her nose as she lapped at nipples that beaded into tiny pebbles under her touch. She skimmed the taut six pack with her lips as she explored lower, licking at the small scar she found. Finally, she looked at her prize. Proudly it bobbed, thick and ready, straining for its own attention. She tentatively tasted the tip.

Wayne bucked, and she took him in her mouth, creating suction as she held him captive.

'Oh God, Tara. I won't last—' he ground out between clenched teeth, and he grabbed her shoulders and dragged her back up. Locking his lips to hers, he moved her under him again. Then slowly put his forehead against hers and while looking into her face, he entered her.

He waited for a moment, as if she might need to get used to him and his size but she arched upwards, begging him for more, her body experiencing a need that only he could satisfy.

She looked into his eyes as he fought nature for authority over his own body, to move slower. To make the moment last for both of them.

'I love you, Wayne, now and forever,' Tara whispered.

Wayne bent his head and kissed her as he immersed himself in her. He took from her, he gave to her, and within a moment they were together, in an age-old rhythm that sent them into a climax. They dived into the vortex of emotion together, as Tara's whole body shook, so did Wayne's, and they shared joy as together they reached the stars, and were joined in their own heaven.

They lay still, him supporting his weight above her, their bodies still locked together. Spent but not wanting to move.

'Is your head okay?' Wayne asked.

'Perfect,' she said as she reached up to kiss him. He met her halfway.

She could feel him inside her, and as she deepened the kiss, she felt the bob of a post orgasmic twitch. She smiled as she clenched her muscles around him, holding him to her.

They stayed together for long moments, and eventually their breathing slowed, returning to almost normal, and Wayne turned onto his back, pulling her close to him. She used his arm as a pillow as she lay on her back.

She could feel his breath on her hair and his warm hand around her shoulder. It was homey, and it was fantastic just to lie there next to Wayne, and breathe in his scent.

She smiled. 'I remember we used to do this in the back of your father's old truck, just lay next to each other. Back then we used to talk about the future.'

'I remember, but none of those dreams came true.'

'Not true. I became a psychologist, just like I wanted to. You actually never knew what you wanted to do back then other than go to varsity, and get a degree.'

'I got all these bursaries to go, and I deferred them to join the army instead. Joined the Recces, and it was there that I learnt that the wildlife in Africa was being decimated, and unless more people take the time to save it, preserve it, there won't be any left for the next generation, or the one after that …'

'So you changed the sugarcane farm into a beautiful game reserve,' Tara said.

'That, and Jamison and I run our Wild Translocation business.'

'Relocation?'

'Translocation. They are living things. You have seen the trucks. We take wild game and transport them for auctions, from farm to farm. It was never meant to grow in to such a large operation. We started it as a way to get our hands on affordable start-up animals, and it grew.'

'All good hobbies grow bigger because of the passion they are started with,' she said and she shuddered as Wayne grazed his short fingernails over the base of her neck and down to her breasts.

'Is that your professional psychologist's opinion?'

'Yes, and people pay me money for my opinions, I'll have you know.'

Wayne laughed.

'So how do you manage to be the superhero, Wayne? To run both your farm and Wild Translocations?' she asked as she reached over and ran her hand through his hair, and then lazily scraped her nails against his scalp. She was rewarded with a shiver from him.

'Not superhero. I just love both sides of doing it. A side business that helps grow the farm. The first advert I posted in the farmers weekly for "free removal of leopards in conflict with human activity," was such a phenomenal success, Jamison and I moved seven leopards in five weeks. Charging the farmers whose property we were removing them from nothing except a cool drink! We collected cats from all over, from the midlands area where a leopard was frequently seen too close to a school and had started foraging in the dirt bins, to a sheep farm in the Karoo that had a problematic leopard taking its lambs. One from not too far up the road from Hluhluwe on a sugarcane farm, and the other four from the Transvaal, where cattle farmers were having their calves taken.'

'Sounds like hot hard work,' she said moving her hands down over his side, and to the front, over his nipple. It puckered again.

He covered his hand over hers. 'Two can play this game,' he said huskily.

'Sure,' she said and she felt the increase in pressure on her breasts as he began to pluck at her raised nipple. 'Just keep talking …'

'You ask for a lot, woman,' he said. 'I'm a mere male, I can't concentrate on two things at once.'

She hugged him to her. 'You were saying how good your relo— translocation business was going—' she prompted.

'I was, wasn't I,' he said. 'All the work was worth it. At first we relied on using the expertise that Jamison already had from his months with the Zimbabwe Wildlife Department, and pooling his expertise with what I had seen of live game capture years before in the Recces. We began translocating the leopards so that they could populate Kujana with a lower cost than we could buy at the available livestock auctions. We had a few incidents along the way. We had to learn to use a *bakkie* with a long rope attached to lift the door of the leopard's crate when we were releasing them into their new environment. Man, those cats can move super fast, and they come out pretty pissed off when they sprint out of the travelling crates.'

'You serious? Did you and Jamison get hurt?' She sat up and looked at him, concerned.

'No, but it was only by luck that we didn't.' He kissed the tip of her nose. She lay back own, this time on her side, pressed into him.

'Soon saving leopards became an obsession, saving those magnificent cats from being shot by the commercial farmers, or stoned and speared to death by the tribal villagers. We would trap, remove and translocate them.' His hand found her shoulder, touching it, stroking her.

'That's so sweet, but surely you couldn't bring them all here?' Tara said as she adjusted herself a little. His hand crept to her back and started drawing erotic lines, from the tip near her shoulders downwards, finishing just at the top of her thigh, and then he would lift his hand, and repeat it, close but not quite in the same place.

By now her arms were pressed up against his chest, but that meant she could explore that with her fingers. His arm looped over her back and he drew lazy circles as he continued to talk about his cats.

'No, it didn't take long before Kujana had as many as the land could sustain. Leopards are extremely territorial. We needed to avoid the male cats fighting over territory overlaps.'

'I love leopards,' Tara said, 'they always look so soft in pictures, like you can stroke them, just big kitties really,' she said, caressing his arm.

Wayne laughed, a deep belly laugh. 'Please don't—'

'I wouldn't, I'm just saying—'

He kissed her again, his lips finding hers and their breath mingling in a lazy satisfied exchange. 'Leopards remind me of you in many ways. They are such solitary animals. And they take great care to avoid one another. Like you did to me when we were teenagers, before we became friends. Regal animals.'

'I'm not regal—'

'To me you are. The female will allow her cubs to stay with her until they are old enough to properly fend for themselves, then eventually they leave, go find a territory of their own. Then she's alone again, until she mates, and has more cubs.'

'That's sad,' she said. 'And that is definitely not me—'

'Not that part, just the part where they look good, and are so strong, so protective,' he corrected.

She smiled. Letting her hand wander across his chest again.

'I remember when I first got to Angola, my team and I were hiding in a crevice, and I saw a mother leopard defend her cubs from an intruding male. It was a fierce fight, and she saved her cubs, but she didn't make it. I always remember feeling devastated that I couldn't run out there and scare the male away, because I would give away my position, and we were in a hot zone, so if I did that, I could have been shot. I was so affected by her, sad that she had died, and yet so proud of her for protecting her cubs no matter what. She gave everything for those cubs. Just like you gave up everything, to move away from your mum, from your home, to save our Josha. The lengths you went to, to disappear so my mother couldn't find you. And then you brought me back into your life, thinking of Josha's future, ensuring that he was safe and looked after by both Gabe and I. Like a wild cat, you did what you had to do to protect your cub.'

Tara hugged Wayne. He hugged her back, holding her tightly to him.

'When I was in the Recces in Angola, we had a pet lion, Terry. We left him behind when we closed the camp after the war, so once Jamison and I had the fences up, and we were able to, we visited my old camp, looking to translocate him if he was still there.'

'Did you find him?' she asked.

'No, I was too late. Later I heard of others who had returned before me, looking for him, wanting to make it right, ensure he was looked after, but no one found any trace of him.'

'That's sad.'

'No, that's good news. No bones means he left, he survived and got away, moved to another area. I like to think that he found a wild pride somewhere, and there are Terry offspring now running around in Namibia or in Botswana.'

'That's a nice thought.'

'I was an idiot. I should have returned for him earlier, maybe the outcome might have been different,' he said as he kissed the top of her head.

'No, it's in the past. Looking back doesn't help,' she said. 'I too was an idiot, I should have got in touch with you so much earlier! I can't bring that time back, but you need to know I'm sorry, Wayne,' she said, and her voice was barely audible as the emotion was so thick in her throat.

'I know,' he said.

After a small silence she asked, 'So, what do your resident leopards think of your tourists?'

Wayne smiled as she snuggled back into him and continued to touch his chest.

'They tolerate them. We have one young male that insists on lying on the pool lounges at the Rooi Vlei Lodge. He marked his territory on that spot and even though we replaced the lounge with a new one, he returned and reclaimed it again. The tourists love taking his photograph in the morning as he catches the first rays of light. They don't even need to leave their camp to view leopards and take stunning photographs of his breath on a cooler morning as he stares at the humans intruding on his peace and quiet, or starts scratching his back. He is such a poser.'

'So, how did leopards become the buffalo you had in that truck with Josha yesterday?' She adjusted herself in the bed again, and Wayne lay back on his back. She lay on his trunk, her arms crossed under her chin on his chest. He threaded his fingers through her hair.

'Our hobby. Jamison's and my passion grew to include translocating animals to other safari farms. Fortunately from the initial advert, we had been inundated with requests from people who were willing to have the animals on their land that caused others problems. So we made it more cost effective to do the translocations, more of a business, less of a hobby, and we would translocate the leopard as close to their original territory as possible. We began a long list of safari farms that wanted one when they become available. A client list with a difference.'

'Your market came to you,' she said, then yawned.

'You okay, don't need your meds?' Wayne asked.

'No, I'm good,' Tara said, shifting again, and this time going back to laying next to him, she put her arm around Wayne's waist and shifted closer so that she absorbed the heat from his body. She closed her eyes.

'Long story short, eventually we were requested by some of the State Parks Boards to move leopards back into the National Parks. Soon farmers offered us other animals. Some we couldn't help and had to pass onto conservation groups, like the cape otters, they eat all the new trout fish stocks in the KwaZulu-Natal Midlands when they restock their dams. While protected within the Tsitsikamma National Park, the otters outside the park area can grow to plague proportions. It's really sad that many farmers simply kill them. But other animals, we could help with, we could transport easily. Springbok, and the smaller game, and it grew from there. Word of mouth spread that we had low fatalities, that we took care with the animals, attempted to keep their stress levels low. You comfy?' he asked.

'Yes, don't stop, I'm listening,' Tara said as she kissed his chest.

'We just grew from there, and pretty soon we were joined by thirty staff including our incredible ex-state vet Donavan Marr, and Ryan Maskell, our helicopter pilot you met the other day.'

'He seems nice. Shy but nice.'

'Don't be fooled by his shyness, he's amazing in his machine, he handles her like a bird in the sky. I have seen him do manoeuvres I didn't think possible, and I've been around lots of helicopters.'

Tara smiled. 'Outside his helicopter, he's a shy man, quiet.'

'That's not bad, it means he doesn't party hard and try to fly with a hangover.' Wayne lapsed in to silence for a moment, lost in thought. What had started as a way to source cheaper leopards back in 1992 had fast become a profitable business and a money spinner to help grow Kujana, and somewhere during that time, Jamison and he had become real friends. Wayne looked down at Tara. Her eyes were closed.

'You awake?' he asked.

'Yes, just enjoying your company,' she said. 'I'm so proud of you and everything you have done here at Kujana, and with your translocation company. You have achieved so much so fast.'

Wayne smiled. It was nice to get the recognition from Tara, but his smile was more for the fact that she was acknowledging that he had done it alone, not just relied on his family to get where he was. He knew that his father had certainly given him a huge leg up, but growing the rest, that was all him and Jamison. He would never forget that night when they had discussed making Wild Translocation into its own company, separating it out from Kujana.

'Thanks,' Wayne said, 'I have to admit that I never imagined that in so few years we would be the proud owners of three huge mobile cranes as well as ten specially fitted out trucks that could transport just about any kind of wild animal.'

'Can you move elephant?'

'We've had one so far, but we are contracted to move a few in a couple of weeks. Of all the animals, they are the ones that we have had to spend the most outfitting for. They are so hard, and Donovan been spending time with Parks Board too, ensuring that he is up to date with dosages for them. You have to knock them out then, using their feet and legs, you lift them with a crane and move them up onto the truck, and manoeuvring them into their crates for transportation is not easy. They need to be at least semi-awake in their crates. They are a specialised move, but I can see a future in being equipped for them, so does Jamison.'

'Seriously, you are moving elephant? Josha is going to be out of his mind when you tell him that one. He's mad about elephants.'

Wayne smiled. 'It will be after your operation, from Addo Park in the Cape. Most likely to the Transvaal, that's where the bigger game farms are expanding already. But if he's here to spend more time with me cooped up in the truck, I'm happy to take him along.'

'He's going to love you more for that one. Huge brownie points coming your way.'

Wayne grinned.

'You know, in a few weeks we are moving some rhino. They are up for a catalogue auction from a well-known farm in the area. This farmer has so much excess wildlife that he's selling and he thought it would be worth his while to cut out the live pens. So he's a first, with an onsite auction on his farm. You can view the animals beforehand on his property, and then bid, or you can look at the pictures in his catalogue. After the auction, we will move the rhinos to their new home, wherever that is.'

'I think I'd like to go with you on that one. Would love to see how you move the rhinos.'

'Serious? That would be amazing. It will be after your operation,' Wayne said and he hugged her to him.

'I want to come back,' she said, 'afterwards, if you will have me here. I will have a long time to recuperate, but I want to come back, stay here.'

'I would love to have you with me. But you have to be coming back for more than just the rhino being moved because I have to tell you, the white rhino is gentle, like a domestic cow, they tame down pretty fast. They are full of mock charges, but because they can't see and can't hear that well, they tend to run away from danger rather than confront it.'

'I'm not only coming back for the rhino!' she said as she smacked him lightly on his arm. 'Your life is so different to mine in Cape Town. I want to come back because I want to be here, but I can't stop thinking that I'm going to lose Josha to you because he'll love it here so much, and want to stay here. And I know it won't be your fault, but I'll just be the boring mother and you the fun dad.'

'No. That's not going to happen,' Wayne said, and she could feel that he was shaking his head. 'You are underestimating your own son. He will love it here, it's all new, it's all wonderful, but he loves you, and he loves Gabe. I wouldn't take him away from you guys. I want to share him with you, but not have him totally. That wouldn't be fair on anyone. Believe me, I won't be the cool dad for much longer, I bet the first time I have to put my foot down on an issue it's going to be interesting ...'

Tara smiled. 'I hope you are right, Wayne, I seriously hope so. But I want to come back, be with you—' But her voice was starting to drift away, as if she was just nodding off. He kissed her gently on the lips.

'Have a good rest my love,' he said as he felt her breathing change and he knew that she was asleep. 'I'll wake you at six-thirty so you can get ready for dinner.'

After a while he wiggled his arm out from under her head, and covered her with the blanket, then he looked around his room. It looked right with her stuff on the dressing table, and he liked that it smelt like her.

He picked up the ring that she had barely looked at. The three diamonds he had chosen, one for each of his family, sparkled back at him. He snapped the box shut. He had told her not to give him an answer yet, but he'd laid his card on the table that he wanted the fairy tale ending.

After what they had just shared he didn't think they needed time to work things out and get reacquainted. They still fitted just perfectly together.

But time might be a factor they were going to run out of.

Ten days and counting to her operation.

Until the dice of life were tossed.

CHAPTER 25

The Operation

Cape Town, South Africa
25th March 1998

'Hi, Mr Brits,' Josha said politely to the man who had just walked into Tara's private suite at the neurological unit in the Newlands Hospital, where she was recovering from the surgery. But his voice chose that time to remember he was a racing bag of hormones and it came out squeaking. He coughed. Mr Brits smiled.

'I'll be outside,' Wayne said as he stood up from the chair next to Tara's bed.

'No. Please stay,' said Tara. 'Emile, this is Wayne, Josha's father.' Wayne and Emile shook hands.

Emile turned his attention back to his patient. He looked over at the heart monitor and scribbled on her chart. 'I have results, would you rather I come back?'

She shook her head slightly. 'No, you can tell us all at the same time. Just Gabe is missing, but we can fill him in.'

'You sure?'

'Yes.'

Wayne noticed Josha grab hold of his mum's hand and squeeze it tightly. If the neurosurgeon was hesitating, it couldn't be good news.

'You were lucky. We got the whole tumour out. It was benign. There's no cancer. You are going to be just fine—'

Josha threw himself into a huge hug of his mum. 'Oh Mum, I thought you were going to die.'

Wayne's legs crumpled beneath him and he sat down heavily on the chair.

Emile was speaking in slow motion as all the blood rushed to Wayne's head. He felt hot and cold at the same time.

Tara wasn't going to die from her brain tumour.

He could hear Emile talking further to Tara but no coherent words reached his brain.

She was going to be okay.

She was not going to die.

Wayne's tuned in again to Emile Brits's voice. '... so your pituitary gland is producing the appropriate levels of hormones again and we won't need to do any drug replacement on that side. I have scheduled you for an MRI in the morning.'

'Another one?' Tara asked.

'Get used to them, they are about to become part of your life. Initially I'll order another in six months' time, to ensure that there is no regrowth, then depending on how that goes, once a year, to ensure that you have no recurrence. It's all precautionary from here on.'

'Thank you so much!' Tara said.

'I'll check back in with you tomorrow after the MRI. I want to keep you in for another day or two, have a look when those bandages come off, just to be certain everything is perfect. We can't rush it, healing a body takes time.'

'Thank you, Emile,' Tara said.

'Pleasure. It's cases like yours that make my job worthwhile. Now I'm glad to see you talking, and having company. Make sure you eat dinner. See you on my rounds tomorrow, Tara,' he said.

'Wayne,' Emile said, and shook his hand. He turned and waved at Josha. 'You did well over the last two days, Josha. Wish more teenagers were like you, being so supportive of their mums.' He walked out the door.

An eerie silence descended on the room. Then suddenly the three of them were talking at once.

'Wow, Wayne. Hear that? I'm in the clear!'

'Yippee,' Josha was chanting.

'Oh thank God!' Wayne said.

They were laughing and hugging each other, all together.

'I need to call Gabe!' Tara said. 'We need to tell Gabe!'

Josha picked up her private telephone that sat on the locker next to her bed. He pushed the buttons for the number, and waited.

'Hey Lucretia, it's Josha,' he said then there was silence while he listened to her on the other side. 'No, it's good news, Lucretia. But can I speak with Uncle Gabe?'

Again silence.

'No, I haven't.'

Silence.

'Awww Lucretia, no I don't.'

A much longer silence.

'Okay, I will. Thanks. Bye.'

'Mum, Uncle Gabe is already on his way here, and Lucretia told me that when he goes home I have to go home too for a shower tonight because she can smell me from there.'

Tara and Wayne both laughed.

'That's a sound that I haven't heard for too long,' Gabe said as he walked through the door.

'Gabriel!' Tara said.

Wayne watched as Gabe strode into the room, and drew Tara into a huge hug. He didn't seem worried about the bandages, or the IV drips, or that she had just had an operation two days before, and he felt nothing but joy that Gabe was such a good friend to her. That he had been able to help her when he couldn't, that he was her friend, and her cousin. Even if it was just second cousins once removed or whatever the connection was that Tara had tried to make him understand.

'Gabe,' Tara said, 'I can't breathe.'

He immediately let Tara go, and although he still held her he no longer held onto her as tight. 'Better,' she said.

'I saw your Mr Emile Brits in the foyer, and he was happy to share your good news with me. Amazing. So totally amazing!' he said. Then he hugged her tight again for a second time, before releasing her.

'Great news, hey, Josha!' Gabe stretched across the bed with his hand up for a high five.

Josha slapped his palm to Gabe's. 'The best, Uncle Gabe!' They did a little hand slapping combination thing after the high five, and Wayne hadn't seen that series of slides and waves before.

Wayne laughed. A few short weeks ago, he might have been jealous of their relationship, but not now.

'Right, I have an article to finish writing, so I need to go home, but I had to see you tonight.' He bent and kissed Tara on the forehead above the bandages. 'You keep out of trouble, you hear. I'll see you tomorrow.'

He shook Wayne's hand. 'You look after her tonight, she is after all your responsibility again.'

Wayne grinned.

'Come on, Josha, say bye, you need a decent night's sleep tonight, your dad is on duty,' Gabe said.

'Bye, Mum,' Josha said as he kissed her softly.

Then he walked up to Wayne. 'Bye, Dad,' he said and lifted his fist just like he had seen Jamison and Wayne do countless times. Wayne touched his fist to Josha's, and Josha breezed out the room.

Wayne stared after him, grinning.

'Alone at last,' Tara said.

'Yes, but I don't think you are up to any monkey business in your state,' Wayne said and grinned, but he sat on the bed next to her, holding her hand.

'Guess what, I'm not dead, and I'm not going to die in a hurry,' she said and giggled.

'It's a good day,' Wayne said and he lifted her hand and kissed it.

'So, can I answer a question you told me not to answer a week ago?'

'No, Tara you don't have to. I said when you were ready—'

'I was ready then and I meant it then, and I mean it again today. Yes, Wayne, I will marry you. I'll wear a white dress and I want the together forever after with you.'

'You have remembered that there still might be a man hunting you?' Wayne said.

'I know and I don't want to wait for him to strike or not strike, to live my life in limbo. This was bad enough. My wake-up call to re-prioritise my life. I want you in it. Permanently. I don't want to wait for a better time, for another opportunity, or anything else. I want to be with you. Forever. I love you, Wayne Simon Botha, and yes, I will marry you.'

'This time I'm accepting,' he said, and he dug in his pocket, 'this time you are putting this ring on and not taking it off ever again!'

He pulled the box from the zip pocket in his jacket, and opened it. Then he took the ring out and slipped it on her finger. 'I love you, Tara. I will love you forever and always.'

He bent down and he sealed their pledge with a kiss.

CHAPTER 26

The Bush Drum

Kujana Farm, Hluhluwe, South Africa
12th February 1999

Jamison's telephone rang at twelve minutes past one in the morning. He dived out of bed, and rushed to silence it before it woke the children.

A loud scream came from the nursery, and Ebony groaned as she too rose from their bed, and trudged down the passage to the nursery. 'That better be a life and death situation,' she said.

'Hello,' Jamison said.

The operator on the other side was asking him to accept a reverse charge call from Gibson Ncube.

'Yes, put him through,' Jamison said, and he ran his hand over his eyes to try and dislodge some of the sleepiness.

If his cousin Gibson was calling him at this time of the morning it was important.

He sat down on the stool, and put his elbows on the dressing table as he waited.

He could hear Ebony in the nursery as she put Joy back to sleep, and quietened down Blessing, who had woken at the alien noise in the house.

'Hello,' Gibson said.

'Gib,' Jamison replied.

'He's coming for you,' Gib said. 'He left the farm in his sheep *bakkie* yesterday, and before he left, he went to his shrine. I followed him.'

'His shrine?'

'I'll check properly when he is gone for a day or so more, but he collected something from his mushroom shed before he went and was muttering about the time being right to find the angel to save Impendla.'

'Where are you?' Jamison asked.

'I walked to the main road, then caught a bus into Tsholotsho last night. I waited until there was no one around, and then I came to use the pay phone here in the street. I didn't want anyone in Nyamandhlovu seeing me using a phone.'

'So you are safe?'

'Yes. He is gone. But I think he knows where you are.'

'How? After all this time?'

'Last week, we took a road trip back to Chinoya and we visited Amarose again. This time he went as a hunter. He took three days just to shoot a lion. Three days. I tracked it in one morning, but he was in no hurry. He was talking to all the staff about how he once knew you and how good you were at your job, and how he wanted to employ you, had to find you …'

'Oh no …'

'He spoke of hearing how you had built up the farm for the Widow Crosby so many years ago, and how he was looking for someone like that, someone reliable.'

'And?'

'Someone told him that they think that when Moeketsi had left, he might have gone to South Africa to find you. To join you.'

Jamison hung his head.

Not now. He looked down the passage where Ebony had just snuck out of the nursery and came towards him. His family.

Tara's operation had been a success, and she had married Wayne, and moved to Kujana. Josha was so happy at the farm, and he was beginning to refer to Wayne as his dad to everyone.

He pinched the top of his nose between two fingers. 'Moeketsi is from a large family. Did he take anyone from his clan?'

'I don't know. Buffel dropped me home, and then he went off again for another two days alone. I suspect he went back, because he came to his farm really late at night, and went straight into his mushroom shed. That is never a good sign. I will dig around a bit in there soon too, but I have to be careful that the other two workers here don't get suspicious of me. They all know me as his tracker. No one knows that I was once a policeman. That I am your cousin.'

'You stay safe, Gibson. You hear me?'

'You too.'

Jamison put the phone down. He stared at Ebony.

'He's coming, isn't he?' she said.

'I think so. He had already been gone for over twenty-four hours before Gibson could call this time, so he might already be here.'

He crossed the short distance to his wife, and hugged her close to him. 'Eb,' he said, 'look at me—' He raised her chin gently with his finger. 'We have state-of-the-art security now, an alarm that would wake a hippo underwater, and smoke detectors, Eb, he can't get to us in our house. We have game guards positioned outside, and travelling with you. We are armed to the hilt. We have made sure that we have everything we needed in this new house. He can't get in without us being able to react. But I need to warn Wayne.'

'I know. Poor Wayne and Tara, just when they are so happy. Now he is coming,' Ebony said. 'Go call him. I'll be here waiting for you.'

CHAPTER
27

The Trigger

Game Auction, Hluhluwe Outskirts, South Africa
17th February 1999
10:30am

Buffel stood at the edge of the crowd at the onsite game auction. He had on the felt hat he always wore when he was going hunting, only now it was pulled down low over his forehead. He had forgone his usual safari suit and worn denims with a white shirt. To anyone else he looked like a farmer who had come to the game farm for the auction, to buy game for his own ranch.

But he was here for a different prey.

The brother of Moeketsi had sung like a Burchell's coucal, warbling on about how Moeketsi had a better life now that he had moved away, and he was now a professional hunter, and he lived on a farm that belonged to a white man who treated his black workers like kings, all the while he and his family were almost starving under his Zimbabwe government. About how unfair life was that he was getting beaten up for his lucky brother again. Just like when they were children together.

Buffel hadn't even needed to torture him for the address. He had given it freely.

Kujana Farm, Hluhluwe, South Africa.

But live men tell tales, so he'd had to be silenced.

Buffel smiled at the memory.

A telephone book, and two phone calls, and Buffel knew where Shilo was going to be. The farm had been easy enough to find, off a main road on the back of Hluhluwe, and everyone in the small town had known the Wild Translocation trucks, pointed them out to him. They had even told him that they would be at a local game auction the next day.

Small tourist towns. The people were always so easy and helpful, especially to strangers.

The ostriches in the boma near him were having a commotion about something. Their loud protest defied anyone close by to have a conversation. He looked at the hessian sacking wrapped around the temporary boma enclosure, but he couldn't see anything out of the ordinary causing their distress.

He checked down the boma line, to where some sable antelope were penned. The meanest bastards to a hunter. A wounded sable would fake death when you shot him, only to impale the hunter with its scimitar-sharp horns if he wasn't careful when he went up to it for a photograph. Aggressive as hell, the sable was an antelope many underestimated in the safari trade and the hunting business. He strolled towards the pen, feigning interest. Counting minutes, straining to see Shilo in the crowd as they milled around him.

The viewing panel in the solid part of the boma was about the size of a standard pillowcase. Made with corrugated iron, it rattled loudly when he opened it. Within a moment, he saw the big black bull rush from the one side of the boma, and slam into where he stood. Only the strength of the boma spared him the wrath of the animal. He stepped back as the attack happened, but eagerly stepped up towards the window to see what damage the sable had inflicted upon itself.

Nothing.

The base of its curved horns was thick, yet this cornered beast was fighting for its freedom, with no regard as to how much pain and suffering it could give itself.

He was magnificent.

Buffel looked at him through the eyes of a hunter, thinking how proud he would look on his wall in his trophy lounge.

The sable slammed at him again. He closed the viewer window, not wanting to draw attention to himself, and not wanting to spoil the trophy beast.

He noticed Shilo the moment he walked around the side of the boma set up outside the tent. In the six years since he had last smoked him out, he had not aged much. He looked from Shilo to his companions.

The farmer. He walked with the swagger of a confident military man. One who was at ease in the bush and in any shithole of war around the world. His short blond hair was typical of one who had served or still served within the SADF.

But it was the person who held his hand who suddenly drew Buffel's full attention. He held his breath. Trying to stop his beating heart. Trying to hold his mouth closed. Stop himself from grinning like a baboon having too many marulas. It was impossible.

His white-haired angel. He knew it was her.

Impendla's saviour. The Butterfly.

Tara Wright was just as beautiful in adulthood as when she had been just about to blossom into a woman. She wore an impractical white dress, close fitting to show off her body, it left her shoulders free for the African sun to kiss lightly. She had on dark sunglasses, but he didn't need her to remove them to know that the colour of her bright blue eyes wouldn't have changed. They would be the same as when they had first looked at him across his veranda table when she was too young.

The same eyes that tormented his dreams.

The same eyes that had the power to call all the butterflies together, and to save Impendla.

He looked to her right, and striding next to her was a boy. He had the same white hair she did, and his eyes were shaded by sunglasses. He walked tall and although he looked a bit like the farmer there was no mistaking he was her son. Bordering on manhood, the boy walked with a purpose that many of the younger men lacked now.

Pride. He strode, he didn't simply walk, he held himself tall.

A worthy warrior to accompany the Butterfly on her journey, he thought.

The last man in the party walked on the other side of the boy. He looked out of place with his denims, and his shirt rolled at the elbows. His hair looked like it had been styled with a dryer, and he held the boy's hand.

Buffel bristled. A *moffie* or a male model. Not a man's man, but a man who thought more like a woman.

He spat in the dust.

Then he turned slightly to the left, so that when they passed by they wouldn't see him. He turned and watched as they walked into the huge white marquee that sat like a giant bullfrog in the middle of the farm. The auctioneer was already inside, and a general hum like millions of bees could be heard from the tent. He walked slowly behind the party.

He couldn't help grinning. He could quieten Shilo and get his angel and her warrior in one clean sweep.

All he had to do was be patient, and strike like an Egyptian cobra when he made his move.

It had to be on his terms.

He had to plan.

CHAPTER
28

Sensory Overload

Game Auction, Hluhluwe Outskirts, South Africa
17th February 1999
11:00am

Moeketsi ran to catch up to the others. Having turned back to the vehicle for his hat, he now wished that he had left it where it was. He was already sweating from the heat, and adding the physical exercise to it, he was going to look like he had run under the sprinkler when he went inside the auction tent.

He noticed the man standing by the boma, and he slowed. Instead of catching up to Jamison and Wayne, he hung back. He had seen the sketch that Gabe had done of the man they thought was responsible not only for Tara's father's death but for the disappearance of a heap of white girls.

He couldn't tell if it was him, but the similarities were too many to dismiss. The height, the set of his jaw. His overall size.

The man turned away as Wayne and his family passed, then he stood staring at their backs for a while. Eventually, he pulled his hat lower on his head, and followed them inside the huge tent.

Moeketsi lifted dirt from the floor and let it drip slowly through his fingers. It stayed vertical, no deviance from ninety degrees.

No wind.

No reason to pull a hat further onto your head.

Unless you were trying to hide under it.

He walked to where the man had stood and began to track his footprints around the boma.

'Come on, Africa, show me his story,' he muttered as he bent to check if he had the print correct, and continued to track what the man had done before standing watching the Wild Translocation party.

Moeketsi followed the spoor to a white king cab *bakkie*. The back was grated, designed to carry animals, like sheep or even small buck, and raised on a higher suspension than normal. Customised. The back had obviously been cleaned and laid with fresh hay for the auction. There were three thick-cut sticks in the back, like a Zulu fighting stick in size with big knobs on the end, but heavier than a normal knobkerrie.

He memorised the Zimbabwe numberplate.

He walked around the vehicle, and tried each door, but it was locked. Peering through the deeply tinted window he couldn't see anything amiss in the *bakkie*, only a small old-fashioned duffel bag that sat on the back seat. In a city, the car would be broken into and the bag stolen, but here the farmer knew that his possessions would be safe at the auction.

Moeketsi walked slowly back towards the tent. The scalloped white edge didn't move as there was still no wind. He looked for the stranger, but couldn't see him outside hovering anywhere. He slipped into the back, letting his eyes adjust to the naturally dim interior.

The auctioneer stood in the front of the tent, a portable steel game pen visible behind him. Farmers in khaki sat in the rows of white plastic chairs which filled the area in front of him. Some were rocking on the back legs of the chairs as they waited for the lots that interested them. Women waved the program, fanning themselves.

The auctioneer's voice rose in pitch as the figure being offered grew higher and higher.

It was easy to spot his colleagues. Madam Tara's hair was very white compared to any other blonde there, and as she sat alongside Wayne and Jamison, she looked tiny. Josha was next to her, not quite as tall as his dad yet but getting there.

His eyes continued their search.

Finally in the opposite back corner he spotted the man.

Still wearing his hat, despite being indoors, he nursed a Coke up close to his face as he stood on one leg, the other crossed over forming a V as his toes tapped an irritated rhythm in the dirt. He didn't seem to be listening to the auction, but his focus was on the back of Tara's head.

Moeketsi watched him for a while, ensuring that he had the trajectory of the stare right, and then he slowly made his way to where there was a spare seat next to Gabe. He sat down and held his position for about thirty seconds, feigning interest in the auction, then he leant forward and snapped his fingers low at knee height to gain Wayne's attention.

Wayne leant towards him to listen.

'He is here. Back left corner, wearing a hat. Madam Tara is being watched.'

Slowly Wayne sat up, then he spoke in hushed tones to Jamison who sat next to him. 'Moeketsi says Tara is being watched by the man in the left corner with a hat. Do you recognise him at all?'

Jamison stretched up his arms above his head and as he yawned, he bent backwards and glanced over his shoulder to the left. Slowly he turned his head back to Wayne and brought his hands down. He didn't have a bidder's card so he didn't need to worry about the distraction to the auctioneer.

'It is him,' Jamison said in a voice just above a whisper.

Wayne felt the adrenaline surge through his body. He let go of Tara's hand and flexed his fist.

'What is it, Wayne?' Tara whispered. 'What's wrong?'

'You and Josha stay with Gabe and Moeketsi, no matter what happens,' Wayne said as he bent towards her and kissed her mouth. He stood up as Jamison did, as if to shield Jamison with his body from Buffel's view, then together they made their way down the aisle of white plastic chairs, and up the passage on the right-hand side. Wayne allowed only his eyes to move to check if the killer was still there, and as he checked, the man ducked out the flap of the tent.

He broke into a run.

Jamison right beside him.

Wayne stopped as he exited the tent, looking left towards where the man had gone, but he saw nothing. Jamison ran to the flap and immediately dropped to his knees. Trying to decipher which footprint belonged to him.

He picked one, and began moving fast, towards the outside of the boma. He motioned to Wayne to split up and head along the other side.

As Wayne obeyed his hand signal, Jamison followed the spoor around to the gate area.

The man was running, the imprint of the footprints were no longer clear and sand was flicked from the front of his foot towards the back.

Jamison increased his pace.

He heard the screaming before he got to end of the long boma.

The shouts of people warning of a danger. Then the sound of hooves beating the hard ground.

He rounded the boma, and could see chaos in front of him as people clung to the sides of the temporary fencing, up out the way of panicked animals. People streamed out of the tent, like ants from a burning log, running to get out of the way. He could see the back end of the herd of sable as it had been funnelled between the boma, and the car park, and directly into the tent.

The sable were unpenned and they were making a break, running for their freedom.

The auction attendees were running for their lives.

'Jamison,' Wayne's shout carried above the noise. He homed in on him as he jumped down from the boma. Wayne pointed towards the car park area.

Jamison ran for the car park.

Wayne ran towards the tent.

Tara head the screaming and the shouting and suddenly there were black buck tearing through the tent. Sable antelope, she realised as one reached the end of the tent where the auctioneer stood and turned around. It hesitated for only a moment before putting its head down and charging to the right, towards an open air flap, and disappeared out the tent. The others followed, some jumping over people who sat on the edge near the aisle between the seats. Farmers and patrons threw themselves to the middle of the seating, giving the beasts room to run freely down and out the other side.

Women screamed.

Men shouted.

One sable stopped halfway down, almost opposite where they crouched on the ground. Gabe had his arm over both her and Josha and somehow Moeketsi had jumped from his seat near Gabe and now shielded her with his body from the side where the sable was.

Tara screeched as it looked like it was about to charge at them.

Someone came barrelling over the chair next to them as the sable started to run, and at the last moment Moeketsi saw the man. He sprung upwards to try to deflect him away and over the top of Tara, tried to help pull him over them, so that he didn't land on her, but the man's boot kicked her in the chest.

Solid steel-capped leather connected with breast bone.

For a moment Tara saw stars as pain shuddered through her whole body. Radiating out from her chest, through her neck up and down. Heaviness pressed in on her.

Moeketsi pushed the man totally off her, and he was apologising and thanking them at the same time, but Tara lay still. Plastic chairs went flying as the sable hooked one onto its horns. Spooked by the white chair, it turned towards the crowd trying to leave. But the men threw their arms in the air, shouting, and the buck snorted and unusually chose flight over fight. It turned around and fled after the rest of its herd, out the top end of the tent, the chair still stuck like a crown above its head.

Slowly people got up off the floor, and dusted themselves down.

Gabe knelt over Tara. 'You okay? Tell me you are okay.'

'Oww,' she said. 'Man that hurts.'

'Oh thank God!' Gabe said.

'Mum!' Josha called as he threw himself down in the dirt next to her.

'Josha, I'm okay. I'm okay. I just feel like something huge is sitting on my chest. Are you hurt at all?'

'I'm good, Mum,' he said and he clung to her.

Wayne burst through the crowd that had begun to mill around. 'Tara! Josha!' he shouted.

'Here, we are here,' Josha said jumping up. 'Mum's hurt. Some guy scrambled to get out the way of the buck and kicked her in the chest.'

Wayne pushed past the people filing out and eventually got to her. 'Shit,' he said, as Moeketsi moved out the way so he could kneel next to her.

'I'm fine, just a bit sore, that's all. It's going to be a bruise from hell but I can breathe again so I should be okay. Just bruised.'

He hugged her, mindful of her sore chest, and he reached for Josha and hugged him too. 'Oh my God, I was terrified that you guys would be caught in a stampede. What the sable could have done to you …'

'One got a chair caught on his horns, and eventually ran out the other side after the rest,' Josha was saying. 'It looked like a crown, but he was as mad as a snake!'

'What happened?' Tara asked, looking at Wayne.

'It was him. Buffel. He was here, he let them out. He's seen you and definitely now knows where you and Josha are.'

'Dad, I can't breathe,' Josha said, 'you are squeezing me in tight here.'

Wayne let Josha and Tara go. He sat down on the plastic chair. Moeketsi asked. '*Baas*, where is Jamison?'

'He followed Buffel into the car park—'

'We must hurry to help him,' Moeketsi said, 'I know where his *bakkie* is parked and he can get out fast.' He began running away, dodging the crowd.

Wayne was torn, to stay with his family, or to go and help Jamison. He knew that in that second, he had to choose because he couldn't do both.

But inside the tent with Gabe and with the crowd, they were safe. Buffel wouldn't try to come back in. Tactically it made sense that he could leave them. But that didn't make the decision any easier.

'I have to go. Jamison needs me,' Wayne said to his family. 'Stay here where there is a crowd. Gabe, don't let them go out of this tent, stay within a crowd!'

He ran after Moeketsi, saying 'excuse me,' to dazed patrons as he passed.

'We will have a short half-hour break, then we will be right back with the auction.' The auctioneer was speaking into his microphone, but Tara didn't think that anyone was listening.

She sat on the chair, and put her head in her hands.

Buffel was here.

They were in immediate danger and Wayne had just rushed out to help Jamison.

Jamison was in danger too.

Gabe asked, 'How sore on a scale of one to ten is your chest, Tara?'

'Eleven and counting,' she admitted, 'but I think I'll be okay, Gabe. I don't think the animals are supposed to get out and run through the auction. Seriously, when last did you ever see such chaos—'

'Until you got kicked in the chest it was running into the home video's funny rank, but I agree with you on the chaos theory,' he said, as he sat down next to her.

She watched Josha as he put his backside on the chair in front of them and he rocked, and bounced the chair. 'You sure you're okay, Josha?'

'I'm good, Mum, you're okay, so I'm good.' He wiggled and put his feet up on the chair in front of him.

She took a few deep breaths. 'Gabe, did you hear Wayne?' she asked quietly, trying to make it so her voice didn't reach her son.

'About Buffel being here. I heard him. I'm staying close, keeping you guys inside the crowd.'

'He's really here at the auction. He's really the one after me. Even after Jamison wouldn't speak his name. You said it, and I still couldn't believe it was him.' She looked around wildly. But people milled around aimlessly, standing to vacate seats as they grouped together to natter and some filed out into the sunshine.

'Mum, we should go back to Cape Town if he is here,' Josha said.

Tara ran her hand over her son's cheek. 'You weren't supposed to hear that,' she said, 'But thank you, Josha, I think we are safer here. I think that Wayne, Jamison and all the game guards in Kujana can keep us safer on our own home ground.'

'You could have a point there,' Gabe said.

Tara continued to rub her chest. Looking around a bit, scanning every face in the crowd.

'When we leave here today, it would be good to have you checked out, Tara, make sure it's just superficial bruising.'

'What's a doctor going to do?' she asked.

'Make sure there are no broken bones. Normal doctoring things,' Gabe said.

'I hate it when you are so practical,' she said. 'There is nothing broken as far as I can tell, just a bad bruise. I'll take some Panado if it's still sore then, and Wayne can rub some onika oil in later.'

'When did you become Miss Tough Nut again? Oh wait, that was when you became a farmer's wife, I remember that day …'

She smiled at Gabe. 'You should. It was just a few months ago and you walked me down that aisle!'

'Oh yeah, that part I would never forget.'

Tara smiled weakly. 'Gabe,' she said. 'How feeble have I become that I'm sitting here inside hiding, and Wayne is out there tracking my own father's killer? I should be strong and out there with them. He has been my burden all these years. It's not fair that I have passed the problem onto Wayne.'

'Not passed, shared. That's what family does, Tara, they share good and bad,' Gabe said.

'Poor Wayne, I seem to be sharing more bad then good.'

'Rubbish. The two of you look like a couple still on honeymoon. You are perfect for each other and I'm so glad that you got back together.'

'I wouldn't have it any other way, Gabe, you are still my best cousin in the whole wide world, and I wouldn't have had this happiness if it wasn't for you,' Tara said.

She watched as Gabe looked around too. Looking for a ghost from their past that was now haunting their future.

'Gabe, I still can't fathom just what the hell Buffel is doing with those girls,' Tara said.

'Jamison won't tell me, he clams up every time I ask him. It's like whatever is happening is so bad that a grown man can't talk about it,' Gabe said. 'My gut is still telling me muti trade, a white man selling white human parts on the market ... it's plausible. *Sangoma*s would come from far and wide to buy muti from him. A white Karoi.'

Movement caught his eye at the front of the tent. 'They're back,' Gabe said and she looked over to where Wayne and Moeketsi hurried towards them.

She could read fear, stress and trouble on Wayne's face.

'Where is Jamison?' she asked.

'He took him. We saw him hit Jamison across his head with a thick stick, and toss him into the back of his *bakkie*. He got away,' Wayne said. 'We need the police to help us. He has kidnapped Jamison in front of witnesses now, we have proof to follow him to the ends of the earth.'

CHAPTER 29

Radio Waves

Hluhluwe Police Station, South Africa
12:30pm

The SAP sergeant behind the counter rubbed his chin. 'Kidnapping. No, that happens in America, not here in Africa.'

'He hit him over the head, and took off in his *bakkie*, I'd say that what he did was kidnapping,' Wayne argued.

The sergeant nodded.

'He has my business partner, I gave you his numberplate, what more do you need to find him?' Wayne asked.

The sergeant scrounged around the counter looking for a pen.

'Oh for Christ's sake,' Wayne swore. 'We are not asking you to solve world peace, just stop him killing Jamison. We have to find him—'

'We will. His *bakkie* is easy enough to spot with his Zimbabwe number plates,' the policeman said. He took the piece of paper that Moeketsi had written the numberplate down on, and disappeared into the back room.

'Why is it always so hard to get the police to move at anything other than Africa speed?' Wayne complained.

Gabe shrugged his shoulders, knowing it was a rhetorical question. 'I'll be with Tara and Josha in the truck. I know Moeketsi is with them, but I—'

'Thank you, Gabe,' Wayne said, putting his hand on Gabe's shoulder. 'It's better with you there too. Can you make sure that Moeketsi has checked in on Ebony again. It's been half an hour already, the extra guards should be at her house.'

'Will do,' Gabe said and he walked out the police station into the parking lot.

He opened the door of the Mack truck. 'No news from any truckers yet?' he asked Moeketsi, as he climbed up and sat next to Josha.

'Nothing. I'll give it another five minutes then repeat the emergency call out. If that *bakkie* is in this area, they will close their net and someone will call it in. The truck drivers will want the reward for information that Wayne offered when he first radioed the details. Big cash offered just for spotting the *bakkie* and keeping tabs on it was a smart thing to do.'

Gabe nodded. 'Only it could create other problems for him further down the track—'

The truck's CB radio crackled and then an African voice shouted loud and clear into the cab.

'Wild Translocations, Wild Translocations, this is Donkey Freight 1, come in—'

Moeketsi reached for the mouthpiece. 'Donkey Freight 1. Moeketsi from Wild Translocations here.'

'Just saw that white *bakkie* with the Zim plates you guys were looking for, driving into your Kujana Farm driveway. I have pulled off and am watching that he doesn't come out again.'

'Thank you, Donkey Freight 1. Either wait now, and once we get there we can sort out your reward, or next time you are in the area, drop in. We will keep a beer cold for you.'

'Counting on it! I have time. I'll wait until I see you, just to make sure he doesn't go anywhere.'

'See you soon. Thank you, Donkey. Wild out.'

'Donkey out.'

Gabe jumped out the truck and ran for the police station. He pushed the station door open. 'He went to your place. Donkey Freight 1 just called his location in on the radio, Buffel turned into Kujana Farm!'

The policeman pushed through the internal door speaking at the same time. 'That registration comes back to a Kirchman Bernard Potgieter.'

'Thank God,' Wayne said. 'Who?'

'So you found him?' the policeman asked, both speaking over each other again.

'Kirchman Bernard Potgieter,' the policeman repeated. 'No Buffel in his name.'

Wayne looked at the policeman. 'Okay, thank you.' He took a moment, then added. 'And yes, the truckers came through for us, they have located him. Now get your vans to Kujana Farm, we are going to need help to stop a murder!'

Together Wayne and Gabe sprinted back to the trucks.

Wayne didn't need to open the driver's door, because Moeketsi was busy jumping out. He already had the engine started and running for him.

'Thanks,' Wayne said as he climbed in, and Moeketsi slammed his door.

'You okay back there, Tara?'

'Dandy. Always wanted to be hunted like an animal, kicked in the chest and travel at high speed in a huge Mack truck. Just get home so we can save Jamison.'

Wayne smiled. This was the woman he knew. The woman he loved. The fighter. The one whose dry sense of humour made him laugh at inappropriate times.

His wife.

He glanced at the gold ring on his own third finger, that she had so recently put there, and he couldn't help but smile. They were together now, and they were living their happy ever after they should have been allowed to choose when they were just teenagers and in love.

He heard Gabe close the passenger side door. 'All aboard?' Wayne asked as he put the truck in gear and took off. 'Josha, how are you holding up?'

'Fine,' Josha said, sitting in the middle seat between his dad and Gabe.

'Would you like to hail Ebony on the radio for me?'

Josha grabbed the CB and called on their private channel. 'Wild Translocations home base two.'

'Home base two,' Ebony said, obviously waiting by the radio for some news on Jamison.

Josha passed the mouthpiece to Wayne.

'Ebony, keep your house locked up and the alarm switched on. Stay inside. Buffel is on his way into Kujana. I'm hoping that the police will not be that far behind us. We just left the station. Only they called him Kirchman Bernard Potgieter, not Buffel.'

'Okay,' Ebony said.

'Hang in there, Eb, we will get him back—'

'I know,' she said quietly.

'Those extra guards should be at your home, Ebony, you know those men. They are all black, don't shoot them. Don't let any white man in that house, Eb, even if he says he is the police. Wait for us.'

'I know him,' she said softly. 'I won't let him in.'

They heard a child start to cry in the background and then someone else soothed it.

'Ebony, who is inside your house with you?' Wayne asked.

'Your mother. She has been listening in on her CB radio, and she put your ridgebacks in her Mercedes Benz and drove down the farm road and came to be with me.'

'My mother?' he said.

'Yes, she wanted to help. I have your dogs inside my fence and I gave her the kids to look after while I got everything else ready.'

'Ebony, you are a genius. Hang in there. Stay safe.'

'Oh Wayne, your mother said she knows how to use a weapon, I'm assuming that giving her a hunting rifle would be alright.'

Wayne smiled. 'I don't remember her ever shooting, but that's not to say she doesn't know how to use a weapon ... I wasn't always at home—'

'Hurry, Wayne,' Ebony said.

'I'm pushing, Eb, we are flying, believe me. We'll get there in no time.'

He handed Josha the mouthpiece, and put both hands on the steering wheel. The junction in the road to turn off left towards the farm was coming up, and he needed both hands and to use his exhaust breaks to slow considerably to navigate it safely. Despite the urgency to get home to Kujana, he had his family in the truck with him and they were precious to him. The Mack slowed down to a crawl and rounded the steep turn, then Wayne pushed his foot on the accelerator and picked up speed again, quickly passing the speed limit.

Suddenly Gabe snapped his finger. 'The connection, I know the connection. I got it, Tara, I found the connection. It's so him! The link as to why Buffel could so be the same man who is killing the girls now, because he saw a killing like that when he was just a kid.'

'What?' she asked from the back.

Gabe turned towards her. 'Impendla. I knew that name. He's one of the dead children mentioned in that newspaper cutting. Now the police have called Buffel by his whole name, Kirchman Bernard Potgieter, it makes perfect sense. Kirchman Bernard Potgieter – the mission reverend's child – was the survivor who didn't get used in the tree ritual from that article that I found when I first worked in the Bulawayo paper. The old one from 1946 about native witchcraft and sacrificing children in the Karoi area when a chief died, and hanging them in a tree.'

'So why would he kill the girls?' Wayne asked.

Tara said, 'It all fits. When Jamison told us of his cousin Gibson watching him, he said Gibson spoke of his mumblings, of wanting the butterfly to save Impendla. In his own warped way, he probably believes that by replicating the ritual he witnessed, that this boy Impendla was involved in, he would save his friend. Save his soul, help him cross over to the light, the other side to be with the ancestors. The belief in the afterlife is strong in the black community in Zimbabwe, perhaps Buffel was influenced more by that than his father's Christian ways.'

'You knew this man's name all this time, Gabe?' Wayne said.

'No. No one called him that when we were growing up, it was always just Buffel. I never put two plus two together. That he was the young missionary's son. The big neighbour from next door. We were kids, Tara was twelve and I was twenty. We didn't have the training or experience we do now. But if it is him, only he knows where the missing girls are, or what happened to them,' Gabe said.

'Shit,' Wayne said.

CHAPTER
30

Bunkering Down

Kujana Farm, Hluhluwe, South Africa
12:30pm

Buffel hated being disorganised.

He hated spur of the moment decisions without planning.

Taking Shilo in front of everyone had been one of those moments.

If only that farmer and Shilo hadn't chased him.

He'd only gone to the auction to check the information he had was correct. Then he was going to stake out their ranch and learn the routines.

He wasn't ready for a confrontation.

He had been spooked when they had recognised him in the tent and given chase. His impromptu kamikaze escape had almost worked. Except Shilo had taken him by surprise when he charged him by his *bakkie*. He didn't think Shilo had it in him to take him on, in hand-to-hand combat. Shilo knew his strength, and even at sixty-three he was a stronger man than most.

He had underestimated Shilo's determination and rage. Grabbing a stick from the back and knocking him out had been his only choice. But then he had thought that if he had Shilo, then the farmer would follow, and that he would bring Tara with him.

He would get his Butterfly for Impendla.

So he had lifted Shilo into his *bakkie* and driven away.

The only place he knew that the man would follow and bring The Butterfly was Kujana Farm. He already knew the way there. He had stopped on the side of the road and tied Shilo up by both his hands and his feet before moving him to the front seat. Shilo had started to groan and wake while he was tying him tightly to the passenger seat.

He cursed that Shilo was too big to fit in the hidden compartment under the back seat where he'd smuggled his little butterflies through the border posts.

He began the drive towards Kujana Farm.

Shilo groaned again.

'Shut up, quit moaning like that!' Buffel said.

'Shit, Buffel, you son of a bitch. What the—' Shilo surfaced enough to realise he was tied up. Tight. 'You fucking lunatic. Untie me. Let me go!' But as he struggled, he hit his head on the headrest, and groaned at the pain.

'I should have hit you harder across that thick head you savage good-for-nothing *kaffir*. Then I wouldn't have to listen to your voice,' Buffel muttered.

'Any harder and I would have been dead,' Shilo said as he attempted to move against the rope that held him to the chair.

'You might still get your wish. Stay still, man. Wriggling is not going to loosen that rope.'

'Fuck it, Buffel! Get these bladdy ropes off me. I know what you do with people you take hostage. No fucking way are you doing that to me!'

'I remember it like it was yesterday! Now shut up before I shut you the fuck up!'

'Buffel, stop this *bakkie* and let me out. You can't do this, people would have seen you at the auction, the police will get involved. This can't end well for you. Think, man, this is not the type of thing you do, you plan things. Untie me!'

'I just want The Butterfly. Then Impendla can cross over and be with his ancestors. He will bring her with him to save you.'

'The Butterfly? Tara? You can't still be after her all these years?' Shilo asked.

Buffel rocked in his seat as he drove. 'The Butterfly. I need her to set Impendla free.' He looked across at Shilo.

'Who is Impendla, for God's sake?'

'He was taken. The *Karoi*, she killed him. She hung him …' Buffel's voice dropped off as if speaking the words pained him too much to talk.

'Buffel, you can stop this, you can end it. Let me go. Piss off back to Zimbabwe. I haven't broken my oath. All these years, I haven't talked. I never told anyone your name. No one needs to know, just leave me here on the road. Let me go!'

'But you might. You still might. Now stop talking,' Buffel said, 'before I stuff something in your mouth to shut you up or better yet, I can stop and get the tranqs from my hunting bag.'

Buffel thought about the tranquillisers, how he might need to adjust the dose for Shilo. The shots he gave the girls when he took them to accompany Impendla would be too weak.

The first girl he had given the tranquiliser to in Cape Town had died too quickly, and he had learnt to decrease the dosage, keeping the girls barely alive, silent and immobilised as they were hidden in his *bakkie* beneath his seat, with the sheep he was transporting covering any noise or smell they made, until he could take them to his shrine. Only there could he spill their blood. Only where it was sacred for Impendla.

He had learnt that a child couldn't have as much of the chemicals as a wild animal.

Soon he might need to give a similar amount to Shilo. He didn't want to kill him just yet.

He wanted Shilo alive.

'Why are we going towards my farm?' Shilo asked, breaking into Buffel's thoughts.

'He will bring The Butterfly home,' Buffel said.

There was a long silence. Then Shilo spoke, 'No. Buffel, listen to me. Wayne is a Recce. A true fucking Recce, an operative, not a desk jock. You know their reputation. They are legendary for being fucking psychos. Do you seriously think that he will let you get away with this? He will never let Tara go, you won't get her. Stop the *bakkie*. Don't try and fight Wayne for Tara. It won't work. He will kill you!'

Buffel stopped the *bakkie* again on the side of the road. He grabbed a rag out of the side panel in the door as he got out and walked around to the passenger side. He climbed in the back, and put the rag over the top of the seat, and against Shilo's mouth.

Shilo clamped his teeth together.

Buffel attempted for a moment to saw the material backwards and forwards against the obstruction.

'Open now or you get a tranquilliser shot!' Buffel said, and Shilo opened his teeth a little. Buffel pulled the rag tight and fastened the gag in place behind his head.

Coming up to the turn off of Kujana Farm, Buffel smiled. There were signs that counted down the kilometres to the entry. He should have expected a flash entrance like it had, the place was a game farm, and by the looks of it, and from what he had got out of the locals, a prosperous one.

Buffel turned in and drove over the extra wide cattle grid. 'He doesn't mess around with his entrance, does he?' he said as he raced down the farm road through the trees that lined the sealed road.

He could see what appeared to be a farmhouse nestled among the old tall trees to the left, but he needed somewhere more quiet to work on Shilo, to set a trap.

To collect his Butterfly and have an escape route out again.

He continued down the road and saw the perfect dwelling.

Behind the sheds there was a house tucked away. It was surrounded by tall, neatly trimmed hedges. He drove to the front gate, and through it. Not bothering to open it, his bull bar on the front caused it to shudder as it sprang back and opened towards the four-string barbed wire fence that hid inside the hedging. He went through the gate and drove slowly up the road towards the front door.

No dogs came running and barking at him. It was a good sign.

He looked around. No one was running to tell him he was in the wrong place for the safari farm experience. Good.

When the road turned to a single separate garage that was attached to the house, he left it and took the thinner concrete path to the front door. He drove over the rose bushes and flowers that lined the pathway. Soon he was as close to the door as he could get without driving up the steps.

He stopped and climbed out of the *bakkie*, taking his keys with him as he walked up the front steps and tried the front door. It was locked. He ran his finger along its edge, finding that it opened inwards.

He took a step back then he lifted his foot and kicked at the lock. The door didn't open, but it did give a little. He stepped backwards again, and slammed into the door with his shoulder.

This time the lock splintered the softer wood on the inside of the door.

He called out into the house. 'Anyone home?'

No one answered him, and no one tried to shoot at him. He poked his head through the open door. Then he turned back to the *bakkie* and went to fetch Shilo.

He wasn't old, but he was getting older. Shilo was a large man, and he huffed and puffed now as he manoeuvred him through the front door.

He dumped Shilo on the white leather couch in the lounge area. He cut a cord from the curtains and he tied it into the rope that already bound Shilo's arms and legs. He tied Shilo to the metal feet of the sofa before taking a look around the house.

It was definitely empty, no one at home. No one hiding in a bedroom or anything.

The house belonged to one classy lady, based on the furnishings. From the white and red harem-styled main bedroom with the huge sleigh bed, to the fancy pink handtowels in the kitchen, the house smelt of expensive perfume.

He returned to the *bakkie*. Shouldering his duffel bag, he pulled his rifle from under the seat. Walking inside, he set both down on the white full pile carpet. But not too close to Shilo, just in case.

He needed to barricade the house and fortify the front. He also needed to ensure that he had a clear escape route planned. He knew that the farmer would come.

He knew that the police might come, but he needed to know from Shilo how much he had told them. He needed to try to trade Shilo for The Butterfly, and, maybe the boy too. He needed to complete the final ritual as close to the original as he could. Four males and two females. Only this time, The Butterfly would be sacrificed, and this time he would save Impedla. The children's voices crying out in his head would be silenced as she walked them all through the light.

He hated that this part was not meticulously planned. It meant there was always an element where something could go wrong.

He kicked Shilo as he passed him and pushed a bookcase against the window near where the TV cabinet was.

This mess was all Shilo's fault.

If he had just kept out of his business in the first place, it would never have come to this.

He lowered all the blinds, and pulled the curtains closed. He moved every piece of furniture that he could to either barricade a door or block a window, except the kitchen door at the back. He left that free of clutter as an escape route.

While he was moving things, he walked into a study, and there he found a CB radio station. He reached for the power button.

There was silence.

No chatter on the airwaves, but he wondered about the presence of a radio in the house, and the whereabouts of its owner.

CHAPTER 31

A Thin Line

Kujana Farm, Hluhulwe, South Africa
13:15pm

As Wayne drove into his property, he took a deep calming breath. First, he needed to find where Buffel was holding Jamison, then he needed to ensure that Tara and Josha were safe. Only then would he go after the son of a bitch. He drove towards his homestead.

Hawk Ngele, one of his game guards, stepped out a distance in front and raised his hands in a stop position. He slowed the Mack truck down to stop next to him and Hawk climbed up onto the outside step to talk to Wayne.

'*Baas*, he's in your mother's house. We didn't try and stop him, just like you instructed. He has taken *Baas* Jamison inside, but he was tied up and had a gag in his mouth.'

'Thank you, Hawk,' Wayne said. A calmness he knew well descended on him, he was in combat mode. His Recce training had now kicked in. His mission was to retrieve Jamison.

'He also took one rifle out his *bakkie*, it looked like a Ruger or some other bigger calibre hunting rifle, and he had a large duffel bag that he carried in too. But other than that, nothing. No movement from inside for the last ten minutes or so.'

'Instruct the men to gather by the tractor shed,' Wayne said.

'Yes, *baas*,' Hawk said and he jumped clear of the track.

Wayne continued to the Mack truck's parking bay inside one of the big sheds, and within moments, Moeketsi was parked along side him in the smaller truck.

'Moeketsi, stay with Tara. If Buffel takes one step towards her or Josha, shoot him. Even if you have to shoot through me or Jamison. Understood?'

'Yes, *baas*.'

'Under no circumstance is he to get his hands on her at all.'

'Yes, *baas*, I understand, I will die before I let him get his hands on Madam Tara.'

Wayne helped Tara out of the truck. He held onto her waist and hugged her gently to him.

'I need to go and get Jamison,' he said.

'How?'

'Still working on that, but I'm going to try talk him out first.'

Tara said, 'I'm coming with you. Gabe and I might be able to help you. He knew us once …'

'I don't want you anywhere near—'

'Wayne, I need to do this.'

He looked at her face, it was set and determined. 'Okay, but you stay beside me, and don't show an inch of yourself where he can shoot it, okay.'

'Sure,' she said and lifted herself to kiss him.

'Josha, go into the house—'

'No way, I'm staying with Mum.'

'Me too,' Gabe said, 'So don't even try tell me—'

'Moeketsi, take Josha with you, bring back arms for everyone from the weapons safe in the office. Bring a tranquiliser gun for

Josha, I don't want him killing anyone at his age. Meet us at the gate into my mother's house.'

'Come, Josha,' Moeketsi said, and they turned to the main Wild Translocation office that took up part of the shed space at the other end.

'Tara, stay close to Gabe. I'll be right back,' he instructed as he crouched down, and headed towards the outside of the sheds. Slowly Wayne crept along the hedging and then peered around the corner.

He could see Buffel's *bakkie* parked against the garage door, facing the gates, as if ready to leave in a hurry if Buffel got the chance. He couldn't see in because of the tinting, but he didn't think that Buffel was in it, his boys would have noticed something like that and reported it to him. The house was silent.

He retraced his steps to the shed.

'Right, we need to get closer, before we do anything else,' he said to Tara and Gabe.

Storm came and stood next to him, and he reached over and gave her a pat. 'Come on, old girl, you need to stay out of the way too,' he said to her.

They walked to the assembly area where ten of his armed game guards stood waiting with Hawk.

He addressed them. 'I'll drive the front end loader in there, the thick metal on the front will give some protection if he opens fire. Hawk will drive behind me with the hay bailer, and come up on the left, blocking the *bakkie* in so Buffel has no escape route. Mark and White, you need to put something across the front of the smaller tractor to protect Hawk as he drives. Bring some of that old corrugated iron from the back of the shed that we have piled there. Be careful of snakes when you lift it. Tie it in place with wire, quickly. My idea is that we drive with five men close behind us, towards the front of the house.' He pointed to a group standing together as a unit. 'I want you to go on the outside of the hedge, crawl under the bush and the wire at the back of the house and stay hidden as close to the back door as you can. If he comes out that door, shoot him. I'll move the tractor in five minutes. Move out!'

The men scattered to do his bidding.

Moeketsi and Josha arrived, both loaded with weaponry.

He gave them a quick rundown of the plan.

'Thank God my mother went to help Ebony with her kids,' Wayne said.

'Poor kids, she's a strict one that,' Moeketsi said. 'Sorry, *baas*. I know she is your mother—'

'No it's okay, you're right. She has tried hard since coming home again, but some things in her nature she simply can't change. But she seemed to have those kids controlled which was what Ebony needed.'

'Talking Ebony—' Moeketsi said and nodded his head.

Ebony had just driven Jamison's dual cab up beside them. She got out, and lifted a .303 rifle behind her.

Wayne's dogs came bounding up behind her, their tongues lolling to the side.

'Heel.' The ridgebacks dropped down at his feet. 'Whoa, Eb. Where you going?'

'To shoot the lowdown shit that has my husband,' she said in a voice as cold as ice. Wayne had never heard that tone from her and he knew that she was in a place that he had to drag her back from.

'No, Ebony,' Wayne said. 'You can't do that. You have two beautiful girls who need you. You can't go to jail for him.'

She seemed to deflate a little, and then she looked at him. 'Wayne, how did it come to this? How did he get the jump on Jamison? He's going to kill him. This man inside, he has no conscience. He tried to burn me alive.'

Wayne opened his arms and she stepped into a hug. He pulled her close. 'Eb, I know. Jamison told us.'

He let her go slowly. 'You obviously want to be nearer the action, like Tara, so wait here at the end of the shed with her, Josha and Moeketsi,' he said.

Ebony nodded. He watched as Tara and Ebony walked to the outside of the shed where Ebony rested her .303, leaning it against the cement, barrel upwards, keeping it close. Josha walked to his mum's house, and his dogs crept towards Josha. 'Go, guard him!' Wayne said and the dogs rushed at Josha, then sat either side of him.

Wayne watched as his son reached down and fussed both of them on their heads.

He turned back to his men. 'Right, move out in three minutes.'

'Moeketsi, don't let the women come out from the shed,' he instructed.

'Yes, *baas*.'

Wayne took a side arm and a rifle from Moeketsi, and extra ammo clips.

'And these,' Moeketsi said as he passed him both a throwing knife and a hunting knife.

'Thanks. Come on, Gabe,' he said as he ran to the front end loader, and climbed up.

Gabe stood at the bottom. 'Am I inside or outside?'

'Get in, hurry, don't let me regret this,' he said as Gabe clambered up and squished into the cab with him.

He started her up, and backed carefully out the shed.

He could see Hawk had finish tying down several sheets of corrugated iron to the front of the baler and was climbing into the driver's seat. Wayne started driving towards his mother's house. Looking back, he saw Hawk was following closely behind him. There were feet running behind Hawk's tractor and he knew that his men were there to back him up.

He drove through the gate, lifting the thick metal bucket in front as he went to protect the glass of the cab. Slowly, he drove over the grass, then over the rose bushes that Buffel had already destroyed. Looking out his side window he judged when he needed to stop outside the front door. If need be, he would be happy to drive the front loader right inside, but he thought he might try to talk to the man first.

He could see Hawk had parked and retreated from his baler and was with his men, now using the vehicles as cover. Some stood, others lay flat, but everyone trained their weapons on the front of the house.

Wayne opened the door on the side of the front loader and shouted out, 'Potgieter. We have you surrounded.'

A short silence followed, and then a single shot rang out.

Everyone dived for cover but they could hear that the shot hadn't hit anything. It appeared as if he had only shot out the window, and upwards, aiming for nothing and no one.

'Potgieter, no more shooting. I have trained guards ready to come in there. But I would rather you come out alive,' he said.

He paused for a moment.

'I'm told by a good authority that you need to save a friend, save Impendla's soul. If you can come out, we can organise that.'

Silence came from the house.

'Potgieter. Buffel. We know what happened. We know you need help and that you are in a dark place at the moment, that the weight of your friend's death is tormenting you. It wasn't you who killed him. Don't feel responsible for another person's death. Let Jamison go. Walk out with your hands above your head. Surrender to us and we can get you help. There are good doctors who can help you.'

He waited for a moment and when he heard nothing, he tried again.

'Buffel. Kirchman. Surrender. Do not harm Jamison in any way. We will get you help for Impendla's soul, we can get a priest or a *sangoma* to help him cross over.'

'Butterfly!' Buffel shouted. 'I want The Butterfly.'

'No fucking way!' Wayne swore.

Buffel shouted back. 'Tara Wright is the only one who can save Impendla's soul. If she comes in here, I will let Shilo go.'

'What if you show some faith and send Jamison out, and she can meet you on the veranda?' Wayne shouted.

'No, then one of your professional hunters will take me out. She comes in or Shilo dies.'

'Then we kill you and you will never get to save your Impendla anyway,' Wayne said. 'Think of Impendla. He will stay in a dark dark place, his soul will always be trapped where he died, and the witch will keep his soul. He will come for you, because you never got a priest to bless him.'

'Tell him to let Jamison speak,' Gabe suggested.

'Let us talk to Jamison to make sure he's still alive, then Tara will talk to you from out here.'

They waited with breaths held.

'Wayne,' Jamison shouted.

'Thank God he is still alive,' Wayne said to Gabe.

'Wayne, don't let him get—' Jamison went silent.

'Shit,' Wayne said.

'Jamison,' he called.

'Shilo won't be talking anymore until I get Tara.'

'I'm here. Start talking, Buffel,' Tara shouted, and Wayne realised that Tara had crept up behind his front end loader.

'Shit!' he cursed at the same time as Gabe.

Then Wayne heard the sirens of the police vans arriving, and his heart sank.

CHAPTER

32

Nyamhika Nehanda

Kujana Farm, Hluhulwe, South Africa
14:30pm

Buffel sat in the lounge area, barricaded in. He rocked back and forth on his haunches. He had tied Shilo to the couch and put the gag in his mouth once more.

He had seen the police arrive, followed closely by the riot police, and he had seen them rush to join Kujana's game guards. He had watched them swarm in and take up positions. He knew that there were more guns pointed at the house than he had seen in many, many years.

'I am lost, Impendla,' he said. 'I have failed you.'

He looked over to where Shilo sat gagged and bound.

He was no threat now.

He was no help either.

He was the one man who had come close to being a friend. Together they had fought side by side. Then he had gone away. He didn't understand. He didn't want to help Impendla, even back then.

He walked over to him and undid the cloth from his mouth before crouching down on the carpet in front of him. 'Tell me, Shilo, how am I going to save Impendla if they have blocked my way out? When I get The Butterfly, how am I going to get out?' he demanded.

'You are not, Buffel. There is no way out,' Shilo said, shaking his head. 'Wayne and his men will never let you walk from here. And now that the police have arrived, you are stuck in here. No escape.'

'The *Nyamhika Nehanda*, she will find a way out. She will get The Butterfly, and she will run. She will escape—'

'There is no escape. You will be killed. There is no way out from this one, Buffel.'

'But Impendla? His soul?' Buffel shouted.

'Why do you think you can save him if you have Tara? How was she going to save him?'

'Now she is a woman, she is ready. She can save him, and all the butterflies she calls to her when she dies, she can set their souls free,' Buffel said.

'Where did you get that crap anyway, that you needed to kill her so long ago?'

'In a dream, I saw it in a dream. She set the children free and their voices stopped crying out and sung as if they were angels instead. The sound was happy because their souls were saved, they were with their ancestors and had crossed over into the light.' Buffel rocked backwards and forwards.

'A dream? Buffel, dreams are not true. It's like the nightmares, they are not real. Just thoughts, old thoughts, they don't mean anything anymore,' Jamison said, his voice level, controlled.

'It's real. He told me I had *Nyamhika Nehanda* inside. I have to save him. *Mwari* told me—'

Jamison shook his head. 'Buffel, you can't save him, it's too late. That was years ago. It's too long ago now. You should have said something years ago, I would have told you the truth then. Your friend, Impendla, his spirit is lost. He can never walk with his ancestors. That is the way. One year. You only had one year to find

Drip water on him. Keep him from the sunlight. Try to restart his brain, say he was sick.

But he wasn't. He was *Nyamhika Nehanda*, and he had served *Mwari* faithfully. So why had she failed Impendla and kept his soul?

All this time he had tried to appease her with sacrifices, and yet it had already been too late. He took his rifle from where he had left it by the window after firing his warning shot and walked back towards Shilo on the couch.

He took a deep breath, he squared his shoulders. He was 1st Psychological Operations Unit.

He was one of the elite.

One of the untouchables.

He heard the riot police breaking the windows as they began their assault on the house.

'They are coming, Shilo,' he said. '*Tiri Tose. We are together.* I have failed you, Impendla, my friend. Forgive me.'

He sank to his knees, and raised his favourite hunting rifle, his 416 Rigby with its wooden handle that reminded him so much of the rifle he had lost when Impendla was taken, and he loaded it.

The explosions from the grenades hurt his ears. He smelt the gas and his eyes watered.

He pulled the trigger as the first human forms appeared in the smoke.

One of the riot police, dressed in full helmet, fatigues and body armour, walked out the front door, his weapon pointed to the floor. He removed his gas mask.

'Clear!' he shouted. The head detective walked to the man.

While they were talking, Wayne could see a body being carried out on a blanket and deposited on the front lawn. He knew the clothes and the shape of the person well. 'Jamison!' Wayne cried and ran towards the riot police. He covered the short distance and threw himself down next to the policemen.

'He's alive. He's got burns from his ropes where he fought them and a nasty bump on the head, so he'll need a hospital to ensure he has no concussion.' The detective spoke from behind him. 'You shouldn't have crossed the barrier.'

'Detective—' Wayne began, but got no further as Ebony pushed through to her husband's side too, despite being told to stay behind the police vans. Wayne noticed that Moeketsi had discreetly picked up her .303 from where she had left it leaning on the wall of the tractor shed, and he watched as he put it inside the Mack truck, out of sight, tucking it behind the driver's seat so that the police didn't give her any trouble about it.

He gave him a thumbs up, and turned back to Jamison.

Jamison was coughing, and Ebony encouraged him to sit up, making it easier.

'What about Buffel?' Gabe asked behind him, as he too ignored the police instructions. 'Detective, where is Buffel?'

'In the house.'

Gabe started to walk to the house but the detective cautioned him. 'Unless you have a cast-iron stomach, don't go in there. Apparently the man's head has been blown apart, and there isn't much of it left attached to his body, and a lot of it is on the ceiling.'

'Where do you think the policemen need to look first?' Jamison asked Gibson.

'I think they should split up. There are two sites of interest. The mushroom shed and the sacred site,' Gibson said as he pointed to the huge shed build half submerged below ground level.

Gabe immediately said, 'I'm with the team who goes to the sacred site.'

'Me too,' said Tara. 'I don't want to go in that shed, it looks really dark.'

The policemen talked between themselves and their teams split up, with Zimbabweans and South Africans in both teams, to make sure that each country could record the same incident and not accuse the other of incompetence should something happen that either of them didn't like.

The detective from the farm was with the sacred site team, and they set off in their vehicles to follow Gibson to the site in the bush. The others were collecting huge spotlights from their *bakkies* and heading for the mushroom shed.

Jamison opted to stay and look through the shed. He had seen the tree re-enacted enough times before many years ago. He didn't need to see it again.

The detective climbed into the back seat of their 4x4, next to Gabe, with Wayne now driving, following the lead vehicle. They drove in the opposite direction to where the road had come into the farm, along a small strip dirt road where the middle *mannetjie* was covered with green grass that brushed the underside of the vehicle. They came to a wall of thorn trees. Gibson stood at the wall where a small game path led into it.

'Great, thorn trees, had to be,' the detective complained.

Fifteen minutes later they came into a clearing. A single tree grew in the clearing, and Gibson pointed to a bag hanging in the tree.

Some of the Zimbabweans had a discussion about carrying on because they were entering a *sangoma*'s private territory, but Gibson assured them that it was Buffel who had put the muti bags there. Gabe took pictures of the bags, keen to photograph everything about the murders he'd been working on for so many years.

As they came out of the bush they could see a large tree in the centre of a clearing. From its branches hung several large objects that looked like five cocoons suspended by thick nylon rope, high enough off the ground to stop wild animals tearing them apart.

There were white bones shattered and lying around on the ground everywhere. Gabe took a photo and then examined one closer. He had been in enough war zones, and seen enough carnage in his life to identify what he was looking at.

'This is human,' he said. 'Everyone, tread with caution, these are the remains of some of his victims.'

The detective shook his head. 'I thought you were mad, I thought that perhaps we were looking for some reporter's pipe dream. I followed this up because you were so insistent, Gabe, but you were right. Look at this.' He pointed to another fragment of human bone.

Gibson sniffed the air. 'Leopard,' he said and he looked up into the tree. 'There, in the branches.'

They could see the leopard that stood in the tree. It was large. Gibson brought his rifle up and got ready to shoot. 'It's seen us and it's not happy,' he said as the leopard hissed and spat at the humans intruding on its territory.

It moved through the branches, and then jumped down along the trunk of the tree and ran off into the bush. Outnumbered by humans, it had chosen to flee.

'We need to make sure that those are bodies in that tree,' the detective said.

They moved closer.

'Old, no smell,' Gibson said, as he lead them carefully to the tree. He gave his weapon to Wayne, and shinnied up into the lower branches and across to where one of the ropes was tied.

'Wait a moment, I need photographs,' Gabe said and again he took multiple photographs with both the cameras he carried. The

GLOSSARY

Achaar	An Indian word for pickle, used generally in Southern Africa for any pickle with an Indian flavour. (Indian – but used in general term in Southern Africa.)
Aiwa	No. (Shona)
Amawarrior	Nguni prefix 'Ama' to warrior. Name used for the raiders of the south, now most commonly known as the Ndebele or amaNdebelen, officially known under British rule as the Matabele. (Nguni)
Ándale	Come on, hurry up. An instruction used in my youth to tell a horse to run fast as it could. (Spanish)
Assegai	A traditional spear, used for fighting. (Generally used in Southern Africa.)
Baas	Boss. Generally used in Southern Africa as a reference for your employer. (Afrikaans)
Bags	Slang, to make a claim for. (English)

Bakkie	South African word for a pickup truck, a ute in Australian English. (Afrikaans)
Balla Balla	Kudu. (Ndebele)
Biltong	A kind of dried meat.
Bladdy	A swear word often used for emphasis, to replace 'really' alongside 'good', 'fantastic', 'great' – can also be used in derogatory terms, like 'that bladdy so and so', meaning that no good/good for nothing, etc. (South African slang)
Bobotie	A curried mince and baked egg traditional Afrikaans dish. (Afrikaans)
Boerewors	A traditional Afrikaans spicy sausage, made in a coil. (Afrikaans)
Boet	Brother. This term is also used for a close friend. (Afrikaans)
Boma	An area surrounded by a fence used to keep animals enclosed, also can refer to an area used for outdoor meals and parties. (Swahili, used generally in Africa)
Bonnox	A type of wire mesh fencing used to keep animals inside.
Bonsella	A bonus, a tip, a gift. (Zulu, used generally across Southern Africa.)
Braai / Braaivleis	A barbecue – to cook meat outdoors. (*Vleis* – meat in Afrikaans.)
Broekies	Knickers, underpants. (Afrikaans)
Budza	A hoe to scrape weeds from the fields. Sharp gardening tool. (Used generally across Southern Africa.)
Baie lekker	Very nice, very good. (Afrikaans)
Bundu	The wild bush. (South African slang)
Bushveld	The bush of Africa. (Southern African English)
Chicken-run	Reference to the people who left Rhodesia during and after the change to Zimbabwe. Term implies they were too scared to stay and fight

	or give the country a chance. (South African slang)
Chinhoyi	Formerly Sinoia
Chinhoyi Caves	Limestone caves located in the Makonde District, Zimbabwe, which have amazingly clear blue deep water in the cave system. Formerly Sinoia Caves.
Chipo	A bonus, A tip. A small gift. (Shona)
Chirorodziva	The biggest blue pool in the Sinoia Cave system. Called The Pool of the Fallen Heroes. (Shona)
Chockers	Filled to the brim – totally filled up. (Zimbabwe slang)
Claymores	During the Rhodesian war, these were often made with smaller old plough disks, packed with nails and other shrapnel and plastic explosives, set with wax. Designed to explode outwards, and damage the person coming into the trap, to slow them down, not necessarily to kill them, but make certain they can't follow the path they are on.
Concession	A hunting concession is when the Parks Board allow a certain number of animals to be hunted for the year. The 'concession' is what the hunter purchases – his quota of animals for the year/season.
Cossie	A swimming costume. (Zimbabwe slang)
Doek	African head scarf worn as part of a maid's uniform, but also as part of the traditional clothing. (Afrikaans)
Donkey boiler	An drum of water kept outside that is heated by fire then feeds hot water into the house area. (South African English)
Donkeyberries	*Grewia bicolor.* A native bush with brownish edible berries. (South African English)

Doppie/s	The shell left after a bullet is spent. This can also be a drink in Afrikaans. (Afrikaans, used in general slang)
Dorp	A small town. (Afrikaans)
Eish	An exclamation used to express anything and everything: from frustration to surprise to disapproval and everything in between. (Slang, used generally in Southern Africa.)
Esse stove	Stove that burns a fossil fuel. Can be anthracite or wood. (English)
FN	Light automatic rifle, standard issue weapon used during the Rhodesian Bush War made by Belgian arms manufacturer Fabrique Nationale de Herstal. (Acronym from Fabrique Nationale de Herstal.)
Four count	After jumping out of a plane, a static line paratrooper counts off four seconds in his head, at which stage he needs to hear and feel things start happening, if they don't, he knows to deploy his own spare chute from his chest. (English)
FRELIMO	Mozambique Liberation Front (FRELIMO) from the Portuguese Frente de Libertação de Moçambique. (Acronym from the English name.)
Geyser	An electric hot water system often placed inside the ceiling. (English)
Gooks	Terrorists were referred to as gooks during the Rhodesian Bush War because they were trained by Chinese and Cuban military. Also influenced by the American soldiers who went to fight in Rhodesia, because of the Vietnam War. Became used for any black terrorist.
Goosie sand	Loose sand in the lowveld. Fine and abundant and almost like beach sand. (Zimbabwean slang)
Groot gat	Big hole. (Afrikaans)

Gudo	Baboon. (Shona)
Hepcooler	A cold box used for keeping things cool. South African brands include Coleman. (Australian: Esky) (English)
Huya pano	Come here. (Shona)
Ice it	Put it on ice to keep for later, to save it for another time. (South African English slang)
Ikhaya	Home, a hut made with mud and thatched roof. (Zulu)
Imbodla	Wild cat, also *'Igola'*. (Zulu/Ndebele)
Impi	Armed body of men or a Zulu fighting regiment, often referred to as the Zulu Impis for their fighting skill under Shaka Zulu reign, and the reputation that remained after that. (Zulu)
Indlulamithi	Giraffe. (Zulu)
Ingutchini	The madhouse. Certifiably crazy. (Zimbabwe slang)
Ingwe	Leopard. (Zulu/Ndebele)
Inkosana	Eldest son, prince, son of a respected person. (Zulu)
Inkosazana	Eldest daughter, princess, or just daughter of a respected person. (Zulu)
Insinkew	Bushbaby. (Ndebele)
Kaalnek	Naked necked, chickens with no feathers on their necks. (Afrikaans)
Kaffir	The word *kaffir* has now evolved into an offensive term for a black person. But it was previously a neutral term for black southern African people. The word was also used of a non-believer, referring to a black person not being of Christian upbringing.
Kaffir oranges	*Strychnos spinosa*. Also known as the monkey orange, hard shell outside, and soft edible fruit inside.

Kapenta	A small fish found in Kariba Dam, it's dried and eaten by the local population.
Karoi	Little witch. Also a town in Zimbabwe near Sinoia. (Shona)
Kaross	Blanket made from animal skins. (Zulu/Ndebele)
Kaylite	Styrofoam / polystyrene. (Zimbabwe slang)
Kist	A blanket box, can be ornately carved or a simple box, used to store linen. (Generally used in Southern Africa.)
Knobkerrie	An African club. These are typically made from wood with large knob at one end and a long stick protruding from that. They can be used for fighting or throwing at animals during hunting. Ideal size to also be used as a walking stick. (From Afrikaans, but now generally used in Southern Africa.)
Komeredes	A New Zimbabwe soldier, referring to the soldiers employed by the Zimbabwe government following the end of the bush war. These soldiers were disliked intensely in Mozambique.
Kraal	An area where animals are kept, usually found inside and African village/settlement, and is usually circular with barricades to keep the stock inside. Can also refer to an African cluster of huts. (Afrikaans, but used commonly in South African English.)
Kujana	A fair distance away. (Zulu)
Laagered	The ox wagons formed a defensive circle called a laager.
Laat-lammetjie	A late lamb, when an older woman has a baby it is referred to as a *laat-lammetjie*. (Afrikaans)
Lowveld	Generally refers to low-altitude areas where the soil is loose and loamy, supporting grasslands, and flatter areas covered in grass or low scrub.

Nguni	A people of Africa, including the Xhosa, Zulu, Swazi, Hlubi, Phithi and Ndebele. Can also refer to a type of hardy African cattle.
Nyamandhlovu	Nyamandhlovu is a village in Matabeleland, northwest of Bulawayo. The name of the village means 'meat of the elephant'. (Ndebele)
Onika oil	An oil used to treat bruising. (South African)
Pan	A flat depression in the land that fills with water only when the rains are very good.
Panado	Paracetamol medication used for headaches and fever.
Penga	Mad in the head, certifiably mentally unstable enough to be institutionalised. (Zimbabwe slang)
Piccaninny	Also spelt as *pickaninny*. A young black child. At one time the word may have been used as a term of affection, but it is now considered derogatory. In this story this word is used with affection. (English)
POU	Psychological Operations Unit. Name used during the Rhodesian Bush War.
ProNutro	A breakfast cereal that has a porridge like consistency when mixed with milk.
PSYOPS	Psychological Operations Unit.
R&R	Military term, meaning rest and relaxation, time off from the military world.
Raviro	Gift from the gods. (Shona)
Recces	The South African Special Forces Brigade.
RENAMO	Mozambican National Resistance, from the Portuguese Resistência Nacional Moçambicana. An anti-Communist political organisation that fought against the FRELIMO during the Mozambican Civil War, and against ZANU from 1975 to 1992. (Acronym from Portuguese)

Riempies	Ropes made with animal hides. (Afrikaans)
Rooi	The colour red. (Afrikaans)
Rooinekke	English people. Can also can be called 'Sauties'. (Afrikaans)
Roora	A dowry, a payment made to a bride's family as a sign of respect. (Shona)
SADF	South African Defence Force. The SADF was all forces within South Africa: black, white, brown, everyone together were under one defence label.
Sadza	The staple food in Zimbabwe of the African people. It is a thick maize meal porridge. (Shona and Ndebele)
Sadza neNyama	*Sadza* and meat. Traditional dish of meat and gravy eaten with *sadza*. (Shona)
Sakubva	A township in Umtali, Rhodesia with a small area and high population density.
Salisbury	Capital of Rhodesia. New name: Harare.
Sangoma	Traditional healers, practitioners of traditional African medicine. Often still holding onto the Sharman aspect of mixing witchcraft with herbal medicines.
SAP	South Africa Police.
SAS	Rhodesia's Special Air Service.
Shongololo	*Jurus Terrestris Millipede.* Giant millipede, has a hard shiny dark brown segmented exoskeleton. (Zimbabwe, from Nguni '*ukusonga*', to roll up.)
Shoosh	Tell someone to keep quiet (sounds like bush). (South African slang)
Sinoia	A town on the road to Kariba from Salisbury. New name: Chinhoyi. (Shona)
Sinoia Caves	Limestone caves located in the Makonde District, Zimbabwe, which have amazingly clear blue deep water in the cave system. New name: Chinhoyi Caves. (Shona)

Siyabonga kakulu	Thank you very much. (Ndebele)
Spoor	Tracks, usually left by animals. (Afrikaans)
Takkies	Sandshoes/trainers, worn for running and exercising. (Afrikaans, general South African slang.)
Ters	Shortened form of terrorist. Term used during the Rhodesia Bush war. (Zimbabwe)
Thinning disease	In Africa, HIV is commonly referred to as the thinning disease. People who lose lots of weight suddenly are more often than not suspected of having HIV. If you have the thinning disease it is assumed that you will be dead soon as there is not a lot of intervention by the government with drugs.
Thuli-makwe	The Thuli-makwe water scheme was a dam built in the Thuli area, supplying irrigation to a vast area of commercially grown crops.
Tiri Tose	We are together. Motto adopted by the PSYOPS and the actual POU unit during the Rhodesia Bush war. (Shona)
Tokoloshe	A really bad spirit. A *tokoloshe* can resemble a zombie, or a poltergeist, or a gremlin, any demon-like thing. A *tokoloshe* in this book refers to something evil.
Tosholotsho	Formerly known as Tjolotjo, a village 65 kilometres north-west of Nyamandhlovu and 98 kilometres north-west of Bulawayo.
Troopie	National Serviceman. (Zimbabwe slang)
TTL	Tribal Trust Land.
Umtali	The third largest city in Zimbabwe in the east of the country. New name: Muture. (1983)
Varsity	University, shortened form in South Africa.
Veld/Veldt/Velt	A generic term defining wide open grass or low scrub rural spaces of Southern Africa. (Afrikaans)

Velskoene/ Veldskoene/ Velskoen	Bush shoes. These are suede leather ankle boots, usually worn without socks. (Afrikaans)
Vlei	A shallow minor lake, mostly of a seasonal or intermittent nature. (Afrikaans)
Xhostas store	The name of the store that sold second-hand goods, and mainly catered to the black trade, and was cheap.
Xolile	Made happy. (Zulu)
Yebo	Yes. (Zulu)
Z-style	A gate that can't fold in on itself; solid outside steel tubing in a Z shape across the inside of the frame, with a wire mesh covering.
ZANLA	Zimbabwe African National Liberation Army, the military wing of the Zimbabwe African National Union.

Madala	An old man. (Ndebele, slang. Also used in parts of South Africa)
Makonde District	Located in north central Zimbabwe. Chinhoyi, its main town, is approximately 125 kilometres by road to Harare.
Mala Mala	Mala Mala was the first privately owned game reserve in South Africa. It is located between the Sabi Sands game reserve and the Kruger National Park, and has international recognition as an outstanding reserve. It is considered to be the blueprint on which the South African safaris are built.
Mandrax	A drug made with Methaqualone that is highly addictive when smoked with Dagga, causes psychological and physical dependency.
Marula	*Sclerocarya birrea*. A medium-sized tree, mainly found in the woodlands of Southern Africa. Now popular for its fruits, which are used in the liqueur Amarula. When ripe, the fruits have a light yellow skin and white flesh. Many animals love this fruit. Even the seed/nut inside is eaten by rodents once the flesh of the fruit has gone.
Matabele	The Ndebele people.
Mfino	A wild African herb, sort of like spinach.
Mhanya	Run. (Shona)
Mhondoro	A royal mudzimu (wandering ancestral spirit) or lion spirit. Can also be a guardian spirit. (Shona)
Mhoroi amai	Hello, Mama. (Shona)
Middle *mannetjie*	The dirt bump in between the two tyre tracks in the road. (Afrikaans, used as a general term in Southern Africa)
Moffie	Male homosexual, used in a derogatory way, expressing distaste. (South African slang)
Moola	Also spelt as mula or moolah. Slang for money (Generally accepted African continent term)

Mudzimu	Wandering ancestral spirit. (Shona)
Mukomana	Boss's son. (Shona)
Mushi	Nice, great, fantastic, good. (Zimbabwe slang)
Musika Wahuku	The chicken market, the trading place in the middle of everything, that everyone comes to. (Shona)
Muti	Traditional medicine in Southern Africa. It is used in South Africa as a slang word for medicine in general. Also spelt as *'umuthi'*. (Zulu, general slang.)
Muture	The third largest city in Zimbabwe in the east of the country. Former name Umtali. (pre-1983)
Mvura	Water. (Shona)
Mwari	Shona god, the High God of the Shona. (Shona)
Mywena	Oh goodness. Literal translation: my you. (Zulu slang – now slang for Southern Africa.)
Mzilikazi	'The Great Road'. He was the Zulu who split from King Shaka, moved north and founded the Matabele kingdom, Matabeleland, Zimbabwe.
Ndebele	The Ndebele are an ethnic group in Zimbabwe, descendants from Mzilikazi.
Nehanda / Nyamhika Neranda	Shona god. *Nehanda*, originally Matope's sister-wife, possessed supernatural powers. She became a guardian spirit, and could transfer her spirit and inhabit other bodies. *Nehanda Charwe Nyakasikana* was considered to be the female incarnation of the oracle spirit *Nyamhika Nehanda*, and considered to be the grandmother of Zimbabwe. Some people, both male and female, claim they are *Nehanda* reincarnated because Shona people believe in spirit possession.
Ngubani igama lakho	What is your name? (Zulu)

ACKNOWLEDGEMENTS

I might string the words on paper to form a book, but a lot of people had their input as always. All mistakes in this book are mine, not those of anyone I consulted with.

Thank you to:

Inacio Antonio Simango and Corn Smith for your help with my Shona.

Gary Fonternel for your help on helicopters, paratroopers and general military from that time. For taking my frantic research calls late at night and somehow always managing to understand my emails.

Cleaver Firearms, thank you for your gunsmith expertise.

To the brilliant men and women who were part of the Grey's Scouts Regiment. Although I have borrowed your name, and many of your nicer mannerisms, the incidents referred to in this book are *fictional* and bear no resemblance to any incident in real life. Thank you for suspending your disbelief while reading this book.

The Grey's Scout Regiment loop on Facebook, including Doug Kriedemann and Mike Watson, who so kindly let me sit in, watch and research, and who answered my questions, both silly and meaningful, thank you. The horses I promised to immortalise in print and didn't make it in this book will be in another one coming. Thank you for sharing your love of your mounts with me. Long life to the mounted war horse!

Gordon Frost, for your time and patience in my deeper research of the Grey's Scouts, of their formation and their everyday lives. For inspiring the idea of a link between books, and for being the gentleman you are. To Gordon's beautiful wife, Lanie, who I had the pleasure of meeting too, thank you for sharing Gordon's mind with me.

Donovan Maskell, who shared so much with me, and scrounged photographs, etc, in South Africa from friends to share in my research.

To the boys who left school in the time of compulsory conscription, my thoughts were with you a lot while I wrote this book. You began your military training as school boys and came home men and heroes.

South African Special Forces League (Recces) for your information and your help. I couldn't have given my hero Wayne a better family to grow into a man in. Thank you especially to the Webmaster of recce.co.za, who was so helpful and prompt with his replies to my search for information. For sharing tales of life within the Forts at that time, for stories of Terry the lion and general information on being a Recce.

To everyone who knew and loved the real Terry the lion so much and made space in your hearts for him. I don't know if his happy ending here helps, but I like to think he was just fine after you left him – remember always he was one of you and would have survived at all costs!

To the real Kwasi, who I met in a shopping centre in Caboolture, Australia, and inspired a character with his hair, thank you for being the beautiful man you are.

To the real Jameson at Ivory Lodge, Zimbabwe, the inspirational name behind Shilo Jamison Khumalo. Thank you for being so patient with my sons, and for entertaining my *Isinkwe* with tales of the Africa bush, you have a heart as big as Zimbabwe herself. I will police officers did the same. They walked around the tree and took different angles, and pictures of the tree and the ground where more bones were scattered around.

'I'm ready,' the police photographer from Zimbabwe said.

'Right, untie one and let it down carefully,' the detective said.

Gibson tried to unknot the rope but it was too tight.

'Cut it,' the detective instructed.

He positioned men under it to try to catch the cocoon.

'Coming down,' said Gibson as he cut the last strand of rope with his hunting knife.

The cocoon landed safely in the arms of the men, and they quickly put it on the ground. More photographs were taken and the detective carefully cut open the thick *riempies* that were wrapped around the *kaross* protecting the chrysalis inside.

It was stiff to open, but eventually they bent it back, to reveal a human skeleton. The flesh had long since been eaten by maggots, the skin shrunken inwards, but the long blonde hair was confirmation that this had once been a girl.

'I was right,' Gabe said. 'I hate that I was right.'

Tara stood still. She looked around her.

Buffel had wanted to put her in a cocoon just like this.

So many children had died because her mother had moved her away, and he had attempted to substitute other girls for her in his sick dream. Her mother's own softness at not wanting to live away from her own family had saved her life.

'The butterflies,' Gibson said as he came and stood next to her. '"Butterflies to hold Impendla's hand and save his soul." It's what he used to say in his shed. I never caught him stealing one, and I was so wary of following him into the *bundu* and having him discovering my tracks. I didn't want him knowing that I was where I shouldn't be. I should have come here, I should have checked inside these *karosses* before today.' He hung his head.

Wayne stood next to Tara, his arm around her. 'I'm so glad that you lived. That you gave me a son and that you are not inside one of those cocoons.'

As they stood there, Tara noticed something she hadn't before. Dancing around her was a mass of small white butterflies. They seemed to be on a migration pattern and were flying through the site. For a moment the area was alive with the butterflies, then they slowed, and only a few could be seen dancing their bourrée fluidly as they floated across the African bush, headed northeast.

'I can only hope that all the souls here find peace now,' she said as one landed on her.

Such a delicate insect, its paper-thin little wings, with dark brown lines. She watched as it closed its wings, and opened them again, as if catching its breath. As if using her as an oasis in its epic migration.

Tara thought of the anguish every victim had undergone at the hands of Buffel, of all the innocence lost. She thought of the happiness he had stolen from her so many years ago. But instead of feeling sad, she felt a weight lift off her.

She was free.

And she hoped that the soul of the original victim in the whole mess, Impendla, was free at last too. That perhaps the butterflies were a sign that he had crossed over, and his soul was saved.

CHAPTER

33

Butterfly Kisses

Piet Retief Farm, Zimbabwe
24th February 1999

Tara remembered it all as they drove past the turnoff she used to take to get to Whispering Winds. She saw landmarks that had never been far from her mind. Everything was just as she remembered it from so many years ago. Nothing had really changed over the last almost twenty years. She rolled down her window and smelled the hot dry Zimbabwean air as it rushed into the air-conditioned 4x4.

She sat in the back seat next to Wayne, while Gabe and Jamison were seated in the front. She kept taking deep breaths, as if she was puffing like a train, taking air in and slowly letting it out again.

'What are you doing?' Wayne asked.

'Lamaze breathing, trying to keep my panicky self under control,' she said. 'I learnt about it when I chose to have Josha by natural birth. They help when I get totally freaked out.'

Wayne unbuckled his safety belt, slid next to her, and hugged her to him. 'I'm right here. Gabe and Jamison are here too. We're all here for you. You know you don't have to do this, we can turn around if you want to?'

'I need to do this. But the memories flooding through me as we drive are getting really heavy. This guilt has been hanging around me all these years since my father and uncle died and I survived. I saw him that day, a big man in camo, crouched over my dad. I should have realised it was Buffel. I blocked it out. I saw him. Now coming here and helping the police look for this tree, knowing that Buffel was sick and obsessed with trying to help his dead friend … It's sad and it's scary too. Such dedication to a friend, and so scary that he wasn't differentiating between reality and dream in the end. If we can find the proof that he was the killer we think he was …'

'The South African police found that hidden compartment in his *bakkie*, and they found girls' clothing in there. They found his tranquilliser darts in his bag. If they didn't think there was merit in what you and Gabe told them, we wouldn't be here. There is no way the Zimbabwe and South African police would have managed to work on this together if they didn't think you two were right.'

'I know, and I want closure for me and for all the families that had their little girls ripped away. They need to know where the girls are. But I can't stop thinking how lucky I was that Jamison was in my life then. He saved me, and now again as an adult he put his life on the line for me. That type of debt, I can never repay.'

'I don't expect repayment, Tara,' Jamison said. 'I just want the same as you, for this nightmare to be over. I can't imagine anything worse than this ritual that he used happening to my girls.'

Gabe stopped the *bakkie* in front of the sheep pens where the Zimbabwean police officers stood. The detective was in his car, which was covered in dust, and there were two police vans from South Africa parked nearby.

Gibson Ncube shook his cousin's hand as he joined the group of people talking in the middle. 'Shilo, it's been a long time.'

Jamison smiled. 'Too long,' he said and introduced Gibson to Wayne, Gabe and Tara.

the worm or the caterpillar on his grave once they removed the stick, after he was buried, and then you could save him. One year. Now, he is part of this world. His spirit is here. That is the way it is in the Shona traditional burials. *Mwari* must have told you that too. You cannot save him now, it's too late. It was always too late, even when you became PSYOPS. But you can save yourself. You can let me go. You can let Tara live, and you can stop the killing.'

'No, I must save him,' Buffel said, shaking his head violently from side to side. 'I have to save him. I have to stop the voices.'

'You need to save yourself, Buffel. You need to think of your own soul. Right now, you need to think of your own safety. Your life.'

'You still don't understand.' He shook his hand at Jamison, pointing, then balled it into a fist. 'My soul was claimed by the devil when I lived, and Impendla died when I was only ten years old. It was me who walked into the *Karoi's* area first. It was me who disturbed her bag of muti, and it was me who didn't believe until he was taken. It should have been me.'

'It could never have been you. You are a white man,' Jamison said. 'The *Karoi*, she would never have taken a white child. It was never meant to be you who was taken. I am a black man, I know the Shona god *Mwari*. I know of the *Karoi*, and her customs. I know that even though she killed your friend Impendla, she would not have taken you. Never.'

Buffel cocked his head to listen. It was too quiet outside.

'So many dead, and for what? For nothing. You can't save him, Buffel. He is lost to you. The police will storm in here any moment and shoot you. With tear gas and stun grenades. You need to surrender. They will shoot you and if you survive, they will take you and put you into an insane asylum, they will put you in the *Ingutchini*, not a prison. Is that what you want? To be inside walls all the time? They will keep you inside and never let you see the sun. Chained to a bed somewhere, like a dog. Never see your farm again. You need to surrender. But perhaps you can save your own soul—'

'No. Shut up with your lies,' Buffel said putting his hands over his ears.

Jamison shouted so he would hear him anyway. 'What will happen to your soul if another POU is killed because of you? All this time, I have kept my oath. Now you are going to kill me, you will not see this through to the end. You are abandoning me, just as you did your friend Impendla when you were a boy. Running away from your true responsibility. You are breaking the oath, Buffel. You are breaking your oath. The others, the POUs, they will come for you. Remember that if you kill me, they will get you even if you walk away from today. You can't save Impendla, that was over fifty years ago, but you can still save you, and you can still save me.'

Buffel got to his feet and put the gag back on Shilo, despite Shilo's struggles. Eventually he had to hold his nose and only when the other man finally opened his mouth to breathe did he manage to force it in.

'No more talking, Shut up! Shut up!' Buffel repeated over and over as he walked over to the barricaded window where he had left one small viewing section between the mattresses and the upended table. He could see the armour-plated vehicle that the riot police had arrived in and the police captain or someone in charge standing with his legs apart, waiting for his moment.

This was never in his plan.

He had not planned, and his impulsiveness had got him trapped.

'What am I to do, Impendla? I don't feel like I am the *Nyamhika Nehanda* now. I am in a hole, like a rabbit. Trapped. The spirit, the voice of *Mwari*, is trapped this day. I cannot be a *mhondoro*, I can not run free and save you. How can I not save the only friend I ever had in this world? If Shilo is right and I only had a year to save you, then all the sacrifices, they have been for nothing. The Butterfly, she is better living than sacrificed to the spirits. It's too late. It's too late for us.'

He looked back at Shilo still trying to get loose.

He could surrender, go outside as they asked.

But Shilo had said that they would put him in a mental hospital. The *Ingutchini*. They would torture him. Shock him with electricity.

bring my 'bushbaby' for another visit, so you can teach us how to make those beautiful elephant hair bracelets.

To the real people of Karoi who on their Facebook page answered so many questions about the town for me.

To my cousin Albert Durant who gave me a condensed version of growing tobacco in Zimbabwe, in four short hours by phone, and whose amazing farming ability has survived a move to a new continent. You are a true farmer, Alby, and I love you.

To Tjaart Boshoff, from Ditjabe Wildlife Services, who spoke at length to some mad woman author on his mobile. For the crash course in translocating different animals, and for being so patient with me running scenarios by him, and for explaining the live game trade in South Africa. For planting the majestic sable in my thoughts and for your tales you told me. To running fast and learning from mistakes as you learnt on the ground in a business that grew in a rapidly changing society.

To my daisy chain of ex-South African and Zimbabwean ladies on my island who support me through the good and the not so good. How you won't let me forget how bad my Afrikaans is, but don't care. Thank you for long lunches, and never letting me change. Especially to Ess Grubb, Jauline Rene Benson, Siobhan Graham and Petro Grobbelaar for all you help in spellings in Afrikaans, Zulu and sayings, and to Jauline, who first told me about the name Buffel in a string of swear words I had asked her for. Thank you to Jauline, Siobhan and Petra for being beta readers and fitting my deadlines into their lives.

Sam Eeles, for your beta reading, correction of my spelling and grammar, and also for putting up with me when I haven't had enough sleep, and when I'm lost in my own creative world.

Rachel Hyndes from Boot Camps Australia, who tries so hard to help me make healthy choices and just keep showing up to get fitter. And everyone at boot camp who see me at my most vulnerable, thanks for the constant encouragement.

Leonie Tyle, who first read a version of this story as a young adult novel years ago, and told me that the real story hidden inside was of Josha's parents. For always encouraging me, and for continually believing in me as an author as well as the CYA Conference organiser.

Dr Sue Eaglesham, psychologist, for your advice on characterisation of PTSD. Thank you for your professional opinion, guidance and help on making my character Buffel believable. But more importantly, for your friendship.

Dr Emile Brits, GP, for your advice on pituitary adenoma. For your friendship through the years and then for smiling when I asked to upgrade you to a neurologist and use your name, for not shooting me down in flames of technical jargon as to why I couldn't!

Wendy Skidmore, for answering even my most untactful question honestly about unwed teenage pregnancy during that time, to her husband, Shane, who is by her side still today. For proving that teenage love is real and worth risking your heart on because it can be forever.

To my mum-in-law, Caroline Clark, for doing general housework, the washing, the folding, the ironing of work shirts, the dishes, and everything else while I was rewriting the main body of this book and you were supposed to be on holiday. Thank you, your help doesn't go unnoticed and is always appreciated.

To my dad-in-crime, William Clark, for doing the school runs, the grocery shopping, the weeding, taking out the bins, watching the forecasts to ensure the boats are tied down in stong wind warnings, and generally picking up the slack while I was writing this book and you were visiting on holiday. Thank you for just being you.

To my son Kyle, who did my original electronic mud maps – thank you for making the life of the design team at Harlequin easier so they didn't have to read my handwriting for most of the process.

To my son Barry, who watches my type of TV programs with me, and often figures out who the killer is before me. For discussing the villains in my stories repeatedly with me, mostly during the school run, and who doesn't mind going over and over different scenarios with me. Because he decided that Buffel was a 'collector', and it pushed my imagination further, to darker places.

To staff at Harlequin Mira Australia, thank you!

Sue Brockhoff, who bought *Shooting Butterflies* after a conversation without a full synopsis. I love you for that as I'm totally useless at those. Thank you for your belief in me and for your help in growing me as an author.

Annabel Blay, who is so great at answering emails so promptly, and for whom nothing is ever too much to ask.

Glenda Downing, for your help in making my stories sparkle in the real world, and in helping shape my book into a better story.

Lilia Kanna, who held my novice hand most of the way through *My Brother-But-One* and made me want to publish more titles with Harlequin, because nothing was ever too much or too hard for her.

The design team, my cover fairies, thank you! May I now upgrade you to gods?

TINA MARIE CLARK

Born in Zimbabwe, Tina Marie completed her primary school years at boarding school in Bulawayo, but weekends and holidays exploring their family ranch in Nyamandhlovu, normally on the back of her horse. Her teenage years were totally different to her idyllic childhood. After her father died, the family of five women moved to Kokstad, a rural town at the foot of the Drakensberg Mountains in South Africa, and the boarding school hostel became her home. In winter she walked to school in the snow and could never get warm, and in summer she sweated having to wear an impractical, but smart, blazer.

She began writing fiction in the UK while a stay-at-home mum to her two sons, following a suggestion from her husband Shaun during a trip to Paris, and she hasn't looked back.

Now living on a small island near Brisbane in Queensland, Australia, Tina Marie combines her passion for storytelling with her love for Africa. When not running around after the men in her life, she gets to enjoy her hobbies, which include boating, reading, sewing, travel, gardening, and lunching with friends. (Not necessarily in that order!)

Passionate about Africa, different cultures and wildlife, most of Tina Marie's books are set somewhere on that ancient continent. Her first book with Harlequin, *My Brother-But-One,* was shortlisted for the Queensland Literary Awards in 2014.

Readers are welcome to find Tina on social media:

Facebook: facebook.com/pages/TMClark-Author/130010083845439

Twitter: @TinaMarieClark2

Or visit on her website: tmclark.com.au

FACT VS FICTION

Hanging sacrifices of children in the muti and witchdoctor trade in Africa are real. The details and ritual I have built around this are fictional.

The Shona name for the Sinoia Caves (Chinhoyi Caves) is Chirorodziva, Pool of the Fallen. The Shona believe that there are ancestors sleeping in this pool, and that you shouldn't throw a stone into the water as the spirits will catch the stone and a curse will fall on to the stone thrower. The sacrifices and further superstitions I have built around these beliefs are fictional.

The Rhodesian Philological Operations Unit – POU – was real. The motto *Tiri Tose* was real. The details and the deeds of my PSYOPS and atrocities they committed are fictional.

Terry the lion in Fort Droppies was real. Please see www.recce.co.za/terry-s-pictures for pictures of his interaction with the troops and some of their first-hand accounts of what Terry got up to within their Fort. Obviously my characters' interactions with Terry are fictional.

PTSD, post-traumatic stress disorder, is real. The term was first used by anti-Vietnam War activists and the anti-war group Vietnam Veterans Against the War (VVAW) in the mid 1970s, but was only formally recognised by the Committee of Reactive Disorders, USA, in 1980. Today many people are diagnosed with PTSD, and while some seek the help they require, many still don't.